THEY CAN'T BURN US ALL

www.penguin.co.uk

Also by Cathryn Kemp

Non-Fiction
Coming Clean: Diary of a Painkiller Addict

Fiction
A Poisoner's Tale

THEY CAN'T BURN US ALL

Cathryn Kemp

bantam

TRANSWORLD PUBLISHERS

UK | USA | Canada | Ireland | Australia
India | New Zealand | South Africa

Transworld is part of the Penguin Random House group of companies
whose addresses can be found at global.penguinrandomhouse.com.

Penguin Random House UK, One Embassy Gardens, 8 Viaduct Gardens, London SW11 7BW

penguin.co.uk

Penguin Random House UK

First published in Great Britain in 2026 by Bantam
an imprint of Transworld Publishers

001

For a full list of works cited, please see pages 395–7.

Map and illustrations drawn by Liane Paine.

Typeset in 12.25/16 pt Granjon LT Std by Falcon Oast Graphic Art Ltd
Printed and bound in Great Britain by Clays Ltd, Elcograf S.p.A.

The authorized representative in the EEA is Penguin Random House Ireland,
Morrison Chambers, 32 Nassau Street, Dublin D02 YH68

A CIP catalogue record for this book is available from the British Library.

ISBNs:
9781787637160 (cased)
9781787637177 (tpb)

FSC www.fsc.org MIX Paper FSC® C018179

For every woman who has ever been silenced

I carve runes on this horn,
redden words with my blood,
I choose words for the trees
of the wild beast's ear-roots (horns)

Egil's Saga

Thou shalt not suffer a witch to live.

Exodus 22:18

Grænland
Bolungarvík
Hnífsdalur
Skutulsfjörður
Eyrakirkja
Eyri
Önundarfjörður
Seljabrekkum
Kirkjuból
Breiðadalsheiði
mountain pass
Holt
Súðavík
Mosvellir
Westfjords
Trékyllisvík
ICELAND
Mount Hekla
Þingvellir
N
0
4 miles

A Note on Icelandic Language and Pronunciation

Icelandic Pronunciation

Many of the Icelandic words used are printed in their Icelandic spelling. Below is a short approximate guide to pronunciation:

á is pronounced *ow* as in *owl*
e is pronounced *e* in *air*
é is pronounced *ye* as in *yes*
í and ý are pronounced *ee* as in *been*
ó is pronounced *o* as in *note*
ö is pronounced *ur* as in *fur*
ú is pronounced *oo* as in *school*
æ is pronounced *i* as in *wife*
au is pronounced like French *oeil*
ei is pronounced *ay* as in *way*
Þ is pronounced *th* as in *thing*
ð is pronounced *th* as in *this*

Icelandic Names

In Iceland, a woman's name remains unaltered after marriage. Traditionally, a patronymic naming system is used, meaning a child's last name is derived from his or her father using the first name together with 'son' or 'dóttir' suffixed according to the sex of the child.

Þuriður Jónsdóttir is thus translated as Þuriður, Jón's daughter, while her brother, Jón Jónsson, is translated as Jón, Jón's son. Therefore, members of the same family may all have different surnames.

Prologue

November 1657

THE CURRENT SHIFTS.

Air brushes the tip of each feather. It is cool, silky, a skyward stream. The raven – coal-black eyes, body, beak – lifts and glides before beginning again to flap its jagged wings. It turns back to shore, the wind carrying it now over the churning sea towards the cliff and its storm-buffeted edges.

If it sees the woman standing alone, too close to this edge, it pays no attention. The bird enjoys the serene clarity of a scavenger seeking its prey. There is movement in the swaying grasses at this woman's feet. A small rodent. A morsel for plucking from the *fjallagrös.* The young woman pulls the shawl around her, face lifted to the darkening skies, but she may as well be a carving in the rockface of the highest point for all the raven cares. She is still, motionless, watching as the bird flaps again. It moves faster now, its velvet wings outstretched. It could be Flóki's raven, his wayfinder, drawing him across wild, white-tipped oceans to this land of ice.

In a few seconds, the raven will descend, a distillation of iridescent fury, of talon and claw, feather and bone. Its only aim: a feast of dismemberment. In a few seconds, the woman's fate will be decided alongside that of the small, hunted animal which now senses its own impending death. Cleanly, quickly, it is snatched into grasping talons and taken into the sky – its life over, its destiny complete. The rodent can do nothing. The raven's sight is honed, sharp, an absolute concentration of hunger and flight. But what will this woman do? Should she too step into nothing? Should she hold her arms aloft and imagine, for a brief moment, she is the bird, weightless and transported?

The wind is cold on her cheek. It rushes against her skin: a fierce caress. The call of winter arrives with grey, leaden skies, glowering clouds forming over the ever-moving seas below, the jutting rocks. There is a sigh. Perhaps the wind itself sees her plight. The ocean too.

She turns.

The bird plummets, snatches, rises again in a jumble of oily feathers. The small creature shrieks a long, high sound.

They are standing behind her.

Three men cloaked in black.

PART ONE

Urðr
Fate

Yggdrasil,
Loam-soaked world-ash,
Keeper of Mimir's well,
Created dew and rain.
From the pool
The three maids entered:
Fated, Becoming, Must-be –
Runesmiths, law-givers.

Völuspá: Prophecy of the Völva

Decree of King Christian IV

As regards genuine sorcerers, who have made themselves over to the devil to be joined in partnership with him or who are confederate with him – all such shall be dealt with according to due process of law. And those who put themselves into the hands of such people, desiring and coveting the realization of some benefit for their own people by means of these men's skill in sorcery – they shall be put to death without mercy.

Moreover, in order that this our gracious and earnest will and decree may be more effectual, to the glory of Almighty God, we do hereby command and strictly enjoin all nobles and officials, all bishops, deans, priests, mayors, councillors, sheriffs, and all who have been appointed and commissioned to positions of authority, as follows: they should one and all, each according to his rank and position, as soon as they become aware of cases covered by this our letter, denounce them publicly and have the culprits punished, provided that they do not wish to be prosecuted themselves for being accessory to people of this sort and consenting to their wickedness.

Published at our palace, Copenhagen, 12 October 1617, under our seal.

I

December 1655

PARISH PRIEST SÍRA Jón Magnússon sits astride his horse.

Snow swirls all around. Behind him, a small harbour created by the spit of land, Eyri, curves into the expanse of the Djúp. The fjord is flat, suffocated by glittering flecks of white, which lie heavy now in the valley ahead. There are no boats for crossing today. Soon, the water will freeze, and so he has ridden from Eyrakirkja, Eyri Church, round the length of the harbour that separates the spit from Kirkjuból, a journey taking less than half a day by foot. Less on a horse even in inclement weather. He pauses before digging his boot heels into the animal's flanks. He grips the reins, though he may as well hold the long, rough mane. The horse snorts, paws the ground, its breath forming wet crystals on the air. Snow falls harder now.

Despite the aching cold, the brutal onset of another Icelandic winter, the priest appears not to notice, so driven is he by his mission. His thick cloak is sodden, his wool gloves too. He brushes off the worst of the snowfall, squinting into the dying light. Ahead lies Kirkjuból, the largest, and richest, farmstead in the district. Beside it, scattered across the undulating land, lie the other, smaller farms, more a series of wind-battered crofts: Seljaland, Tunga, Hafrafell, Engidalur, Fossar. Each contains several households, their servants and farmworkers. It is these people he has come to preach to as the day fades quickly to night.

If the light was different, if the midnight sun was shining and exposing all to its honey-gaze, he might have been able to see the series of squat buildings that lie nestled in the lush pasture south of the harbour: the *skáli* for drying fish with lines of pale, hardening cod and haddock strung up in rows like crooked teeth; the sheds for cattle, for chopping foraged wood, for storing the things that keep each household alive through the onslaught that comes each year – tar and coal, kindling and barrels of dried fish, straw for winter feed, rope and nets looped over the rafters. He might have glimpsed long grasses where sheep graze in summer, wildflowers moving in the slight breeze, terns screeching as they defend their nests. Instead, all is muffled, quiet. Looming over are the mountain ranges that encircle the valley. They rise up, reaching into the cloud cover with relentless brown rock, a smattering of green moss underneath the forming ice, disappearing into encroaching blackness.

Síra Jón sees only the firmament, the light leaching from the sky, leaden clouds that hang heavy overhead. He has come for a reason. A line has been crossed, a scar riven into the two communities that must exist together for survival. How deep the line goes is yet to be determined. The priest knows only that he has work to do this evening at the service he will hold among the godless of Kirkjuból, those who still hold on to their beliefs in the pagan Norse gods. It will not be an easy task, but it must be done. The future of Eyri, the saving of the souls of all who live here, may depend upon what happens next. He cannot doubt his conviction, his *righteousness*, now.

He must be as a shepherd, herding his flock back towards the holy light of God. He must act, and act quickly. There are dark forces at work in Iceland, as in the world beyond. News comes from the Danish merchants who trade food and wool. He has had confirmation in letters from clergy in Denmark, in Norway, even from Scotland. And now the Danish king's decree has been published here in Iceland, though the monarch himself now lies dead in his sarcophagus.

Black magic is a crime, a sin, with which he is all too familiar as for months he has suffered grievous bodily attacks: hallucinations, fevers, pains that wrack his body, that come from nowhere and disappear as quickly. The source of these attacks has become plain to him and his household. They are too violent, too strange to have any earthly cause. His gaze has fixed upon this place, on two men who proclaim themselves sorcerers, on two men who have cause to hate him.

Eventually, he digs his heels into the warm round belly of the horse. He pulls his cloak back over his head, clumsy with gloved hands. He moves off, grateful to head onward. Ahead lies a nest of wickedness and witchcraft, one he has sworn to God and to the sheriff to convert back to the Church – or destroy. He takes another breath. Cold, merciless air fills his lungs. It is time.

2

THE WIND SCREAMS as the priest dismounts.

I watch him through the opening in the stone wall of my father's croft, the *skjár,* a membrane of sheep's stomach stretched to form a pane, pulled to one side. The night is bitter cold. Beside our farmhouse sits a small wooden chapel, crouching beside the croft as if sheltering from the storm that is whipping through the valley. One of the farmhands grabs the reins and leads the horse off to shelter, their heads down against the gusts that have travelled across glaciers and volcanic rock to reach this place.

'Welcome, reverend,' the man says, but his voice is almost lost in the sound of the wilderness.

I cannot hear Síra Jón Magnússon's reply. I gesture to my father, Jón Jónsson, and my brother, named after him. I do not speak. I have not spoken for many years, and so rely upon signs made with my hands or expressions made by my face to communicate. I rap on the table, making them both look up, and point urgently to the church.

'So, our benevolent priest has arrived,' my father says, without moving from the hearth. 'Gracing us with his presence, when for years he has refused to come to Kirkjuból. The letter he sent to all the households here was infuriatingly vague. He will give a service. We must all attend. Why now? Why not stay inside his big wooden church on the spit with those who want the hand of the Lord God on their heads?'

My father and brother exchange a glance.

'I think we know why,' my brother, Jón Jónsson the Younger, says. He puts down the iron scribe used to carve *galdrastafir,* magical runes, upon a twisted length of foraged birch, scented sweet by its sap.

'Go over there if you must, Þuriður. We may follow.'

'Or we may not,' my brother says, eyes glinting. I throw the ball of yarn I have wound together, catching him above his cheek. He grins, but we all know they must attend. Not to do so would mark them out even more than they are marked already. The priest and my family have history.

I point again, this time scowling. The messages sent to each household were clear: attend, or be damned. The wind howls again. I do not relish the thought of stepping into the winter night, but I see Síra Jón is already inside the chapel, along with most of the residents who live and work on this side of the harbour. Our maidservant, Margrét, went earlier with the farmhands, giggling as they went, as if this was a feast day, and so now I throw my thickest shawl around me, pull on gloves, a hat. Descend into the maelstrom.

Pushing open the wooden door, I stamp the snow off my fish-skin boots and shuffle into the small space now crammed with people standing, since the chapel has no pews, my cheeks smarting from the cold. Here are the families who have lived on this land for generations, their maidservants and workers, the young men and women who wander from settlement to settlement each summer, those without homes or kin. All waiting for this strange service to start. Wondering, no doubt, why we are ordered here.

It has been a long time since a priest stepped onto the land at Kirkjuból. It has been a decade or more since holy communion was taken by his predecessor. Our small chapel has lain empty ever since. Some of the women clean it now and again, though it has an air of neglect.

The two communities of Kirkjuból and Eyri, divided by the harbour, are distinct and separate, yet bound under the same parish district and the same priest. Síra Jón Magnússon preaches at the church in Eyri on the spit of land that cradles the fjord. We are expected to attend services there, though in practice many do not, or, at most, attend irregularly. Here, we hold close our old gods, those our ancestors have worshipped for centuries. These beliefs are not welcome across the watery boundary that both divides and joins us.

The priest has already taken his place at the back of the church by the altar, such as it is, which is bereft of anything except a small silver chalice. It is the only treasure we have left. On the wall hangs a crude picture of the crooked body of Christ on the cross daubed on wood, now cracked. There is little else except a lamp, casting its oily orange glow. It was a Catholic chapel once. When the Reformation swept through the country by order of King Christian, this chapel, like so many others, was changed, its few gilded contents dispersed. Not that people here cared much. The new god merged with the old gods, and somewhere between them all evolved a faith of sorts unique to Icelanders. Faith in nature. Faith in Óðinn and Þórr, the All-Father and the God of Thunder. Faith in this Jesus Christ who died to save us, though from what, or from whom?

I squeeze in beside my oldest friends, Anna and Freyja, who smile. Each takes a hand, rubbing the warmth back into my fingers. I pull off my coverings, causing my bone-white hair to tumble down my back. We share a glance: the same puzzlement on our faces. Anna's grey-blue eyes widen under blonde lashes; Freyja's amber-flecked placid gaze directed now at the priest. We wait.

None of us knows what will happen tonight. The mood inside this chapel, littered with rat droppings underfoot, is wary. The priest gathers himself. He looks around at us. He nods at some he recognizes from their attendance at Eyrakirkja. Frowns at others. The women wearing simple linen caps, the men bearded, some with inked markings on their faces and hands, all swathed in thick wool clothing. A baby cries in a woman's arms. Already the air is stale with the scent of unwashed bodies and sheep shit. Many are glad to be given a reason to leave the dark confines of their soot-scoured crofts. Each household will be largely confined until Várblót, Spring Solstice, except to dig paths through the snow to tend the animals. I look back towards the door. Will my father and brother come?

The chatter and gossiping die down. Síra Jón Magnússon adjusts his cloak, clears his throat.

'You will all be wondering why I called this service, why I asked you to be here,' he begins. Several people turn to each other. The priest holds his arms up. The last of the murmuring voices stop. The chapel falls silent.

'These are difficult times, dangerous times,' the priest says, looking up as if waiting for an answer to a question he is yet to pose.

'We must all be on our guard, for Satan's demons are here among us. They have infiltrated our small community. This can be no surprise to anyone standing here. For centuries, Iceland has been steeped in superstition. People have worshipped the old gods – and continued to do so even though we have been a Christian nation for six hundred *years*!'

A prickling sensation creeps down the back of my neck. Anna squeezes my hand again. Her sister-in-law, Ólina, and her daughters, Kristín and Kaðlin, stand close too. We each exchange glances.

'When popery was driven out by the forces of Luther, it should've been a new start for all of us. Yet there are still many who cling to the old ways.'

People shuffle, accompanied by whispers.

'Life is hard here. We rely upon each other for our survival. This has created an abominable tolerance between those who fear God's word – and those who dabble in sorcery and pray to the Norse gods. Here, in Kirkjuból, it has long been known that witchcraft is at work: black magic and sorcery.'

He looks around. I feel a slight itch of sweat. A sense of foreboding. *Who does he look for?*

'I am here to tell you it ends now,' he declares. 'Those responsible will be punished if they do not come back to the Church. You *all* will return, or face the wrath of the Almighty . . .'

'Or the Danes . . .' someone says under their breath.

A moment's pause. The priest's deep brown eyes burn in their sockets. Unusually dark-skinned for an Icelander, he pushes his thick hair off his face. He opens his mouth to begin again, but the door to the chapel crashes open. I turn, along with everyone else in the room.

My father and brother step into the chapel as if they own it. Both tear off their tail caps, revealing their golden hair and freckled faces, both nodding with barely concealed arrogance. People move over, make space for them, yet they seem to fill up the room. My father, Jón Jónsson the Elder, leads the way, moving through the crowd to stand beside me. Both Anna and Freyja let go of my hands, frowning. My brother, Jón Jónsson the Younger, shoves through behind him.

The priest stands straighter, raising himself higher. He watches them with undisguised loathing. He isn't the only one. Many people around here dislike my kin and their power. They are the richest landowners by way of their craft as *seid-menn*, magic men, who never fail to remind those who seek them out of their importance and prowess. I have heard what people say.

Bigger pricks than brains.

Too full of their own regard.

Arrogant. Mean. Spiteful.

Much is true. But even though most treat me with the same distrust, they are the only family I have and so I stand with them. Not for the first time, I curse their rash, stubborn, belligerent character.

'Evil thrives in Kirkjuból. Evil that has spread beyond these farmsteads and into Eyri. It will continue to spread if it is not cauterized.' Síra Jón Magnússon's voice is too loud now for this small space.

'The new laws created by the Danish king are clear. Those who harbour witches will themselves face persecution. Those who tolerate these old practices will be punished. Those who practise witchery will *burn*.'

The place falls utterly still, as if even the babes-in-arms and sheep in their huts have heard this declaration too and are stunned.

Witches will be burned. Here?

'You!'

The priest points, first to my father, then to my brother.

'You are known sorcerers! All Eyri knows of your malice and your magic. I have written to the sheriff. I have told him you sent a league of demons after me.'

I feel my heart's beat grow fast. New laws mean new punishments, and the priest is right. My family are witches, men who wear their proud lineage like precious stones. Sorcerers of many generations past. They cannot deny it. Their trade is based upon it. And we are proud of it! My family is learned, unlike many here. They have studied grimoires and magical texts. They help people, though they also hinder – and worse. But this is their history. I feel the indignation my father surely feels as if it is my own.

Despite this, I look to my kin, expecting, or hoping, they will show contrition, even if it is false. They do not.

My father is shaking his head and smiling. Smiling? My brother is openly laughing. Why don't they understand? Publicly, he has declared my father and brother are to blame for his sickness. If things have really changed as he claims, they must repent or face terrible consequences. Why won't they listen?

Síra Jón Magnússon's voice rises, higher, louder.

'See how they taunt us! Servants of the devil!' The priest looks around at the congregation.

'Look at them. Their sorcery is a threat to us all.'

Around us, sideward glances become openly hostile stares. Several move away from us as if, suddenly, we have shit on our boots. These are people I have known since birth.

The priest walks slowly towards us. Every head swivels between Jón Jónsson the Elder and the clergyman, faces writ with shock. The crowd parts like the sea for Moses. I reach for the hem of Anna's sleeve.

'How dare you talk to us this way,' my father says.

Fokk, Father! Can't you see he's serious?

'You insult us!' my brother adds.

Idiot brother!

My father, the tallest of the three men, steps forward, towering over the priest.

'You dare to come to our farmstead, to try to destroy our traditions. Let us all hear the evidence. Let us judge for ourselves the truth of your words!'

'God shall be the judge of us all,' Síra Jón Magnússon counters. 'Don't deny you sent the devil in the form of a black dog to haunt me. You have cast spells against me. You have left me in agonies so severe that I have begged God to end my life. Don't deny any of it!'

'What proof do you have, preacher?'

'I will get proof, I promise you, and when I do –' here his voice lowers – 'I will see you both burn.'

An audible gasp. Several cross themselves in the Catholic way, forgetful of their Lutheran conversion. There is a moment where no one knows what to do. There have been few trials and burnings in Iceland. Only one to date in the Westfjords, in Trékyllisvík. This threat seems to break an invisible cord that runs round this place, these people, binding us together.

Jón Jónsson the Younger laughs. 'This is a fucking joke.' My father nods in agreement. They turn and stalk out, just as I thought they would, neither saying another word. The congregation stares after them, then back at the priest, who breathes in a long, sated breath. Some stare at me too.

Síra Jón Magnússon walks back to the makeshift altar. He closes his eyes and dips his head.

'Let us pray,' he says.

3

I HAVE NEVER seen my father nor brother challenged before. No one has ever dared, until now.

The gap where they stood opens. Even our maidservant, whom I have known since a child, edges to the wall of the chapel. I am alone until Anna and Freyja step back beside me. I am the daughter of sorcerers, but as I am only a woman no one here suspects me. Even so, there is a shift – seismic, like the earth that moves, rumbling under our feet at times. I am tainted by association – and always have been – even though I have helped birth most of the squalling babies in here.

'Þuriður, what are you doing?' my practical, sensible, beloved friend Anna whispers as I turn.

'You mustn't go. You'll look like you're guilty too!' she hisses as I move towards the door.

I shake my head and continue.

I cannot stay here and listen to the priest and his prayers after what has been said!

Both my friends, close as sisters, move with me. Freyja has hold of my arm now, but I shrug her off.

'Þuriður Jónsdóttir, you must stay. Anna's right. It won't look good if you go with them . . .' Freyja says. Her usual easy nature has vanished. She looks scared. I smile, trying to reassure her. It does not work. Her plump, round face stares back at me, imploring.

'Stay,' she says, her voice low.

If I could reply, I would say I am in no danger. It is not I accused of sorcery against the clergyman. After all, women in Iceland cannot be witches; we do not have the learning, nor the ability, or so the men say. They have said this for centuries, and so it must be true. It does not mean I should be here, though, murmuring to this preacher's God as if He was my own, rather than with my kin.

I use a particular gesture. A slicing motion with my flat hand. It says a definitive 'no'. An absolute. A finality. I do this now and see the exasperation on my friends' faces.

Wilful, they call me. *Stubborn. Defiant*, at times. *Walking her own path, just like her mother*. There are many things said about me. I ignore them. My thoughts and feelings are my own. I do not owe anyone in the settlement the knowing of them, except my friends and, with Anna and Freyja, I have ways of saying things with looks and gestures that go far beyond words.

I do not reply to them. I have not replied to a single person since the day my father told me my mother was dead.

Dead?

I recall saying it aloud, but maybe not. Drowned in the fjord after swimming out too far. Dragged into silt depths. Chill water claiming her as its own. Lured by the enchanted song of the Nykur, the horse-like spirit who rides the unwary to their death. Her bones sinking down into the gravel and choking weeds, lost to me.

Dead?

I remember, even at eight years old, thinking how could someone so *alive*, who had sung me to sleep the night before, who had braided my hair that morning, be dead? It was an utter impossibility. My father's grim expression told me it was not. I ran from him, all the way up to my sanctuary, high above Kirkjuból, scrambling up the rockface to *Naustahvilft*, the place known as the troll seat, a large flat dip in the side of the mountain where a troll woman's arse may once have rested. There, drawing my knees to my chest, I sat on the cool *fjallagrös* and waited for the churning, heaving panic to subside. Silenced by sadness, I allowed the rushing wind to speak for me, the tidal fjord, the croaking ravens coasting on the breezes. I stayed there for a long while, until I felt safe, knowing I had to return to a home now changed forever, now empty of her. Never again would I assist her during the labours of local women. Never would I catch her smiling at me, feel the light touch of her hand on the crown of my head, hear her hum as she walked through wildflowers, gathering plants for medicine and cooking.

Grief submerged me just like the waterfall at Bunárfoss, washing away all desire to communicate, to interact with the world outside my broken heart. For a long time, I could barely breathe let alone talk. It took many months, many tears, before I discovered I did not *want* to speak and so I withdrew my voice, my words, fancying the world was not kind enough to receive them. Now? Now, I wonder if I will ever speak again. I have lost the knowledge. I cannot imagine how to blend breath and sound to make solid my thinking. I am not sure I want to. My silence gives me something my words could not. After all, silence is a form of defiance.

My father urged me to speak. My brother too. Then, they became angry.

'Wilful child! What use is a daughter who doesn't talk?'

'She's doing it for attention!' my brother replied, as I stood, glaring at them, mute. There was no sign then that my brother would become the bridge between my father and myself, allowing something akin to communication, translating my silence when I refused to, and then later when I could not.

'Why are you doing this?'

Father wanted me to tell him what the fishermen's wives were saying about the traders, which goods they might be bringing next time, when they might berth in our harbour surrounded by its yawning stretch of mountains. I learned then that silence was power. It was mine and mine alone.

'*Fokk*, Þuriður, why are you so . . . so *difficult*?'

I grinned back at my brother, only two years older than me but already becoming a man. He had a strong frame, a lean body, already scarred from the lash of a broken net he pulled from under their small boat. I stuck my tongue out. Smiled. Walked off, knowing my brother was scowling behind me.

'She's doing it for attention,' my brother repeated, grumbling into his supper. Whether my father replied, I do not recall. But I knew from that day onward, I had something over them, almost like a spell. They could not take this from me, no one could.

Anna and Freyja accepted my silence as if it was natural. They never spoke of it. They never questioned me nor tried to make me anything other than what I was. The settlement women gossiped for a while, saying the grief had stolen my tongue, but even they, after a time, accepted it. They always thought I was strange, anyway, because I alone had inherited my mother's colouring: skin the blue-white of the heart of a glacier where it is coldest. Hair whiter than snow and pale ice-blue eyes. There was talk of me being an elf child and my mother an elf woman. There still is. Some said she left rather than died, returning to the *álfar*, beyond the troll rocks, back to a world of plenty and pleasure. Her body was never found, her drowning witnessed only by my father. Swept out to sea, her beauty dissolving in salted decay. She was my world. Without her, there seemed no point in saying anything ever again.

'Come on, little one. Tell me a story,' my father would say over the years to make me talk, trying to wheedle a saga from my closed lips. He knew I'd listened as if enchanted when my mother spoke of the great women from the old stories. The shield maidens who fought with swords alongside the warriors. The explorers who stood at the helms of ships and searched for new lands. These were the women I wanted to become. Their stories became my own. Their rage. Their bravery. Their murderous fury. I absorbed it all because, deep down, I always knew I felt the same.

The memory vanishes, a thin thread of remembering that spools away. My body is already leaving the chapel: legs, torso, arms, neck in motion. Snow-melt on boots. Wind-rush through holes in the turf roof. People part, flattening themselves against the wall. I ignore them. I also ignore the priest, who has begun to pray – loud, insistent – as if for my ears alone.

The door bangs shut behind me. The storm strikes my face like a blow from a fist, taking my breath away. Pushing against the incessant flurry that is thrown down from the skies, I struggle to our croft. As I open the large wooden door, it feels as heavy as the tree trunks washed ashore in a seaweed tangle. Ours is the only farmhouse occupied by just one family – my father, my brother and me – as well as our maidservant, Margrét, and the farmhands, who sleep in the *skáli* adjoining the kitchen.

'Þuriður?'

Who else? I stamp off slush, remove my wool hat, my gloves, my outer shawl. A trickle of ice freed slides down the back of my dress. I shiver.

'You should've stayed,' my father calls out to me. 'At least that way the shit-for-brains priest couldn't accuse you of being ungodly too.'

'Did Margrét or the labourers come back with you?' My brother, Jón, stands by the fireplace, warming his hands. 'No? Well, I guess they don't want to associate with us tonight. Fucking cowards!'

Already, I wonder if I should've stayed. It feels as if we are splitting, moving slowly apart like a fissure running through rock. Outside: the silence is now of *mjöll*, fresh-fallen, the kind of absence of noise that opens up like a ravine and swallows sound whole. Soon, our neighbours on this side of the spit will spill out, complaining about the frost, the barraging gusts, the lengthy prayers and whatever else they may grumble about. Until then, only us: here. Wondering what the priest intends next.

My brother looks over at our father. Jón Jónsson the Elder is already halfway through a cup of mead. He drains it, reaches for the jug.

'The magic'll come next,' Jón the Younger says, spitting onto the floor. He wipes his mouth, pours himself a cup. 'He'll cast a malignant curse against the priest – you'll see. If he thinks he has suffered until now, he won't have another moment's peace for the rest of his days.'

I raise a pale eyebrow.

He is right. As soon as a second measure is drunk, my father stands up, kicks back his chair. He reaches for his cloak of animal skins, crude stitches knitting them together, then hangs a necklace made of rope, carrying a small metal Hammer of Þor, round his neck. He puts on his peaked fur cap, and picks up his rattling shards of whalebone each carved with a different rune for protection.

'Give me your ankle. He'll need your blood for this curse.' My brother draws the ceremonial brass-handled knife and makes a tiny cut in my proffered leg, releasing a thin stream of rust-red into a bowl used for spell work. It hurts only a little. He has chosen a spot where there are no fresh scars, small drops of my virginal young blood being an essential element for their magical practice.

I watch as my father draws the Ægishjálm, hear the scratch of the sharpened feather quill on parchment. Careful not to blot the seep of clotting liquid, he draws the eight lines of the rune. Each with three branches. Each with three lines crossed through, a circle at the centre, eight half-circles at the ends. A symbol of power, striking fear into enemies with a single glance. As the marks dry brown on the sheath of goatskin, he pours water into the rune bowl. He dabs the small cut in my leg with a wad of linen, then uses this to draw a circle in the dust of the floor. Steps inside it.

Placing the parchment between his eyes, my father stares back at me, glazed, unseeing, just as if he is Fáfnir, the great serpent worm from the Völsunga and Reginsmàl sagas, the owner of the helm.

My brother has a hunger on his face, greedy for this magical power in the half-light of the hearth. Declared sorcerers. Declared enemies of the priest, a man fervent and righteous. One who has turned his brimstone gaze to Kirkjuból.

The fire flares as a piece of dried dung collapses, cascading a shower of sparks. Earlier, I drew protective runes in the ashes to keep the croft safe from burning. An old practice. Something my mother did, and her mother too, though few think of it now that the Christian prayers have replaced our heathen ways. I lean over and, using the prong, nudge the largest of the coals back into the heat. My father summons the devil himself to unleash all hell upon the preacher.

4

THE PRIEST TOSSES and turns in the bed he shares with his wife, Þorkatla Bjárnadóttir.

His skin burns: invisible flames shoot up his body, their burning tongues an agony of suffering. His eyes flutter open.

'Lord,' he croaks, 'free me from this curse.' He speaks into the winter darkness, the ghoulish white of snowfall glazed by moonlight. His flesh feels singed as if subjected to flames in truth. His throat is dry, his nightshirt stuck in wet clumps to his body, thin from fasting, drenched in sweat.

'God save me,' he utters.

His wife stirs. 'Husband?' Her bed cap slightly askew, brown hair tangled, she leans over. 'What ails you?' Her voice is still muffled by sleep.

'Much ails me, though I do not think it is sickness of the body or mind.'

'You're feverish,' Þorkatla says.

He grabs her hand. 'This is punishment for going into the nest of witchery, for going to Kirkjuból. I can think of no other cause for sufferings such as this.'

He recoils as she begins to pull the damp shift from his trembling body. Then, a clean shirt is pulled over him with difficulty, the action made clumsy by the fact that he cannot remain still. His limbs seem to move without his instruction, the trembling beyond his control. He sees her frown.

'The devil continues his attacks upon me, but they're stronger this time. I cannot fight them.'

Þorkatla mutters a prayer, glancing around the *baðstofa.* There is little for her to see: their marital bed, carved from imported pine that sits on the *pallur*, the sleeping platform; a small table; a cupboard, dusty and piled with scuffed leather-bound Bibles. A single decoration: a wooden Jesus Christ enduring his torments upon a wooden cross; a candle, its buttery wax puddled.

'You're shivering.' She gets up, walks away, her light footsteps padding across the earth floor. Before long, a light bobs as it is carried back to his bedside.

'Is it the same as the last?'

The priest nods. He struggles to raise his head.

'I fear it is worse,' she says.

'Every part of me aches,' he cries. 'My limbs are heavy, as if demons lie prostrate upon me. Indeed, they came to me in my sleep. Terrible visions: lurking and prowling around this very chamber. The black dog too.' His voice is stronger now. 'It growled in the corner, baring teeth yellow and foul!'

He sinks back onto his straw-stuffed pillow. His terror begins to abate, yet the night is not over.

Þorkatla tucks the woollen blankets and sheepskins over Síra Jón.

These attacks have come nightly at times. They wrench them both from their slumber. She has learned to dread their ferocity, their intensity. There have been none for weeks and so this comes as a shock once again.

'It is the work of the sorcerers,' her husband moans. 'Can't you see the demons? Can't you hear them? They whisper crude words and incantations. They scratch at me with their claws and teeth . . . they tell me I was wrong to do what I did . . .'

'Be calm, husband,' Þorkatla says, the light in her hand shaking now. The small flame flickers. 'You must be still and seek the Lord's protection with your prayers.' She hears a noise from the small kitchen, which is situated down a narrow corridor that runs the length of the croft. Footsteps: at first cautious, and then louder. They have woken the servants.

Pale faces appear at the door to the *baðstofa*. She waves them away.

'There is nothing to fear,' she says, though she feels her own spreading panic. 'Leave us – there's little you can do.'

The faces squint at the orange glow from the lamp. For a moment, they do not move.

'Go,' says the priest's wife, sharp this time. She pulls her shawl tighter around her back. More snow is falling; the dull smudge of movement visible as the pane grows whiter.

'The elder sorcerer spoke to me in a visitation. He said these pains are for thwarting them . . .'

She places a warm hand on his forehead, making him wince.

'There's devilry at work, and we must trust in God,' she replies in a whisper, feeling her heart skip its beat.

She kneels now, begins to pray under her crumpled linen cap, her face wan with exhaustion. She recites the Holy Bible. When Þorkatla opens her eyes, she half expects to see herself surrounded by foul creatures sticking out their fiery tongues; black eyes that glint and forked tails that point to the rafters. Claws, rough hair, teeth that gnash and froth.

Her knees feel stiff. Not for the first time, she resents the poverty of their situation: the damp earth beneath their feet that needs to be washed down and scraped clean each spring; the chill of the room, its small hearth throwing out smoke from smouldering dried animal dung; the bestial stench of tallow candles; the sour fish odour of the lamp. But, worse than this, is the sight of the man she married, his face grey and clammy. She feels the dull timbre of fear only someone widowed can truly know. The terror of being cast into the world with her daughter, unprotected again.

She dips a clean linen cloth in a dish of water one of the maidservants thought to bring. She wrings the water out until it is merely damp and lays it gently across her husband's brow.

'Sleep, husband. Sleep and let the Lord do His work. None can harm you here.' She does not know if this is true, but it seems to calm him. His eyes droop a little, then shut. His limbs slacken. His breathing returns to a regular rhythm. In. Out. In. Out.

Þorkatla prays again, but as much to calm her own disquiet as for the priest's salvation. When she has finished, she climbs into their bed, one in which she will sleep alone, if but for an hour or two. Outside, there is silence except for the lowing of cattle, the bleats of sheep as they wait for light to dawn.

5

A WEEK PASSES. The priest's wife, Þorkatla, is busy shooing away a stray goat from the kitchen of the rectory on the spit when she hears the sound of a horse whinnying, the bustle of an arrival.

'Find someone to take it back to the *skáli*, or do it yourself, and quickly! The dignitaries will be here soon!' she calls to one of the servants, a surly girl who arrived last summer, whom Þorkatla has already decided to send on her way come the thaw.

Then comes the sound of a man shouting for the reins. Another in greeting while the wind blows up the thick snowfall, *skafrenningur*, that had already settled.

'They're early! I'm not ready!' Þorkatla unties her stained apron and throws it into the food store. She pushes her hair back under her cap, and straightens her skirt, hoping the sheriff will not see where she has darned the hem countless times. She might be a poor parish priest's wife, but she has status in their community. She will stand with her head high, her pride smarting, hoping none shall guess her shame at their lowly state.

'Get that goat out now!' she snaps at the servant, who is still trying to push the reluctant beast out into the cold. The storm has, thankfully, passed, though more will come tonight. Winter arrived early this year. They were barely beyond the long summer nights before the days of digging paths and breaking ice off the animals' troughs began.

'Where's my daughter?'

Þorkatla hurries into the *baðstofa*. Her husband is on his knees, praying in front of the carved cross. She manages to stop herself tutting. His knees will be damp, his smock stained. On her husband's stipend, they must suffer cold, dank ground beneath their feet and tallow rather than wooden boards or good wax candles. She does not care for this reminder of their situation, though her husband tells her humility is dearer than riches to God. Nor does she care for the sheriff's scrutiny.

'Husband?'

When Síra Jón Magnússon does not reply, she steps a pace forward.

'Husband. Our guests are here. The sheriff must be greeted properly.'

With a whispered 'amen', the priest opens his eyes. He looks up to the cross then back to his wife, who stands, barely concealing her impatience. He nods.

The priest can feel his wife's discontent.

It rolls off her like fog peeling off the mountaintops. He knows how much she hates this rectory and the meagre living they must endure. He sees her displeasure, her wanting more than this life. He pities her for it.

It has always been the custom for new priests to wed the previous parson's widow alongside the safekeeping of a parish's souls. Despite having no particular affection for Þorkatla, Síra Jón did his duty, marrying her and taking on her daughter as his own. He has never baulked from what God has asked of him. But there remains a coolness between the couple, a mismatching, a space that hovers between them that rubs, a friction.

She stands before him, frowning, making the lines already showing around her eyes deepen, though she has lived ten fewer winters than he.

'The sheriff is here. We cannot keep him waiting.'

The priest gets to his feet, with some difficulty. The pains have come and gone since that night after he returned from Kirkjuból, each time throwing the household into disarray. He must hold the edge of the wooden bedframe for support. This day, he feels sore, scalded by the devil's breath that blows hot and stinking into this rectory.

'Bring me my surplice,' he says.

'Yes, of course,' Þorkatla replies, and hurries to him with the garment. He knows he infuriates her, and she does her best not to show it. She once said that he is like this place: a man of fire and ice, of volcanic fury and passion, of stern, unbending duty. He could not disagree. He still cannot.

'Thank you.'

He stands upright. Something of the nights that have passed falls away. He was born to faith, to responsibility, to diligence. He is unquenchable in his love of God, an austere, fierce love reserved for Him and Him alone, like the land that ends where it meets the ocean in jutting rocks and flint-hard stone. He guesses at the pain this causes Þorkatla, though nothing is ever said between them. He does his duty, as she does hers. He has tried to love her.

At the doorway to the rectory, the priest, with stained knees, stands alongside his wife. Outside, the air is chilled, grey skies heavy overhead. Farmworkers have been busy all morning clearing a path for the visitors, on Þorkatla's orders.

'*Komdu sæll*,' the priest says, anticipating the usual greetings.

He leans heavily upon his wife, though she says nothing to acknowledge this.

'*Sæll vertu, sæl vertu.*' The district sheriff dips the brim of his riding hat first to Síra Jón and then to his wife, who sinks into a small curtsy. The priest sees her size up the lawman's fine wool coat with shining buttons, his good leather boots with silver spurs, the soft wool hat bought from Danish traders. He sees her blush with shame, knowing already the contrast between them: her scuffed boots, patched hem, faded linen cap.

The sheriff, Sýslumaður Magnús Sigurdsson, is not tall. He is rather a man with girth: a portly, self-regarding person who appears to enjoy the power he wields, bringing as he does the authority of law, of worlds beyond Eyri, though he is younger than the priest by ten winters or more. He strides over, not looking back to see who has taken the reins of his horse. As a person of his authority expects, it is already being led away, stepping gingerly through the ice. A younger man, wearing layers of moth-eaten woollen clothing over which lies a rough-hewn wooden cross, dismounts. He is busy taking what looks like a bundle of sacking off another horse. It takes the priest a moment to realize that the sacking is, in fact, the tiny, drooping form of an old woman, more sack-of-grain than human. Her clothes are ragged, her skin flayed by many winters. Instantly, he realizes the woman is blind; milk-white eyes stare without seeing from her hollowed-out face.

'Welcome, Sheriff Sigurdsson . . .' Here the priest stops. Stares over at the aged woman.

'May I introduce you to the noted seer Randiður Ólafsdóttir, and her son, who attends her. I have brought her on your instruction in the last of many letters you have sent me on this matter. You wanted someone who can give you proof of witchcraft, and so here she is. Blind and lame and –' he wrinkles his nose – 'pungent.'

The priest stands, mouth gaping. He steps forward, gestures to the open doorway.

'Please, come inside and get warm, Randiður Ólafsdóttir. Your journey has been long, and fraught with difficulty, I imagine. It is an honour, a *privilege*, to welcome you.'

Síra Jón leads them into the *baðstofa*, where a servant has piled dried dung onto the hearth. It emits a dry, choking heat. The old woman walks with difficulty. Supported by the younger man, her hand, calloused, grips a simple wooden staff. She shakes with cold, emitting a yeasty odour like dough left too long in the sun.

'Come closer to the fire. Please sit,' he says, fussing. He turns to his wife and stepdaughter, who has now joined them. 'Fetch ale and skyr for our honoured guests.'

6

'DON'T LOOK AT me like that,' Jón says as he crouches over a bleating sheep.

Kneeling beside my brother, I hold the animal's head as he inspects its leg, glancing back at me now and again. We are inside the largest of the *skáli*, a stone hut where our flock lives out the winter. Animals huddle together, chewing with stolid purpose from hay bales stacked haphazardly against one of the walls.

I look 'like that' again to make my point.

'I know what we did to the priest wasn't good, sister. But can you blame us?' He looks back at me again. 'How is it, Þuriður, that you can say so much without words?'

I consider his face, angular in just the right proportions to make many of the local girls blush and cast down their eyes. Yellow hair. Wind-burnt skin. Deep blue eyes framed by eyebrows that arch when he looks at me. A man now, young and headstrong, his character already shaping the contours of his face: the beginnings of lines at each corner of his mouth from laughing and shouting and all manner of boisterous utterings, and deep-etched frown and smile lines from fishing out at sea. He looks so much like our father. From what I remember of our mother, there is little to see of her in him, yet always I search. Her features are just out of my remembering, a chimera, a memory I have built rather than recalled. At night, I still think of her, what she would have looked like now, how cool her hand would have felt brushing my cheek. She would have cautioned my father against goading the priest, or, at least, I think she would have done. It was too long ago. Ten winters. I was a child of eight, my brother a boy of ten. Too young to lose a mother.

I allow Jón a small smile, but my feelings run harsh with judgement. I want to reprimand him, tell him how foolish they have been to invite the wrath of such a man, yet I would not condemn them. They are men of standing in our community. Not to fight back would have been a sign of weakness.

The ewe struggles.

'She's lame. Look, she's injured her front leg, which means she'll bring infection to the rest of them if we don't cull her. You were a good lamber, weren't you, girl?' My brother speaks to the creature as if to a babe in his arms. Soft and placating. 'How did you damage that foot so badly? Did you get trampled by the bigger mothers, pushing you away from the hay?'

He strokes the sheep's face, her unblinking eyes staring back at him.

'We have to send you back to the gods where you came from. Óðinn will feast on you at Jólblot, at Yule, so the gods won't know hunger.'

It is touching, this little scene. My brother staring into the sheep's devoted gaze, but the truth is he has courted disaster. Things have been said that cannot be unsaid, threats made that cannot be rescinded. Síra Jón Magnússon was clear – but my brother and father seem not to care, carrying on as if the service – and the priest's public attacks on them – did not happen.

As if they were not threatened with burning.

As if they did not send hellfire in the form of black magic after the service. Upon waking, a pallid brume settling across the valley, I heard their voices outside, talking to the farmhands, insulting the priest, laughing at his audacity in naming them. *Them*. I heard also the catch in my brother's throat as he laughed along. Fear underneath the bravado – fear that seems to have evaporated with the dew-threaded mist.

I touch Jón's shoulder after he releases the ewe. She limps away, back into the thickening of sheep, of wool and bleating and chewing. When he turns round, I make the sign of the Christian cross and hold my hands as if in prayer. I know my eyes dance with amusement, but I also know the same trepidation lurks there too.

'The priest,' my brother says, guessing instantly. 'What can he do? It was worth it to see him frothing at the mouth. Men like him are too busy on their knees in front of an altar to be a threat to us. Of all the *seid-menn* in Iceland, our father is the most powerful. This snivelling priest can't touch us. Don't waste your time thinking of it. We will send more demons to him this night – and every night hereafter. He tried to make a fool of us, but we have ways to keep him on his knees.'

Prick.

Arrogant prick!

'You don't agree? You could always actually fucking speak to me, sister, rather than make me guess what you're thinking.'

My regard must soften, because he smiles back. There is a sudden movement somewhere and a high bleat. Jón jumps up and wades through the moving woollen mass.

'I knew it. She's being stamped on by one of the other mothers. Get away, you fucker, and leave her alone!'

The injured ewe lost a lamb last year. She tried to suckle the other mothers' newborns, which is why they kick her away even now their lambs are full grown. I look around, draw in the odour of the hut.

There is little to see except the low turf roof of the thick-walled shelter that will contain them until the days lengthen and the thaw begins. We are just like them. We too will crouch in the darkness of our crofts until warmth creeps back across the land, bringing spring rain and long summer nights.

My brother drags the bullied mother sheep away from the others, pulls her to the small wooden door of the *skáli.* I pick up my pail of milk, freshly harvested, and stroke the nearest sheep to me, a ewe with cream-white wool pitted black and brown.

'Let's go. Father will be calling for his meal.'

I follow him back out into the bitter fray. Tiny shards of ice swirl in the frigid air, and deep snow lies underfoot, though a pathway was cleared by the labourers yesterday.

A caw.

Like shadow in motion, the raven rustles its feathers, perched on the post that marks our croft. It makes a soft, clicking sound as I approach. Hand out, palm flat. A small piece of gristle as bait. It rises, flaps, lands on my arm, talons sharp as they grip my flesh. Heavy and blinking, it dips its beak, snatching the meat, gulping it down.

My brother stands back. He knows not to disturb us. I feel the weight of the bird, its unrelenting nature that runs so completely alongside my own.

Deep, throaty croak. It moves its head from side to side, then launches. Midnight sheen. Sky spirit. My soul made with feathers.

'Come, sister. Is your shawl warm enough?' he says, eyeing the large bird as it settles once again on the post.

Linking arms, we walk together. I once saw him do that with a plain girl from Eyri called Rannveig, with brown hair, brown eyes, one I know wanted marriage with my wayward brother. A line he should never have crossed. For all his blustering, Jón has a heart. I cannot deny him that, but he is a fool. And so is my father.

7

ÞORKATLA BJARNADÓTTIR WRINKLES her nose.

She looks over at the old woman and the man who must be a relative of some kind. She thinks: *Save the good yallow-brewed ale for when the sheriff visits alone*. Rannveig, her daughter, walks rather too quickly down to the kitchen. Þorkatla knows she resents her time spent indoors, away from her beloved sheep. More than that, Þorkatla knows she tries not to be in the same room as her mother after what happened. It is something that is never mentioned; there is a name never breathed in this household. But, like white cloud-mould that grows on winter barley, it spreads its spores, contaminating them all, growing in the silence.

There seems to be nothing she can say to mend her daughter's opinion of her. So this dance continues: Rannveig and her. Never saying what needs to be said. Never fixing this schism that stretches between them, this division. Whenever Þorkatla tries to speak, the words do not appear at the right time, in the right order. When this happens, her daughter looks at her with scorn, making her falter, words intended to build a bridge between them shrivelling and dying on her tongue.

Rannveig is already gathering what they have. She scoops late-autumn berries onto a plate, finds a dish of skyr from the stores. The surly maidservant has already put a kettle on the fire to boil water for tea.

'Don't waste the firewood. Your master says they must drink ale. Go fetch a barrel. Make sure it isn't our best sort,' the priest's wife says. 'Rannveig, when you've prepared their food, take it through. Our guests need sustenance.'

Her daughter will not meet her eyes, but she nods. This is how it has been for four months now. How long will this continue?

'What are they doing here?' the maidservant asks.

Rannveig still says nothing. Instead, she pushes a stray lock of the same earth-coloured brown hair back under her cap. Þorkatla bustles now, finding enough cups, making sure they are clean. She wipes one with the end of her apron, retrieved from where she flung it earlier.

'None of your business,' she snaps. At the same time, she glances over at her daughter. Rannveig is the image of her mother: the same unremarkable brown hair, the same sallow skin and mud-brown eyes. She has a smattering of freckles across her nose that serves to make her face pretty in the right light.

'Be careful! Don't spill the skyr. We need every bit to last this winter.'

The maidservant scowls.

'Why are they here, Mother? Is it to do with the Jón Jonssons?' Rannveig stops now. A dollop of thick curd slides off her spoon onto the table. The maidservant looks between the two women. Acting fast, she drags her finger across the spill. Sucks it off her finger.

'Clean that table now!' the priest's wife says, aiming a slap at the maidservant's arm. The girl is too quick. She dodges out of the way, suppressing a giggle.

'That girl. It's not as if I don't feed her. She'll be going in spring, mark my words.' Þorkatla tuts, thankful for the distraction. She turns back to her daughter, unsure what to say. She hesitates. Words prick like brambles. They twist and turn, spiky in her mouth.

'Daughter, I can't talk about it. You must forget them. They mean nothing to you – or our family – any longer . . .'

But as she speaks Þorkatla feels the sting of her lie. Sýslumaður Sigurdsson is here because her husband gathers evidence against the sorcerer and his apprentice, Jón Jónsson the Younger. The boy who courted her daughter. Who brought all this upon them. Þorkatla bites her lip. She imagines the thorny brambles growing from her throat, up out of her mouth as she tells falsehoods to her daughter.

Rannveig, who looks older than her sixteen winters, throws her mother a look that says she does not believe her.

'After you've taken in the food, you can go back to our *skáli*. There should be hay enough to feed your precious sheep.'

Þorkatla instantly regrets the tone of her voice, the implied sneer in her choice of words.

Rannveig nods as if she expected the remark, walks out, her head held high, carrying the skyr to feed their guests.

The priest steps into the kitchen. He leans back against the wall to let her pass.

'I was checking when they might eat, but I see all is in hand,' he says.

Þorkatla, her insides churning, regret and sadness pulling at her with invisible cords, nods.

'Husband, may I speak with you?'

'What is it? We mustn't keep them waiting.' The priest makes as if to turn. Þorkatla places a cool hand on his arm to stop him.

'Rannveig—'

'Yes? What about her? I must get back to our guests.'

For a moment, she hesitates, as if unsure of herself.

'Will you tell her what it is you're doing? Will you tell her you are gathering evidence to use against the Jón Jónssons? Don't you think she should know?'

Síra Jón Magnússon looks momentarily startled. He soon recovers. Shakes his head.

'This is the business of the law and the Church. Rannveig must be protected at all costs. Do you forget, she was almost the victim of their wiles, their witchery? Do not tell her anything. This is my command to you as my wife.'

Þorkatla's face reveals the battle raging inside her. There is an agony playing out in her eyes and heart. The priest sees it and waits.

Her daughter's interests or her husband's? There can, of course, be no question whom she must obey, but he can see it pains her.

'Of course, husband,' she says at last. Satisfied, he turns away. Again, the hand on his arm. This time, clutching his sleeve.

'What now? I must go to our guests.' His voice is coolly impatient. He makes to pull away from her. She does not let go.

'That woman? The seer, Randiður Ólafsdóttir?' Þorkatla says. Her eyes flick towards the doorway of the *baðstofa*. 'It can't be the one they talk of throughout the Westfjords . . . that woman stinks of the cattle shed! The famed seer saw devils sucking the life out of her husband as he lay dying. That woman sitting on our good chairs, drinking our ale, is . . . is . . . as unlike a clairvoyant as any person I have ever set eyes upon.'

The priest looks down at his feet, shod in leather that has seen better days. He notices the smears of earth upon his surplice, the rim of dirt under his fingernails. He draws in a long inhalation as if anchoring himself here, with this woman, in this life. At last, he speaks.

'Yes, we are indeed *privileged* to have the famous seer in this rectory. She is a woman of *absolute humility*. She has no riches nor finery to flaunt, yet she does *God's work* for the benefit of us all. Look again, Þorkatla. Look past the poor nature of her dress, her rough manner.

Look into her soul and see the wealth of God's love. She is medicine. She will see what there is to see. She will uncover the devilry that has been sent to injure and taunt me, and she will do so with righteousness and faith that shines beyond the lustre of any gemstone.'

He gives his wife a long, hard look. She steps back, takes her hand off his arm. He does not wait for her reply. Instead, he walks back to sit with the visitors, leaving his wife staring after him, her mind a tumult of things she cannot say.

The district sheriff has taken off his riding hat and smoothed down his shoulder-length hair, greyer even than his beard. He is still wrapped in a thick outer coat though the fire is stoked, a servant piling on a good quantity of fuel. The seer refuses all offers of food, her son too. In contrast, the sheriff scoops spoonfuls of thick, white skyr into his mouth, wiping his beard occasionally on a piece of linen placed by the side of the dish. His face is fleshy, his lips red, flecks of skyr clinging to his bristles. Only when he has finished can they begin.

'Thank you for travelling from Súðavik, a day's ride in bitter weather,' Síra Jón says, directing his gaze first to the *sýslumaður* then the old woman, and finally, the young man.

Sýslumaður Sigurdsson grunts a response. Finishes his mouthful. Looks around the small, squat croft, meanly furnished, at the bare rafters overhead packed tight with turf, the trampled dirt of the floor, at the bed, the hearth, the cross.

Weak sunlight casts its haze-glow on each stick of furniture, each person within.

It is a strange tableau: the sheriff, the priest, his wife, who stands now at the side of the room, the ageing seer and her son.

Just then, the seer makes a high-pitched sound.

'I see it!' she says, her voice querulous, wavering.

Randiður Ólafsdóttir looks with her unseeing eyes, pointing towards the window.

'It is there . . . It is there now.' She shuffles off her seat. Edges her bony frame closer to the wall.

'It looks straight in on you.'

All heads turn. The membrane stretched across the hole in the wall reveals nothing.

'What do you see, Mother?' The young man stands up, grips an arm to steady her.

The priest feels a sudden chill. It spreads through his body. He stands, unsure what to say, what to do.

The elderly widow steps towards the small window again, holding her staff aloft now. Her arm – and soon her whole body – trembling.

'It's there, and it's looking at you, Síra Jón Magnússon.' When she turns her face to the priest, her wild grey hair tangles around her face, her eyes, as opaque as the sheath pane, stare straight at him. Though how can they?

'What is it?' the priest says. 'What is there, looking at me?'

'The one who harms you, preacher,' Randiður replies. 'Be warned. He watches you in the shape of a black dog. He is there now. Be warned . . .'

The old woman sags, spent. She leans back into her son's embrace. The priest feels a sudden piercing sensation near his heart. Clutches his hand to his chest. He moves towards the small square of light. His body quivers. He cannot control the shaking. There is nothing there he can see. He rips back the veined skin. There is nobody in the yard, not even the younger of the maidservants, who dallies there in the hope of catching sight of one of the young farmhands, despite the chill. The large wooden cross of the church dominates the skyline. If this was summer, it would throw down its shadow onto this croft, blocking the light.

'There is nothing there,' the priest says. He cannot tell if this frightens him more.

'Oh, it is there, Síra Jón Magnússon. A black dog growls, with hackles raised.' The seer coughs, her mucus-speckled lungs discharging phlegm, which she spits with some force. The yellowing wad of spittle lands at the sheriff's feet, causing him to step back, disgust on his features.

There is a pause.

'A black dog . . . See, sheriff? See! The seer has confirmed it. There are dark forces unleashed upon me and my household, though it is I who am hunted. It is the work of the sorcerer Jón Jónsson the Elder and his son, the Younger. Can any now say it isn't true?'

Again, the silence.

Sýslumaður Sigurdsson clears his throat.

'I see nothing. The word of the seer, however godly, is not enough evidence to convict those who call themselves sorcerers of a campaign against you.'

'This is the word of Randiður Ólafsdóttir!' Síra Jón says, his breath short, his mind buzzing like insects in long grass. 'She is no ordinary seer. She is renowned throughout the Westfjords. Her word must count.'

The buzzing increases.

The face of the sheriff is blurred. He is wiping his beard, picking up his hat as if making ready to leave.

Horror, absolute, engulfs Síra Jón. The sheriff denies the truth. He, Síra Jón, is alone, fighting the devil sent by the sorcerers. He pictures, for the briefest moment, a sheep's stomach bloated by disease, the animal corpse lying abandoned in a summer pasture. He recalls the round swelling burst, spewing rot and maggots from its greying flesh. A release of darkness and decay. A release of death. He understands that his faith alone cannot save him. The darkness is unquenchable.

The priest collapses.

*

'My love? Husband? Síra Jón's eyes are opening, bring water . . .'

Þorkatla's voice washes into his hearing, then recedes like glacial tides from Grænland. The priest's head feels light, too light, as if he has drifted, unmoored, away from the shore of his physical body.

'Splash his face!' comes now the sound of Sýslumaður Sigurdsson, barking a command like he does to the hounds that follow his horse.

The sheriff's face peers down. His pale blue eyes blink. When the priest's gaze meets his, they narrow, briefly.

'He's alive. Well, he's conscious, anyway,' the sheriff says. He is already sitting back in his chair, his hand stroking his beard as Þorkatla and the seer's son help the stricken priest to his feet. Unsteady, Síra Jón sits heavily on a chair.

The sheriff calls for brandy, which the surly maidservant brings, dipping a curtsy and gasping aloud when she sees the strange gathering: the priest hunched in his seat, the seer hitched to her son now, her mistress flapping and fussing around her husband. The sheriff eyes the girl, who blushes and walks back to the kitchen slower than she should, her hips swaying. Sýslumaður Sigurdsson swigs the dark liquid as if this is a social call, wetting his fleshy lips.

'He has been fasting more than usual and is weakened. He says he must do it so God will hear him and rid him of this terror,' Þorkatla says as she moves. One blanket or two? Some ale, warmed. A pillow, arranged, to rest against.

'Enough, thank you,' he says. 'I am well enough.'

Síra Jón Magnússon turns to the sheriff. Just as he opens his mouth to speak, the seer speaks. Her voice, thin and reedy: 'The dog has gone. It has taken its foul breath and its stinking hide away from here. It follows the spirit as it walks back towards Kirkjuból. As the dog trots away, the fjord waters rise to greet it.' Her voice rises. 'They know of its diabolical origin. They know it is one of the devil's instruments. The sea is churning into waves as if an earthquake has shaken under it.'

A candle flares with a sudden draught. The seer's arm is raised again and this time she looks upwards, beyond the driftwood rafters, the turf mounds packed together to make a roof, upwards to the celestial heavens.

'God save us!' the priest whispers.

There is silence now in the room. Noise has been sucked out, like an unfriendly tide, leaving only a fearful gap where the sounds of the farmhands and servants, the clattering of pails and the sluicing of water for washing, should be.

The old woman shrinks back further into her son's arms. He nods at Sýslumaður Magnús Sigurdsson, who lowers his head a little in response. With the sheriff's approval, the son leads his withered mother out of the croft. Þorkatla follows and the priest watches them go. A great pull of tiredness takes over, dragging him downwards.

The sheriff looks back at him, slumped in the chair.

'I'll send for the witchfinder,' he says.

8

February 1656

THE WITCHFINDER ÞORLEIFUR Kortsson inspects the room.

He spies the wooden chest, unpacked and open; his leather-bound books lining the shelf; his documents, sheaves of curling vellum patterned with lines of careful notes, placed upon a table. He traces a finger along the fronds of a carved leaf on the back of his chair. Notes the window containing a clear glass pane. Adjusts a quill that lies at a slight angle next to the ink pot, bringing it back into alignment. He is, if not pleased, then at least satisfied with the accommodation for the duration of his stay in Eyri.

It is here, in his chamber inside the Danish trading station, that he will conduct this investigation into the Jón Jónssons and their practices. A fire leaps in the hearth, which is welcome despite the fine wool of his dark jacket. He catches his reflection in the glass. A man of forty winters. Trimmed beard streaked silver, his thick hair the same, eyes that are piercing in their focus: relentless, rigorous. The smell of cooking meat wafts in from the nearby kitchen, making his mouth water. In contrast, the tiny gaol that sits at the far end of the long building contains only a bucket and filthy straw. The window, such as it is, sits at the top of the wall and is barred, while the wooden door, hewn from oak brought from the still-lush forests of Denmark, is as thick as his fist. There is little wood nor trees to be found in Iceland after the first settlers burned it for fuel.

He thinks briefly of his wife left in their farmstead, a large, sprawling estate with a croft and outbuildings, many acres of land for grazing and crops, a small army of servants, labourers and farmhands. He carries a small painting of Ingibjörg and their four children, a rare token of the human feeling he disguises with exquisite care.

His reputation arrived here before him, travelling through endless harsh wilderness to this isolated series of farms around the Djúp. He is gratified to see the confusion, then the dawning understanding, the *recognition*, upon the faces of those he has encountered at Eyrakirkja. Then, the quick-hidden fear, the knowledge of others he has prosecuted, has killed, that has reached even here, on a windswept spit of gravel.

He saw the same thing at Trékyllisvík; the expressions of the three men who thought themselves protected by Satan and his demons. As each sorcerer stood before him at their trial, he felt the earth rise up to claim them, to remove them. He felt an outpouring of his powers, singeing all in its path, the beginning of the purification of this land. Of course, he is a man devoted to God and to His authority and dominance. He knows he is but a servant, a devoted, dedicated servant, and all thoughts of the supernatural are forbidden. However, he sees that fear is a power all of its own. One, if used on the path to righteousness, worth exercising in the name of Frederick III of Denmark, the witch-hunting King Christian IV's second son and unlikely heir.

One of his documents from that trial lies open: a testimony, several oaths, a verdict: all writ in his meticulous, steady hand, though there are flourishes of the quill nib: two 't's crossed through with a curving swoop that loops back on itself, the spine of each 'ð' flowing upwards into the path of the letters above it. He prides himself on the neatness of his records, the completeness of his account of each prosecution, each burning, entombed inside these parchments that will form part of the history of his frozen homeland. One day, he muses, in the far-distant future, someone will look through them, will learn of the battles fought upon this volcanic rock. He only hopes and prays they will look from a place of victory, where the Christian Church is triumphant, and magic but an echo, a long-stubbed-out memory from the past.

At the window, he watches snow dancing as the wind swoops and whistles off the fjord. The sky is blank, grey, forbidding.

He sees Síra Jón Magnússon, swathed in a thick brown cloak, head down against the buffeting gale, walk the short distance from the rectory to the church. He carries books under one arm, most likely Bibles for the day's service. He thinks of Sýslumaður Magnús Sigurdsson, the lawman who will preside over these activities.

Tonight, they will act. Tonight, it begins.

9

'HE'S COME! I saw him with my own eyes!'

My friend Anna's face is flushed as she stumbles into my croft, holding her daughter, Fjola. I am sitting at my loom. The river stones weighting the warp threads clack together as I draw the stick shuttle, wound with wool, through the threads. Winter light falls in a single shaft onto my hands as they work. Behind me are the women of the settlements around us, discussing the weather, their husbands, how best to brew their next batch of mead, how best to entice a lover. Together, we weave and sew like the three Norns, the female deities determining our fates: Urðr, Verðandi and Skuld, who weave the threads of fate and the destiny of souls. Children squabble and chatter, milk-beaded smiles on grubby faces, an occasional swipe aimed in their direction.

I give a small shake of my head. Lift my shoulders.

Who? Who has come?

'Þuriður! The witchfinder is here. The one who killed three *seid-menn* at Trékyllisvík! He's feared from here to Copenhagen.' Anna places Fjola down, and begins to peel the thick layers of clothing from them both.

My father and brother are out feeding our livestock winter hay stores with the men. Margrét looks up from her darning, as do the other women.

'The fishermen's wives told me he was standing there, next to the altar on Sunday, with Síra Jón,' Anna gushes.

'It's true, there have been rumours the witchfinder would come for days now,' Margrét says, pricking her thumb, drawing a red orb of blood. 'Everyone's talking about it. As soon as the service ended, I came back straight away. I was going to tell you . . . Anyway, the boatman rowed faster for me. He always does . . .' she adds, smiling to herself as if her flirtations are news to us while she sucks her finger.

Our maidservant is the same age as me; we have both seen eighteen winters, though I fancy I am the elder. Blonde, pink-cheeked Margrét arrived one spring, an orphan, asking for work and a warm bed, and has stayed ever since. She usually hums to herself as she drops stitches, making a poor attempt at repairing my brother's socks. She is looking at me now as if suddenly wary.

I turn to look at her, then Anna.

My friend's eyes are wide, her face flushed from windchill. She divests herself of layers of patterned wool.

Inside, within thick stone walls, it is warm enough. I wear only one shawl and fingerless woollen gloves. Outside, the sky glowers grey while the wind shrieks, throwing snow down from darkened skies. Almost everyone now makes their way each Sunday morning to Eyrakirkja in knee-high snow, but my family and I do not.

'The witchfinder said your father and brother are a disease, and he is the cure. He says they – and all like them – must face purification by fire, just as the priest said.'

My kin have practised magic since I was a suckling babe, and their forefathers before them. Why now? Through the cold summers and failed harvests, we have stuck together to survive, by magic or whatever means. My father and brother have never made any attempt to hide their sorcery. Why should they? Most local people have used them in one form or another. If a sheep goes lame or a cow cannot be milked; if a fox decimates your flock, or a harsh wind destroys your crop; if you want to marry this maiden or that farmhand; if you want to avoid trouble in childbirth; or dangers at sea, then come to Jón Jónsson the Elder and the Younger. They can work with the old gods and the new, with Óðinn's fury and God's wrath. It is here you will find help, for the price of a bale of hay or an ell of cloth, your desires can be magicked into existence.

They never had a problem coming to my kin for help. What has changed? Anger flares like a lit torch.

'Þuriður?'

The stick I was threading through the warp has now, inexplicably, dropped to the floor. I stand, my heart pounding, a feeling of being squeezed, choked, making it hard to breathe. I open my mouth like a fish gulping air instead of briny sea water. I close it again. The words are falling over themselves to be spoken, but I have forgotten, my mouth has forgotten. I am bound to silence. My throat is tight, my pulse hammering now as the dread of this unfurls.

I make a soundless gesture familiar to us both. I move both hands, opening the palms outwards and upwards, reaching up but a little as my shoulders hunch. A gesture of surprise, of consternation, of questioning.

When will he come for them?

Anna has both hands on my shoulders. She grips me tight to steady me. I know my skin, translucent and white, blue veins threading underneath its surface, will show the marks.

I look around the croft. Here, we live surrounded by the tools of their trade: the rune sticks; grimoires; feathers; shells; markings scratched into bone and wood; nameless parts of birds, small calcified creatures; prayers rendered in blood on thin, stretched calfskins; *galdraletur* inscribed upon the rafters; and all manner of spells and curses that have soaked into the walls and turf roof. People – men usually – come here every day to ask for a charm to help a birthing cow, or a curse to stop an enemy fishing at sea. It could be any manner of problems or worries that, with a spell, can be magicked away, for a price. This is the way of things. It has always been the way of things. There are always those who wish to have power over something in their lives. Or at least there used to be. No one has come since that night in the chapel.

I look back at her and shake my head.

Fokk.

She nods as if she reads my mind.

'You have to do something, Þuriður.'

They are not in the outhouses nor the *skáli*.

Wading through snow, Margrét grumbles at my side. I pulled her from the fireside out into the frozen pasture to look everywhere I can think of, sending the other women back to their homes. We have to find them. Their lives may depend upon it. Cursing silently, I admit defeat when I see their horses are missing. They must have gone to trade hay or livestock with an outlying farmstead.

While I wait, I find weaving does not calm me as it usually does. The gentle rattle of the stones, the pull of the warp, the slow threading. Each section of the cloth forming almost without seeming to. Each movement an incantation woven into the fabric. Usually, it stills the wildness in my soul, but not today. I pace. I fret. I look outside though darkness has fallen. When I hear their horses, a surge of anger comes so fierce it seems to burn away my fear.

My father and Jón clatter in.

'We're hungry!' my brother shouts. They are throwing off their snow-wet cloaks, talking loudly, laughing at some stupid joke. I gesture for them to stop. I shake my head.

No.

'What, Þuriður? We're tired. Make the dinner and help me get these boots off.' My father sits down heavily at the table, reaching down to pull off the worn leather, soaked through.

I shake my head again. I grab his hands to stop him.

No.

I point outside, towards the spit in the distance.

'What now? We don't know what you're trying to say!' He glances over at Jón.

Father has teased the boot off. He grunts as he lets it fall, starts to drag off the other.

Again, I grab his hands, scowling. *No!*

'*Fokk*, Þuriður, why can't you just say the fucking words,' Jón says, rolling his eyes. I stamp my foot and march towards him. He moves to shield himself until he realizes I carry nothing that could be used as a weapon: a ladle, a sharpened knife for gutting fish. I have slashed at him before, as a child, catching him on the side of his cheek. He has a small scar still. He had been teasing me mercilessly. What did he expect?

I point again in the direction of the spit, vigorously. Anna and Freyja would understand.

My brother sighs. With an exaggerated shrug, he sits down, does the same as my father.

I pick up my father's boot.

Put it back on! You need to leave!

I jab at the mountains behind us this time.

You must run away and hide. You must go now!

My fury makes them laugh. They return to talking about another farmer, sniggering at something. I cannot make them listen.

I look around. I can write but badly. Girls are not taught, but I know how to draw the runes and the magical sigils, because I have watched my brother's feeble, halting attempts. There is a good quantity of ash by the fire. Kneeling down, careless of the grey powder covering my skirt that is sewn with plants and flowers, my own decoration, I draw *vegvísir*, a sigil of warning, of an approaching storm. Then, I point again. This should do it.

Neither man is watching.

Both are peeling off layers of wool jumpers, the sour smell of sweat and sheep wool permeating the *baðstofa*.

I want to shout: *Get your own fucking dinner – and when you've done that, listen to me. You need to go tonight!*

My brother has begun sharpening his knife with its brass handle, slouched at the table. My father is already preparing a spell for a fisherman in Bolungarvík to change the direction of the wind. A bird lies scattered upon the wooden surface – a wing here, the beak and head there, eyes glassy and still.

'Food, daughter, please,' Father says, without looking at me.

Then, a warning.

Outside, a fox screams.

10

THE BANGING COMES: forceful, insistent.

My father and brother share a quick glance. There are other noises – horses whinnying, the muffled drop of feet into snowdrift, low chatter – though the storm blankets the sounds. They stand up, presumably to go to the doorway to see who is there.

They do not need to.

The door crashes open, the tail end of the blizzard following. A sudden draught. A moment's silence as the freezing air rushes in and forms itself around the three men striding into our croft. The fire flares and then dies back. A lone candle sputters out. The men move like harbingers of doom, biblical in their grievances, rolling in on the late-winter tide, their boots covered in snow.

The priest Síra Jón Magnússon, Sýslumaður Magnús Sigurdsson and another man, a stranger. A man dressed entirely in black: cloak, hat, boots. I have already guessed who he is. They stand in our *baðstofa*. The silence is broken by my father:

'What brings you all here this treacherous night?' he says as if they have met by chance.

The men glance around the room. They see the lengths of netting, the large hearth piled up on stones upon which a kettle is warming, the two rows of wooden beds with carved edging along each side of the raised platform, the furs and oilskins. They see the signs of a farm that is flourishing, its land in good heart, its workers well fed and warm.

The sheriff clears his throat.

'You know why we're here,' the priest interjects, standing forward. 'You are both accused of sorcery. No, do not deny it here!' He raises a hand to stop whatever it is that might be said in protest. 'Save it for your trial.'

'Our what?' Father says. 'Our trial?'

'This is fucking ridiculous. You're insane, priest.' My brother this time.

'We're here to arrest you.' The sheriff, Sýslumaður Magnús Sigurdsson, speaks. The stranger says nothing. The candle smokes behind him.

My brother laughs.

Idiot. He doesn't realize how dangerous these men are. He's so slow. The sheriff coughs. The air is dry from the wood and dung on the fire.

'Þuriður, please fetch the sheriff, Magnús Sigurdsson, a cup of water.'

Before I can move to do my father's bidding, the priest shakes his head.

'We will take nothing here from you this night except the air we breathe. You must come with us now.'

Jón's face is changing, his expression sliding from a sneer to shock, to bald fear.

'You can't arrest us!' he says.

'Why not?' the priest replies. 'Because you are feared and powerful *seid-menn*?'

'What harm have we done? We perform only white magic, good

magic to help with crops or cattle or other problems. Every man in these parts has called on our help. It's what we've always done.' My father's voice is raised. He turns to the priest.

'What do any of you know of this magic, of our ways, *þumlungar*?'

Fokk. Fokk. Fokk.

My father has spoken his nickname for the priest aloud. It is an insult, an unmanning. It implies smallness, of stature – and of manhood.

There is silence for a brief moment.

'You must come with us. Now.' The sheriff is half a head shorter than my father, but he seems to grow, to enlarge in the gloom. His dark coat with silver buttons that glint as they catch the firelight expands until he fills the *baðstofa*.

I look at my father and see his arrogance as if it is drawn on his skin like the inked markings, the special signs and sigils that mark him as sorcerer. I shiver though the room is becoming warmer again, the heat rising from the fire into the rafters.

'Arrest them, sheriff. These two men have tortured me. They've been guilty of serious and dangerous crimes. They've practised sorcery against me with vicious acts of witchcraft, which is forbidden under God's laws—'

'And those of the Danes . . .' my brother mutters.

Shut the fuck up, brother.

'They've summoned the devil to appear to me, causing pains in my body and mind, and all of Eyri knows of my sufferings. Many can – and will – testify.'

'We practise white magic. Our family has done so for generations, as long as there have been settlers here in Iceland,' my father says. He places a hand on my brother's shoulder. He does it to calm my brother, or to stop him speaking. God – and Óðinn – know how stupid he can be at times.

With surprising dignity, my father continues.

'These are our traditions, our ways. We've lived alongside the Christian God and His preachers for centuries – though this priest has been determined to ruin our names and standing. For months now, he's been making these accusations at Mass, telling any who would listen, or so people say . . .'

'You wouldn't know because you have not been to Mass!' the priest counters.

'You both know as well as I that King Christian the fourth banned all sorcery – black and white – as sinful,' the sheriff says, stepping in. 'You know his son Frederick, whom it pleased God to ascend the throne after his death, follows his father's lead. Both are now punishable by death. What might once have been . . . tolerated, is now a crime—'

'And a sin!' the priest says. Still, the stranger says nothing. He has a brooding, unquiet presence; an Arctic fox stalking, back crouched, dark eyes set, paws picking through snow.

'The Danish Witchcraft Act, made law here in 1630, tells us so.' It is this man who speaks. When he opens his mouth, the fire seems to draw down, the lamplight too. The air in the large room seems all at once to stifle and suffocate. His speech is eloquent, the clothing on his back fine, his boots good leather.

The witchfinder.

There is silence, again.

'You are accused of flouting this law, of continuing your sorcery and using your powers to harm the local priest,' the sheriff says. It is clear to me he has wearied of this conversation. As if in agreement, the wind rattles the doorframe, sending a shower of ice in through the *skjár*.

'We meant no harm,' my father says.

I look over at my father. I know without checking he will have bunched up his fists, readying himself. Each skin-hardened finger will curl into each palm, both scaly with blisters from carving, chopping, herding, dragging nets both in and out of the water. The salt crust of the sea has chafed his strong hands. Meddlesome winds have scored lines into his face. He too is a handsome man, all the women say. He is the only parent I have. He is also a witch, a man of magic, a sorcerer.

Yet, when the time comes, my father walks out of our homestead as meekly as Christ's lamb to the slaughter. It is my brother who almost knocks over the priest in a fit of temper. He has finally realized these men mean what they say, that his life is now threatened in the time it takes a smile to turn into a frown. My brother: loutish, often drunk, a man who hollers rather than shouts, who slams his fists onto tables rather than talks. They have brought peril to our door on this storm-blown night.

Father steps outside first, closely followed by the priest, who mutters a prayer as they open the door to the frozen night, the gusting wind. The shimmer of moonlight lays bare the white pastures, the steel-slashed ice of the fjord. Inside, a lamp flares then dies, leaving only one small halo of light. The fire brightens, the embers glow hot and red. The sheriff goes next. He puts his hat back on, arranges his cloak, nodding to me as if he finally notices my presence.

Take a coat, I want to say. *Take food, water, gloves. Take a fur to wrap yourselves in. Take the herbs to cast a spell to free yourselves.*

My brother shouts and curses. His voice carries through the door, out into the storm, along the rough track Father dug out only today, a pathway of sorts towards the direction of the fjord. The horses stamp their hooves and snort. The man in black is the last to leave. He turns to look at me as if he knows me. I did not think he had noticed I am here.

II

March 1656

A COIN SLIPPED into a waiting hand.

The clink of metal on metal. The scrape of a key turning in a lock. The stench of piss and shit and dirt. Footsteps on the slimy flagstone floor. Two sets of eyes blinking back at me in the darkness.

The gaoler grunts as I nod my thanks and enter. My father, who it appears can still command a little of the respect given to *seid-menn*, has negotiated this visit. Sending word to me. Telling me to come.

The door shuts behind me. The key turns. The rats scuttle. There is little light except for the candle in my hand and a window, barred.

'Þuriður, you brought us food?' My father, his face already thinner, looks up at me as I scrabble through my bag made of sacking. Both men are chained to the wall. There is a bucket to piss in and fetid straw to lie upon. My father pulls at the cloth in my hands, taking a chunk of rye crust. Devouring it. My brother pulls himself up from lying in the filth. His hair is streaked dark with grime, his trousers torn. Neither is wearing enough to counter the flaying whip of the season's chill, which is itself a form of torture in Iceland.

My brother snatches at the cod and the last piece of the bread. He does not look at me. He turns his face away, scatters crumbs as he eats. He has been humbled. When they have swallowed their final mouthfuls, with difficulty without fresh water, they sit back down again on the straw, backs against the wooden wall. I kneel down, place the candle on the hard floor, take them both in. My father, bloodied, has a cut on the side of his face where a bruise blooms dark purple and yellow. Their gaolers are not treating them well.

They both wince as they move. I see the dried blood caked on their sleeves, their collars, their bare feet. They are pale in the gloom, their skin grey underneath the beards that are growing on both their chins. The pallor of the prison.

My father coughs and does not stop. I look around for a pail of water. Finding none, I get up and run to the door, banging for the gaoler.

'Something to drink, please,' my father says, gasping when the guard appears.

The gaoler looks between us. Finding nothing of sorcery or witchcraft about this request, he walks off. He returns with a single cup and a slop-stained bucket, which contains water, brackish and cold.

'Thank you,' my father says.

'Arsehole,' my brother, Jón, mutters. Outside a goat bleats. 'Fucking goat. I wish it was dead. It keeps us from sleep!' he says loud enough for the gaoler to hear this time. The key turns, locking us in. The gaoler glowers behind the barred door.

I ignore my brother, and scoop up the liquid, holding it out to my father. The weight of the irons round his wrists makes holding it difficult. He takes it, drinks, leans back against the wooden walls, built from timber brought in by the Danish fleet. When the hacking eases, he looks at me.

'We need your help.'

I nod.

That's obvious.

'We need twelve men to swear the *tylftareiður*, the sworn testimony that will set us free.'

I nod again.

Again, obvious.

Everyone in Iceland knows the law. If twelve good men swear your innocence, you are free, no matter the charges. My father looks at me: expectant, hopeful. My brother says something under his breath I cannot make out.

I nod for the third time. This seems to satisfy my father. Of course, I know to approach the men of our community.

'Daughter, you must gather men from Eyri and Kirkjuból. There'll be enough who'll take the oath at our trial. We've helped many more than that, so why wouldn't they help us in return?'

'If they don't, they'll be the worse off without our magic,' says Jón the Younger.

There is something unsaid. I can feel it. It sits like a sea mist uncurling within this cramped space, this place of containment and capture.

'All they have to do is swear our innocence on a Bible, and then we'll be free,' my father says, looking at me with rare tenderness.

'But how's she going to ask people to help when she doesn't speak? And she's only a girl – what can she do?' My brother casts a glance at me with less concern. When I was younger, I would have stuck my tongue out at him or whispered some insult. I might have stolen his knife or thrown his eating spoon or a boot off the side of the mountain. Now? Things are different. My silence is my power, a rockface neither can climb.

'Because she's Þuriður. She's got more balls than half the farmstead. If anyone can find a way to help us, it's her.'

I wonder about my father. So often, I feel invisible in our home, kept away from the closed lives of men fishing at sea, herding cattle, drinking mead, performing magic. It seems I have not escaped his notice, however. I am unsure how I feel about this new-felt exposure, this *pride* in me.

I cast my gaze down to my hands. They are clasped together, entwined. I pull them apart, slowly, space appearing between each digit until they are separated.

But what if they won't swear the tylftareiður? What then?

It appears neither my father nor brother has thought of this. They stare back as if this is settled. As if the chains that bind them will snap apart and they will glide out of here back to our farm.

I know this will be a hard task. But these two men – these two frustrating, foolish, arrogant men – are my only family. I have no fear of begging for help. I have no pride that will stop me asking people, then asking again. If anyone can do this, it is I. Yet, I feel it. The unspoken thought. The silent accusation.

My father and brother are guilty, and everyone knows it.

12

THE RIDE BACK to Kirkjuból is hard.

Ink-black like the sky, the fjord harbour has hardened, each lap of the water forming into icy ridges, patterned back from the shoreline flanked by white-sheeted mountains. My eyelashes are ice. My fingers too. I grip the reins, though I barely feel my hands. Another storm is coming. I can feel the wind-whipped spray of it as it forms out at sea. I cannot remove the sight of my once-proud father and brother chained and shackled from my mind as I urge my horse onward.

I do not go straight to our croft.

'*Komdu sæl og blessaður, Þuriður*.' There is a pause. 'We know why you've come.'

Anna's husband, Ari Björnsson, opens the croft door to me after I knock three times on the window, one each for the Holy Trinity. I cannot knock on the door as the light is dying. Everyone knows only evil spirits knock on doors in darkness. We kiss on the mouth as is the custom, but his words are clear. He shakes his head, offering his hand to guide me into the *baðstofa*.

I duck as I enter, stamping my boots in the small area between the outer and inner doors. My horse stands, tied to a fence. I cannot leave him outside for long. Even inside, it is cool. Frigid air leeches through the stone walls of the dwelling. A fish-oil lamp burns at one end.

I move around the room, greeting each person in turn with a nod and a smile. Three families live in this turf croft that sits to the west of Kirkjuból: Ari, Anna and their children; Ari's older brother, Egil, his wife, Ólina, and their children; and his younger brother, Ólafur, as yet unmarried. The servants live here too yet it is the same size as our dwelling: a sizeable room with a corridor leading to the kitchen and then onward to the outhouses and *skáli*.

After being blessed many times in return, I am back facing Ari. He is a tall man, with the strong arms and frame of someone used to the rigours of fishing at sea. His two brothers, Egil and Ólafur, sit at the table, both almost identical in looks. Ari has dark blond hair and a darker beard, and he is frowning at me. His face is weathered, his eyes lined, the skin lighter inside the creases like pale cuts from a gutting knife. It is a good face, a kind, working face. One I trust.

Ari's large hands are now hidden in his crossed arms.

'We guess you've come to ask us to swear the *tylftareiður*?' he says.

I nod.

He shakes his head, glances at the other men. They do the same.

'Many think your father and brother have brought this upon themselves. They've spoken of their hatred of the priest countless times. Not everyone feels the same way your kin do, Þuriður Jónsdóttir . . .'

I place my hands on my hips. I look him straight in the eye.

You have to swear the oath.

'You're going to struggle to find twelve men to swear to their innocence on the Bible,' he continues, as if this is, indeed, a conversation. 'People here don't want trouble. They want to make sure their crops ripen, and their cattle survive. They don't like this. It's a bad business, Þuriður – you must see that?'

I shake my head. I know he is right, but this is my family, my only living family. I circle my arms in a gesture that means everyone here sought them out at one time or another.

They accepted my father's help enough times when they wanted their crops to ripen or their livestock to live! They didn't worry about their immortal souls while they were saying their Pater Nosters backwards and inscribing runes on runesticks to thwart an enemy or make a woman want to bed them. No. They weren't so worried about God – or the witchfinder – then.

'I'm sorry, Þuriður. We won't swear the oath, and neither will any man in these parts.' This time, it is Ólafur who speaks. He puts down the net he repairs in preparation for the thaw. He stands now, taller than Ari, his expression frank.

'It would bring trouble to our door – and your father and brother have done enough of that already. Prepare yourself. You cannot save them.' His words may be harsh, but his pale blue eyes are soft as he looks at me. I rub my cheek, a gesture I used to make when I was small. It signifies uncertainty, upset, confusion. It is I who turns away from Ólafur's gaze first. I do not want him knowing the pain his words cause me.

There is a low murmur of assent from each of the three men.

I have to try!

'Anna and the children are in the kitchen preparing our meal. Please, stay. Eat with us. We can, at least, do this for you . . .'

The same flare of anger. These are my friends. I have known them since I was born, yet they will not help me. I turn and make to leave, but Ari takes hold of my arm.

'Peace, Þuriður Jónsdóttir. Please, find Anna. She can comfort you. There's no more you can do tonight.'

I know my eyes are hard as I stare back, but a wave of exhaustion, and something else – the powerlessness of this – stops me.

'Anna!' he shouts down the corridor. 'Your friend Þuriður is here . . .'

She appears quickly, meaning she must have been listening close by. Her face is a mix of regret and pain. Her baby son, birthed only three months ago, is asleep in her arms, his head lolling, tiny eyelashes quivering as he dreams.

'Come, let's talk away from the menfolk. You must be hungry and cold.'

My friend leads me to the kitchen, where Egil's wife, Ólina, is stirring a pot on the hearth. Next to her, fifteen-year-old Kristín holds Anna's daughter, Fjola, who is trying to braid the older girl's long dark blonde hair. Kaðlin, a young woman of seventeen, and soon to be married, is spooning skyr into a dish. The fire is a welcome sight.

'Sit down. Get warm. Your cloak is soaked through.' Anna fusses like a mother over me and I find I do not mind it. I am still shivering from my journey, and reeling from the refusal of the men to help. Without their support, my task ahead will be made harder. Why would any man stand by my kin if even our nearest friends do not?

Anna places the warm bundle of her infant into the crease of my elbow. He looks up at me, awakening. His eyes of deepest blue, his cheeks pink against pale skin, a covering of downy blond hair on his head. He is already sucking for his next feed. I bend my head and sniff. He smells of warm milk and the faint scent of sheep from the blanket inside which he is swaddled.

'See? He knows you already. Don't you, little one?' Anna smiles, then turns away, lifting her daughter into her arms as Kristín, the same long dark blonde hair and high forehead as her sister, gets up to help her mother.

'You won't find a man around here with enough guts to stand up against the witchfinder, including my husband and his brothers,' says Ólina. She has a heavy-set face and light brown hair. And though she is only twelve or so years older than me she has a natural authority among the women of the Kirkjuból farmsteads.

Ólina's words are harsh but they are true.

I look down at the boy in my arms. He should know me. I was there for his birth along with Anna's mother, sisters and sister-in-law. I rubbed her back when she moaned as they sang the old songs for birthing women to ease her labours. I threw dried *umfeðmingur*, vetch plants, into the blazing hearth as my mother had taught me, to bind the pain away from my friend's body. They recited Psalm 91 for protection, chanted the words *hugrekki*, courage, and *þrek*, endurance: words that hold power in the birthing room, until he slid out from between Anna's quivering, blood-streaked thighs and into my arms. I held him for those first liminal seconds where he hovered between death and life, waiting for the gods to decide. He should know me. I was the first to smile when the spell broke, when he opened his lungs to scream his first, primal, guttural sound – his call for sustenance, for life. He blinks up at me now, and it is as if the world entire is held within his gaze.

'You won't find six people to stand either side of your father or brother to swear the full oath of innocence. They attest this in front of God with a clear conscience. No one here would imperil their own immortal souls – or attract the attention of the man who burned three sorcerers at Trékyllisvík. You may call them hypocrites, but this is the truth of it. I'm sorry, Þuriður.'

Hyprocrites.

'You know my husband and his brothers would help you if they could . . .' Anna says, halting, supplicating. She is trying to make me feel better. Her daughter, Fjola, is singing to herself, a pudgy hand grasping a length of my friend's long blonde tresses now, while I struggle with my temper rising. I know they must protect their own, their menfolk, but what about mine?

Anna places her daughter down on the floor where the young girl begins to grizzle. Before long, she is led away by another child, an older boy, Gísli, Anna's nephew. For a moment, I watch my friend. Always practical. Always her head leading her actions. It's been like that since we were children. Anna would be the one to remind us the sun was setting and we should return from the pastures or mountainside back to our crofts. Freyja and I would have stayed out until the foxes shrieked and the moon shone silver in the night sky.

A jug of fresh milk and a bowl of soft cheese is set down beside me by Kaðlin. I smile, though, inside, the heat of their rejection simmers.

Again, Anna looks at me like a mother might – or would do if I had one to worry about me. Around us, everyone goes back to normal, now that the proper customs for greeting a visitor, albeit one known to them since birth, are complete. The child Fjola waddles back into the room with a doll made of rags held aloft for her mother to delight in. Outside, the skies darken to black.

They're going to try to kill them.

Anna and I exchange a frank gaze.

Our connection has always been beyond words. Handy when one of us is mute.

Ffffokk.

I screw up my eyes. If they won't swear the oath, then I will have to try harder, ride out to the other farms. I cast a look towards the door.

'Not tonight,' Anna says, making me start. Sometimes her understanding almost frightens me. Both her and Freyja read me like an open sheaf of parchment or a page in their Bibles.

The baby makes a small snuffling sound then a whine: the moment just before a cry for food. Anna reaches for him, pulls him to her.

'How strange it must be to have come to earth, Þuriður, born from an elvish mother to live among the brutish ways of the Icelanders,' she murmurs, touching a lock of my bone-white hair that tangles to my waist. 'How lonely it must be without her. You miss her – I know you do. We all do. She was kind to all of us children. She helped give us all life. She was beautiful in a strange way, just as you are, my dear friend. Don't go back to your croft and sleep alone. There are spaces in the children's beds. The fire is lit here. Stay with us. We're your family now.'

I hear her voice as if from the other side of a waterfall, the water a curtain of sound between us. A sudden flash of memory. A face: pale. Hair: as wild and as white as my own. Eyes of sudden ice-blue. A flower-scented kiss on each of my cheeks, the hazy trail of wild grasses. The warm sensation of being held. It vanishes as soon as it arrives, leaving the same bitter-sweet emptiness, the echo of her in my heart. I wish she was here.

I feel my eyes closing. I must find twelve men of good standing. My father expressly asked me, and I agreed. How could I not? The sight of them in their gaol. The knowledge of how cold they must be, how dark is their cell, how hungry they are kept, means I cannot let my family be swept up by the fates like dust under Ólina's broom. Anna shakes her head as if, again, she sees my thoughts.

'My husband has spoken to every farmhand here at Kirkjuból. They know the only way the Jón Jónssons can be saved is the *tylfta-reiður*. Your father and brother . . . well, they . . .'

I open my eyes. Stare at her.

'You know what I'm going to say! They weren't liked. They used their powers to harm people – this you know. I'm only grateful they didn't draw you into their devilry.'

The look I give my friend stops her.

'I'm sorry, Þuriður. I'm tired. This one keeps me up all night, just like his father . . .'

We both look at the infant that sucks greedily on a piece of linen dipped in sheep's milk, then back to each other and smile.

'Oh, I know we all used them for their spells and charms. Your father carved runes for protection for both my births. Your brother gave Ari the wrestling magic and didn't charge him like he did the others.' Anna sighs. 'Everyone from here to Súðavik has either benefited from their powers or been troubled by them. What people don't like, what they've never liked, is that they boasted of their prowess as sorcerers. You can't deny it. They weren't humble, Þuriður. They made sure everyone knew they had the richest farm, the largest flock of sheep, all because of their witchcraft.'

In my mind's eye, I see my brother, his wrists sore, his pride now reduced to dust inside the gaol. I see my father, shackled and dirty, cold and thirsty, and I feel the sudden urge to weep.

'They mocked the priest,' Anna says. 'They did it to his face. How could they think they'd escape punishment, even from a holy man?'

There is silence between us now as I digest my friend's words.

The trial date has not been set, but it will come, and soon. I know this because the urgency of the raven's flight, beating an airward path against the leaden sky – tells me so. The wind-seared hills and mountaintops whisper to me: *Soon, it will be too late.*

'Could the priest's wife help? She might intercede for you,' Anna says, almost as an afterthought.

Þorkatla Bjarnadóttir's face swims into my vision. I have barely ever set eyes upon her, only when I have walked to the harbour to see the Danish ships dock to trade, or when the smaller boats come in with their cargoes of fish. Then, at the waterside, I have seen her.

'Maybe not,' Anna says. 'People say she's envious of anyone who has land and livestock, having only a meagre hearth and a few sheep to pray over . . .'

I snort with laughter.

The priest's wife will not help me. To her, I must be more witch than woman, born as I am from sorcerers, born as I was in Kirkjuból.

I will have to find another way.

The bowl of soft cheese lies untouched, though I have drunk from the milk. It is thick, creamy. It bubbles now inside my belly, churning like whey for butter with the fear that grows inside me. I stand up, leaving Anna rocking the infant to sleep. I kiss her on her forehead, and walk back to the *baðstofa,* my sodden cloak heavy on my shoulders. Ari and Ólafur look up.

'We're sorry,' my friend's husband says, putting down a piece of rope, three twisting yarns bound together. His other brother, Egil, who sits beside him, hunched as he drags a fishbone needle through a length of netting, mutters something indistinct, but I take it as agreement.

'Our quarrel is not with you . . .' Ólafur says. He blushes a little when our eyes meet.

Anna reaches out and takes my hand. Mine, so white it is almost blue. Hers pink, already roughened from scrubbing clouts and shifts and caps. Together, our hands meet, our foreheads too.

Her husband leads me back to the door. I do not need a lamp when I leave them to walk home. Every tuft of grass, every stone and winding trickle from the mountain streams is known to me, even under a blanket of snow. I do not need the light to know the darkness.

I have taken a few paces when someone runs out of the croft.

'Þuriður Jónsdóttir, wait!'

It is Ólafur's voice.

'Stop, please.'

I turn to face him, suddenly conscious of the tear tracks down my dirt-streaked face.

'We won't let you do this alone. We know you'll go to every farmstead in the district, so I've decided I'll come with you. We go at first light.'

A feeling I cannot explain sits in my chest. I nod, walking away, the night sky punctured by stars as the clouds part. They glint in the vastness above. When I stop and look up, it is as if they are falling down, showering me in their brilliance.

He does not go inside until I reach my croft.

13

THERE IS A knock on the door of Þorleifur Kortsson's chamber.

'Enter.'

He sits behind his desk on the fronded chair, the quill and ink pot by his hand.

Síra Jón Magnússon walks in, his dark hair flecked with snowflakes, his cloak too.

'*Sæll vertu*,' Þorleifur Kortsson says, gesturing for the priest to take the only other seat in the room.

'*Sæll vertu*,' Síra Jón replies, stepping forward. He strides rather than walks, the witchfinder notes. He has an urgent look, a sincere, stern expression. The witchfinder gets up, walks to the door, peers round it and summons a maidservant, who scurries off for refreshments. When finally he sits opposite the priest, he flips his fine coat back so that he does not crumple the ends. He does not speak at first. He notices that this does not faze the preacher, as it does so many others.

'You may be wondering why I have invited you here?'

Before Síra Jón Magnússon can answer, the door opens. A young woman wearing a grey dress and black shawl, her eyes downcast, comes in carrying a tray. She bobs a curtsy, lays a platter of dried herring with two cups of warmed ale on the table, then she curtsies again. The witchfinder does not acknowledge her. He is sitting, apparently at peace with the world, his elbows on the desk, his fingers touching, making the shape of a boat's underside, like wood sculpted and bent to make a skeleton of sorts. The priest murmurs his thanks as the young woman passes him.

When she has gone, Þorleifur pushes one of the cups towards Síra Jón.

'Drink,' he commands. 'You'll need this. It's bitter out there.'

The room is warm. The priest removes his cloak. Melting snow drips onto the rug at his feet.

'Thank you. Your presence is greatly appreciated here in Eyri. I had written many times to Sýslumaður Magnús Sigurdsson about the wickedness abroad here, but what now?'

The witchfinder nods. He would like to make haste with the trials. He is keen to return home as soon as the spring thaw begins.

'I have called you here for a specific reason.' He sits back, stares directly at the priest, who blinks back at him. *He may struggle with the task ahead*, the witchfinder thinks. He knows his type. Has seen so many churchmen like him. Driven by zeal rather than position, by faith rather than gain. They are the hardest to work with. They seem to think God should have a say in the business, and not just Þorleifur Kortsson. The witchfinder prefers dealing with men like the sheriff: a lazy, self-satisfied lawman with an eye for his own enrichment at every opportunity. Present the easiest path, or the one that will benefit him the most, and he will take it. The priest, on the other hand, will need to be coaxed, or led without realizing he is being pulled like a bull to market.

But what both men fail to see, the witchfinder muses, is that no one can afford a conscience when it comes to rooting out witchcraft. All measures are justified. All actions forgivable. The threat sorcery poses to a well-ordered society is absolute and irreversible. Without the harsh cruelty of law, without using the full extent of their powers, sorcery can only flourish; a root that cannot be pulled out. And so, regardless of the price to each, it must be hacked away with as much brutality as possible. There is no other way.

'Our work is that of the Lord, and I am your servant as well as His,' the priest says.

'You are aware the Christian world is moving against sorcery. Here in Iceland, we have only just begun the work of our lifetimes, banishing it using the full force of the law.'

Síra Jón nods, sips his ale.

'And you are aware of the impact sorcery has in persecuting the godly and those of us without sin. Naturally, you are. You have felt the full weight of its wickedness . . .' Þorleifur Kortsson continues.

'Every night now,' the priest says, 'I fall into an unnatural sleep and am plagued by terrible dreams. Evil is at work in Kirkjuból, even now, even as those responsible are caught.' He glances towards the door. Further down the passageway is the gaol.

A moment's silence.

The witchfinder smiles, though his eyes remain narrowed.

'Good,' he says, his voice soft. 'Good, Síra Jón Magnússon, you are a man of virtue and righteousness. I see it within you. I see, also, you do not shrink away from what we must do, from those practices we may use to draw out information, to question these men using the powers given to us by my master the king – and, in doing so, save their souls for eternity.'

He leans forward.

'We need to take more . . . *effective* . . . action. We need to use those tactics that will truly root out the darkness within these men. We cannot tremble before the devil. We cannot baulk at the methods we must use. This is why I asked you here today.'

Síra Jón blinks. Clears his throat.

'Methods?' he says, swallowing with difficulty.

'Of course, we have carried out the usual punishments,' Þorleifur Kortsson says. His voice is a smooth seduction, as if discussing simple Church matters. 'The Jón Jónssons have been argumentative, sullen, defiant even. And so, naturally, we have used some force; some beatings, some physical ways of releasing their tongues, though with limited success. They have withstood all reasonable requests for their confessions.'

'I will entreat God. I will ask Him to work on their consciences,' the priest begins.

'But what if they have none?'

In the following quiet, there is a sound from behind the barred door. A small scratching. A niggling. It could be a rat – or a man. Síra Jón grasps the edges of his chair seat. His knuckles yellow.

'You are learned, Síra Jón Magnússon. You know as well as I that if the devil takes a soul, evil grows canker-like, unchecked. We need those instruments and, yes, methods that will overcome their reluctance entirely, that will uncover their evil deeds in the fullness of their confession. They must repent – but, more than that, they must confess to save their immortal souls and vanquish the darkness.'

When the witchfinder pauses, the priest shifts a little in his seat. At first, he looks puzzled. Then, understanding dawns.

'You wish to use torture?' His voice wavers.

Þorleifur Kortsson demurs. He leans back, unclasps his hands.

'Torture is a strong word, yet surely you agree we must use the strongest methods if we are to remove the devil and his imps from these lands?'

The priest's face has drained grey-pale. He looks like he may refuse.

The witchfinder observes a flush growing now in his cheeks, blotching across the pallor of his face. He smiles – a smile of reassurance in the powers vested in him by the Danish crown. Just a moment longer. He can feel the swell of the man's thoughts. His reluctance, his feelings that run like stormwater, changing from alarm to disgust to – agreement? It is this, the witchfinder savours. If he could roll this moment into a good clay pipe, he would inhale it deep into his lungs, a rich sediment, a vein from which runs a kind of power.

He wants to refuse, but he won't. Þorleifur Kortsson suppresses the urge to laugh out loud.

'Yes, y-yes, of course, we must remove the devil . . .' Síra Jón Magnússon stammers.

'And we must use the most effective course of action,' the witchfinder agrees, as if this was indeed the priest's idea. 'We must match the devil's power with our own. No method should remain unused. Surely you see that?'

'Yes, but—'

'Then it is agreed,' Þorleifur Kortsson says with finality. 'I have sent for the executioner, a man singularly skilled in methods known to extract information. He will bring prongs and other such equipment used in the trials of the Trékyllisvík witches. All we need is coal for the furnace. It will be done in the name of the Lord. You will, of course, need to supply a statement for the court, and what other evidence you can procure. I take it this can be produced?'

The priest looks as if he still wrestles with his thoughts, as if the path ahead, one he has now chosen to walk, has narrowed – the way forged with fire, from which he can never turn back.

An uneasy silence falls.

'That is all for today. I thank you for your time. My servants will see you to the door.'

Síra Jón Magnússon takes a second to realize his audience with the witchfinder is over. He nods a response, scrapes his chair as he stands. He gathers his cloak and, without another word, walks out of the room. Þorleifur Kortsson stares after him. Outside, a raven jumps from its perch on the gable of the trading station. Its wings beat black against the mercury sky.

14

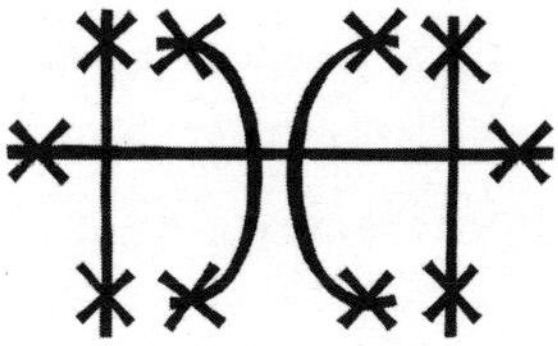

I, the undersigned, appointed to be a servant of God's word, face torments due to vicious acts of witchcraft, by the permissive will of God, because of my zeal for the duties laid upon me by my office, as the evidence for the antecedents and the beginnings of the affair indicate. I publicly declare that I consider the father and son, Jón Jónsson the Elder and the Younger of Kirkjuból, to be fully responsible for the sorcery and acts of witchcraft which this winter have befallen this parish, my household and my own person, from the nineteenth Sunday after Trinity up to the present. I make this declaration in the light of all those happenings, conformations, arguments, and relevant antecedent events that may and will be adduced as pertinent to this affair, and that may be granted to me to give consistently with truthfulness and the law. In token of this, I hereby sign my name by my own hand below.

(signed) Síra Jón Magnússon, preacher at the parish church of Eyri at Skutulsfjörður, March 1656

THE QUILL DROPS from the priest's hand.

It lies, the parchment where his statement dries curling round the feather. He pinches the narrow part of his nose near his brows. Looks down at what he has written. The day has darkened into night, leaving most of the room in shadow. Síra Jón Magnússon exhales. His wife hovers beside him with bread and skyr. He had not noticed she was there, and he starts. She places a cup of fresh milk next to his hand, trying to peer over his shoulder, though she cannot read well.

'Husband, rest now,' Þorkatla says, not moving away. 'You've done enough for tonight.'

The priest does not reply. He murmurs his thanks for the food, hoping she will retreat. He wishes to think his thoughts. He wants reassurance from God that he is doing the right thing. The witch-finder has rattled him, he admits to himself. His *certainty*. His *methods*. Neither sits well with him tonight, though it was he who embarked upon this crusade. He has set a train of action in motion, which he is beginning to realize is irreversible.

A memory comes to him: troubling, unsettling. The young man. His hand in Rannveig's as he inked her wrist, the point where a pulse flutters, placing kisses as he did so. He sees again the guilt on her face as she realized they were discovered. The smirk on Jón Jónsson the Younger's face. At first, he does not let go. The priest feels again the rage that hit him, the molten fury that engulfed him when he caught them, alone, unsupervised, in an outbuilding while hunting for his thickest cloak. He recalls not what he said, but the shouting, gesticulating, then, later, solemn regret. Síra Jón Magnússon tries to exorcize the recollection, but it stays, mocking him just as keenly as the men themselves have done. Are his motives as pure, as righteous, as he believes? Was it his pride that flared at the sight of one so unworthy as the apprentice? At the deceit, the betrayal, existing behind his back? Was it that moment that sealed the Jón Jónssons' fate?

Next to him, Þorkatla shuffles. He had forgotten she was there.

'You mustn't *doubt* yourself, my love,' she says. The priest winces. Is it so obvious?

'Those men are an affront to all that is good and holy. They must be stopped. You have said so yourself many times. You are doing the Lord's work in punishing them.'

He recalls the look on his wife's face when Rannveig ran to her, expecting her to allow this ungodly betrothal. He recalls running behind his stepdaughter, telling his wife what her daughter had done. Þorkatla had looked just as pale, her face just as pinched. Strangely, when she walked away from Rannveig, he had almost pitied the young woman, who sank to the floor, sobbing, the half-inked rune smeared on her skirts.

The fire burns, but the room is barely warmed. Draughts whistle through this gnarled building with its cracks between the stone walls, loose roots shedding dust and soil from the turf roof. They are exposed on the spit, subjected to the worst of the season's onslaught. He pulls his rough woollen blanket round his shoulders. Around them are the sounds of people going about the business that marks the end of each day: the creaking door as a pile of fuel for the fire appears, closely followed by the manservant who carries it. The sound of women gossiping as they sweep and scrub the kitchen. The whistle, shrill and piercing, of a farmhand herding a stray sheep into a *skáli* somewhere close by as snow falls soundless from the evening sky.

'Husband?' Þorkatla places her hand on his arm. He cannot help it. He recoils. She removes her hand as if scalded.

'I'm sorry. I'm tired. As you say, I need to rest. I have written my statement for the witchfinder. He will use harsher ways of gaining information – and I have agreed to it.'

'But how else can the investigation proceed? You've done the right thing in agreeing. The devil can't be coaxed out into the light of God. He must be forced!' Þorkatla says with fervour. 'And why should they have the biggest farm, the most livestock? They who mock you with their riches as well as their sorcery! No, this cannot go on. They are an affront to you and to God . . .' Her voice tails off.

It is not often the priest chooses to confide in her. He knows this frustrates her too, makes her all the more willing to listen when he does. Why does it have to be this way? When God called him to priesthood, He also called him into this marriage. The priest vows, silently, to make amends. To try harder with her.

She steps towards him again.

'You must do everything, *everything*, in your power to prosecute these men who have brought Satan's fiends into this home and attacked your body and mind . . .'

Síra Jón looks again at his wife. He sees the proud set of her chin, the gleam in her eyes. He sees a woman he does not love well enough.

'Will you pray with me?' he asks.

'Yes, husband, of course.'

They kneel down in front of the wooden cross. The priest feels the soft heat of her body next to him though they do not touch. She bends her head, closes her palms together. She shuts her eyes. It is the way Þorkatla gives herself to the Lord. Every time she begins to pray, she performs the same small ritual, the same surrender. She shuffles. Moves a little, finding the right position. She sniffs, a sharp inhalation, a beginning. The priest feels she is lost to him then. The moment she is furthest from him is the moment he feels closest to her. Does Þorkatla sense this? Does she realize she is a revelation to him when she prays? Her lips move even before Síra Jón speaks.

Þorkatla knows even as she kneels beside him that she cannot please him as a wife, as a companion, as a woman. Her husband is like the mountain stream that trickles down, shaping mountain crags, becoming a deluge and overpowering all. What piety she possesses feels like *his*. What little gaiety she has is washed away by his conviction. She is an empty vessel and yet he fills her with his sermons and prayers until she is sated, and can take no more, yet still they come. Does he guess at her thoughts? Are they hers, or do they leak from Þorkatla's head like milk from the hole in a bucket? She prays, not for the sorcerers, nor for her husband, but for herself. Long has she wanted another child, and so far their halting, infrequent union has been barren.

Neither of her marriages was by choice. The first was arranged by her father to secure her future, and it was a good marriage to the former priest of Eyrakirkja. A calm, solid man who gave her the child she craved. When he died, she felt as if she'd fallen through a crevasse. Down, down, down. Tumbling towards the jagged ice below. If his replacement, Síra Jón Magnússon, had refused to marry her, she'd have been cast out of the rectory, homeless. Forced to look for temporary work, a farmstead to shelter in each winter, subjected to any number of cruel masters with a young daughter to protect. She was grateful. She knew she had been saved from an uncertain future. She felt her heart flutter when first she saw him. Handsome. Tall enough. Dark hair and eyes, as well as being a Christian man. But he was as unlike her father and first husband as it was possible to be. Where they were steady, reasoned, he was mercurial, prone to moods that ebbed and flowed like the tides. She had adjusted herself. She knew he did not love her.

Perhaps tonight. He might come to her now they have prayed together, and soon she will feel again the quickening that would herald a baby in her womb. A second chance at motherhood, even as her daughter refuses to speak to her. A second chance at their marriage. Surely, when he has a child in his arms, he will grow to love her, as a woman, as his wife.

Her knees are already sore, her body weary. A prayer book lies open on a small cupboard by the window. She casts her eyes down and hears his voice. Always his voice. She wonders if it will always be so.

15

I HAVE RIDDEN in snow, in gales, in the dark heart of winter.

I have dug a path through where snowfall is thickest to reach the farms that lie beyond Kirkjuból. I have tried every farmstead, every household within fifty *akrlengd* of the spit, accompanied by Ólafur Björnsson, who would not let me ride alone. I am grateful for his company, his *solidity*, beside me.

Yet each 'no', each shake of the head, each person who is unable to look me in the face, fells me. They flinch when I come to their door. The sorcerer's daughter. Outcast girl.

Despite this, I held my head high. I even tried to speak.

Nothing happened, of course.

What came instead was strangled noise. Each time I tried, Ólafur stayed silent, letting me attempt without shame or hurry. Each time I failed, he nodded and said the words for me. He asks nothing of me in return.

Together, we have ridden with difficulty to every part of the district. The only real welcome was at Freyja's, the last of the crofts we visit on our return to Kirkjuból. There, my friend took us in, warmed our cloaks and gloves by the fireside. Made us eat, hot broth, bread, even though there is little grain left to last until spring.

'You should both sleep here. Ólafur can stay by the fire in Father's chair, while you can fit in with me and my sisters. There are enough blankets. My friend, I can't let you go back alone to your croft tonight.'

For once, I am too tired to resist.

Freyja takes my hand, my fingers cold as ice. She rubs them, cooing as if I am one of her mother's younger brood. My friend is aptly named for the goddess of beauty and fertility. She is gentle, her nature sweet, her laugh like a contagion, spreading to all around her. She wrinkles her nose when she is confused. She is slow to anger, quick to forgive.

We should have nothing in common.

Yet, what one of us lacks, the other balances out. I am comforted being in her presence, but I must keep searching for those who are not too shit-scared to stand by my kin. Those who will lie to the court to keep them alive. Those who will insist they have never seen them perform magic, when all along they have gone every year to them for charms and curses.

Strangely, it is Freyja's tenderness that overwhelms me tonight. I lean my head against the back of her chair, catching a glance pass between her and Ólafur. Already, I see their relief that I will not refuse her offer. When the fish-oil lamp fizzles out, I let myself be taken up the short ladder to the bed in which I will sleep under blankets and skins of goats, next to Freyja's sisters, who wriggle and sigh as they dream, and I am cast into the welcome oblivion of sleep.

A shadow glides across untouched snow.

I look up. The raven passes overhead. Dark, shifting shadow against the whiteness below. Another warning.

Ólafur brought me back at first light. I was up before the weak dawn washed over the fjord, and we left without waking Freyja's family. I hugged my friend, taking sustenance from her touch, from her whispered farewell. We shared a long look. One of friendship, one of understanding. I will not stop searching for men to swear the oath. Freyja is too wise to tell me I should do otherwise.

I have armfuls of driftwood to build up the fire, taken from the store by my croft. Before he left for Ari's farmhouse, Ólafur offered to carry it for me. With a shake of my head, I refused, preferring to stack my own fuel for my hearth, thoughts knotted like the wood lying rough in my hands.

I walk with some difficulty, slipping on snow-mush left by farm-hands. The dull sound of hooves and wind-rush carries across the stillness. A horse approaches, galloping across flattened ice tracks like a benediction. I squint into the low sunlight. It is the priest.

His cloak flaps like a bird in flight as he rides, his head lowered, staring straight ahead towards me. I do not move. I do not curtsy when finally he arrives, steed snorting, shaking its long mane. This is my home, my croft, my land. What more can this man want from me?

'*Sæll vertu*,' he says as he dismounts and ties the horse to the stake hammered into hard ground. Upon it, my father carved *galdrastafir*, magical runes: a deliberation of intersecting lines and marks, offering our homestead protection and blessings. Above the door hangs the skull of a sheep and a single white feather.

I stare back at him.

Why have you come?

'I know I am an unwelcome visitor, but I am here to collect evidence for the trial of your father and brother. Please step aside, Þuriður Jónsdóttir,' Síra Jón Magnússon says.

There is a pause. Does he expect me to reply?

I do not step aside.

He will have to barge past me to get back into my home. There will be no door banging open, no flurry of snow, no trampling of boots this time.

I shake my head.

No.

You are right. You are not welcome. Go. Get back to your windswept spit and your vengeful God.

We stand facing each other. I shiver as the punishing wind blows. Pale smoke rises into the sky from the *skjár* in the turf roof. Around us soar the black mountains, the crags and ripples of stone that scar the caustic surface, all covered now in ethereal white that will stay until long past spring.

What happens now?

Has the priest has been expecting this? Maybe his wife warned him of me. She will have heard the gossip from the other women of Eyri: the unruly elf maiden who refuses to speak, who will bar her doorway and not let him pass.

'So be it,' he mutters, and walks forward.

I hold my ground, forcing him to push past me, almost knocking the wood from my arms. With both hands, he thrusts open the door to my croft. I admit, I am shocked at his persistence.

'I need everything. The magic books, the spells, everything. The witchfinder has sent me, and I will not return empty-handed.' Though his words are an affront, his tone is flat. I see he does not relish this task.

Once inside, he seems to lose his confidence. He stands in the centre of the long *baðstofa* and looks around him as if seeing it for the first time. I can, at least, enjoy his discomfort.

Much of the detritus of my father's magical work is easy enough to find. The preacher begins by scooping books, rune staves, pieces of bone and animal skeletons, a bird's wing, its separated head and beak, and calcified remains of several spells and charms into a large piece of sacking taken from the folds of his cloak. Inside it goes a sea mouse's body, caught in tendrils of my virginal human hair to call in wealth, the head of a ling fish carved with the rune-stave *vindgapi* to whip up an unfriendly storm, a raven's feather encrusted with blood taken from my right foot and applied to the rune to enhance its powers. Directed at the place where the land meets the sea, it can conjure up a tempest to make the seas boil. He finds strips of curling brown vellum, consecrated, marked with incantations in Latin to invoke healing when wrapped around a suffering person's body.

When the sacking is half full, Síra Jón stops, yet he does not look at me, so I stand beside him, eyes blazing, hands on hips, furious. This is a violation. It is my father's croft – and, by rights, mine. How dare he enter without my permission? How dare he think to treat us in this way? If the priest guesses what I am thinking, he does not say. He looks to the sleeping area, the raised platform lined with our beds, and climbs up into our private space.

Just then, Margrét pokes her head round the doorway from the corridor that leads to the kitchen and *skáli*. I shake my head and point back where she came. The serving girl casts an uncertain, quizzical look at the priest's boots that are the only part of him visible as he climbs the ladder. She retreats, her fish-skin shoes making a hollow muffled sound on the floorboards.

Again, I follow the preacher.

He seems unnerved by my presence now. He seems to shrink a little in the smaller space. The tense silence is broken by the whinny of his horse.

'What else is there? What have you hidden? It will do you no good to keep secrets from the Church or the law. Your father and brother can be helped only with compliance, with truth and penitence.'

Liar.

His voice shakes a little. I am rooted, solid and unmoveable, in the place that is so familiar to me. This is the bed where my mother birthed me, a hard labour, not easy like my brother. From the moment I arrived, I was her miracle, her delight. I had not been expected to survive, and neither had she. My father was born in that same bed too. Many were given life by the old gods and birthed here. What match is this priest against our history, our lineage, our ancestral power? Sheepskins lie on blankets. Candle stubs sit in blackened wax puddles. A Bible lies shut and incongruous by a wooden bed. The same things any family in these farmsteads has. The same woodsmoke, the same dark beams, the same crooked ladder. The same things a priest might own.

His brow wrinkles. He wants to leave, but he can't.

My brother's bed, the blankets still crumpled, his shirts thrown careless across the pillow, a woollen sock missing several stitches. It has been weeks since he was arrested, but I cannot bring myself to tidy this space. It looks as if at any moment he will climb the steps leading to the sleeping area and yawn as he pulls the unwashed blankets over him. The priest reaches into the unmade mess, his arm extending under the covers. Finding nothing, he pads under the wool mattress and here he stops. He draws out a parcel of cloth. He unwraps it with fumbling hands, a lock of hair tied round a small bunch of dried wildflowers: stalks and stems of *sýkigras*, asphodel, tiny white petals that scatter, releasing the scent of dust and resin. Gathered before dawn, it is a gentle herb for love, to aid the magic of desire.

Uninterested, the priest drops the cloth, moves to the pelts of animal skins that hang from the rafters, pulling several from the metal hooks. He moves to my father's bed as I bend to scoop up what is left of the posy, the hair the colour of darkened earth, Rannveig's hair.

Before I can think what this means, Síra Jón, apparently finding nothing more in any of the beds or cupboards, ties up the sacking. I block his path back to the ladder. The ceiling is lower than the *baðstofa* below. Again, we face each other, breathing the same musty air. It is dark up here. There is but a small light from the tiny window, and though it is not long after noon it is already fading from the day.

'Þuriður Jónsdóttir, you must accept God's will. Your father and brother have sinned most grievously . . .'

My fists clench, anger rising. It would be the work of a moment to grab the shearing scissors and slice this priest's throat. One swift laceration and it would be done. I imagine the shock of the blade, its deep cut instantly drawing blood. The recognition of death approaching. His terrified eyes that would scan my face, arms grasping at air, falling backwards. My hands itch with the effort of not moving. I breathe. Drop my gaze. Step aside.

He fumbles with the bulk of his bag as he descends, but I do not follow him. I sit down heavily on my bed, still clutching the length of hair, the exhilaration of an action not taken but imagined, my heart beating hard and fast in my chest.

I hear the priest mount his horse. The raven, startled, rises from the gable where it perches over the doorway, croaking as the mare and its rider gallop away.

Smiling, I look up to the rafters. Here is where my father's most important magical text and objects lie hidden. The secrets he spoke to my brother about in hushed tones when he thought I was not listening. The spells from his *galdrabók*, his grimoire, used for black magic: to frighten away spirits, to wreak revenge on an enemy, to deal death to the men in fishing boats that bobbed far out in the ocean's swells, to call on the wrath of the old gods and to reawaken the dead from their earthly slumbers, an act of sacrilege performed for a grieving widow in Bolungarvík. These, I will keep. The priest and lawmen can have the rest, though I did not wish to make it easy for them to collect. I knew not to hide the simple domestic charms and spells stored or discarded on every surface in our home. I knew not to burn them, or they would have searched the croft properly. I knew they would come and so I let them have trinkets when all along I had hidden away treasure.

Are the helpful spells enough to convict them? Maybe, though each may be argued a folly or a child's charm. Let them not have the most powerful of the *galdrabækur*, the books of magic containing incantations steeped in darkness, in the basest of human desires and hungers. Those alone are my legacy. Those alone belong to me, their rightful guardian, though I am but a woman.

'*Þakka þér kærlega fyrir mig*,' he said as he left. It strikes me now as strange, awkward. He thanked me for the evidence he will use to try to kill my kin. I climb down, slowly this time, and walk to the door, check it is shut and bolted. Leaning back on the wooden frame, my knees give way and I sink to the floor.

16

7 April 1656

THE NEXT DAY, I am searching for my father's grimoires. The important ones. The powerful ones. Those I hid from the bed-wetting priest, who left with other books and magical objects more fit for a child's ill-wishing.

Balancing on a stool, I lean up into the rafters on tiptoes, sliding my hand along the largest beam. Feeling across the knotted wood, its uneven surface, following its sea-sculpted form, I find them among the dust and mouse droppings. My fingers scrape the edge of the box, towards which I lean precariously. Pulling it to me, I wipe away clods of dried earth that have fallen from the turf roof.

Inside is the most precious of my father's *galdrabækur* and some of his magical things. I scrabble through what is left of the spell work, knocking over a spent candle, its wick upright in a congealed lava of tallow. Where are the staves carved with runes and where are the parchments? Where is the *Pater Noster*, written on vellum in my father's confident, meticulous hand?

'What are you looking for, Þuriður?'

I look down from my viewpoint on tiptoes from my stool. I had almost forgotten Freyja is here with Anna, who has baby Ari in her arms, both staring up at me. Margrét has left for church. Freyja wears an expression that veers somewhere between exasperation and pity. She slides the cap off her deep auburn hair and drops it on the bed beside her.

When she sees what lies on it, she gasps.

'Þuriður! What's all this here? Those are your father's grimoires, aren't they? How do you have these? I thought the priest took everything!'

Shaking my head, I grin.

There is a small, heavy, pocket-sized book. Dust drifts off the veined calfskin cover. I open it to find strange sigils, delicate runes written in ink, drawings of spells and enchantments, scratched in a tiny, legible hand.

'Þuriður!' Anna exclaims. She moves sideways as if to shield her son from their potency. 'You were meant to hand over everything! What happens if the sheriff or priest finds you with these?'

I'll be fettered and chained, just like they are.

I open the vellum pages of the grimoire. I have not, of course, been taught to read. That pleasure fell to my brother, who spent hours kicking the table legs, dropping his quill, sloshing ink, anything to avoid the lessons my father gave him. He was a reluctant pupil, but I was not. Though no instruction was given to me, I absorbed everything. I watched as my brother fumbled his first letters. I listened when Father made him do it all again, learning everything by my brother's mistakes, and there were many of them.

I flick through the pages. Each is littered with tiny writing as if a spider has dropped in the ink and skittered across the page. Can anything inside here be of use when it is only a woman whispering the words?

Freyja says: 'But what will you do with all this? Women can't perform magic, only *seid-menn* can. What use to you is any of this?' Here she stops, takes a small rodent skull in her hands then shivers. Puts it down.

'Þuriður, you're not meant to have this,' Anna says. 'Please listen to us. You put yourself in danger.'

I wonder if she remembers.

Freyja looks at us both, and something passes between us three, a chill like a cloud sliding across the silvery moon.

It was not long after my mother died.

I disappeared. My friends had spent the day looking for me in all the usual places: my croft, each of the *skáli*, the farmsteads and pastures, even Eyrakirkja on the spit. They called my name and yet I would not answer. A darkness had fallen upon me. My father had been drunk the night before. He raged about her as if she still lived. The next morning, as soon as light dawned, I fled up, up to my place halfway between Kirkjuból and the gods.

Their voices grew louder as they got closer. Inside me, a furnace burned, a storm thundered and flashed. I had run to my sanctuary: the troll's seat up high in the mountains, though I could make out the small figures of my friends below, which got bigger as they climbed upwards.

'Þuriður! Didn't you hear us?' Anna was the first to appear, her face pink with exertion. Freyja followed, tongue sticking out to the side of her mouth as she concentrated on the final few steps up to my perch. Here, I could see everything. Each shifting undulation of the glittering ocean. Each gull dipping down, white and grey feathers streaking through the soft cloud cover. Sunbeams shone in strips, but I could sense something was coming, a low, creeping raincloud, a gentle breeze that might grow and billow.

'We thought we'd lost you! Why did you run off?' Anna said, hands on hips just like her mother. We were eight winters old. Girls pretending to be women. Freyja flopped down on the *fjallagrös* next to me, panting.

There was a waver, a thin vibration coming off the expanse of water. I stared hard at it, ignoring my friends. The air was soon thick with it. A surge ran through me as if I was the ocean and the waves and the clouds overhead.

I stood up, raised my arms out to the sea, without thinking what I was doing. It felt like it was *speaking* to me: *warning* me.

'Þuriður, what are you doing?' Anna said, her voice strange.

As she spoke, a cloud, greyer and larger than any other, moved across the sun, throwing all into shadow like the devil himself had flattened his snarling, shit-smelling hide across the afternoon sky.

The wind rose. I felt my hair untangle and move in the breeze that was becoming a gale. I reached up, higher, shutting my eyes, feeling its power. Darker and darker. Fat raindrops began to fall. Out at sea, far, far out, the waves showed white eagle-talon tips.

'Stop this,' Freyja said. Her voice trembled. 'She's making a storm. Make her stop.'

'She can't do that! She's a girl and girls can't make storms.' Anna's voice was small against the tempest arising.

'But she is! She's making a storm, I tell you! Stop, Þuriður. Stop!' Freyja shouted.

Anna grabbed my arm and began pulling me away.

Shaken from the completeness of this reverie, I stumbled. Opened my eyes to see them staring at me, pinch-white faces in the sudden inky darkness.

'Stop, Þuriður!'

I cannot recall who said it then. We three stood, like hags on the hillside, the biting wind pulling at our clothing; our hair, our caps now tied under our chins. I laughed as if *I* were this uncanny storm: alive, free, unquenchable. It pulsed through my body, running through each fingertip, each strand of hair, each limb.

'I want to go home,' Freyja said, her lip quivering. Her eyes were wide, glowing amber in the darkness. Both ran, pulling me with them, reluctant as swirling black clouds gathered above us. A black shape hovered overhead. A single raven's plume smudged the endless grey, jerking to the ground by my feet. It shone, its oily black sheen gleaming in my hand: a gift from the wilderness.

As I ran back to the farmsteads, the feather gripped in my hand, I remember the thrill, the summoning. I remember feeling as if salt blood ran through my veins, the song of the storm humming inside me.

We never spoke about it. What was there to say?

Later, one of the fishing boats far out at sea was lost. Three men from Súðavik: drowned.

Is Freyja thinking of that storm now?

Our eyes meet, and this time my gaze is softer. I must do everything I can to turn the tide that laps at the feet of my father and brother, whether she is afeared or not. I must take their implements and texts and find a way to touch their magic, to force the hand of the executioner away from my kin. How to say that without words, without speech?

I shrug.

It has to do.

Anna looks back at me now, her eyes narrow. I see she struggles to comprehend my meaning.

'Have a care. If they find out . . .'

If they find out.

Who would tell them? You?

The spell is easy to find. I turn to the page I am looking for: it contains a ritual that counters the wrath of powerful men. I saw my father perform it many years ago for a man accused of killing his brother. Then, he said the words I am about to say inside my mind.

'Stop. Þuriður, please . . .' Freyja says. In my mind's eye, we are back on that mountaintop, three young girls, the elements broiling and furious. The same alarm. The same fear. But it is not my fear. This is where I feel most alive: when danger and necessity collide.

I shake my head.

Don't try to stop me. I will do this my way.

I pour what is left of the water from the pitcher into the rune bowl. I do it too quickly and it slaps over the sides. I take the parchment, unfurl it, find a part that is free of my father's markings. I cut this part away with the shearing scissors.

'My friend, hear me. This is wrong!' Freyja stamps her foot.

I am rushing now. My hand trembles as I draw the rune. The ink drips onto the surface, obscuring one of its lines. Freyja's expression grows darker by the second. I must do this. I must try to weave some magic to free them. The ink blots again, but the Helm of Awe is unmistakeable.

Anna's face is pale.

'The *Ægishjálm*! . . . Þuriður, you must stop now. This is men's magic; this is forbidden magic. We don't know what the symbol will do!'

For a second, a mere breath of air, I pause. She is right. I might unleash *something*. And if I do? What happens next? Without my father's instruction, I am blind to its path beyond my unsteady hand. Then I remember the shackles round my father's wrists and ankles. The bruised-grey circles already formed round my brother's eyes. I smell the rancid straw, the overflowing chamber pot, the dirt of the gaol. I must fight back.

'What are you doing now? Why aren't you stopping? You can't

save your father and brother!' Freyja grabs my wrist, but I will not listen. I will not stop. Heart thudding, I wet the parchment and slap it onto my face, between my brows. My friend gasps. She steps back from me now. I had not noticed before, but I am crying as I cup my palms together. Then, the cold shock of the water on my face, the spell beginning. Inside, I think the words: *Ægishjálm er ég ber, milli brúna mér*.

I call in the powers that my family might be executed for. At least, I hope I do.

I wash away the enemies of the Jón Jónsson men, my father and brother. I discharge accusations made by powerful men . . .

Another splash.

Let God see them. Let every man look upon them with gentle eyes. I bear the Helm of Awe between my brows. May the world and the land now be gracious to them . . .

A crash. The dull clang of metal hitting wood. Disorientated, I realize my embroidered skirts are soaked. The words die inside my mind.

'I won't let you do it,' Anna says. She steps in front of me, eyes blazing after knocking the rune bowl forcibly from the table.

They both stare at me as if we were back on that mountainside, the storm seething, the sky darkening. Freyja gives me a strange look, but I back away from those who are like sisters to me. We have shared everything as a three. We have picked *vallhumall*, yarrow, and made decorations to garland each other's hair. We have carded wool, sung on washing day, paddled in streams so cold we shrieked with its ice-burn. We have grown together, three girls who now stand at the threshold of womanhood as my world crumbles to dust. My face is wet as I wipe the wildness of my hair back off my face. The spell is broken, if it ever existed at all. As if to make the point, the parchment slips from my forehead and tumbles to the floor.

17

8 April 1656

AGAIN, THE GAOLER, my coin slipping into his waiting hand.

Again, the stench, the dirt, the cold.

Again, the bruises on their faces, the cuts that weep blood, the brackish water and stale bread amid the filth.

This is the place where my father and brother have no power. This is the place where their strength has been broken over the months they have spent incarcerated.

'The witchfinder came with a poker and coals. He set a fire . . .'

My brother avoids my gaze, his words sinking into the dank straw.

'The sheriff and the priest joined him. They . . . questioned us . . .'

They did more than that. Your wounds tell me this.

'Yes, and I gave them nothing!' My father interjects, emerging from the shadows. 'I said nothing they didn't already know.' He takes hold of the rags his shirt has become and lifts it up, his hand trembling. Lines slashed into his skin lie red and weeping. Welts burned into his back and belly.

'It was your brother who told them our secrets, the death wishes, the spells for injury and maiming. It was he who crumbled at the sight of the glowing coals,' he spits.

My brother watches me now, his eyes red, raw. Has he been crying? His hands are streaked with blood where once his fingernails were before they were wrenched from his fingers.

'Þuriður . . .' My father urges me forward. 'There's a reason why we bribed the gaoler to send for you. Gave him a spell that'll make his prick hard and his purse heavy . . .' Father licks his cracked lips. 'Listen, this is important. When Sýslumaður Magnús Sigurdsson came two days ago, he told us our trial is set for tomorrow.'

'We have no more time,' he continues. 'Gather all those who will swear the *tylftareiður*. Tell them to be ready.' He is nothing but skin stretched over bone, yet his voice is still the same. He commands me as if I was a fisherman on his boat. Despite that, I fancy I hear a thin note of pleading, but his grip is firm, his voice steady.

My brother, on the other hand, looks broken.

'Go now. Leave us the food. Tell everyone they need to be there.'

My silence stretches on.

There were two men, only two, who said they would swear if I paid them. They were farmers from one of the outlying crofts, and the only ones who did not shut their door in our faces. They wanted payment in the form of livestock. I refused by walking away. I am happy I cannot tell you this. It is enough that we fell short, that we failed.

Jón Jónsson the Younger holds his face in cupped hands. He understands.

Strangely, when he speaks, it is not rage I hear but something quieter and more devastating: disappointment.

'Father,' he almost sighs, 'there are no men who'll take the oath. Can't you see? They're shit-scared of the witchfinder. They won't help save our arses. They'll watch us burn rather than piss off Þorleifur Kortsson. I'd probably do the same in their boots.'

'No men?' My father echoes. He lets go of my arm, his eyes travelling around the small room, as if the answer can be found in musty straw.

'Fucking cowards!' my brother mutters.

My thoughts exactly.

'They begged us for spells! They came from every part of the Westfjords! All wanting our help. All wanting *something* from us!' Rage suits Jón Jónsson the Elder better than despair. Better he is angry than defeated. Then he turns it on me.

'If I didn't have these fetters, I'd slap you!'

You wouldn't fucking dare.

I've held my ground many times, especially in the weeks and months after my mother died when he was more drunk than sober. I am quick, ready. I could duck and weave away from his blows. Now? Now, he could not hurt a child with his emaciated limbs and iron chains that hold him to a ring on the wall like a chained beast.

I almost feel sorry for him. It cannot be easy to know you have no friends in the world.

Even so, I stand stock-still, feet planted on the floor, as if he is a ram about to charge.

'Leave her, Father. She'll have gone to everyone, and you know it. If Þuriður can't find twelve who'll swear the *tylftareiður*, then no one can.' Jón the Younger looks away.

My father shuts his eyes as if he cannot bear to look upon either of us.

Why cannot they fly from the barred window or break out of the locked door? Where is their magical power? Has it deserted them like everything and everyone else?

'Do they have the *galdrabækur*? I assume they came back after we were arrested and searched the croft?'

My father has not asked this before. I have dreaded this question since the priest came. Until the questioning started proper, they felt untouchable. And now I must answer, in my own way.

I stare back at my father, unblinking.

'They have everything,' Jón says, not unkindly, watching my expression. I make a see-saw gesture with my right hand, fingers apart, my hand rotating right and left.

Not everything.

'They have enough,' my brother says in sharp, pointed words that slash at the air.

I'm sorry.

My brother often tried to translate my silence to our father when I was younger, even though he was frustratingly slow to understand my meaning. Growing up, we fought. We were not especially close nor tender together. I was jealous of his authority as first-born son. He was irritated by me, the usurper, who did not know her place. He pulled my hair. I attempted to pull his back. He sneered behind our mother's back as she told me off for some misdemeanour. I stuck out my tongue at him and earned myself a cuff round the ear. Many years later, as young adults, we settled upon an uneasy truce that has grown into a kind of fondness, yet still we fight: both too strong-willed to exist together in peace.

My father groans. He attempts to smash his chains against the wall.

'How could you, Þuriður? Have we taught you nothing? They should have been destroyed! *Fokk*, Þuriður. Why didn't you burn them?'

'Stop, Father. Can't you see she isn't to blame?' my brother sounds weary, as if we have had this conversation before.

'They know who we are, what we do. They've known for years. We've hardly hidden ourselves! Our farmstead is scored with *galdraletur*. Whether they have the grimoires or not, it makes no difference. Everyone knows us as the sorcerer and his son,' Jón says, and

I hear the bitterness he has always felt at being the apprentice. Now, of course, he won't inherit the title of sorcerer. He will die an apprentice: a boy, still, in so many ways.

Before our father can reply, I open the sack bag I have with me. Inside it are the herbs and plants I gathered for their injuries. There is something else in here too. I carried it from our croft, the burden of it weighing heavy. Heart beating, I pull out a knife. Not the brass-handled one. That was confiscated by the gaoler when first they were captured. No, it is an ordinary knife, but one I have honed so the blade glints sharp in the weak daylight. Strangely, again, it is my brother who gleans my meaning.

His eyes widen. He whistles a long note.

'*Fokk!* Þuriður, you don't mean?'

I nod.

If they are going to find them guilty and burn them as sorcerers, then this may be the only way out.

My brother whistles again, but he takes the knife, holds it in his rust-stained hands, draws a finger along the blade. His blood shows red from this new cut in the pad of his finger.

'You treat us like cowards! You think we would cut our own throats to avoid walking in front of those lawmen? That'll never happen, never. The Jón Jónsson men have wielded great power for centuries. We'll never relinquish that power! Let them kill us! That way, they'll always be looking into the shadowy corners of their lives, fearing our retaliation as ghosts come back to haunt them. I will haunt those men of law, and by Óðinn and Þórr I swear on my own grave that I will, but I want them to fear it first. I want to look them in the eye and send them a curse that will carry through their bloodline for centuries to come.' My father stops. He coughs with the effort of avenging his enemies. I put my arm round him and feel his ribs where once there was flesh and muscle.

Powerful magic-men they once were, but no longer. Now, they are just men, as close to the earth and the land as everyone else. Their magic has been stripped from them, pulled out with pliers, just like their nails. They are lost – and now they know it.

The journey back to Kirkjuból is the same as it ever is, yet everything is different.

Meltwater laps at the small boat as the oarsman pulls us closer to the mainland, rippling through the green-brown reflection of the mountain ranges that encircle the spit and shoreline. The sky hangs low and grey, stretching off beyond the snow-clad mountaintops. I sit. I breathe. I hear the screech of the terns as we come closer to the landing place. Their white wings beat overhead, black faces emboldened. They screech again and I shield my face as I step out of the boat. I do not feel the small stones underfoot, the chill of the fjord water, the slap of the small waves made by our movement.

'Tomorrow?' the oarsman says. So he knows. That means everyone knows. News travels fast between the spit and Kirkjuból. Tonight, I must prepare myself, but how? How can anyone prepare for their world collapsing, as it has done before, as it will do again?

I nod.

Tomorrow.

18

9 April 1656, Eyri

THE PRIEST STEPS forward.

The trial is taking place on the exposed land outside the Danish trading station on the spit, where the Jón Jónssons are held. It is bitterly cold, the grey sky threatening snow.

A hush falls as all who gather turn their gaze to him.

'Many of you have come today to witness the trial of two men who have unleashed a campaign of witchery against me. Before we begin, let us pray together. Let us ask the Lord God Almighty to bless these proceedings and bathe us in the light of righteousness.'

He bows his head. All follow. The wind whips at the hem of Síra Jón Magnússon's cloak. A smattering of rain follows from grey, lowering clouds. He speaks the words, muffled by the squall. Around him cluster parishioners, their gloved hands held in prayer.

'Let your Holy Angel be with me, that the evil foe may have no power over me.'

'Amen,' the onlookers say.

'We have welcomed Þorleifur Kortsson here to Eyri to oversee this trial on behalf of the king himself.' The priest pauses, letting the authority of these words sink down from the skies to the crowd below. He stands on a higher mound of turf, gazing downwards. He turns to the witchfinder, who hesitates before the words pour out of him.

'I convene this court in the name of His Majesty, King Frederick the Third of Denmark, along with His Highness's honourable men of the district.' Behind him are the sheriff's men. They each wear an expression of stone; flint-hard, unyielding.

The priest's wife, Þorkatla Bjarnadóttir, stands alone behind them. Síra Jón banned his stepdaughter, Rannveig, from coming. This time, she did not bother to appeal to her mother, glaring at her with a whey-pale face.

'Bring out the prisoners!'

The door to the trading house opens. Sýslumaður Magnús Sigurdsson strides out wearing a red wool coat, fine boots and a wide-brimmed hat. Stooped like old men, the Jón Jónssons appear, dragging irons, the prison-rot following in their wake.

They do not look like sorcerers. They look maimed, bloodied, broken.

The priest sees the scars from those methods used by the witchfinder. He shuts his eyes. Mouths a prayer. It tastes sour on his tongue.

'Both men were lawfully arrested and held according to the provisions of the twentieth paragraph of the *Jónsbók* and held in custody by royal authority,' the witchfinder announces.

'Sýslumaður Sigurdsson will now read out the evidence and accounts of the accuser, Síra Jón Magnússon, preacher at the parish church of Eyri at Skutulsfjörður.'

The sheriff steps forward. He has the air of a man pleased to be in front of an audience. He nods to the witchfinder, then turns to the company, clears his throat. He holds up a sheath of vellum.

'The elder Jón Jónsson is accused of practising sorcery. As evidence of this charge, let it be known that magical items were found at the farm of Kirkjuból, owned by the same man, Jón Jónsson the Elder: grimoires containing spells, charms and curses, a piece of parchment covered with magical runes, alongside many other diabolical objects. There was also a ceremonial knife used for magic, but it has disappeared – witched away and existing no longer!'

The sheriff holds up a small piece of browning goatskin covered in tiny markings, and waits for the muttering and craning of necks to finish. He shouts above the sound of the angry wind as it rushes across the gravel spit.

'Síra Jón Magnússon has written a statement publicly declaring that Jón Jónsson the Elder and Jón Jónsson the Younger are *fully* responsible for the acts of witchcraft that have befallen him.'

Síra Jón listens to his words as they are read out to the assembly. The timbre and flow of them. The sparse nature of them. How can they explain the torments he has suffered? How can they convey the depths to which he has descended, his soul ripped and tattered like netting left outside in winter storms? He arose this very day from a night without slumber. One haunted by the sensation of rats running over his thin body. The scratch of their feet on his skin.

Did he do enough? Did he try hard enough to save their souls before denouncing them? He cannot answer. God has brought them here. This is the Almighty's will. As a humble servant, he must obey. He must face this day with courage.

'The gaoler offered evidence that Jón Jónsson the Younger cursed a goat within his hearing and did point his foot in the direction of the creature. Five days later, it lay dead.'

Gasps from the assembled crowds. Sýslumaður Magnús Sigurdsson continues.

'Lastly, and most gravely, it is stated that the devil in the form of both Jón Jónssons frequently appeared before the preacher as a black dog. This was witnessed by the holy widow Randiður Ólafsdóttir.'

The priest steps forward. Rain falls heavy now. He catches sight of the sorcerer's daughter standing at the edge of the crowd staring at him, a woman on either side of her linking arms. Her wind-whipped hair. Her searing eyes. Her expression fierce, not fearful at all. She appears more apparition than woman.

He feels a sudden jolt of fear, as if she has pulled the darkening ferment down.

The chill wind blows in from the ocean.

The priest shivers. A devil's wind.

The witchfinder, Þorleifur Kortsson, appears not to notice. He points to both accused men, each in turn.

'We have carefully examined and interrogated these men. The Elder has *confessed*, in the presence of God, that these are his books of magical objects and papers, as has his son, the Younger. Both men stand before you all, stripped bare of their wickedness. They have *confessed* to sending demons to the priest to cause sickness of the mind and body. Síra Jón Magnússon, what say you?'

'Take not these words as truth,' the priest replies. 'No, let us hear instead from those who have caused these afflictions. Let us hear from the sinners who stand before you, who have sent this evil into the heart of our community!'

He turns to the elder of the *seid-menn*. Several in the crowd clutch wooden crosses strung round their necks. All stand silent.

'Jón Jónsson the Elder, did you, or did you not, practise dark magic, summoning a storm at sea to kill an enemy?'

His voice, when it comes, is rasping but defiant.

'I did.'

More gasping.

'And did you summon the devil in the form of a black dog to inflict harm upon my person and my household?'

'I did!' Jón Jónsson raises his voice, though it cannot compete against the indignant whistle of storm winds.

'I can't hear you! *They* can't hear you!' the priest cries as the gusts blow stronger. 'Repeat your confession, sorcerer!' His voice seems to echo off the high slopes of the mountains, ricocheting off the rockface.

'I did – and I would do it again!' he says, this time louder.

The sorcerer looks around those here, seeming to challenge those friends and neighbours who did nothing to help.

The priest inhales. He takes his time to exhale. The hard shape of the metal cross Síra Jón Magnússon holds up cuts into his palm.

'Did you, or did you not, *both* work with the devil to cause a plague of demonic disturbance in Eyri?'

The whole spit seems to quieten, though the sea breaks against the shore ever more urgently. Flecks of snow begin to swirl, hurled down from the heavens.

'Answer me or face the wrath of Our Lord God Almighty.'

Jón Jónsson the Younger weeps. He is trying to clutch his head, but his body shakes. He cannot hold up his hands due to the weight of the manacles. Meanwhile, the elder, the sorcerer, holds the priest's gaze with abominable confidence.

'Answer him,' comes the voice of Þorleifur Kortsson.

'Síra Jón Magnússon, you insulted us when you refused my son's request for your stepdaughter's hand – an insult no man with any pride could let go unanswered.'

A flash of memory. The tearstained face of Rannveig. Her skirts pooling on the earthen floor as she beseeched her mother, his wife. The look of concern, then dismay, from Þorkatla. He stalls. Words slip away from him. His heart stammers as he recalls again the moment he discovered their dishonour.

The witchfinder turns to the crowd.

'Pride is a sin no man can afford. See how the Younger weeps and repents of his crimes. Come, tell us all what you have done and your soul may still be salvaged . . .'

The sorcerer's apprentice falls to his knees. He drags himself along the ground, trying to kiss the feet of the witchfinder. He is almost incoherent, so quick is he to trip over his tongue.

'We did many bad things. Too many to count. Too many to tell.'

'But we have some time. Come, Apprentice Jón, unburden yourself . . .' An uneasy titter travels through the onlookers. There is a collective intake of breath.

Jón Jónsson the Younger hesitates.

The priest sees his sister, the wild-haired maiden, shake her head. A small movement, almost indiscernible. Her brother smiles, though the effect is terrible. Black-blood encrusted lips open to reveal missing teeth. A tear slides down his bruised cheek. The sheen of youth. The golden hair curling at the nape. The strength and vitality of this young man – all gone. Taken from him.

'Yes, I drew the rune *fjölnir* on my palm and shook the priest's hand to send a curse under his skin,' he says. The priest looks down at his hand as if the spell lies there still. In that moment, he understands they have to die. Doubt falls away. He glances up at the delicate webs of snow falling onto his cheeks. He thanks God for this deliverance.

'I . . . I carved *fretrúnir*, farting runes, to get back at a girl,' the sorcerer's apprentice continues, his voice a whisper. 'I carved the sigils *golnisþey*, *hagallinn blá* and *augnaþuss* to work charms. I carved runes to help Markús bed the girl he wanted. And I drew this –' at which point, he starts to draw marks in the earth beneath his feet, scratching out the lines with a stone. In the crowd, there is movement where the man Markús stands. He shakes his head, issuing loud denials.

'These were for protection at sea, to prevent us drowning when we fished,' he continues. At his feet, appears a jumble of criss-crossing lines and shapes, more like the squiggles of a boy than symbols of magical power. The witchfinder grinds his heel into the patterns.

'I sold *glímagaldur*, wrestling magic, staves to protect the fighter, to ensure victory. Many came to me wanting them. Most men here have, and they can't deny it . . .'

'And yet it is you who are on trial here today,' Þorleifur Kortsson says. There is a rumble from above as if the thunder agrees. 'And among the many things you have said, there was one curse, was there not, that was central to your campaign against Síra Jón Magnússon? Let us hear what you carved upon whalebone, which you were seen by witnesses throwing to the winds as you spoke the words.'

Jón Jónsson the Younger looks up and catches the eye of the priest. He is foolish enough to say them aloud.

'May the accursed fire blaze forth and assail you with your hatred. May all the evil that you intend for me, turn back on you and pursue you.'

A moan escapes from someone's lips. Such words should not have been spoken. They bring damnation. But it seems the apprentice has not finished confessing. He is like a trickle from a dam ready to burst.

'Yes, I did many things and I've confessed them all under torture! I used my own sister's blood to make our spells strong and potent. I have made spells to make a woman want to fuck me. Oh, and that isn't all. We've done far worse. We've made spells to bring back the dead . . .'

'Enough!' The witchfinder stands in front of the kneeling man.

There is an expectant, fearful silence.

Þorleifur Kortsson draws himself up. He turns to the wide-eyed audience, all thoughts of their warm hearths forgotten.

'Good Christian people of Eyri, you have heard from the lips of these sinners. You have heard their extraordinary crimes, and how they endanger every man, woman and child here today. The final test of their crimes is to call upon you, good people, and ask if any will step forward and swear the oath. Do so now.'

No one moves, except for the daughter who spits, hard, on the still-frozen ground.

The witchfinder smiles.

'Again, I ask. Who here will stand up for these men? Who will deny their guilt and swear the *tylftareiður*, the oath that will set them free?'

The sorcerer's daughter alone seems to stand upright, without shame. The priest cannot take his eyes from her. There is a watchfulness, a knowing, that lies behind her eyes. Something that persists.

'No man here has come forward.' He turns to the men. 'No one!' the witchfinder says with glee.

'This court sees no reason for leniency or mercy. Does not the Bible say: "A man also or woman that hath a familiar spirit, or that is a wizard, shall surely be put to death: they shall stone them with stones: their blood shall be upon them!"'

Leviticus 20, the priest thinks.

'And does not our own *Jónsbók* state in the second section of the Personal Rights: "those who are executed for murder, black magic, sorcery, any form of soothsaying, or outdoor vigils for the purpose of conjuring up trolls or practising heathen rites – these are criminals without rights, whose death is not to be compensated"?

'Furthermore, did not the old king himself, in his letter of the year 1617, declare that men such as these are to be put to death in accordance with God's word and the laws and ordinances – by fire or sword according to the actions of each, for the wickedness that is most widespread, and rages most destructively, must be punished most harshly?'

Þorleifur Kortsson takes a breath.

He looks between them. The Elder still stands defiant, while the Younger raises himself to his feet. Snow falls in earnest now.

'In the name of our Lord Jesus Christ to whom all authority is given in heaven and on earth, and who will come again to judge the living and the dead, we, the aforementioned members of the court, do pronounce with the full force of the law that this father and son, Jón Jónsson the Elder and the Younger, have both forfeited their lives and are condemned to death.'

The witchfinder's voice rises.

'They shall be burned to ashes in a fire in view of their evildoing as proven criminals with no rights in law. This will take place at Seljabrekkum near Kirkjuból, the killing stones by the fjord. May their witchcraft be now ended.'

Then comes another voice.

The father.

He shuts his eyes, throws back his head as if summoning the devil himself. A crack of lightning snakes down from the sky, causing the crowd to cry out.

'I speak the words of spell forty-six of the *galdrabók*!' His voice and the storm seem to have merged. Each rages and throws down terror. 'May you all become as weak as the fiend Flóki, who was snared by all the gods. This is *my* curse to you all. May you be *forever* haunted by the ghosts of the Jón Jónssons. May you *never* know another night's peace . . .'

Someone screams. Another shouts. People pray and begin to run away.

Sýslumaður Sigurdsson pushes one and then the other towards the gaol, yet still the man rails at all here. The sheriff uses a staff this time to touch their miserable ragged clothing, to poke into the ribcages beneath, as if to touch any part of them would scald.

Two men, condemned to die at his hand, and all the priest can feel now is relief mingled with shock. With a prayer, he turns and strides away, mind whirring. Their mortal bodies will be consumed by purifying fires, but will Jón Jónsson the Elder's curse defy the flames? Will his magic linger after their charred remains are cooled and blown away, its potency unquenched, its malignancy unchecked?

19

THE BUNDLES OF sticks and branches weigh heavy on their shoulders. My father and brother stagger as they carry the materials needed to build their pyre, their once-golden hair now matted and streaked with grime, their sacking hanging off their wasted frames. Wood and branches collected from our stores at Kirkjuból by the sheriff's men is tied to their backs, alongside pots filled with sticky black tar and bunches of kindling. This wood I foraged and stored through winters past, will now be used to kill my family.

My Jón Jónsson men arrived by water from their gaol across the harbour inlet. The boat barely made a sound; two oars cut through clear fjord water reflecting the mountain range and sky. Terns screamed and dived, protecting their nests the closer the boat got to shore. Both men stared ahead: dazed. If they had hoped to escape, to be freed, then hope had died by the time they stepped onto pebbled shore. I saw my father glance around as if he expected twelve good men to step forward even now. Of course, there was no one.

I follow behind them. A strange procession: a silent one. Ahead, a crowd has gathered. My friends Anna and Freyja wait for me by the killing stones. The priest, witchfinder and sheriff too. All of Eyri and Kirkjuból are here, as well as faces I do not recognize from outlying districts. Many do not catch my eye. They stare past me, they stare past my father and my brother, as if we are spectres: invisible, roaming, restless.

Finally, we reach the ancient killing stones, Seljabrekkum, though there have been no executions here in my memory. Here, the pyre is built. Stick lands on stick, bushel upon bushel. Twisted bark of sea driftwood cast off from Grænland's shores lies atop pieces cut for the hearth. Hours collecting, searching, foraging for it all. Now it will burn them.

'Good people of Eyri,' the sheriff begins with relish, 'today you will witness justice by command of King Frederick the Third. Two men have been found guilty of sorcery, of magical practices that undermine the will of God Almighty. They've been found guilty of witchcraft.'

Above, a raven calls. It casts its black shadow as it flies, circling the long grass along the bank. As the sheriff speaks, someone is trying to light the wood with a taper from a fish-oil lamp. There is the sharp tang of salt, soot and coal as the jumble of wooden stakes and branches finally catches. The flame is jarring, too bright against the muted landscape. The first crackle, a thin line of orange-red, snakes along a branch. Smoke, thick and black, plumes. They stand, bare feet on grassy mounds beside the stones. It's this that horrifies me the most. Their feet: chilled and sore. Two proud *seid-menn*, subjugated.

It is time for the priest to speak. 'These men have shown their wickedness and must be punished for it. Only then can their evil be purified in the flames that are a mere breath of wind compared to those they will face in hell . . .' He raises both arms. Suddenly, the pyre roars into life. Flames jump into the air, greedy, devouring.

I see my brother step back as if the heat is too strong even there. Two of the sheriff's men grip both his arms. The same for my father, though both try to shake them off. There is alarm now on my father's face as if awoken from a spell.

They should've slit their throats while they had the chance.

I feel a similar hold on my arms, but I am fortunate. It is the grip of my two friends who stand either side of me as if to hold me up. I am in no danger of fainting, more of running at the sheriff's men to bite and kick and claw their faces.

The witchfinder watches me from under his black hat. I bare my teeth like a she-wolf and catch the eye of the priest's wife dressed in her Sunday best as if this is a holy day. She looks shocked, for a second, then glances away. Rannveig is, again, missing. In this moment, I have no fear of any lawman. I feel only anger-madness, as hot and unpredictable as the conflagration is becoming.

Þorleifur Kortsson steps forward.

'Jón Jónsson the Elder and the Younger have been found guilty and are sentenced to death.'

If silence can fall upon the swelling sea and on keening birdlife then it does so now.

Bastards and hypocrites.

The witchfinder turns to my father, who stands as proud as he is able. My brother, on the other hand, has dropped to his knees onto the damp earth and looks like he might be praying.

That won't save you, brother. Nothing will now. At least hold your ground, show some dignity. They cannot take that from you – unless you let them.

'What say you? Do you have any last words? Do you repent your terrible crimes against the godly of Eyri?'

All eyes seem to travel now to Síra Jón Magnússon. He stands a little behind, back straight, eyes blazing, holding the metal cross that sits round his neck. His lips move in prayer, presumably.

My father draws the spittle in his mouth. He rolls it on his tongue then hurls it into Þorleifur Kortsson's face.

With studied calm, the witchfinder wipes his cheek. He opens his mouth, but my father interjects.

'I do have something to say. Oh yes. By Þórr's hammer and Óðinn's rage, my son, Jón, and I will haunt you all until you die, and we won't stop there. We'll chase you fuckers through the gates of the underworld, and we'll laugh while we're doing it. We'll laugh . . .'

Tears slide down his cheeks, making rivulets in the dirt caked into his skin. Then, my father's voice rises above the murmurings in the crowd.

'Magic will outlast us in Skutulsfjörður even though we depart. Be warned. All of you, be warned! There is worse to come . . .'

A shocked hush. A moment where no one seems to know what to do. My brother breaks the silence. He wails, crying for mercy. He drags himself along the tufted grass, his arms outstretched though he struggles with the chains.

The witchfinder ignores him, gestures for the sheriff's men who step forward to grab them both, to drag them to a place above the killing stones. The fire reaches higher and higher into the sky. A soft rain has begun to fall, making the flames hiss.

Then, they push my father.

Into the furnace he falls, yet it is my brother who screams. It rents the air. By the look of his sacking, he has pissed himself. There is a sound like air escaping from a folded sail, then he too is thrown down, screaming as he goes. Both men writhe as the heat melts them down, their skin bubbling; hair and sacking alight, eyes becoming sightless.

My father goes silent first.

He seems to sink into the ground and disappear inside the tarry flames, greasy smoke drifting up towards the mountain ridge. The raven alights further up the craggy incline as if watching. Its flight distracts me, but not for long. Then, in a shock of charred wood and terrible motion, my brother, Jón Jónsson the Younger, appears out of the depths of his pyre like an imp from hell. Flapping burning arms, he runs blindly. His mouth, half melted, is still open, a scream aborted.

Shrieks from the crowd. People fall back. My friends tighten their grip on my arms. I wriggle to be freed. *My brother. My brother. My brother.*

'*Andskotans*,' Anna mutters. 'By the devil . . .'

'Þuriður, look away! You can't help him,' says Freyja.

No. I won't look away. I can't.

I struggle still, but the shock makes my limbs heavy. My strength is gone. My brother, unrecognizable even to me, moans a long, hollow sound before collapsing to the ground, trailing orange and red and soot.

'*Fokk!*' I hear my friends say in unison. They start to pull me away, but I will not move from this spot. There is ash on my lips. Rain falls in sheets, dampening the pyre. I try again to break free their grip and run to him.

'The sorcerer lives!'

The priest steps forward. He seems to grow larger as the fire burns behind him.

'The devil walks among us. It runs from the fires of hell. Mercy, Lord. Mercy be upon us all!'

'Enough,' Þorleifur Kortsson says. Rainfall seems to slough off him. 'He must go back into the fire. Kick him into the flames, there can be nothing left for the devil to work with.'

Farðu til helvítis.

Go to hell.

Nausea rises in me. I have sunk onto the cold wet grass. Anna and Freyja pull me up again, this time helped by Ólafur Björnsson. They take me away. I turn to see the witchfinder staring at me as the men of Eyri kick my brother's remains back into the place where he will burn to cinders.

PART TWO

Verðandi
Becoming

Earth's warden, Thor,
Grapples with the snake.
But poisoned by its breath,
Nine paces back, he sinks.
Sun blackens, earth crumbles,
Stars tumble from heaven,
Fire laps the ash,
Flames lick the sky.

Völuspá: Prophecy of the Völva

Then the fire of the Lord fell, and consumed the burnt sacrifice, and the wood, and the stones, and the dust, and licked up the water that was in the trench.

1 Kings 18:38

20

THE RAVEN PERCHES, the wind ruffling its onyx feathers.

Its black eyes scan the mountainside from the top of the stake. Below him, *galdrastafir* carved into the wooden post. Behind him lies a croft with a single white feather above the door that sways in the breeze. A world of movement and colour is laid bare to this bird. It surveys its territory stretching onward beyond the scope of the human eye. A world teeming with insects, small rodents: the bird is a scavenger before the hunt. The wind changes direction, causing it to shuffle on the spot, twitching its feathers.

The barrenness of winter is passing. The streams and rivers begin to sing with life. The grass begins to show, green and vivid, underneath melting snow. Creatures come out from hibernation, from beneath the earth. He can smell them. He can sense them as they burrow, noses quivering. He can feel the earth awakening, and he regards it like a lawman before a courtroom, seeing all, knowing all.

The raven is unaware of its reputation as a harbinger of death. Or it knows and cares not. The bird is a spell incarnate, a death wish made physical. It is an incantation of malevolent intent, a spirit wayfinder, with its solid, jagged bulk. It shuffles its wings again, testing the current, feeling the cool draught, making *click*, *click* sounds. Then, it launches. Great wings seem to glide effortlessly above the terrain. Individual blades of grass fade into the distance, small rodents too, though the bird can still feel the movement: the scuttling and quivering. The raven moves higher, using each silken breath of winter's air, each passing current, to move this way and that, climbing ever higher.

Below it now is the farmstead. Its three large crofts and many smaller outbuildings recede. The shining waters of the fjord lie ahead, marked only by a small spit of land upon which is a human settlement: a church, a trading station and storerooms, a cluster of gale-battered crofts and huts as well as boats bobbing in the small harbour. The bird thinks nothing of this.

It moves onward, just like Óðinn's ravens – Huginn and Muninn, thought and memory – collecting the wisdom of the old world to perch on the raven-god's shoulders and croak in his ears, messengers of all that is seen and all that is heard. Huginn flew to the hanged. Munnin to the slain. Perhaps that is why this raven circles now above the crowd that has gathered at the mouth of the fjord by soot-blackened stones. The *lap*, *lap* of the water is veiled by murmurs. Thick, choking smoke fills the air. The raven lands on the peak of the rock that climbs up not far from the water's edge. It ruffles itself. It jumps once or twice. It settles, eyes darting. It sees two men stumble and a single female, moving slowly this way.

If the raven wished to hear their thoughts, it would know of the anger and fear, the rage and shame of those men. It would understand that the hearts of men are as wide as the sea and as shallow as the harbour. That treachery and kindness walk side by side, and none is spared. It sees the troubles of people, and it soars above them, honed by storms, sea spray and snow-flecked skies. It watches, shuffles, comes back to stillness. It scans the horizon then stares back at the mountaintops.

Just then, the bird catches sight of another raven, a male, far in the distance, and caws its warning. The intruder flaps away in a clumsy jumble of flight, the warning heeded.

The raven chooses this moment to leap into the sky. It glides. It flaps, flaps again, and catches the breeze, carried by it down to the valley where a rodent scurries: in deadly pursuit.

21

I STUMBLE BACK to my father's croft.

The raven's shadow falls black across my path. This day must end just as their lives have: in fire, in soot and charring. I sink onto my bed. Someone, Anna or Freyja, I cannot tell, tucks the blanket around me, but my mind has turned in on itself. I crave darkness now, for the light to die, for sleep to drown me, for it to take me into the churning, restless waters of my dreams. Within seconds, my wish is granted.

22

May 1656

'WAKE UP!' A woman's voice comes from far away.

'Wake up! You were dreaming . . .'

Eyes flutter open. A brow, damp with sweat. Hair, tangled on the pillow. Slowly, a body raised and now sitting. A single candle flame bobs in the black of night. A face stares back, alarm and worry in the creasing of her brow, her dark, dilated pupils. Þorkatla Bjarnadóttir's eyes appear to flash blue, the colour of frozen water. A momentary shock then they are restored to brown. The priest blinks. The vision recedes, but it shakes him.

'You were shouting, saying all manner of strange things. You said moths were skimming your face and hair, and there were rats running up and down your legs again.'

The priest's wife, Þorkatla, is not alone. Around Síra Jón Magnússon's bed are most of his household: two maidservants, three farmhands and his wife.

He blinks, the memory of his nightmares receding. They leave behind a detritus of fearful imaginings, just as a wave pulls back from the shore dragging seaweed and knotted wood in its wake.

'I . . . I . . . I saw the black dog . . .' he mumbles now. His wife leans in closer to hear him. It has been almost a month since the burnings. Days and weeks of calm, of dampened flames and peace. A mist has hung over the valley, blurring the edges of the rocks and stones. It settled down upon the ashes of the men, their coal-glow still smouldering.

'Do you remember?' he says.

'Remember what, my love?' Þorkatla replies, glancing back at one of the maids. Her hand is cool when it touches his forehead.

'You're burning hot! The master has a fever. Bring water and a clean linen cloth,' she says to the same servant, who dips a small curtsy and runs from the *baðstofa*.

'No, no fever. This is different. It was a message.' The priest tries to pull himself up.

His wife rushes around to prevent him, pulling the blankets back over his legs.

'Help me – he's unwell,' she says to one of the men, who goes to the other side, holds the priest's shoulder so he cannot move.

'Listen to me,' Síra Jón says. 'It was there. I saw it with my own eyes . . .' He falls back against the sweat-stained pillow, the effort of lifting his head apparently too much for him in this state of distress. His strength has failed him. It has been taken away by those whose maleficence has continued beyond their dying breaths.

'The black dog. It growled. Saliva dripped from its jaws. There was blood and gore and the stench of hell.'

'He's ill. Tell the men to bring more light. And stoke the hearth fire,' Þorkatla says, looking back but remaining where she is, sitting on the side of the bed, her hand in her husband's. It is damp, clammy. He shivers.

'It came to me to tell me something.'

'Hush, husband. Try to rest. These dreams are just that: dreams. They cannot harm you . . .'

'You're wrong! They *can* harm me. That's exactly it! The devil has not left Kirkjuból!' It is all so clear to him. 'You heard the sorcerer say those words.'

He coughs. Each rasping breath is filled with stale air so his chest swells and shrivels in turn.

Þorkatla takes a cup from a wide-eyed manservant's outstretched hand. Holds it to the priest's lips, but the water dribbles down his chin, his mouth slack, body rigid. How can he make himself understood? Why do they gape at him? Don't they realize the danger?

The ferocity of this attack has shown him the truth.

The sorcerer and his son live through another. But who? And how can he stop this legacy of hate against him, one that appears to have no end?

23

June 1656

A HORSE: GALLOPING, it neighs and snorts.

A set of boots hits the ground. I look up from the rune bowl I am holding and wonder what new disaster comes. It has been weeks since they were killed, and still I dream of them. Or not so much *them* as the echo of them, the imprint they left behind. The space where they used to be.

Each night, I dream of three cups, three bowls, three spoons laid on the table. I dream of their footprints left in deep snow, leading from the outer door of the *baðstofa* to the wood store or the cattle shed. I know that, in my slumber, I am trying to find them. I see curling wood scrapings littered on the floor under their chairs from hours spent spell-carving; feel the sudden shock of cold air as the inner door opened, announcing their return from fishing far out at sea, making the hearth glow red and the fish-oil lamp flicker; hear their sounds: boots stamped in the entrance, low muttering by candlelight, raucous shouts and jeers while drinking mead. I dream of their shadows falling against the stone walls, the endless reeking fug of fish and smoke that hung around them, their oiled and darned sealskins, their knotted woollen jumpers. How is it that they are *gone*? How can they have evaporated to nothing, like water for tea left too long on the stove?

My anger is like the hearth fire. It burns silent and strange in this absence. I stay away from Mass though Anna and Freyja come each Sunday to try to convince me to go. I would rather slit my own throat than breathe the same air as my family's killers.

I look down at the rune bowl I hid. Inside, the rune stones rattle faintly as I run my hand across them. They were my father's – and now they are mine. They are a sorcerer's tools for divination, instruction from our old gods. Each one is carved with a sign, a symbol of wisdom long passed, of stories untold until they are shaken and thrown into the air to announce what may come to pass.

Each pebble has been foraged from the streams that run from the mountains to the edge of the fjord, washed in clear mountain water and presented here like treasure: new, glistening, sacred. Now, they are covered with a thin coating of dust. They lie lifeless in my hands, their magic gone, their nature returned to its original state of blank, unseeing nothing.

'Þuriður Jónsdóttir? Þuriður Jónsdóttir, are you there?'

I recognize the voice. One of the fishermen from Hnífsdalur who drank mead with my father.

'My wife has been in labour for many hours. She needs help. Are you home?'

I hear him come to the doorway.

His knock comes next. A hesitant fist against the wooden door.

'Þuriður?'

I have looked back to this moment to inspect it. To turn it in my hands and see it from all angles. Should I have opened the door? Was this the moment that the gods' gaze fell upon me, and picked me for battle?

The rune bowl must be hidden, so I place it under a sheepskin in a small pile of clothing waiting to be embroidered.

I open the door. The man, a strong, sturdy-looking fisherman with a thick blond beard and lined face steps back. There is a look on his face I have seen before men cut a sheep's throat. A wariness. As if they guess the beast for slaughter knows what is coming, and judges them for it.

'You must come. My wife's calling for you. She's been labouring for days now and grows weaker. She says only you can help . . .'

It takes only a moment to gather what I need. I tie it all in a bag made from sacking and nod. I catch the man peering around the croft as if he is looking for something: a stray demon or two clip-clopping around the place.

I walk out. The door bangs behind me. He is forced to wrench it open as I am already halfway to his horse, tied to the post. I mount it, my hair trailing down my back, my cloak wrapped tight against the early-summer chill. I take hold of the rope reins as he gets up behind me, holds my waist as I dig my boots into the flank of the long-maned creature, spurring it onward.

'The baby refuses to be born,' a young woman says, running over, wringing her hands as we jump down off the sweating mare. The breeze blows strong here on this exposed hillside where sits a cluster of small windswept crofts. Behind, the mountain ranges look down upon us, impassive and solid. The fisherman does not follow me into the house. I glance back and see his face. He looks conflicted, uneasy.

'She can't come in here!' An older woman, probably the labouring girl's mother, says with vigour as I walk into the small *baðstofa*. I ignore her. I set my bag down and begin to take out those things that may help: *vallhumall*, yarrow for wound healing; *fjallagrös*, dried moss used as tea to bring on a mother's milk. Inwardly, I begin to mutter the special birthing words sacred to women: *hugrekki*, *þrek*, *hugrekki*, *þrek*, *hugrekki*, *þrek*. They are like a spell.

'We need her skills, Mother. We should've gone for her sooner,' the younger of the two women says. A sister, who is roughly the same age as me, but I do not know these women well. I have seen them with the other fish wives and daughters at the fjord side when the boats come in, keening gulls overhead. They gossip together about the weather, the likelihood of storms, the way one of their friends eyes up another's husband. Nothing I would wish to be part of, but sometimes I felt the rub of exclusion like a bruise.

I look around. Other women from the settlement are here. I am unsure for what reason as they do nothing except take up space, eyeing me with undisguised hostility. There is little that is clean in their hovel. I walk to the tiny kitchen, trailing the older woman and her caustic voice behind me.

'What's she doing? Why is she always so . . . so odd? Why doesn't she act like a normal young woman? Here, stop! Don't touch my linens! What d'you think you're doing, touching our good things?'

I turn to glare at the mother. She wears a thick shawl tied across her full chest, underneath which is a yellowing linen blouse tucked into a plain brown-coloured skirt. She scowls. Steps back a little.

I continue sluicing my arms with cool water, rolling up my sleeves until I am ready to begin. The young woman is making whimpering sounds from a pallet bed in one corner of the *baðstofa*.

What does it look like I'm doing? I'm cleaning myself so that I bring no more dirt to your daughter, who is fighting for her life, and that of her child. Ignorant woman! Go and nag your cunt-whipped husband and leave us to birth this child!

Taking a handful of dried *umfeðmingur*, I throw it into the small flames of the fire, just as I always do.

Take away the pains. Take them into the fire and burn them away.

'What's she doing now?' the woman shrieks. 'She's thrown dried plants into the hearth! I'm not happy. She's the daughter of sorcerers.'

'Peace, Mother,' the sister says. 'She can do no harm. Her blood may be the same as the *seid-menn*, but she's just a girl, no more capable of magic than you or I. Go and sit by the warmth of the fire. Stoke it up to keep my sister, Sigrún, and her child warm. Make tea. We must let Þuriður do what she has come to do.'

'But what is that, huh? What more can she do that we haven't already? And is it God's or the devil's work?'

Before anyone can answer, the squat *baðstofa* is filled with a long, loud moan.

Lying on the pallet, Sigrún is pale as death, sweating and shaking. Her sister now holds her hand, whispering soothing words to the young woman.

Let them stare.

The straw beneath her is soaked a startling red. This baby must be born soon or they will both perish.

I nod at the sister. Her face is pallid too, her mouth set in a grim line. I get to work.

24

DEATH IS PATIENT.

It waits, silent and still. It listens for the slowing heart rate, the wheezing breath, the pull away of life. Death is waiting in this room. I can feel it. There is a sickly, bestial odour: the scent of blood and fear.

An hour later, I am down on all fours.

Like this, see? Do this. It will help you. Do this now.

She nods. Between us all, we lift her as carefully as we are able. Move her into the same position. Together, they pull her on to her knees though her legs tremble and her head lowers to the clot-red straw beneath her. Her blood-stained shift drags under her, sodden. Her limbs shake and can barely hold her up. The baby has not yet turned and is stuck. Sigrún, her eyes wide, her hair damp and knotted, asks: 'Where is my baby? Where is my child?' Her voice is small and weak.

'He'll come soon,' her sister says, 'very soon, my love.' With a gentle hand, the woman strokes her cheek. I have crumbled sweet-smelling *maríusstakkur*, lady's mantle, into a dish of water, the yellow star-shaped petals that aid a woman's womb, its life-giving power. She takes a scrap of linen, soaks it, squeezes out the excess to dab the young woman's flushed skin.

'He's not coming. He doesn't want to be born.' Her voice threads a high, trembling note.

'Hush, sister. He's coming. Keep pushing and he'll come.'

The sister, whose name I do not know, and I share a look of warning. I smear fat mixed with *ljónslappi*, Alpine lady'smantle, onto Sigrún's back, in a pressing, circular motion. To push the baby out. To force the hand of life that holds us all in its grip.

The other women hold back. They form a circle round the girl. They watch as I mouth the birthing words silently. They pray, yet her labour continues.

Somebody stokes up the fire, someone else pours water from a pitcher, another brings cloths from their own croft. The young woman pushes and pushes. Yet still no child is born. The whispers start. Worried looks are exchanged. They hover, waiting. I press into her swollen belly, trying to turn this child who refuses to be born.

Come out into the world, little one. Come and join us. Your mother longs for you.

I breathe with quick, panting inhalations then pause, making sure the birthing woman watches me, then do it again. I press harder as she copies my breaths, and I feel the child move.

A small foot appears. Blue, smeared, and each woman watching glances to the other. They know what this means. It is death for the child, and most likely the mother too. I know this, but I refuse to give up.

Keep pushing. I will not let Death claim you, little one.

Keep pushing.

Sigrún does not falter though her breath is ragged. I reach inside as gently as I am able, as we do with the livestock when a calf is born in a tangle of limbs. The woman has life enough to yell while two of the waiting women hold her. Red soaks everywhere: the makeshift bed, the *pallur*, the straw. I guide out the infant until a head appears, chin first, then a nose, squashed, then two eyes, closed. At last, the child comes away from its mother's body. She seems to deflate, collapses back. There is silence.

I catch sight of myself in a pail of water: hair now pink with blood, arms stained brown and rust-red. I point to the sister, then to a clout of cloth-wrapped moss, and the bruised opening of the woman.

Staunch the bleeding while I see to the baby.

I take the newborn. I wipe her cheeks, her forehead with tenderness, but all the while her eyes remain closed, lips unmoving. The infant is unresponsive, quiet. I blow gently onto her face. She does not respond. My mouth moves again. This time, the words call for this child to pass through the place that sits between life and death and enter the world of men. My mother taught me these words, sacred to women. If I hope to feel her spirit with me at this moment, conjured by the words she gave me, then I am disappointed. She is nowhere inside this birthing room except for my heart. I blow again on the child's face, this time with more force.

Stay with us.

Around me I hear several of the women murmur.

Then, a cry.

It is a small, weak squall. Greeted by a collective exhalation. The young woman's mother leans over her dying daughter, strokes her white face. Tells her she has a daughter who lives.

But the woman does not move. Only her eyelids flutter as if she hears but cannot respond. Already, one woman is urging her to sip a cup of broth. Another is cleaning her clammy face with a cloth, but Sigrún lies silent and still.

Outside: a raven feasts on the carcass of a sheep already half devoured by a nocturnal fox. The ewe must have been dead for two days or more as maggots have already begun to swarm over the meat. The bird looks up and around as if something passes by, a spirit or a wayward ghost, a troubled soul. It senses a passing and an arrival. It knows the work of this night is almost done and it must return to the land near the spit.

Inside: a woman takes the child quickly from my arms.

There are renewed mutterings. This woman looks her over, sniffs her. Passes her to the older woman as she lets out a yell that would rival the hounds of hell. I know they are checking to see I have not put a changeling, an elf child, in place of the human girl.

'Praise be! She has strong lungs!' the woman who sniffed says, and several put their hands together in prayer. 'Amen,' they respond, throwing sideward glances in my direction.

Preparations are underway now. The thin membrane stretched across the window nearest the bed has already been removed. Her soul can escape and travel onward. Tears are shed. The child, at least, is saved. She has passed over the threshold and lives.

I gather my things. Without looking back, I go to leave but the sister takes my arm.

'Thank you, Þuriður. Without you, we'd have lost the baby, my niece, as well. Go with God.'

I am weary, but I smile back at her. There is grief in her eyes.

A motherless girl. A woman's life taken as lightly as snuffing out a candle. I dip my head down and tread out into the early-morning air. The setting sun colours the sky bronze and gold as the earth moves to sleeping. The men are nowhere to be seen. I decide to take a horse and travel back alone, knowing they will ride over to collect it in the morning, but I hear a sound.

Another long moan of distress.

This time, a cow. I walk to the hut where the birthing mothers are kept and see a heavy-bellied cow lying on her side in straw already black with blood. A young woman, possibly a servant, is there. She looks up at me, panicked. I hear the raven, its wings slicing against the air current as it rises off its perch nearby. I look up, before bending to wash the dead woman's blood off my hands in a pail of water that reflects the changing sky. It catches the bird's broken reflection as it flies away.

When I am clean, I kneel down in the straw. Place my hand on the cow's flank, feel the awkward shape of a calf lodged inside. Again, I roll up my sleeve. I feel inside her, making her groan. The serving girl watches me, stepping back to the side of the *skáli*. It is obvious the creature is stuck. I have no choice. I inhale, then, gripping hold of two back hooves, I pull. For a moment, nothing happens. Eventually, the calf slips out, limp and loose, flopping onto the hay, making me stagger back. The maidservant is praying, her eyes cast upwards, her hands held together.

That won't help it now. It's too late for prayer.

The calf is born dead. Another soul passing through to the other worlds. The mother lies still now. I stroke her back, leave the calf. It is beyond earthly help. On the night-scented breeze, I catch the hum of a quiet melody my mother sang to me when I was small. Her face is a smudge, as if I am peering through a *skjár* at her, blurring her features, all except for her startling blue eyes, her snow-white hair. My knees are stiff. I shake off tendrils of straw and glance at the girl who quivers in the corner.

It was no one's fault. We did what we could.

She is praying, but her expression is one of fear. I do not wait for her response. I leave, breathing in the briny evening air, salt mixed with peat smoke. The horse is waiting for me. I take the reins and mount her. A small child runs in the grass. I turn the horse and ride without looking back. Far ahead of me, the raven caws, its call echoing across the darkening valley.

25

July 1656

ÞORLEIFUR KORTSSON WALKS across the spit.

The day is grey, a fine drizzle coating everything, clouds scudding across the sky. His destination is the rectory adjoining Eyrakirkja, where he intends to speak to Síra Jón Magnússon. Under his arm, he carries a large object folded in linen cloth, a protection against inclement summer weather.

Tomorrow, the witchfinder leaves for Copenhagen, recalled by the king, a move that cannot come soon enough. Already, he has stayed longer than he'd planned. The administration of the sorcerers' deaths created work he had not foreseen: monies to count, debts to settle, legalities to draw up. As he packed his belongings, placing each book into the travelling chest himself, he drew out a tome, weighty and thick, its yellowing pages curling with damp. He is loath to leave it. It forms the absolute heart of his work, containing as it does the central arguments that form the pinnacle of his mission, his conviction. He has thought hard about his decision to leave it behind, but leave it he must. He cannot risk it being damaged or lost during the crossing. And there is something else as well. He knows his gaze falls wider than the priest's. Evil can grow anywhere: in hearts young and old, in plain sight, among the righteous, the weak, the invisible.

Men nod or bow as he walks. Women, still wrapped in thick shawls, bob curtsies and are greeted by scowls. He distrusts them. He distrusts everyone. None dares meet his gaze.

He pulls up his collar against the breeze, not for the first time wondering how these people can live in such a place where the wind strips your bones each everlasting winter. He thinks of his estates in Bær on land that forms a basin, weathering the climate better than here. Here, storms direct from Grænland assault them in a tumult of driving snow and shrieking gales – even in summer. No, this place is not for him. He wants to see the sun-dappled pastures of his home again, feel the softer air on his skin, see his children, who will have grown taller since he departed. First, he must report his findings in Kirkjuból to the Danish authorities.

He knocks on the door.

A maidservant opens it. He sees her eyes widen when she realizes who stands before her.

'Is your master here?' Þorleifur Kortsson never needs to raise his voice. Somehow, his presence is always enough.

'Yes, yes, he's here,' she gabbles.

'Lead me to him,' he commands, stepping into the gloom of the entrance, the grey light disappearing. He ducks his head. The rafters are low. Tendrils of grass and the trailing roots of plants hang down from the low ceiling. He brushes away a stray clod of earth that drops onto his fine woollen coat. There is a musty smell originating, he supposes, from the earthen floor. It muffles the footsteps of the priest's wife as she appears, dips into a low curtsy.

'*Sæll vertu*,' she says, pushing a loose strand of brown hair under her cap.

He nods. Returns the greeting.

'I wish to see Síra Jón Magnússon. It is a matter of some importance.' Removing his black hat, he hands it to the maidservant who hovers behind him, without looking at her.

'Bring our guest refreshments.' Þorkatla gestures for the witchfinder to follow into the small *baðstofa*. It reeks of dung, fish bones and the faint odour of sleep-rumpled bedding.

'Husband?'

The man in question is scratching words in his careful hand at a small table, preparing a sermon for Mass. It is obvious he has not heard his wife, so deep is he in concentration. He squeezes the skin between his brows where it meets the bridge of his nose. He writes. Crosses out full lines. Starts again. The parchment is crammed with inky threads of words, lines running through them.

'Síra Jón Magnússon, my apologies for intruding upon you and your household . . .'

The priest starts.

'Forgive me. I did not mean to startle you.'

The witchfinder's eyes appraise the priest coolly. There is the shadow of stubble on his chin, unkempt hair. Beside him is evidence of many candle stubs, wax congealing on the wooden table. Signs of late, sleepless nights. Signs of a man struggling.

In contrast, Þorleifur Kortsson sleeps soundly. Not for a moment has the sight of a demented, roasting man running from his own pyre haunted him. Once the fires dampened down, the men were declared dead and the ashes sifted through, looking for charred organs. Once every part of the two men was burned to cinders, his mind turned to administrative matters: documents that had to be gathered along with records and statements, all compiled and ready for the king's courts.

'*Sæll vertu.*' The priest makes to stand, almost knocking the ink well off his desk.

'*Sæll vertu.* Please, don't get up. I see you are busy . . .' The witch-finder looks around the small chamber containing only the barest of comfort: a small hearth, a bed draped in animal skins with a rough woollen curtain. Curdled morning light filters through the sheath of a small window near the table at which the priest is sitting. There are the usual crosses and stacks of Bibles and other Lutheran books, but little else. A corridor leads off this, the main room, towards the kitchen and small outbuildings where the servants and animals are surely housed. He can hear the priest's wife, Þorkatla, chastise a serving girl somewhere nearby.

Þorleifur Kortsson thinks momentarily of his own quarters at his estate again. The long, wide corridor that runs down the length of his croft, so unlike this small, squat building, off which are rooms either side, each larger than this *baðstofa.* His foreman writes from the farmstead with news of lambing and crops. He feels suddenly claustrophobic, consumed by a desire to turn round and walk out, which he manages to subdue. This one last thing, and then he will go.

He sits without invitation in the only other chair, and places the heavy object down beside him.

'How can I help you?' Síra Jón Magnússon puts down his quill, noticing he has smudged the fresh ink. It is too late to blot it. It has already dried, leaving a black smear on his shirt sleeve.

Before the lawman can reply, Þorkatla appears carrying a small tray. She places it down on the table between the two men where it sits on top of the aborted sermon.

'For refreshment. You might convince my husband to eat.'

Upon it lies two plates with moss bread, pats of yellow butter and a hunk of sheep cheese marbled white, two cups and a flagon of mead.

'There's also skyr,' she adds.

'Thank you, Þorkatla Bjarnadóttir. This is more than sufficient for an unexpected guest. You keep a fine table.'

Her cheeks colour with the compliment. Only the witchfinder picks up a knife and spreads the churned butter onto a single slice of bread.

The priest gestures for his wife to leave them. The atmosphere in the room changes, the real business of this visit unfolding. Þorleifur Kortsson leans forward in his chair, his polished leather boots pushed out in front of him.

'I was educated in Germany as a young man,' he begins, pausing as he pours a small measure of mead into two glasses, handing one to Síra Jón.

'When my father died, I was sent to my grandparents in Hamburg. It was there I was educated in the strictest Lutheran manner and saw the birth of the greatest movement of our time, the reformation of our Church.'

The priest nods, wondering why this man is here in the rectory. He feels a buzzing sound in his ears as if insects hover nearby. He has not slept, or at least very little. His dreams have changed. Each night, when he shuts his eyes – reluctant, anxious – he discovers the black dog appears no longer. Instead, a serpent, coiled and glittering, moves without sound under his bed.

'It was in Hamburg during my instruction that I learned of the diabolical arts of sorcery,' Þorleifur Kortsson continues. 'I saw how vigorously men of God have set themselves to destroying it. I was given tracts to read, tracts written by men of standing, which lay out before our eyes the methods used by the devil to destroy the world we wish to create in God's grace. When I returned to Iceland as a man full grown, I vowed to continue the good and necessary work I had seen over there.'

He sips from the cup.

'King James of England and Scotland lays out these arguments in *Dæmonologie*, whereupon the king himself tells how we must hunt for witches and punish them most severely in a Christian society. His work in Scotland goes further than so many in destroying this evil, cutting it down at its source.'

The priest nods again. He has heard something of the work of clergymen in Europe, the fight against evil raging there.

'But none of this may be news to you! You are a godly man and are already embarked upon a crusade against the forces of darkness.'

Outside, a sheep herder whistles. A dog barks. There is the clatter of something being dropped in another part of the croft and a loud exclamation.

The witchfinder taps his fingers on the table. He appears to choose his next words with precision.

'The devil is not stopped by the deaths of two of his followers. Satan and his fiends are engaged in a battle to destroy all right-thinking men and God's light here in Iceland.'

Þorleifur Kortsson drains his glass.

The priest glances down at his sermon, now marked with oil and a ring of mead from the witchfinder's cup.

'Do you remember what the sorcerer said before he died?'

Síra Jón, who has said nothing until now, says. 'Yes, he said something strange. It sounded like a threat. He said he would haunt us all.'

'Yes, a threat, exactly that. He was a man facing his own agonizing death and would've said anything. But what interests me is what he said after that. He said *magic* would outlast them in Skutulsfjörður.'

The priest sits up, his sufferings temporarily forgotten.

'Yes, I have thought of this day and night! They vowed to continue their sorcery against me – against all who dwell here – and the proof is shown for all to see. My pains have not vanished with their deaths. I have been the target of more attacks, more torments . . .'

The witchfinder nods as if this is not news to him.

'Your work here is far from finished. They as good as told us there is another, a sorcerer or sorcerers, still at work. Síra Jón, you must be on your guard. You must stay vigilant to the workings of the devil here in the Westfjords – it is vital. The time has come for me to leave – and for you to continue the fight against Satan in all his forms. I must inform the king of these developments and so, today, I sail to Danmörku. I have much to do, and many letters to send. News of the burnings has already reached some parts of Iceland, where pastors and lawmen write in need of guidance. The roots of witchcraft are buried deep.'

'Amen,' replies the priest. 'We must burn away its potency, destroy these roots before they strangle us all.' His eyes are alight with fervour.

The witchfinder picks up the large object sitting at his feet. He motions for the tray to be cleared, and so the priest lifts it off the table and onto the floor. Þorleifur Kortsson unwraps the bundle. In his hands is a book, bound in brown speckled leather.

'Pigskin, a binding used in Nuremberg,' he says. Its edges are stained; mould blooms on the sheaves. The priest turns it over so he can read the words written in ink on the spine: *Malleus Maleficarum*, 1494.

'No doubt, you will cast away all thoughts of the age of this text when you read what is contained within,' the witchfinder says. 'Take it. I am entrusting you with my most important text while I am away doing God's work. You will see why it is so important you read and understand this. How your view of the darkness that assails us must be informed by this text.'

Síra Jón opens the rusty clasp. The book jumps open in his hands. It contains words of Latin and illustrations rendered in black ink.

'These are . . . these are visions of hell!' the priest exclaims. He turns another page, and another. Before his eyes are fetid hallucinations, vile imaginings brought to life. Nausea rises. He shuts the book.

'I will take my leave of you.' The witchfinder stands up. 'There are other matters closer to home of which the sheriff will inform you in due course. I leave those administration matters in his hands.'

'Administration matters?' Síra Jón is confused. His head spins.

'Sýslumaður Magnús Sigurdsson will explain all.'

The priest shows the witchfinder to the door, giving the proper farewells. His mouth says the words but the pictures he has seen, the abominations laid bare upon each page of parchment, beat against his brain, making understanding impossible: the devil: black eyes, black wings, black forked tail. Around him figures, drawn roughly with pointed chins, eyes that seem to beseech hell's creature to accept their offerings, infants held up to Satan's imp by their willing servants. Fear and disgust run in waves through him. He has seen depictions of potions being brewed. Pacts being sealed with the devil. Supernatural flights being taken on the backs of goats and wild, dancing figures at secret meetings.

They are all women.

26

A CACOPHONY OF sound greets Þorkatla Bjarnadóttir and her daughter, Rannveig, as they walk over to the edge of the spit, each carrying woven baskets.

Several small rowing boats bob at the shoreline. Men pass heavy barrels to those waiting on land, hollering instructions. Above their heads, white-winged birds screech at the orgy of fish that is contained within them. They dip and soar, waiting for the moment they can snatch at the slippery silver bodies, still wriggling.

Þorkatla wraps her shawl tighter round her shoulders. Clusters of women, the wives and daughters of the fishermen, stand nearby, ready to begin their work drying the catch, leaving enough to trade with the Danes for timber and grain. Among them, children weave in and out, their noses running with snot, their legs already burned brown by the summer wind.

Several of the women acknowledge them as they approach.

'The wind blows fresh today,' says one, whose greying hair whips about her face as she attempts to tuck it back under her cap.

'A good haul. God was smiling on my sons and husband,' says another, surveying the scene.

'I'm glad to hear it,' Þorkatla replies. 'We will all have full bellies this winter, though some around here have full bellies all year.'

Rannveig throws her a look she cannot decipher.

'What? I'm only saying what most around here are thinking, may it please God.'

'Mother, it may please God more if you held your peace sometimes,' her daughter says, giving a small wave in greeting to the girls who beckon her over, making the women titter. 'I'm going to say hello, Mother. Don't worry, I won't stay. I'll come back with you to the croft to help with mead-brewing.'

Þorkatla swallows down her response as her daughter walks off. The eldest among the women shares a sideways glance with the others before they start gutting herring and cod to hang on the frames that zigzag up from the waterside.

'Daughters. Sent to test us, I'm sure,' Þorkatla sniffs, feeling her daughter's snub. Despite this, she likes seeing the fish come in. The noise and activity remind her of happy days as a child spent watching the bustle of a good harvest. She liked the industry of it, the completion of something. As an only child, she looked on, hungry for company, aware too of the distance between herself and the other children. She was the priest's daughter, so she had to be an example to them, her father had told her often enough. She must be godly in all things. So many times had she wanted to run free, to feel her limbs move and the laughter bubble in her throat, but she understood her father's position forbade it. Now, she is the wife of such a man, but at least she can be here to watch, maybe even help. Besides, it is the gossip she comes for.

Rannveig has been swallowed by the group of younger women, and Þorkatla can hear her voice amid the chatter and whistles, though she is quiet at home: sullen. If Þorkatla feels a pang of envy at the ease, the simplicity, in the way her daughter is accepted into their huddle, some of whom wear their babies on their backs as they work, she does not admit it to herself. She is too busy sizing up each man's catch, frowning when she sees the men from the Kirkjuból farmsteads across the spit with a bounty at least double in size than those from Eyri.

'There's almost as much fish as in Flóki's nets!' hollers one woman, her cheeks reddened by the effort of lifting the barrel. She tips it onto the spit gravel. Hundreds of greenish-silver fish spill out. The air is filled with the tang of salt and brine.

A tall, sunburnt man walks past, a single barrel on his left shoulder, whistling. He winks at one of the younger women, who smiles back from under her lashes.

'Did you see that?' the older woman who greeted her says. 'That's my friend's husband. Look how he leads on the younger girls. He has a wandering eye—'

'And a wandering dick,' replies another, making them all snigger and look his way. He sees them and grins, continuing on his way as if without a care in the world.

'He won't be grinning when I tell Greta her husband is at it again,' the older woman mutters. 'How she hasn't cut it off with her fish knife, I'll never know.'

One of the younger women stands up, stares at Þorkatla then nudges the older woman.

'Shhh, not in front of the preacher's wife. Behave yourself or wash your mouth out! She's a god-fearing woman. She doesn't want to hear this.'

Some of the other women exchange amused glances.

Þorkatla holds her head high, a prim expression on her face. If she feels a sinking feeling, born of exclusion from this joke, she does not show it; she does not allow herself to feel it. Her boots may be worn, her skirts hemmed over and over again, but she has status. She is the wife of the district priest and must hold herself as such.

Even so, sometimes, it smarts.

'Forget Greta's husband and his wandering prick – did you hear what happened when the sorcerer's daughter came?' This time it is one of the younger women who speaks, a maidservant from a farmstead further up the coast in Hnífsdalur. Þorkatla recognizes Ingibjörg Ívarsdóttir from church.

'Tongues haven't stopped since. She brought a baby back from the dead . . .'

'Superstition! How can a woman do that?' the elder scoffs, leaning down to slice her knife through a cod's belly, slapping the fleshy white halves down either side of its exposed spine and tying thread-straggled twine to its jaw before stringing it up.

'Not superstition! It was real. I saw it with my own eyes, or at least my mistress did!' Ingibjörg says. She has plump cheeks and brown eyes, with light brown hair that lies thick down the length of her back. She is shorter than the others, and younger. When her father was lost at sea two years ago, her family was thrown out of her farmstead. Ordered by the sheriff to separate, each went to different farms and households across the district to be unpaid labourers, while their lands were auctioned off to pay off the man's debts. A bad business.

'I heard that poor young woman died giving birth and Þuriður Jónsdóttir was unable to save her. She's a good midwife, a friend to the women of Eyri,' the elder tuts. As she speaks, grey clouds are forming, a storm blowing up on the horizon.

'A good thing the men came back when they did for the sea turns angry,' she says, staring out towards where the ocean turns deepest grey with white-tipped waves. 'It's coming up sudden.'

Ingibjörg shakes her head. 'My good mistress would never lie. She says the elf maiden tried to put a changeling in the baby's place and that's why she stopped Death coming and claiming it. The infant girl died before her very eyes! Þuriður brought her back from the spirit world using magic. She brought special plants with her, which she threw in the fire. Then, she blew on the child's face, and it came alive. I swear it! After that, she went out and saved a cow and killed its calf to restore the balance between life and death. This I saw, so I know it to be true.'

'You are a gullible young woman, and you don't know what you're talking about,' the elder woman grumbles. 'Get back to work. I don't want to hear your stories about elves and changelings. Þuriður cannot help being the daughter of two idiots who brought their own deaths upon themselves. Neither of the Jón Jónsson men had the wit to summon anything, let alone the devil, and so why would their daughter?'

'The Jón Jónssons used evil spells, and not just on the priest. I say good riddance to them. They brought nothing but trouble to this land,' one of the other women, a plump fisherman's wife, interjects with a grimace.

'They're dead – and the priest had good reason. Why would you defend them?' says another, but there is little heat in the words. The fish must be dried. The winds must scald the curling carcasses or most will starve this winter. There is more important work to do than argue over the scorched remains of two dead wizards.

'You say you saw what?' Þorkatla speaks now, turning to the young girl, whose face has coloured pink.

'I saw her kill our cow's calf. I swear to you. She came into the *skáli*. Her eyes were strange. Her lips moved without making a sound. I prayed and prayed. I kept as far away from her as I could, but I saw everything.'

'Don't listen to her. This is how rumours start,' the older woman says, 'and it does none of us any good if there's more talk of witchcraft.'

There is a silence.

Ragged snippets of news come in with each tide. In other places, it is said there are witches, women, stalking the lands, trailing black imps. The killing fires are burning hot across Europe.

At this moment, Rannveig reappears. Her basket is full of grey-white pitted fish.

'We must get back to the rectory,' Þorkatla says, reluctant to leave despite the frigid ocean winds. 'Your stepfather will be waiting for us and we can prepare a good meal for tonight.'

Rannveig, her face thinner than it used to be, nods.

'Yes, Mother,' she says, looking at each woman in turn as if to understand what has taken place.

'Rannveig, you need to eat more of the fish you dry,' the elder says, touching her arm with affection and smiling. 'With more flesh on you, you'll be beautiful again and the men will buzz around you like insects to the wildflowers.'

There is something unspoken. An echo of the sorcerer's apprentice. Most here saw them holding hands in the fields; the blush on Rannveig's cheek; the way he walked across the pasture towards her, smiling.

Rannveig takes the woman's hand, planting a small kiss on it. 'You always say that. I eat! My mother knows it. She tells me often I eat too much, and we will starve in winter—'

'I do nothing of the kind,' Þorkatla snaps. She is rattled by this talk of elves and babies coming back to life, as well as her daughter's grief being so publicly acknowledged. She has seen the shadows under her daughter's eyes. The loss of sheen about her hair, her blotched face evidence of the tears she sheds in secret. Since the burnings, Rannveig has barely spoken to her, except for the occasional 'yes, Mother' or 'no, Mother', each one a stab in her heart, the gulf between them unbreachable.

'Come, daughter. We must go or your stepfather will complain he is ill-attended.'

As they turn to go, there is someone walking towards them. Actually, it is three women, arm in arm. Two of them talking, one of them, the one in the middle, silent. The wind blows up, a sudden gust that tugs at the hair and clothing of the women. Þorkatla feels as if she has been slapped, and almost drops her empty basket. The women are so close now they could almost be touching. Time slows to a halt. The woman in the middle turns her head and stares into the eyes of the priest's wife. Her ice-blue gaze seems to sweep through her. Þorkatla steps back, almost treading on Rannveig's foot.

She turns. Catches sight of her daughter smiling at Þuriður as if there is some friendship between them.

The priest's wife feels her heart beat faster in her chest. She holds her hand there to steady herself.

'Are you well, Þorkatla Bjarnadóttir?' the older woman says, looking between the two as Þuriður, Anna and Freyja continue on their way to barter fish.

'Quite well, thank you,' the priest's wife answers, though inside she feels her throat tighten. A sense of unease moves through her like the ripples from a stone dropped in the fjord.

27

August 1656

WE SIT IN a circle in my croft, Freyja, Anna and her sister-in-law, Ólina, as they card the soft inner wool, *þel*, to make yarn for knitting. Next to them sits old Þóra Einarsdóttir, mother of one of the farmstead women who chooses to go to Eyri each week for Mass rather than sit with us. She squints at her knitting, her hands gnarled, her face lined, but her mind is as clear as the translucent waters of the harbour.

I am sitting at the loom, pulling the stick looped with yarn through the warp threads, the stones *click, clacking* as I work. The day is warm, the sheath pane pulled open, the doors too.

Ólina sits beside me, a frown between her brows as she bends to squint at a misplaced cross-stitch. She has a large bed cover rumpled over her legs and is pulling at a length of green woollen thread.

'Tell us about this man who makes you look like a bitch in heat,' she says, raising an eyebrow. Ólina is a plain-speaking woman.

'Sister-in-law! Leave Freyja alone. She'll tell us when she's ready.

And, anyway, it's none of your business,' Anna says, throwing Freyja an amused glance.

Our friend blushes. I stop work and turn round.

Many of the women do not sit with us now. We used to move between each other's crofts, bringing our chairs and our knitting, our darning and our fleece, to work together, but now it is just us. The others stay away. We see them head to the spit to meet with wives and daughters of Eyri, those who attend Mass regularly. Even Margrét, our maidservant, goes as if she fears spending her time under the same turf roof as a sorcerer's daughter. None of us mentions this split in the weave of our small community, the broken thread fraying between Kirkjuból and the spit.

'Anna, I don't mind telling your sister-in-law. She enjoys the gossip too much to deprive her.' Freyja smiles. A shaft of sunlight falls on her hair, released from its cap. It burns fox-red, dust motes rising up to the light as if an enchantment has been placed upon her.

'His name is Finnur and he fishes at Súðavik. His family is good. My father has made the match, of course, but it's a good one. I like him.'

Freyja blushes again, returns to her stitching with intense concentration.

'Then I'm happy for you,' Ólina says. 'There's no happiness like the love of a good man in your bed. Believe me, I know – and so does Anna.'

'Ólina!' Anna laughs again. 'Stop your gossip! For shame, you're making me blush too!'

'It's the truth and thank the gods it is so. A bad man means a bad life – we all know this . . .'

If anyone thinks to glance in my direction, they stop themselves. There is an uncomfortable sensation, of knowledge, of intuition, maybe. I assume they think of my mother and father. I recall arguments. Thrown bowls and the doors slammed. I can still hear her crying as she milked the cows when I tumbled into the *skáli* to find her. My mother always tried to hide it from me, wiping her face with her sleeve, her eyes red. She was a strong Icelandic woman. She did not take any shit from my father. If he hurled bad words, then she returned them. If he hit her, she struck him back. But happiness is not found in those places, except for making up afterwards. The sound of my father grunting and my mother's sighs when I should have been asleep were commonplace, until they weren't. It was when they stopped, when there was silence punctuated by suppressed sobs in the darkest part of the night, that everything changed.

Anna's daughter runs in, her cheeks red, her blonde-streaked hair tousled.

'Gísli hit me. He tooked my doll! He says he'll throw it in the stream!' she wails, pointing in the direction of her cousin.

'Go and grab it back off him, then! You can't let a boy treat you that way. Be strong,' Anna says, picking up a skein of wool.

'I'll go and remind him of his manners,' Ólina grumbles. 'Where are my daughters, Kaðlin and Kristín? Why aren't they keeping an eye on him? They know how he runs wild when his father isn't here.' She gets up off the chair she brought over to sit upon with a small 'oof' sound and drapes the blanket over it. She walks over to the door to find her son, but someone is already there at the threshold, blocking the sunshine.

'Síra Jón Magnússon!'

It is a name we do not expect to hear. Every woman and child in the *baðstofa* pauses.

'For what reason do we have the pleasure of your company here today?' Ólina asks.

I gape over at my doorway.

Anna and Freyja exchange a glance, which I catch out of the corner of my eye.

The room seems to change: the air stifles, the mood dampens.

What are you doing here?

'I have come to see Þuriður Jónsdóttir,' he says, stepping into the room without invitation. His eyes widen at the sight of women clustered together, speaking freely without their caps, sitting around my table.

He appears awkward, but he does not move. He stands in my croft, breathing the pungent floral air, surrounded by bunches of drying plants gathered over the past weeks for medicines.

'Then you have come to the right place, Síra Jón,' Ólina says.

I stare back at this imposter who dares to come here.

The women, all except Ólina, step outside, clutching their sewing, adjusting their caps tied hastily on their heads. The priest takes in my flushed face, my hair that lies uncontained, my bare feet poking out from my skirts. He clears his throat.

'*Sæll vertu.*'

Why are you here?

There is a deep crease between his brows, and streaks of grey at his temples. He looks like a man aged.

'Þuriður Jónsdóttir,' he stumbles a little over the words. I glare. I will not make this easy for him. He clears his throat again.

'I have come to tell you that there has been a second verdict against the sorcerers.'

A second verdict? What do I care about his courts and his verdicts?

'I am to be compensated,' he continues. 'In a court of twelve lawmen, it has been decided . . . the sheriff has decided that . . . that I am to be given Kirkjuból.'

Given Kirkjuból?

How can you be given something that is mine? You lie.

'This farm, your father's homestead and your livestock, has been passed into my possession. As proven sorcerers, everything that was once theirs is forfeit. I am here to tell you that you must leave.'

I find I am standing. A rush of shock. A misplacement. The river stones knock together as I move.

From the doorway, Ólina gasps.

I must leave? On whose authority?

The sheriff can't just hand my inheritance away!

Around me, every stick of furniture, every pot and pan, every limp hanging net, every heavy length of rope thrown over the rafters, every round barrel of dried fish or dish of skyr – this is all mine. This is everything I have. I meet his gaze. He has the grace, at least, to look away.

'I am a fair man. I have come to give you warning and to tell you that, seven days from now, I will be back to claim what is now legally mine.'

He clears his throat and smiles. A righteous, self-satisfied smile.

My pulse roars. My throat constricts. One curve of my arm, a slashing blow with a knife, and he would crumple to the floor in a mess of blood and gristle.

'I am also here to bring you this news along with God's love and His redemption, if you choose to take it. No one is beyond God's love nor His judgement, not even the daughter of *seid-menn*. Come to Eyrakirkja. Be welcomed back to Christ as your saviour.'

I blink.

Neither of us moves.

Outside, Gísli is shrieking, running wild, just as his mother said.

'Think on my words. I will leave you now, Þuriður Jónsdóttir.'

The priest turns tail and stalks out. He leaves me standing stock-still in my *baðstofa*, the only home I have ever known, a home that is now his.

28

'WHAT IS IT, Þuriður? What did he say?' Anna's voice pierces the fog that has shrouded my brain. My mind seems to have slowed. I cannot make sense of anything.

'He said she must leave. The priest has taken the farm and all her cattle,' Ólina says, eyes wide. 'In one week, Þuriður will have nowhere to live.'

Anna looks at me, uncomprehending. I am stunned, silent, bereft. The others come back inside. Evidently, they heard most of what just passed because they stare back at me too.

I won't let this happen. I'll find that fucking sheriff and I'll find a way to demand my croft is returned to me. No one is taking what's mine. No one – and especially not this priest.

Before I know it, I have torn past my friends, and am running, grass underfoot, still wet with the night's dew, though shadows begin to lengthen into afternoon. Heart racing, limbs pushing and pounding, breath short and quick, I run – and almost knock over the man who walks up to my croft: Ólafur Björnsson, my friend's brother-in-law.

'Don't let her go!' Freyja shouts from behind me.

'What? Why not?' Ólafur says. His arms reach for me. Caught, I struggle a little, but I need to draw breath.

'The priest came . . . he told her . . . the sheriff has taken her croft and all her livestock and given it to him . . . They're throwing her out of her own home!' Freyja bends double, panting.

'Where are you going?' Ólafur is a tall, muscular man, but even he is unable to hold me still.

I struggle again.

Get off me!

'Where is she going?' he repeats as Anna arrives.

'I don't know, but go with her at least. You know what she's like! When she's got an idea in her head, no one but the devil can stop her!'

'Those are dangerous words – don't speak them,' Freyja says, her tone short.

Let me go!

I take advantage of this distraction and pull my arm from Ólafur's grip, heading off towards the water, the mountains tall and dark surrounding me. Inside my chest burns a flame. It is a furnace of rage that has ignited, becoming an inferno that is unquenchable. Ólafur follows. Catches up with me.

'I'm coming with you,' he says, barely out of breath. 'I won't let you go to the spit alone.'

We reach the fjord and wave at the boatman to take us to Eyri. I hold my fingers up to show I will bring him an extra basket of *harðfiskur* the next time I come as payment. Before we reach the rocky foreshore, I jump out and wade through the water, impatient and headstrong. I hear a splash behind me and know Ólafur follows. He seems to know where I am heading. His footsteps do not stumble nor falter as I shoot across the gravelled spit.

I push on the door of the Danish trading station, but it is locked shut.

Bang. Bang. Bang.

The seconds lengthen, but soon someone approaches. It is a young maidservant who half opens the door. When she sees me – tousled, wild, furious – she steps back as if I have thrown a curse at her.

'She wants to see Sýslumaður Magnús Sigurdsson,' Ólafur says by way of explanation.

'Well, she can't. He's eating and he doesn't like to be disturbed,' the girl replies. She has an upturned nose and a smattering of freckles.

'Tell the sheriff he must see her.'

Ólafur steps into the doorway. The girl looks between us, then turns and almost runs to a nearby chamber. There are muffled voices, an indignant response, then Sýslumaður Sigurdsson appears. He wipes his mouth, pink and wet, and his beard, on a piece of good linen.

'What is so urgent you disturb my meal?' The sheriff's small eyes narrow.

'You've taken something that wasn't yours to give,' my companion says.

I want to speak. I can feel words bubbling up, but it seems an impossible task to say them. I stamp my foot, anger and fear overcoming me. I look to Ólafur to say more, but what?

Give my home back to me. Give me back my father's lands that are rightfully mine! How dare you take what isn't yours and give it to the man who destroyed him.

'This is Þuriður Jónsdóttir—'

'I know who she is,' the sheriff retorts, distaste writ upon his face. There is something else there too. A wariness.

I want to scream. Instead, I rub my cheek, this familiar gesture from childhood, something I do when I am scared or tired or desperate, as I am now.

'So, then, you know that you've given her farmstead to Síra Jón Magnússon. Why? What has Þuriður done to you? Why should she suffer for the crimes of her father and brother?'

Sýslumaður Magnús Sigurdsson raises himself to as much height as he is capable, though my companion stands taller.

'It's done,' he drawls. 'There's nothing the sorcerer's daughter can do. Those who suffered at her father and brother's hands must be compensated. It's been agreed through the proper channels, in the king's Court of Justice, convened here in Eyri yesterday. Heed my words: move away. Go elsewhere, Þuriður Jónsdóttir. Take heart that you still live and go far from here.'

Ólafur frowns.

'Is that a threat?' he says. He seems to expand in the dim-lit space. Appears twice the height, twice the width of this self-regarding lawman.

'It is . . . advice,' the sheriff replies, looking the fisherman up and down as if seeing him for the first time.

I tug at Ólafur's sleeve. I cannot stay here a moment longer. As we turn to leave, a raven lands high above us, on the roof of the trading station. It turns its head up to the sky, beady black eyes glinting. It croaks and the sound seems to echo across the wind-shredded spit, glancing like hail across the leaden ocean.

29

MY THIGHS ACHE as I climb.

Far below, I make out the wooden cross of Eyrakirkja, the dotted settlements, people smaller than ants as they move on the spit, and across the harbour the farmsteads of Kirkjuból. Lying in green pasture, sheep, smudged white, black and brown on the hillsides lean upwards into the mountains. Two communities. Two friends who are now enemies. I see my croft, the largest, the wealthiest, though I care not for that. I see the place my mother lived, and it is of her I think as I count down the hours until I am evicted. Almost a week has passed since the priest came and shattered my world. There are two nights left. Two nights then a lifetime of love and loss to leave behind.

How can I save my farm?

My words, if spoken, would fly far away from me up here.

I have tried the sheriff. I went back each day to bang on his door, which was not opened again to me. Anger rises inside me, but so does grief. I cannot believe I will be forced from my father's home. There must be something I can do.

Today, I have a croft. In two days' time, I will have no home. Were my father and brother not enough for this hungry priest? Was he so ravenous for my life that he ripped each part of it like a wolf pulling meat from the corpse of a lamb separated from its mother?

Two days.

I remember something my mother said, many years ago: the warp symbolizes what we are given by life, the weft is what we do with it. My life is unravelling like yarn from a skein of wool that lies tangled, discarded under foot, but when I remember what my mother taught me, I know what it is I must do.

I look down, along jutting rocks, to the fjord. The breeze is strong up here. As I hold my head back, the fierce desire for revenge builds inside me, running like lava, its crust black and scorched, its liquid core red and dancing: a summoning.

The light is waning as I scramble down the mountainside, the soft glow of the fish-oil lamps just visible through the small window of the croft. Margrét must still be inside. I head straight to the *skáli*.

The hut is dark, the air thick with the resinous stench of tar and pitch for caulking the seams of the boats. Hidden behind the barrels of black sticky liquids is a large basket containing jars filled with plants I have foraged and dried. These plants must be kept here, away from the croft, away from prying eyes – away from Margrét, who is always watching me now. When I catch her, she twists her head away quickly. Not before I see the expression on her pink-cheeked face: wary, suspicious.

I know which jar I will take, which one has the potency I desire.

Before long, I see Margrét head out, the shearing scissors and leaky pail in her hands. She stops to speak to one of the local farmhands who carries a bleating lamb in his arms. I hear her giggle, brush her hair back before continuing. Inside the croft, I find the smallest of my father's knives, one I have sharpened so the point is a thin trace. I work, swiftly.

Two nights.

Enough time to conjure words albeit silently: imaginings made real, silent invocations and desires. I have work to do.

Later, when the summer light has dimmed to blue, I walk out into the pasture. Margrét has a bucking ewe between her thighs. On her face: a scowl.

'Where have you been? You've been gone all day,' she grumbles. 'This one won't stay still, and there are still many to shear before nightfall.'

Strange that she still expects a response. She continues as if I have given one.

'I shouldn't have to do this! When I came, I asked for light duties, for cooking and cleaning or, at worst, milking cows. I could've gone to your neighbour Anna. She wouldn't make me do this.'

I smile.

Poor Margrét. Ever disappointed. Ever complaining.

The sheep bleats, its eyes rolling in its head.

I grab the ewe, locking her head underneath my left arm, mouthing calming words, lullabies to settle her, just like those my mother sang to me as a baby. Within seconds, she settles, allowing us to hack away at the course outer wool. Soon, the pail is full, and we release her. She kicks her back legs as she goes, skittering away to her two lambs, who are almost as large as her now.

'What did you do to her?' Margrét, one hand on her hip, glares.

I shrug.

'It looked like a spell,' she says, biting her lower lip. 'The women at the harbour gossip about you . . .'

I wait, sensing more is to come.

'Is it true what they say? Is it true you're a witch?' She looks discomfited, unsure, as if today she has seen me for the first time.

I drop the pail. It tips over. Shorn wool spills onto the grass.

'That's what they're saying at church as well. The women say you're a sorceress and you'll be burned, just like your father and brother. They say you learned everything from them, their tricks and their curses . . .'

Before I realize what I am doing, I have stepped over and slapped her face. It smarts red, the imprint of my fingers on her cheek.

Margrét stares back at me, horror writ on her face.

I could reach for her and kiss her hand, show remorse, but I do not. I feel none, so why should I? It is a mistake. One I will come to regret.

Without a word, she turns and walks away. I watch her go, the prickle of fear on my skin.

30

September 1656

IT IS LATE but I do not sleep.

My small bag is packed. Inside: my father's calfskin *galdrabók*, wrapped in cloth and placed in sacking. Tomorrow, I leave. It is a strange thought. It eludes me, skipping just out of reach, and I cannot settle.

My last evening. I run my fingers along the uneven stone walls, across the hearth, along each wooden bedframe. Here, the sigils left by my father's hand, carved into the wooden beams, to bring protection and blessings. A poor protection, it seems. Here, a scratch in the wood by my bedside, a bird in flight, its wings made tattered by my clumsy hand. Each step is a prayer, an offering. I lay claim to my father's croft with invisible threads as it is all I can do. Tomorrow, I walk out of here for the last time, but I go out fighting, in my own way: calling in sadness and grief, calling in vengeance.

Every part of this croft holds something I will now lose. What is sure is that they will pay for it, with their peace of mind, with their luck and love and happiness. All will be lost for them too. All will be reckoned.

The next morning, I walk to Anna's as expected. She opens her door, shows me a bed and a pitcher of water to wash with. I have lost something vital, the last thing I can lose – except for my life – and I already know this is not the end.

'The sheriff's servant tells me she's coming today.' I look around to see Þóra Einarsdóttir arriving with her daughter, who looks as if she would rather be anywhere else but here.

The old woman Þóra carries her own chair despite her age. I take it from her, scowling at her daughter to admonish her for not helping, and follow inside. It is our weaving day and as we cannot sit together in my home we will now sit in Anna's, squeezed in beside the repaired fishing rope and oilskins.

'She?' Freyja asks, throwing me a warm smile, and I am grateful. It has been only days since I left my father's farmstead, but it feels like another lifetime ago.

'Þorkatla Bjarnadóttir, Síra Jón Magnússon's wife. She's been crowing about her good luck, thinking herself a fine lady like those from the Danish court,' says Þóra, frowning. 'She's bringing her daughter, Rannveig, and the priest across from the rectory in Eyri. She'll be warming herself by your hearth before night falls.'

May it burn her arse.

'Þuriður's better off here with us.' Anna touches my shoulder with gentle care.

'That woman is spiteful. She might hide it under her holy ways, but she'll have had her eyes on the Jón Jónssons' farmstead long before all of this happened.' Þóra Einarsdóttir sits down with a grimace on her chair, which I placed near the hearth.

'It's going to be a long winter. The snow will come soon,' she says, sucking her teeth, staring at the flames that leap beside her.

'Mother! How can you speak of the priest's wife so? She's a good

Christian woman. A wife and mother, and you should hold your tongue more,' Þóra's whey-faced daughter bites.

'Pah! A good Christian woman indeed!' The older woman sits back, pulls out her knitting. 'You know what I think about that!'

Freya and I exchange a smile. She sits, threading her fishbone needle and peering at the jumper she is darning. It is too small to be her father's, too big to be hers. She sees me looking, and she blushes. 'It's Finnur's. We're betrothed and will marry in the spring.'

'Freyja! You kept that a secret from us! Why didn't you tell us so we can celebrate? I just know you'll be happy together . . .' Anna walks over to her, carrying her son, Ari, named after his father, on her hip.

'Óðinn's blessings upon you, child,' Þóra says. She squints at her knitting, at the small, concise loops in neat rows.

'Shhh, you mustn't say that any more, Þóra. We can't use the names of the old gods. We have one god now – in public at least,' Ólina says. She is carding wool beside her daughter, Kristin, a froth of fine, fibrous strands between the wooden paddles.

'I can speak as I wish. I'm too old to worry about which god I'm allowed to worship, and, besides, no one here would report me to the preacher and his holier-than-thou wife . . .'

Both Kristín and Kaðlin snort with laughter, hiding their faces in their linen work. I throw an amused glance at Anna, who raises her eyebrows. The wool for carding lies in a basket on my lap, but I cannot settle. The *baðstofa* is warm, the autumn breeze gentle. It feels like a day when nothing calamitous can happen, but I am wrong. A great calamity is coming, stepping into the sharp cold of the fjord water lapping at the shoreline. Þorkatla Bjarnadóttir is coming – to live in my croft, to burn my wood, to sit in my chairs and milk my cows. The priest's wife is coming and, if I could, I would unleash all hell upon her.

31

THE BEAT OF Þorkatla's breath stills.

Rune signs: everywhere. She steps into the *baðstofa*, sunlight streaming in through the doorway. Carved into every beam, every rafter and doorway, are sigils and runes, some crude and hewn with a large implement, some small and intricate, carved by a smaller hand. Rannveig moves her finger along one of the markings.

'Don't touch that!' Þorkatla's voice betrays her fear. 'We'll cut them out. By tomorrow, they'll all be gone. I won't sleep under their malignant gaze.' She shudders.

'They're just symbols,' her daughter says. 'Surely Jón and his father would've drawn good sigils in their own home.'

'I've told you – don't say their names!'

The air smells sweet, of drying flowers and the faint odour of brewed mead.

'Why not, Mother? Why can't I say their names? It is all I have left of Jón – at least allow me that.'

Before the older woman can reply, Margrét barrels in, tipping her bundle onto the floor and forgetting to curtsy. Her cap is askew, her apron far from clean. She pulls out a chair and sits down with an 'oomf'.

'You've no business sitting down!' the priest's wife says, scowling. 'This may once have been your home, but you're my servant now, and I do things differently. Get up and set to work. We need to remove anything suspicious. Begin with that post outside, the one with the devil marks. I want that gone before nightfall.'

The maidservant mutters something under her breath.

Þorkatla catches the end.

'Will you repeat that so all can hear?'

Margrét blushes.

'I said . . . I said . . . I saw a ball of fire blazing over this croft as you approached. It was there, clear as day when I was checking the livestock. I happened to look up into the sky. The light was so bright . . .'

'What else did you say?' The priest's wife glares at the maidservant.

She coughs. Fidgets.

In a small voice: 'Only that the fire was put there by Þuriður Jónsdóttir to scare you out of her home, and I didn't blame her . . . I meant nothing by it.'

'I'll hear no more wickedness from you,' Þorkatla says, though her tone is uncertain. 'Get to work. Lazy girl.'

The maidservant glowers. She scrapes back her chair, and slopes out of the doorway, where some of the farmhands are gathered.

'Tell the men to stop talking and start chopping down that post. Get rid of that witchery. It has no place in a Christian house and will make a good fire tonight,' the priest's wife shouts after her. Just then, the sound of men's voices outside. Her husband walks into the *baðstofa*.

'I can't stay here,' she says. Þorkatla's head aches, brought on, no doubt, by their proximity to the markings. At the same time, she cannot deny how her heart leaps at the sight of the hearth, which is almost three times larger than her own. The wooden floors under her boots. The array of pots and pans hanging over the fireplace, clean and orderly. What had she been expecting? A den of sorcery, dirty and stinking of sin?

Her thoughts are interrupted by men carrying flagons, upended chairs, the small table, armfuls of parchment rolls, her few things: a comb, a small Bible of her own given to her by her first husband, shawls and a poor mattress that sheds straw, making Þorkatla blush for want of feathers. Last comes the bed, bumping through the doorway, and the large cross, a wooden Jesus twisting upon it.

'I must work on my sermon.' Síra Jón Magnússon avoids her eyes. She stands, surrounded by walls that seem to whisper magic.

'Even Margrét is spreading tittle-tattle about this croft being cursed. She said she saw a ball of fire above the farmstead as we arrived.' But he has left, taking his frown with him, and so she cannot be sure he heard.

For Rannveig, the night passes slowly. Her mother and stepfather's discordant breath, the slight snores, her only companions as she waits for dawn.

She dips her face into the pillow, trying again to glean Jón's scent: a masculine mix of sweat, bitter herbs and sea-brine. It is musty, but she thinks she may smell something of him, and it brings her, what? Comfort? Grief? She is not sure, even now, more than six months since his death. She has lain awake for days since learning she would come to live in Jón's croft, surrounded by his things, his clothing, his knives, his nets and woollen gloves, surrounded by his *essence*. Her feelings, already raw, threaten to overspill. Her mother and stepfather seem unaware of this. She watched Þorkatla discuss the move, the things they will need to bring from the rectory, with glee, as if this is what they deserved. Rannveig sensed the gap between them widen, a fissure that feels impassable.

She wonders if she will ever look upon the priest and her mother, who allowed all this to happen, with love again. She ponders: if her family were a blanket, it would be a thin thing, barely covering her. It would need time spent darning and patching. She is not sure she would want to repair it. She did not want to come here, to lie where he lay, to sit where he sat. The idea of it did not feel right. It still does not, though it is an unexpected comfort to be close to where he once was. To breathe the air he may once have breathed. All his aliveness, his charm, his wicked humour had left along with his body and soul, and her world has been greyer, bleaker without him.

She knew what the gossips said about the sorcerer's apprentice when first he'd courted her. He was handsome and made her laugh. She couldn't believe he could like her, love her even. He'd had many lovers, many girls left disappointed and some left in trouble and married off swiftly. Jón told Rannveig everything. It was as if he was asking her for redemption, as if her love granted him some kind of absolution.

He was boisterous when drunk, too loud at times, and could be mean if pushed too far, but with her he was different. He brought her posies of flowers plucked from summer pastures before they were scythed to make sweet-smelling hay. He stroked her hand in the meadows. He cut a lock from her hair and told her he would bind it with special flowers to seal their love. He kissed her gently in stolen moments in the *skáli* where the winter stores were kept. That's where her stepfather found them, as Jón inked a sign on her wrist to pledge himself to her, to offer marriage. That's when Rannveig's stepfather's anger against her lover and his father ignited, when his campaign against the Jón Jónssons began. He'd signed their death warrant that day without any of them realizing. Jón's proposal was refused. Rannveig begged her mother to intercede, but Þorkatla turned away, choosing her husband over her daughter, an act Rannveig may never forgive.

'Oh, Lord! What devilry is this? What evil lies above my head!'

Rannveig looks over to Þorkatla, who shrieks. Her memories curl up and hide like a flower drawing in against the cool night air.

'What is it?'

Her mother sits bolt upright in bed. The priest had risen early. Two other beds lie empty and unmade. Early-morning light filters through the *skjár*.

'The beams! Marks, but many of them this time!'

Rannveig turns over, pulls off the blankets and steps out of the bed, her heart heavier than a barrel of tar. She squints up at the rafters above her mother's head, and gasps.

Etched into the wood are exquisite rune symbols and signs, cut with a thin blade by a careful hand. These marks have been made recently. The wood exposed is new, clean. Most of the markings in the *baðstofa* below are rough grooves, the exposed wood blackened by soot and age. These are different. They *feel* different. They look like scars, small parts of secret code. What language or instruction do they contain? Are they curses or blessings?

'But what do they mean?' Rannveig reaches up to trace one of the sigils with a finger. It feels scratched and hollowed.

'They mean witchcraft. They're bad spells.' Þorkatla scrabbles out of bed, throwing her shawl round her nightshirt. She climbs down to the lower part of the croft, her padding feet disappearing along the corridor. In just a few moments, Rannveig hears her return. Þorkatla appears, flushed and flustered, brandishing the knife for gutting fish.

'I'll cut them out myself,' she mutters, and begins hacking at the symbols.

'Mother, it's still early. Let the farmhands do that, if that's what you want.'

Rannveig has a sick feeling in her stomach. Her mother's fear only serves to irritate her. There are markings, made by a rougher hand, probably Jón's, next to her head where the rafter slopes upwards. It is crude, but follows the same design. Lots of lines, with more lines and circles dissecting them.

They are beautiful and strange, she thinks.

'The farmhands are lazy! No, I'll do it myself. I cannot live like this . . .'

'Mother, just because there are runes, doesn't mean it's magic,' Rannveig offers, her voice quiet. 'The runes are just another language, an older language than ours. It doesn't mean there's a spell there. In fact, they can be more like a prayer . . .'

Her mother stops.

Rannveig waits, not caring if she has upset her, not caring about much at all these days.

'What you are saying is blasphemy. I will forget you ever said such a thing. You will never repeat it,' the priest's wife says, her voice sharp.

'Jón told me.' Rannveig turns to look her mother in the eye. She sees her wince. Despite this, or perhaps because of this, she continues: 'He told me many things. He liked everyone to think he was powerful and frightening, but, really, he was a sweet boy. He painted the rune for love on my wrist. Surely you remember that?'

Þorkatla remembers her husband and daughter raging at each other, running to her with talk of a betrothal to the sorcerer's apprentice, forcing a decision that would divide her small family, that broke her daughter's trust even though she'd brought it upon herself. She says nothing. Stunned into silence. Or silenced by the power of the markings. They dance in front of her eyes.

'Daughter?' Þorkatla reaches for Rannveig's arm.

The younger woman shrugs off her touch as if scalded, makes to walk away but stops suddenly.

'What's this?' Rannveig bends over at her mother's bed, picks up a blue-violet plant, dried and spiked.

'*Þistill*,' she says. Thistle.

Þorkatla pays little heed, thinking it has been dropped by a servant and forgotten. Rannveig peers at it.

'Look.' She holds it out to her mother, who takes it, not thinking what this means except they have found somewhere the sorcerer's daughter did not reach with her broom.

Then she inhales.

There, on the thick dried stalk, a thin white bloom coating it, is a series of tiny markings. Tiny intersecting lines, each one with a star shape at its end. It is too precise, too careful, to be nature's marks. They are deliberate, that is clear, but why would it sit beside this bed? Had it been dropped or was it placed there?

Þorkatla lets it go. The plant drops to the floor and rolls before coming to a standstill. Both women turn to each other, fear on their faces. Rannveig appears to recover first.

'Probably to banish nightmares, or a charm to bring sleep. Pay it no heed, Mother.' Rannveig picks up the plant and, taking care not to drop it again, climbs down the ladder to the *baðstofa*.

The priest's wife hears her stoke the hearth below, breaking the crust so the heat flares, bringing the flame back to life. She hears her take a bucket and clank out of the door to get water from the stream. Þorkatla descends. Looking over at the fire, she sees the thistle as it catches alight on last night's embers.

32

DAYLIGHT CASTS A different view of the croft.

The priest's wife walks to the kitchen. Why did she not spot them before? A row of jars containing dried plants not noticed last night. Animal bones tied up with rope and strung over a rafter. Runes and symbols everywhere she looks. The sheer volume of sorcery in plain sight is astonishing. She has no choice but to take her knife to the walls and rafters.

By the time the sun is high in the sky, she has chipped out many of the markings, with Margrét's help. She has removed the bones, the jars and another piece of thistle, marked the same as before, secreted above the front door. It pricked her hand as she ran her fingers along the ledge above the doorway, drawing blood. She shuddered, sucked her finger, ordered her servant to take it down. That finding disturbed her more than all the others. A thistle does not usually come to be sitting above a door. With the others, she could pretend to herself they were discarded or forgotten, but for this one she cannot. It was placed there for a reason. But by whom? And, more importantly, why?

*

It takes a couple of days before she sees her.

Peeling open the *skjár* to let in the dawn air, she catches sight of the elf maiden, standing outside the fisherman Ari's croft that lies west.

White, wild hair. Skin translucent it is so pale: she stands, stares without blinking at Þorkatla.

The elf maiden.

The sorcerer's daughter.

The mist forms an unnatural blanket, concealing her, then, just as suddenly, she is revealed again: the spectral hue of her ghostly and strange.

The priest's wife makes a sound close to a moan. She steps back from the small window, holds her hand to her chest.

When she looks again, Þuriður Jónsdóttir is still there: otherworldly, unnerving. Þorkatla pulls back the sheep stomach, veined and opaque. Flustered, she shouts at Rannveig for dropping a measure of precious grain, while giving the same orders twice to Margrét.

'This place has been cursed,' Þorkatla says to her husband that evening. 'We cannot stay.'

The priest looks up from his plate of *harðfiskur*. Sucking the dried fish off its bones, he frowns.

'We must stay here, Þorkatla. This place is ours now, thanks be to God. We must show Eyri and Kirkjuból that the Lord's light is greater than the darkness of Satan. How can we do that if we turn tail and flee?' Síra Jón Magnússon's voice is slow, careful, as if explaining a point of scripture to a troublesome child.

Þorkatla bites her lip.

'I don't know what has taken place here, but I *feel* it. I feel wrong here. I don't like it here.'

Her husband puts down the sinewy spine of wolffish, and looks down at his hands.

'We cannot fail,' he replies. His face is drawn. She notices the shadows under his eyes. He writes until late into each night. Missives to Bær, letters to Denmark and further afield. Sermons and pronouncements that travel across glacier and mountain to lands beyond here.

'But—' She wants to explain the sense of dread that has arrived, a feeling that did not exist before.

He waves his hand to stop her.

'To leave would be defeat. It would say to all of Kirkjuból, Eyri and beyond that the devil has more power than God. Don't you see? We must stay, whatever it costs us.'

What is happening to her? Days ago, she arrived with righteousness and, yes, victory in her heart. Now? Now she feels as if she is defeated before she has begun. What was a dream of a better life may have been nothing but a confusion, an imagining, like snow blindness in a blizzard.

33

SÍRA JÓN MAGNÚSSON barely makes it to Eyrakirkja on horseback before the seizure hits.

It comes with a force stronger than any before. Stricken, he reaches out for the doorframe but misses and instead collapses to the floor. The last thing he sees is the large wooden cross that sits above the entrance. It looks like it falls upon him, but it is he who tumbles.

Þorkatla Bjarnadóttir is dusting the altar cloth and candle holders in preparation for the day's service, when the priest falls into the chapel with a crash.

She is jolted out of her reverie, almost knocking over the altar cross.

'Husband! What's happened?' Before she can stop it, the thought flashes through her mind. *What if he dies? What happens then to a twice-widowed woman and a fatherless girl?* She runs over and kneels beside him.

'I was attacked . . . this time by a swarm of biting gnats. They engulfed me as I rode here. And I have pains running through me,' the priest says. His face is deathly white, the colour of soured milk.

'Everywhere: my heart, my arms, my legs . . . It's worse than before.'

'Shush, my love. Calm yourself,' Þorkatla says in response to this sudden calamity.

'I can't be silent. I have been cursed again. Don't you see? The threat to me, to the Church, has never been greater than it is now. Þorleifur Kortsson was right. Satan is at work again in Kirkjuból . . . and this time his powers are stronger, the maleficium deeper . . .'

Þorkatla takes a pained arm and helps pull him back to his feet.

She checks his forehead, his pulse, his eyes that are bloodshot but lucid. He sways a little before being led to a pew.

'Sit, husband. Take your time,' she says. 'Take some water. Let me get you a cooling draught—'

'Don't go. Stay here,' the priest says.

She rubs his hands that are chilled to the bone though it is a mild autumn day.

'It is Kirkjuból – it is because I am the new owner of the farmstead . . . Go to the back of the chapel, please. Open the locked cabinet there and bring me the largest book. It is time you see for yourself. I didn't want to alarm you before now . . .'

Þorkatla obeys, though she would like to say that she'd warned him, that she'd known the place was evil from the moment they first entered. She takes the key he holds out to her and half runs to the back where the leather-bound books are kept locked away.

'Be careful. It's precious.' The priest squints into the shadowy half-light of the nave.

'What is it? What can you see?' Þorkatla is unnerved. She glances around, sees nothing unusual.

'Look! In the corner behind the altar . . . can't you see it?'

'Husband?'

Þorkatla can feel her heart race. She tries to swallow, but her throat is unaccountably constricted.

'I'm dizzy. I'm weakened, but now I know why. I know who the sorcerers meant when they all but said there was another . . .'

She takes hold of the book. It is heavy and old, its bindings stained and musty.

'The witchfinder, Þorleifur Kortsson, gave it to me. It is the work of Reverend Kramer, a man of great piety. Look, wife. Look inside. You will discover what the most learned men of Europe have long understood . . .'

He coughs.

The book lies heavy on her lap.

'This book reveals the truth. Look at the pages, read what you are able, then tell me what I know you already suspect . . .'

'The truth?' Þorkatla says. She looks down and sees there are words written on the spine.

She spells them out loud.

'M.a.l.l.e.u.s. M.a.l.e.f.i.c.a.r.u.m.'

Puzzled, she opens it. She flicks between the pages. It is written in Latin, a tongue she is yet to master. But there are words she recognizes. A sheaf falls open. Falteringly, Þorkatla reads. Midwives killing infants in the womb, offering their unbaptized bodies to the devil. Raising hailstorms, hurtful tempests and lightning. Travelling through the air. Making horses go mad. Pacts and spells and unspeakable acts of lewdness. Carnal copulation with devils. Fornication and lust.

'*The Hammer of Witches*. Across Europe, they're burning and hanging those who've made pacts with the Evil One.'

'But they're women?' Þorkatla draws breath. She feels her cheeks colour. The intimacy of their relations with the devil is beyond imagining. Shocked, she cannot seem to help turning another page, and another, her head reeling.

'Yes, yes!' the priest says, leaning towards her. 'This is what our brethren beyond these shores have discovered. Women who have sinned grievously. Who devour babies. Who rip men's members from their bodies and put them in birds' nests or boxes where they move around like living members, eating oats and corn! Women who cure. Women who injure. Women who do both. Oh, there is wickedness we could never have conceived of – and it is alive in Iceland. It is here—'

'In Kirkjuból,' Þorkatla finishes.

A pair of ice-blue eyes flashes into her mind. *Was it really so clear? Was the cause of their troubles really so near all this time?*

'Satan beguiled Eve and so Adam was fallen,' the priest continues. 'Is it not, therefore, obvious that women who are the weaker sex will be the carriers of the devil's evil thoughts and deeds? Instruments used by Satan himself to assault the holy word of Our Lord? A great crusade is happening – and we must play our part.'

'But who?' she says, though, already, she knows.

'Can't you guess?' he whispers. 'Haven't there been signs? Who has most to gain from my suffering?'

The priest stares into her brown eyes.

'Þuriður Jónsdóttir,' she says slowly. 'It's her. She's the witch.'

Síra Jón Magnússon nods.

'It's been her all along.'

Just then: a sound from the doorway.

A flagon dropped. Milk, white and creamy, pooling on the floor. They both turn and see Rannveig. She is gazing at them, her eyes wide, her face in shadow.

'How long have you been standing there?'

Her daughter says nothing. Rannveig turns and, without looking back, walks from the church.

34

THOUGH IT IS not yet winter, the fjord holds the same deadening chill.

Anna walks beside me, humming. Both of us bare-footed, splashing in and out of the water. I feel the vibration of her song in my throat. We are foraging for driftwood before the snows come. Weak sunshine filters through low clouds. If this was summer, terns would attempt to batter us with their flight and wild insects would croak in the long grasses.

As the long darkness approaches, we must be content with gifts from the sea: mussel shells glinting with sea water, feathers drying on the shore, broken conches and gnarled, battered driftwood, which we scoop up in our already-filled arms. Though the water is bitter, we skip as much as we are able with the load we carry and smile to each other, the brutality of winter to come receding from our minds.

'I wish it could be summer all year,' Anna sighs. She looks out to the horizon, past the harbour that frames our view.

Just then, I see something in the shallows. I put down my load and paddle into the water, my skirt tucked into its waist. Before me, lying on the bed of the bay, is a large stone. It is polished smooth and round, with a perfect hole in the centre. I reach down and pick it up, drying it on my skirt. I hold it up to my eye and peer through the hole, squinting as I look towards the light.

'Þuriður! What are you doing?' Anna hisses, her voice suddenly fearful.

I shrug.

It is just a stone.

'Put it down. Drop it!' my friend urges.

But I cannot put it down. I scan the horizon through the hole, which makes things appear more colourful, more vital: sunlight bounces off the surface of the fjord. I look out towards the deepest part of the inlet, the place my father saw my mother die. I imagine the moment when she knew she was drowning, the water claiming her as its own, the tidal pull dragging her down beneath the surface where light glinted just like today, skirts heavy, hair tangled, breath short. If I squint through the stone, I can almost see her hair like seaweed floating, the last air bubbles reaching the surface, the slow slide downwards.

What I would say if I could is: *I'm looking through this perfect stone, out into our world laid bare before me. Through it, I can concentrate my vision. Here, a ripple that runs with precision through the fjord. There, a floating piece of driftwood blown in from further out beyond the bay. All around is a blue so complete, so achingly vast, that I can feel the colour in my bones. Why wouldn't I look through this, even if just for a chance to catch the echo of my mother's last sigh as she descended to her watery grave?*

So I continue my investigations into the world I normally see with both my eyes open.

'Þuriður! Listen to me! It's a witch's stone! If anyone sees you doing that, they'll think you're looking through to Mount Hekla, the devil's kingdom!'

I snort.

I turn and hold out my hand, offering the stone to Anna.

It is a stone, a piece of the earth's bounty, a honed, purified natural thing that has travelled through the oceans and lands beyond our understanding. Perhaps it has seen the nine worlds? It may once have sat at the base of the great tree Yggdrasil, in the waters of Mimir's well! Who knows where this stone has been and what formed the hole that is so smooth, so rounded, so perfectly matched to fit one eye comfortably to see the world anew?

Anna looks at me as if I have handed her a burning ember.

She steps back, shakes her head. Born in the summer months, we were nursed and weaned together. When Freyja was delivered in the early winter, our mothers sang and wove while we suckled. We grew up enmeshed, like threads running through a loom.

Anna frowns, making small lines appear on her forehead.

'Give it to me,' she says, holding her hand out. I see the set of her face, the knit of her brow, and I know what she intends doing with it.

No. It's mine. It's just a stone.

'Þuriður, listen to me. For all that we are to each other, please listen.'

I feel my resolve waver.

'These are dangerous times. You mustn't give them anything more they can use against you . . .'

The hagstone sits, innocent enough, in my hand still.

'They're casting their net wider,' Anna continues. 'The wives of the fishermen say they're burning women as witches in the lands beyond Iceland. Women! Ari says the Danish crews and merchants at the harbour say this is true. Who's to say they won't do that here? Who's to say they won't look around and see whatever it is they want to see? Just because we're women doesn't mean we won't be suspected. Our sex doesn't give us the same protection it used to, or so my husband says. In my heart, I know this is true. Don't you *feel* it too, my friend, my Þuriður?'

I hear her words and I look up to the sky, shutting my eyes. I have a sudden vision. The smudged light behind my eyes is strong, becoming stronger. It is orange and red and it leaps up like flames. I feel it too. My senses tell me we are not safe, though our learning and status have not changed. There is a chill that settles now between our crofts and the spit. We are not safe.

Anna looks at me with such fear that I feel myself release the stone, dropping it quickly. The fjord-water swallows it with a sucking noise, taking it back under the shifting flotsam. By now, I cannot feel my feet, so cold are they. A shiver runs through my body. Without another glance at my friend, I wade back to the shore.

'Don't be angry with me! Þuriður, I know you're angry.' Anna runs after me, hopping as she stumbles across the gravelled bed. I shake my head, but she is right. My practical, sensible, maternal friend is generally always right, and we must all have a care.

Despite this, I huff down onto the bank. A shadow falls on the shoreline. Large wings flap, blocking out the light. The raven flies low overhead. Instantly, I turn round and see him. The priest. He is hunched, on horseback, where the sky-mirrored water edges the curving bank. He looks ill, unnatural. He is swathed in cloaks though the weather is mild. With all the fuss about the stone, I had not heard his approach.

'Put your cap back on,' Anna hisses, throwing mine to me. We fumble with the ties as we pull them hurriedly onto the tops of our heads. Síra Jón Magnússon does not look away, though he should. He stares while we gather the wood, brush the grass stains and burrs from our skirts and hurry back to the farmstead.

35

'YOU'RE COMING WITH me to church.'

I let go of the long-handled paddle forming clumps of milk fat inside the barrel, the liquid sloshing with the abrupt movement. Anna stands opposite me, her sleeves rolled up, her stained apron tied round her waist. We have been churning cream into butter in turns.

What are you talking about? I can't go there. I can't stand in front of that priest and his wife who live in my croft and farm my livestock.

'Þuriður, your face tells me everything you're thinking, but you must. You'll come and make a show of obedience and redemption and whatever else the priest demands of you. I don't need to tell you that your father and Jón didn't do this. I told Ari what happened. My husband says the rumour is he's called the witchfinder back, though he'll have to hurry before the storms arrive. You have to come to Mass. You don't have a choice any more.'

I shake my head. Feel the same prickle of unease. Wiping my hands on my apron, I step back, but Anna has thought this through. She picks up little Ari, who crawls at my feet, and passes him to me. She unties her bindings, throws the linen cloth onto the table and grabs her shawl.

'Come.' It is not a request.

No.

'We have to go.'

I don't want to.

Ólina and her children appear from outside.

'It's time to leave for Eyri. Anna, are you ready?'

'Wait. Þuriður's coming with us.'

I scowl.

No.

Anna takes my hand. Her fingers feel rough in mine.

'You must, my friend. Please, you endanger yourself, and us too. Please come.'

I relent. I kiss her hand and nod, knowing I would do nothing more to place my friends in harm's way. There is a thick beat inside my chest that speaks of fear.

Together, we walk to the water's edge, across the valley, in silence. I pull my shawl closer round my shoulders as the wind bites. It will soon be time to gather the sheep and house them in their winter huts.

Rannveig appears out of one of the *skáli* as if she has been waiting for us. She runs down the pasture, holding her skirts.

'Þuriður! Þuriður Jónsdóttir, there's something you need to know. I have little time! My mother is milking the cows—'

'Þuriður's cows . . .' Ólina says to the young woman as she catches up with us.

'Yes, of course, Þuriður's cows. Listen. Please, I don't have long—'

'We have to get to the spit for church. Our quarrel isn't with you, Rannveig; please know this.' Anna starts to walk away. 'Come!'

'No, Þuriður, please. You *must* listen,' Rannveig begins, but from somewhere near the croft Þorkatla's voice sounds, calling for her daughter.

Rannveig takes my arm, forcing me to stop.

'Be careful. There's much to be scared of . . . You should leave this place.'

Leave?

'Go. Go tonight. I must attend to my mother. Do what I say and leave Kirkjuból. It may be your only hope . . .'

She grasps my hand and something passes between us. A wordless acknowledgement. She turns, hitches up her skirts again and runs back to the farmstead.

I stare after her, foreboding leeching into every part of me.

'Come or we'll miss the boat!' Anna is hurrying to the water's edge. My head is still reeling from Rannveig's words. She may have been my brother's sweetheart, but she rarely came to Kirkjuból – probably banned by her mother. She kept to Eyri, and that's where Jón would go, though he barely told me a thing. It is strange she and I are not close. I think, in another place, another time, we could have been friends.

Þóra is already waiting, accompanied by her daughter, who sniffs and looks away from us. Her grandchildren scamper like lambs in the pastures, earning them a sharp word from their mother. I stroke the hair of one of the boys who comes over to say hello. He gives me a handful of berries he has picked, small red-purple beads in my palm.

'Don't do that!' Þóra's daughter snaps.

'But she's one of the *huldufólk*! We have to bring them gifts or we'll have bad luck!' the boy says, indignant.

'Shhhh.' Þóra holds a finger to her pursed mouth. 'Forgive his manners, Þuriður. He's only a child and listening to too many tall tales . . .'

'I heard it at Mass!' the child replies.

I look at Anna. She looks back, unsure how to react. What should we fear more: this child's offering, or the casual way in which I am spoken about as an elf maiden by someone outside our circle?

'We'll wait,' Þóra's daughter says, grabbing her son and pulling him away from the water's edge, away from me.

Ólina steps into the boat. Her children follow.

'We'll take the seats, then.' It is her turn to sniff. She bunches up her skirts and plonks herself down as I help the elderly Þóra climb on board.

'I'll come with you. My daughter can learn her manners too,' the older woman huffs.

'Ignore them, Þuriður. It's all just superstitious ignorance,' Anna says. 'We've teased you for years, but it was with love, not fear.'

I understand it has always been a way to make sense of my strangeness. But now? It feels like an accusation.

As the boat casts ripples across the harbour, I let my hand trail in the cold water. I open my grip and the berries drift into the fjord, scattering before sinking. Rannveig was warning me. With every movement of the oar, the sky darkens. A storm approaches.

As we enter the chapel, my heart sinks. I am sure every man, woman and child turns to look in my direction as we walk into the gloom. There are whispers and heads shaken, narrowed eyes and mutterings.

We shouldn't have come.

Anna sees my hesitation. She takes my arm and soon we are standing with Freyja, who takes my other arm. The interest in us abates as the priest steps in front of the altar. In his white surplice he resembles a ghost come back from the grave. He is gaunt, the hollows of his cheeks so deep he truly looks more phantom than man.

Then he sees me; on his face, shock.

He walks slowly, the crowd parting as he comes. A question is starting to form in everyone's minds.

My throat feels dry.

He stalls before me. Opens his mouth but before he speaks there is a gurgled cry.

I catch sight of Margrét from the corner of my eye. She points at me as she trembles. There is fear on her face as if seeing me for the first time. The gossips have swayed her against me. My slap probably did not help, either. Flighty, suggestible, foolish, poor Margrét cries out that she is in agony with pains of the stomach. There are a few mutters that she should have used the chamber pot before she came. She grips her stomach then her head before dropping to the floor, convulsing in the dust. Around us, people exclaim. One woman shouts. Another falls to her knees in prayer. Children cry, high-pitched and frightened. I try to step over to my old maidservant.

Margrét, I want to say. *Come away. We will find healing* sigurskufur, *willow bark, and you will be well.* I want to tell people to stand back, to give her air, to put something soft under her head so she does not injure herself. I have heard tell of illnesses that cause fits: high fevers, malignancies of the mind and body. I watch, helpless, as she slams her head, her frothing mouth, against the floor. There is consternation from the other side of the chapel. Someone else is wailing on the ground. I cannot move. My path is blocked by the priest.

Then, he speaks.

'Witch.'

The black smoke of the tallow candles seems to pour from him. I blink, thinking it a vision, but the familiar choking smell of them tells me it is not.

The assembly gasps as one.

'Servant of Satan.'

Long, high moans reverberate around me.

He steps forward again, his face now in front of mine.

'Originator of the sorcery that torments me and will not stop. From this moment, you are outcast. You are banned from this church and from receiving communion. As long as I have a tongue in my mouth, I shall call upon the Lord to rescue me from your foul practices, from your savage witchcraft.'

I should be frightened but I am not. Inside, I am exultant. My blood rises, and, strangely, I smile.

This enrages him.

That is the effect I wanted. Then I catch myself. My brother and father did the same. They goaded him just as I do. Despite this, I cannot move away.

'Leave this church. Now. You're not welcome here.'

Anna yanks me back, her grip tight on my arm. Freyja pushes people out of our way as we move. I cannot help myself. I turn back and smile again. It is not wise. I know the danger. He has called me a witch in front of everyone. It is no longer the gossips who whisper it. I am forever branded.

'You shall not stand in Eyrakirkja,' the priest calls out. 'You've unleashed the same demons upon me as your father and brother. Or possibly it was your witchery all along!' He raises his voice so all can hear. Heads turn from him to me. Is this how it was that night in the Kirkjuból chapel? Have I been blind to him all this time? People move away from me.

Someone, a man, shouts: 'The witch Þuriður has sent evil spirits that have jumped into the servant girl!'

I try to free myself while my friends push me to the front entrance.

Someone help her! She needs calming herbs. She needs air and rest. It is not a demon – it is an illness!

The priest takes up the cry. His face is ashen though his sunken cheeks are reddening as he points at Margrét, his arm shaking.

'Look! Look what the witch has done! You are all witnesses to the tortures Þuriður Jónsdóttir can inflict upon a person. She has done this to me too. She has driven away my peace of mind, and now she wants to destroy us all. She has unleashed a wicked curse upon this maidservant. No one is safe.'

'Get out. We need to get out of here.' Anna's voice is harsh.

I do not wish to run. I want to face this priest who dares banish me. I am willing to face anyone who dares call me a witch to my face. I will not shrink under these accusations. They destroyed my father and brother, but I will not let them destroy me.

'Move,' Anna commands. The crowd begins to surge towards me, and finally I see the wisdom in flight, in removal. People cross themselves. Others pray in the Lutheran way, their hands clasped together, their lips moving. We are expelled. Ólina and the children follow.

The priest's voice carries: 'Your prayers will not be acceptable to God! He sees through you, to the depths of your soul. Repent, for you are a sinner, and we will uncover all in the investigation . . .'

We shove past people we have all known since we were children. I glance back at Margrét and am relieved to see some of the women kneeling on the floor beside her, though they know absolutely nothing about healing her. Behind us, the priest's voice, though it fades with each step forward. He is now giving thanks to God for my departure, but not just that.

The investigation.

History is repeating itself. His words echo in the back of my mind and I wonder, fleetingly, what this means too.

The investigation.

Together, we scramble away. We run to the edge of the spit. We run on the mainland once we have crossed the water. We do not stop until the entrance of Anna's croft is barred behind us all.

Panting, we each stand, babes put down, children accounted for. My friend reaches for something in a cupboard, places a small leather pouch in my hand. Heart-shaped leaves curl inside. Aspen. I do not have time to think what this means.

It is Freyja who is the first to speak, who walks up to me and takes my hands, peeling them from my waist. Her pretty face is solemn, her eyes awash with tears. She strokes my hair and holds my cheek.

'You have to go, Þuriður,' she says, her voice a lament.

We all look at her. She may have tears in her beautiful brown eyes, but her mouth is set in a hard line.

'You have to go tonight.'

PART THREE

Skuld
Destiny

Thence come maidens,
much knowing,
three from the hall,
which under that tree stands;
Urd hight the one,
the second Verdandi,
on a tablet they graved,
Skuld the third;
laws they established,
life allotted
to the sons of men,
destinies pronounced.

Völuspá: Prophecy of the Völva

Witches are so called on account of the blackness of their guilt, that is to say, their deeds are more evil than those of any other malefactors . . . They stir up and confound the elements by the aid of the devil, and arouse terrible hailstorms and tempests. Moreover, he says they distract the minds of men, driving them to madness, insane hatred and inordinate lusts . . . by the terrible influence of their spells alone, as it were by a draught of poison, they can destroy life.

Malleus Maleficarum, Part One, Question II

'Let thy tender mercies come unto me, that I may live: for thy law is my delight.'

Psalm 119:77

36

I RISE, MY mouth gasping for air, heaving out of the churning water.

A thick hand with scabrous fingers scratches my face as it finds strands of my hair, pushing me back down underneath where there is only death waiting. I kick out, my legs constrained by the sacking I am wearing. My arms flail, though now they find the arm, the shoulder of my assailant, and I rip through flesh, trying to peel the hands off me.

Overpowered.

My strength is failing.

My kicks meet nothing. My scrabbling fingers touch only water. I choke, vomit. The water enters my lungs and I cough, spitting out as much as I can, rearing my head, before being shoved under again.

I feel the seconds roll over me. I know they will not roll forever, and soon I will be motionless, drifting towards the bottom, my makeshift clothing billowing around me.

I try again but I cannot find purchase. The slippery rocks. The numbing cold. The panic rising again and again.

Water closes over my head.

I sink.

With a cry, I wake. Tears wet my face, though it was only a dream. The mountainside is dark still, but I must continue on.

37

November 1656

ON THE NIGHT I was banished from Eyri's parish church, I ran and ran and ran.

Along the valley, the still-light sky overhead, moonlight guiding my way, I clambered over rocks and waterfalls, ascending with every step until I was climbing up the narrow boot-trodden pass that winds up and away from Kirkjuból. I did not look back. I kept my eyes on each stone, each snow-covered blade of grass, until I reached the summit and traversed over and beyond the valley I once called home. I knew if I looked behind me, I would not be able to leave.

It takes many days, stopping only to drink from streams and creeks that will soon freeze, and to lie in the hollows of sheltered knolls to rest before continuing. By the time I begin my descent, I am chilled to my marrow and, more than that, I am grief-stricken.

In the distance, a smattering of crofts and outhouses are white with frost. A sun-sparkled inlet, the water glassy and still, lies beneath rich pastures that in summer will be dotted with sheep, as well as the moving shapes of farmhands and children. Winter is setting in, bringing another type of descent: this time into the harsh weather that may serve to keep Síra Jón Magnússon and his witchfinder on the other side of the mountain.

Eventually, I arrive in the small fishing village of Holt, hungry and cold.

Breathless, I reach the outskirts. I stop for a moment, unsure of my next steps.

Holt, chosen for its inaccessibility, especially in winter. Chosen for the fact it stands in a different parish, beholden to different masters than Kirkjuból. The priest's long fingers cannot touch me here. Here, it is isolated, contained by the fjord and mountains, much like the home I have left behind. I felt like my feet propelled me here as if by a different will than my own, the moon leading me, the land calling me. Yet, I know no one here. I have run to a place with no friends, no connections, and now I have arrived I find I do not know what to do next.

The sun is high by the time I reach the first croft, the largest in the settlement. If I was not so tired and famished, I might have noticed things that are strange about the farmstead. Things that mark it as different. But I am not. I am weak and thirsty, already missing my friends and wondering if there is any way I can ever return. I knock. It is then I catch sight of the runes to keep away enemies etched into the doorway mantel. A sprig of *burnirót*, rose root, tied to the turf on top of the stone croft to confer protection.

When the door opens, everything changes.

As if walking into a dreamscape, I am presented with a mirror, a reflection: white hair, pale skin, glacier-blue eyes. The young girl stares back at me. She could be me as a child of eight or nine. A girl who had not yet lost her mother.

'Mömmu!' she cries, and bolts back inside.

My head reels.

There are others like me?

My shock makes me foolish. So stupid not to guess, not to *feel* her before landing here like a fish thrown, slapping, onto land. Then, a woman appears in front of me, each contour of her face at once familiar and strange. Her skin is threaded with tiny lines that crinkle around eyes that shine the same intense colour as mine. Her skin so pale. Her hair the colour of exposed bone. She stifles an exclamation, a cry.

'Is it you?' she says, stepping towards me, a hand held out, which shakes. The wind blows us, gently.

A long pause. I hold her in my sight as if she is a spirit made flesh. All is revealed to me.

I turn and run.

'Þuriður!'

You know my name!

But of course she does.

Her voice follows, but I pretend not to hear as I run, wild and ragged, my skirts tangling around my legs. When I fall, slipping on a patch of ice, I hit the undulating grassland and find myself staring up at a dark grey drifting cloud: dazed.

'Þuriður? Are you hurt?' she pants, arriving seconds after me. She is lean, well used to physical labour. She kneels beside me. My vision is filled now with *her*. Her hair, her eyes, her face, the intense certainty of the woman I once called 'mother'.

'Let me help you. You must come to the croft, and I'll make a poultice for your ankle.'

I look down to see a large gash on the side of my foot where I fell. When I stand, I find I can only hobble. I rub my face, knowing I betray myself to her, to the woman who has risen from the dead, if, in fact, she was ever dead at all. My addled mind still cannot determine if she is a phantom or real. My yearning for her is so strong that it has rebuilt her, sinew by sinew, muscle by muscle.

'Hold on to my arm. That's it. Now try to put your weight on it.'

Children gather around me. I can see more from across the pasture. They are pointing at me.

Easing myself onto my ankle, it is soon clear it is too sore to walk upon. Wincing, I limp, leaning on my mother's arm. Her scent is a mixture of hazy resinous plants – thyme, sorrel, the faint odour of wool, warmed hay and sunshine – her translucent skin warm and soft.

'Who is she, Mother?' the eldest girl says, looking at me with the same puzzled expression that mirrors mine. 'Why does she look like me?'

'Come, Guðrún. Let's get her home. Run ahead. Find some clean cloth and the jar of salve.'

Eyes wide, the children stare at me. Only the older girl shares my complexion and hair. The other children have ruddy, windswept skin, dark blonde or red hair streaked golden by late-summer light.

The world has distilled to this point, this moment. Insects dance around us as, slowly, we make our way back. I enter the doorway with the sigils and the tied yellow-headed plants. The breeze moves between us, and I feel as if the sun will not set again, nor the tides move. She looks at me. On her face, every emotion it is possible to witness passes like the shadows of clouds across the fields.

Eventually, she leads me inside the *baðstofa*. Around me, is all the usual detritus of a working farmstead, though the furnishings are richer than I am used to, the chairs carved rather than hewn from wood, the table spotless and shining, a pile of woollens for darning at one end beside a small jar of dried wildflowers. There is a large loom, a rug or blanket half woven and weighted down with river stones, just like mine.

'Thank you, daughter,' she says, and I look up, expecting her to be speaking to me. It is another shock to learn she is talking to the older of the girls. We exchange a glance. She has guessed.

My mother – it is strange even to think those words – fusses a little, her head bowed over my foot, her gentle hands cleaning the wound. When she has finished, the girl whose name I now know is Guðrún hands her the jar containing the cooling salve. My mother applies it liberally, wraps my ankle in clean linen, then looks up at me.

'You came,' is all she says.

You came.

Had she been waiting for me all along?

I shake my head. It buzzes like summer flies.

You were dead. Why did my father tell me you'd drowned?

I think I will vomit. Everything is different; I can be sure of nothing. Even my heartbeat seems to slow.

'Will you not speak to me, daughter?' she asks, and this time she is looking at me, her gaze as direct as I remember.

How can I speak with the dead? You were dead and now you're alive. What other lies did they tell me?

'Maybe she can't speak . . .' Guðrún says, as if it is obvious. Already, there is a thread of understanding winding between us.

'Of course she speaks! Don't you, Þuriður. Þuriður?'

My mother studies me. She gets off her knees, steps closer. I recoil.

'Can you not greet me?' she says, her voice gentle.

I shake my head, trembling from the roots of my hair to the soles of my feet. It is like falling into a dream, except the dream is now my reality. I feel dizzy. In blood, she gave me life. I became myself with my pain and my grief and my yearning. In this blood, we are joined. Except I am broken. Shattered.

'When did this start? Are you ill?'

It is my sister Guðrún who takes my hand.

'She isn't ill. She doesn't speak, and that is all we can know.'

Queasy, nausea overcomes me. This time, I lean over and heave the small contents of my stomach onto the clean floor.

'Fetch a pail,' my mother says.

I wipe my mouth, unable to look at her.

Two of the other children tumble in, the younger girl and a boy. He is the image of my brother, Jón, as a boy, the same wildness apparent already, the same grin.

'Þorgerður! Hrafn! Did I not ask you to milk the cows? Where are your buckets? Go and get them . . .'

The boy, Hrafn, pouts.

'I won't go! Who's she and why does she look like you and Guðrún?'

'This isn't the time for questions. All will be explained later. All of you, please go.'

All will be explained.

'Daughter, go with them—'

'But—' Guðrún the Younger interjects.

Daughter.

'Please just go. I promise we'll talk later.'

My sister – *my sister* – throws me a strange glance, one of curiosity rather than hostility. She does what our mother says and goes, shutting the door.

I am familiar with anger, with boiling, revenge-lust, but this feeling is a twisted version. It is the fury of a child thwarted. A sickening, helpless rage that is formed from loss, absolute and terrifying. I am dazzled by it. It is a large wave, cresting then breaking, sweeping me under and turning me in the current, rolling me over and over until I have no notion of where sky nor land lie.

She sits on the chair opposite me as tears run down my face. I do not attempt to hide them. I cannot.

'I've prayed for this day. Oh, not like *that*. Not to God. No, I've begged Óðinn to bring you to me, to explain . . .'

You want to explain?

Did you have a choice?

Somehow, in all of this, I have not yet considered my mother may have chosen her path. She has gone from dead woman, to resurrected mother, to a person who lives this other life. She does not know I thought her dead. She thinks I knew she left, and does not know of my father's lies. I can barely untangle them myself.

'I've wanted to tell you so much, to say sorry . . . I've begged the old gods to forgive me when I've never had the courage to forgive myself.'

The sick feeling rises again.

My face forms a scowl of disbelief. I feel the muscles move downwards, contracting.

'There were reasons, daughter, *good* reasons . . .'

What reasons could there be to leave your children, me and Jón?

Then, a worse thought: *Did Jón know our mother was alive?*

Did you lie to me too, Jón?

These questions will never be answered. I feel a jolt of grief, so complete, so piercing, it feels like the silent entry of a dagger. Sharp. Slicing.

'I tried to come back, but I couldn't . . . It's hard to explain.'

Try. Give me that, at least. I would spit these words.

Before she can continue, the door to the *baðstofa* opens. A tall man with a serious face steps inside. He greets her as 'wife'. She replies to him as 'husband'. She walks over to him as if she is relieved he is here. Together, they turn to face me.

38

'THIS IS LEIF Árnason, my husband.'

My mother's face betrays her guilt. I do the calculation. She must have been pregnant with their eldest, Guðrún, when she left for Holt, a girl named after her. None named after me; the one left behind.

'This is Þuriður . . .'

'Welcome, Þuriður Jónsdóttir,' he says, and nothing more. He has hair the colour of the sunset – red and orange run through with grey – and a beard cut close to his jaw. He wears leather boots, as do they all, and carries a leather bag. He has the air of an important man, but he smiles, looks down at my ankle.

'Your mother will heal that wound in no time,' he says, waiting for a response.

'She doesn't speak,' my mother says. 'I think she stopped when I left her. She always felt things deeply. I think I took her ability to talk . . .'

A catch in her voice. A single tear slides down her face, which she wipes away as if furious with it. I'd forgotten that gesture – *my gesture* is an echo of hers.

You left me?

There. It is said. The truth of it.

She left me.

I rub my cheek.

I look towards the door, thinking I will run, but my legs refuse to move. I feel weak as a newborn. I know, this time, I will not get far.

She didn't care for me. She abandoned me. She left me with a new child in her belly and a new life ahead of her. She tired of us. Of me.

I move my mouth, trying to form words, but they slide away, just out of reach. My heart burns. It incinerates. So many things I need to say, but they are buried too deep inside me. There is confusion. There is love and hatred, and a desperate need to be held. All battle and rage. All keep me silent, strange, impotent. I put my hand to my throat. It feels as if someone is squeezing it tight. Tears sting my eyes and I blink them away, furious at myself.

I hate you.

'She's tired. Has she walked alone from Kirkjuból in this cold?' Leif says. 'If so, she's lucky she wasn't eaten by wolves or frozen on the mountainside. It's a long walk, more than three thousand *akrlengd*.'

'Þuriður, speak to us, please,' my mother urges. More tears fall. She wipes them away, eyes already red and swollen.

Yes, cry, Mother. Cry for doing what you did. Cry and cry because I'll never forgive you.

'Guðrún, leave her now. She needs sleep and food. Nothing can be fixed today.'

This man Leif is tender with my mother, and unperturbed by my sudden appearance. He sits beside me as I glare back at him, nods as if he sees all my terrible thoughts and does not judge me. So different from my father. I push away the thought, the sick feeling receding a little.

'You've walked a long way. You must rest now. There is a bed at the far end of the sleeping area where your two sisters sleep. Go there.

Nothing can be done until you've slept off your journey.'

He has a calm way of speaking that makes me want to obey him. The fight is draining from me. My eyes are heavy, my limbs too. Sleep, when it comes, is deep, dreamless. It consumes me whole.

I do not know how long I have slept.

The beds are neater than when I crawled up the small ladder and sank onto a mattress of feathers. Looking outside, though the window is tiny, I see late-morning light, grey-blue skies heavy with clouds. If I did not need to piss so badly, I would probably gather my things and tiptoe out. Descending into the *baðstofa*, I find a woman sitting at the table, haughty as a noblewoman, or so I guess, never having seen one. She must be the same age as my mother and is wearing the *faldbúningur*, a costume revealing her high status, with a tight-fitted bodice decorated with rich embroidery, and a red woollen dress. Her deep brown hair shines, silver strands catching the morning light. Next to her sits an old woman with long greying hair and lined gold-brown eyes, squinting as she darns.

'She's awake,' the well-dressed woman calls to someone, somewhere, glancing at me and pushing a chair out from the table with her foot.

'Sit down, please, Þuriður,' she says.

Yawning, I do as she asks, before remembering I need a chamber pot. I signal to the outside, then to my skirt.

'She needs to piss!' The crone sniffs, pointing outside. 'Nothing wrong with doing it out there. We've done it for generations that way. I don't hold to this new idea of having a pot kept inside. It'll attract flies, I say to my daughter-in-law, but she won't listen. Guðrún! Come and keep an eye on this one. She'll bolt at the first opportunity. She looks like a ewe who has lost her lamb and will escape to find it.'

My mother appears from the corridor that links parts of the croft, exchanges a look with the richly dressed mistress. The spectral shock of her is as strong as if this is the first time I set eyes upon her again. This ghost has come back from the dead to claim me as her own. I do not know what to feel, how to act. Do I run? Do I stay? Do I try to find a way to tell her I thought her dead?

'Let her go, if she wants, Birta.' My mother's words are a pool of sadness. 'She must choose her own path, as I chose mine. I won't force her to stay.'

She turns to go back down the corridor. Before she goes, I almost reach for her. I feel cast into her net now, squirming and gasping for air. In that moment, I know I will not run, though my questions almost burst from me.

Why did you leave me? How could you leave me, your beloved daughter, one who loved you? One who needed you? Who are these people? Where do I fit, if I even fit at all?

She walks away, and it is a fresh grief piled upon all the others.

After I have squatted behind a *skáli*, I come back inside to find the table laden with food: whale blubber preserved in whey, unleavened bread, *harðfiskur* and *siginn fiskur*. I eat, though every mouthful feels like a betrayal.

The old woman has shuffled off. My mother sits now at the table with the haughty woman beside her, waiting for me to finish. Both eye me, wary, curious. Every bite weighs heavy in my stomach.

'At least you have an appetite,' the stranger says. She takes another long look at me, then stands up.

'I must away back to my husband, Gissur. He likes me with him when he convenes the local assembly, says I see through all the bluster to the heart of each case. He is right, of course. I tell him he is always right, and so we get on very well indeed.'

Her cloak is thick and coloured red. I have never seen anything so fine. I look down at my skirt, my stitching making the course linen fine: soft hues of green, pink, yellow and brown from yarn I dyed myself form a decorative moat around me. My garments are different, but no less striking, though they are grass-stained and grubby.

'Thank you for coming here, Halladóra Einarsdóttir,' my mother says.

'We are friends – of course I came. Leif is my husband's most loyal officer, and so I will always help if I can. But now you need time alone together. The past cannot so easily be shrugged off. Goodbye, Þuriður Jónsdóttir. Your mother has longed for this day. May you both find solace in each other.'

I stare after this creature, watch her leave, pulling on gloves lined with fur, ordering one of the farmhands to hold her black mare. She is bold and strong-willed and – to me at least – powerful. I have never seen a woman like her.

'Did your father tell you anything about me leaving?'

I push away my plate, shake my head.

'No, I didn't think he would,' she sighs. She pulls a thread hanging from her blouse, winds it round her finger, making the tip pink.

'I don't know how much you know?'

Again, I shake my head. *Nothing, or at least nothing true.*

My heart beats faster. I fold my hands together to stop them trembling.

'Jón – your father – told you nothing? What on earth did you think happened to me?'

My face reads like an open book.

She gasps.

'You cannot mean . . . ?'

She makes a sound somewhere between outrage and distress.

'He told you I was dead? Can he really have been so cruel? *Fokk*, Jón, you were always a stupid, arrogant man, but to lie to your daughter? How could you?' She slams her hand onto the table.

'Then, you know nothing, absolutely nothing. No wonder you won't speak to me! You must have thought you saw a spirit come to haunt you.'

I shudder.

There are many stories of the dead returning. My father and brother even boasted of raising corpses, restoring them, in temperament and character if not in physical form. I do not wish to tempt the gods into showing me those who still walk the land, unfettered by life. Again, my face reveals too much.

'Þuriður, I'm alive, though I think you would not wish me to be now you know the truth . . .'

The truth? All I know is I am torn between wanting to claw at you and, at the same time, wanting to run into your arms and weep for the mother I barely knew.

I want to hear her reasons, but, also, I do not. Underneath this raw, guttural hatred is a hurt so complete, so deep, it takes my breath away.

She sighs again.

'The truth is . . . the truth is a difficult thing. There's so much I wanted to tell you, but you were a child.'

I was eight years old when you left. Eight. Didn't I deserve an explanation, even then?

'Your father wasn't a good husband to me. I'm sorry, Þuriður, but I think you already know this. All of Kirkjuból feared him. He threatened people with bad magic. He thought he owned the world, and me included. He tried to stop me meeting my friends, even helping on the days the fishing boats came in. He was jealous and mean and drank too much. There were rumours of him with other women, but you know the worst of it? I wanted those rumours to be true, so he'd leave me, so he'd take his petty spite away.'

She paces the room. Sits down.

Beside her is a basket filled with skeins of fibrous wool. The large fireplace contains the ashes from the night before, a large pile of dried dung and logs, and a poker. Above it hangs a large cauldron along with strips of drying mutton. An ordinary domestic scene, within which rages a tempest. My mother's home. Her real family home.

'Daughter? Please forgive me. I wanted to bring you with me, I promise. I thought your father would come and take you away to punish me. I didn't want that to happen to you. I didn't want him to take away the life I needed to live, either.' She grasps for my hand. I feel the shock of her warm skin against mine.

'Sorry.' My mother is weeping now. 'I wanted to come and get you. I begged Leif to bring me back to Kirkjuból, but he said they'd stop me, or worse . . . I'd fallen in love, of course, and that's why I had to leave. I told your father when he confronted me by the fjord one summer day. By then, I was already with child. Your father was furious. I'd never seen him so angry. He told me he'd kill me if I didn't leave that night. He wouldn't let me say goodbye . . .

'I should've begged him. I should've told him I wasn't scared of him and come back to get you anyway, but the truth is I *was* scared of him. I walked here, to Holt, over the mountains to the man I loved. With every step, I knew I'd failed you and your brother. When I got here, Leif held me. He told me I couldn't go back. Our love was stronger than the ocean storms. We had to be together. Every saga has a love story, Þuriður, even mine.'

And a revenge story. One of hate and fury where old grievances end in blood and mayhem.

Father, I should've slit your throat when I had the chance, as you wasted away in that fetid gaol. If I'd have known, I'd have done it. I swear that to you.

'Leif promised me a new life when we felt a child stir within me. I wanted to bring you. Walking away from you and your brother was the hardest thing I have ever done. I have regretted the pain I caused you every single day.

'And now you're here. It feels like a miracle, but in my mind I'm asking if the gods are playing tricks upon us. I had to leave – please see that, Þuriður. When the rumours arrived on a fishing boat that your father and my son, my eldest born, were burned as sorcerers, I wanted to come and take you away, but I thought you wouldn't come with me. By then, you were grown. You were a woman. In my heart, I knew if I appeared you'd hate me. I was wrong to leave you there, alone and unprotected. Can you ever forgive me?'

I wasn't alone. I didn't have you, but I had my friends, and they didn't run away. They held their ground with me. They proved their love for me – unlike you. And you didn't come back. You never came back for me . . . Forgive you? When the river flows up the steep crags of Hekla. When the salt brine of the sea runs outwards. When the fjord waters are stronger than stone. Then, I will forgive you.

Suddenly, I want air. Lungfuls of fresh, salted, eddying air. I want to feel alive and purged of this bitterness. I get up. Walk to the door. It crosses my mind to leave her, yet I cannot. The unloved child within me cries silently for her mother.

Outside, I run my hand along the sigils and turn my face to the skies.

My father lied to me – and everyone in our community – because he could not face the truth. His wife did not love him. She slept with another, making him a cuckhold. He was humiliated and a weaker, more cowardly man than I ever realized.

Bed-wetting fucker.

Yet, even now, when I cannot bear the sight of her, I recognize she was not wholly to blame. My father's reaction was not her fault. Would he truly have killed her? A pulse of intuition whispers he might. Whether he would have carried out his threat is something only he can answer – except his voice is silent, his body burned to ashes. To assuage his manhood, his pride, he made up the story of her death, thinking one day it would come true if she ever came back. I wonder how the news that she was alive never reached me. The fishermen here have some connections to our own in Kirkjuból and Eyri. The men gossip as much as their wives, though they deny it. Yet my mother managed to stay hidden from me. Perhaps people knew, but were too scared to tell me. Or did they wish to protect her from my father's bitter revenge?

I find, as I take long, slow breaths, my lungs filling with clean mountain air, that I am glad she was kept safe. The loss of her cost me my childhood, but I am a woman grown now.

Another shudder. The wind blows. A familiar shape wends overhead. The long black shadow of a bird's wing. The raven glides like a messenger. Here to tell us how the old stories play out in the nine worlds of the gods, and how they play out down here, where darkness seethes behind the light.

39

To the Dean of Holt, Gissur Sveinson,

May Almighty God have mercy upon you, bless you, and preserve you now and forever.

I, Jón Magnússon, a poor servant of God's word, by the grace of God was freed from the torments inflicted by sorcerers and brought back from death to life by the mercy of God. But now, my honourable, learned and pious dean of this district, I must inform your honour of the following fact: a crescendo of new attacks of sorcery has befallen me and swept over me, so that once again I have been in doubt whether my life will be preserved.

This has been evident to my household and to my congregation. For this reason, I was obliged to send a message north to that devout man Þorleifur Kortsson, demanding, in view of his high office and the gracious letter of His Royal Majesty, that he should return to Kirkjuból and conduct a new investigation of she whom the evidence points to, as I have recently discovered she has taken up residence in the district over which you preside. Devilish activity has been on the increase, therefore I request and demand that you take those measures to which you are obligated by your office, the gracious letter of His Royal Majesty and the glory of God, so that those who may be proved guilty of causing these effects may be examined, exposed and punished.

I commit you to the Lord and to the word of His grace, and likewise all those who are obedient to God in this life and in eternity. Amen.

(signed) Síra Jón Magnússon, preacher at the parish church of Eyri at Skutulsfjörður, March 1657

40

April 1657

THE SIGNS ARE all there.

Þorkatla stands in a shaft of weak spring sunlight, smoothing her skirts over her as yet un-formed belly. There has been no blood for three months now. Every morning, she feels nauseous and cannot touch her dish of skyr. She watches her husband, Síra Jón Magnússon, his quill scratching on sheaves of parchment. His untouched bowl lies on the table beside hers. The frown that lines his forehead seems to deepen each day that passes. All winter long, he has had an unquenchable desire to fulfil his duty and rid the Westfjords of sorcery. This very morning, he is writing again to the Dean of Holt.

The rumours reached the fishermen and their wives three months into this year of Our Lord, 1657, that the witch Þuriður Jónsdóttir was hiding out in that place. Until then, no one in Kirkjuból would say where she had gone. The waist-high snow prevented news spreading as no one could travel to find her. The priest's wife believes if her husband could have gone in search, he would have done so. Every morning, he stood outside from dawn, even on days when he was barely able to move the door open after heavy snowfall. He would look around, his eyes following the horseshoe of the mountain range as if he was a white-tailed sea eagle, yellow claws outstretched, large wings casting their long shadows: hunting.

Then, a parishioner, a fisherman who deals with some of the men in Holt, brought the news. She survived the mountains and landed, scrawny and lost, in the small hamlet that sits outside of Síra Jón Magnússon's jurisdiction.

The sorcerer's daughter is cunning; the priest's wife will give her that. The Dean of Holt and his headstrong wife will not take kindly to being instructed on how to deal with their own parishioners. Gissur Sveinson is a notoriously tolerant man. He is from an ancient, wealthy family, his wife, Halladóra, too. They are untouchable, unimpeachable. They accept the old ways over that side of the mountain range, a tolerance the sorcerer's daughter has not hesitated to exploit. Yet Þorkatla can already feel her interest waning. The longing to bear a healthy child has swamped all else. She finds she has other matters to attend to now the witch has run away and the sorcerers are dead.

Inside her grows a seed that will become a babe-in-arms, taking root in her womb, drawing its nourishment from her bones and blood and marrow. She imagines the weight of her child after he is born, the solid milk-warmth of him. She is sure it is a boy. Though it has been many years since she last carried a child, she is sure this feels different. Þorkatla has longed for him. Every night, unbeknown to her husband, she prayed for him when she should have been following her husband's prayers. She has wished on stars, though it is pagan nonsense, and pleaded with God. Well, finally, He has listened. Years of trying to conceive, of hoping she wasn't left barren by her first birth, checking clouts for blood each moon cycle. Washing away the red-brown stains and hoping, next time. Next time.

'The milk is sour.'

Her husband interrupts her thoughts.

He scowls, noticing her for the first time this morning.

'Sour?' Þorkatla echoes, her reverie broken.

'Yes, sour. Again. Why does the milk curdle so quickly?' he adds, looking up from his missive as if his wife would know the answer.

'I'll speak to the servants,' she replies, biting her lip. 'The cows were milked this morning. They must've mixed up the pails with the milk intended for skyr . . .'

'No.' He looks back at his letter. She sees the slant of his neat, tidy hand, the undoubted efficiency of his arguments presented like sermons. 'I saw Margrét bring the pail straight into the kitchen. There was no mistake.'

'Husband?' she begins, ignoring all question of milk being soured or otherwise.

She can see his mind is elsewhere. Hopefully, her news will bring him back here, to this room, as they sit surrounded by crude hollowed-out carvings left in the wooden rafters by her gutting knife.

'God be praised, I'm carrying a child.' She flushes as she speaks, happiness rising, colouring her cheeks. A baby will be born to them. A new life. A new beginning.

'You're carrying a child.' It is the turn of the priest to echo his wife's words. Then he stops. With a careful hand, he lays down his quill.

'Yes, it's true. I'm having our son, if it pleases God. It is wonderful news, isn't it?' If Þorkatla thinks, *Why didn't you notice?* she does not say.

Despite the hint of better weather, the tail end of winter is hard. She is swaddled in thick woollen layers. She sent Margrét and Rannveig to the *skáli* to check on the sheep, some of which are alarmingly close to their time. The priest's wife pities them: birthing in the straw, in the bitter cold, lying in their own filth. A shudder runs through her. Any birthing, be it woman or beast, carries risk. No woman is ever sure of her survival. She decides to pray with renewed intensity, to put her doubts and fears, her loneliness, aside and trust in God.

'We are having a child,' Síra Jón repeats. He smiles. The effect is like sun rays slanting through clouds. 'The Lord is generous indeed.'

She waits to see if he has more to say to her.

'And are you quite well?'

'I am, husband. I am well, God be praised.'

He looks down as if all is settled. Þorkatla looks at the top of his head as he bends to write again. His dark hair falls over his forehead. He screws up his mouth as he thinks of the next word. She marvels at men, at their world. So different to her own. They act like it is so much *bigger*. So much more *serious*. Yet what could be more important than bringing a new baby into the world? Didn't the Virgin birth the Son of God? Wasn't that big enough, serious enough, for men?

It seems not.

The priest is soon puzzling over a word, his lips moving as he reads what he has written. Þorkatla watches him, observes the easy flow of his attention away from their news – *her* news. Disappointment sits like a stone in the hollow pit of her stomach. She picks up the dishes, making ready to clear the table.

41

THE BREEZE BLOWS cold on my face.

I walk up the mountainside, looking out to sea, the late-April wind dragging against me, snow and ice still underfoot. When finally I reach the summit, all the land and sea are mine. I draw in air and exhale into the ether. Down below, the huddle of crofts sits quiet as evening draws in. I do not want to go back inside yet, though I know I am expected.

I sometimes wonder if my mother whispered a binding spell, holding me with invisible threads to this place. But now I find I cannot leave this new family simply because they are now all I have. I wanted to remain angry with my mother. It was easier than allowing in what lay hidden underneath: sadness, loss, a chasm of things unfelt. It was easier to throw her black looks. To refuse to try to speak, though she encouraged me every night. To shut myself tighter within my silence.

I love you. I hate you.

This became my mantra, even as I sat at her table, drank her mead, swallowed her skyr and good rye bread, listened as they talked together as a family. My family.

One night, not long after I appeared, the smaller of my sisters could not sleep. She crept down the ladder to the *baðstofa* where my mother's voice, muffled, followed her back up to the sleeping platform. I lay awake, eyes raking the blackness. Unable to settle even though I knew I was safe, at least. There was a hush, except for gentle snores from the other two children and low murmurs from the cattle in the *skáli* nearest the turf house. Even the skies were silent. The wind had dropped. I could not see my mother as she knelt by the side of the bed her youngest two sleep in, but I heard her.

Móðir mín í kví, kví,
Kvíddu ekki því, því;
ég skal ljá þér duluna mína,
duluna mina að dansa í,
ég skal ljá þér duluna mína,
duluna mina að dansa í . . .

She sounded like a spectre, her wisp of song dancing like the green and violet lights that appear on winter nights. I remembered the lullaby from nights I could not sleep when I was young. The haunting echo of a ghost child, one of the bastard *útburður*, those left abandoned, wrapped in rags, to die alone in the cold forest. She sang the same song to my sister. Rage flared in my chest. For a moment, I could not breathe, so strong, so incendiary, was the fury. I heard the same love, the same care, and I realized she felt that for me too, then, at least. The song hummed in my veins. It moved through me and, with it, came an avalanche of grief. I bit my hand, relishing the sharp pain of my teeth sinking into flesh to stop the noise of my sobs.

She had loved me too. Whatever she had done, she had loved me too.

The next morning, I returned her smile. Her face froze. For the briefest moment, I saw her delight, which she dampened down like ashes at the end of the night, turning away, but not before I caught the expression on her face. Relief. Joy too. The ice of my frozen heart began melting just enough.

The light fades.

There is a purple tint to the sky, and I wonder if it will snow. The cold, now intensified, wraps around me. With reluctance, I start my descent, my new leather boots sturdy and warm compared to my fish-skin ones. I do not falter as I jump from rock to rock, across tufts of iced earth, down where the freeze is melting. Eventually, I reach the flat pastureland surrounding the settlement. As I walk the last few lengths to the entrance, a black wing flashes against the clouded sky. I look up and see the tail end of the bird that followed me across from Kirkjuból. It swoops, then rushes upwards on the air, beating tar-black wings in coarse, raw-boned flight.

'What do we do with her? Has she spoken yet?'

I hear Leif's voice as I enter through the main entrance to the croft. I pause. Rub my hand against my cheek as if wiping an imaginary smut of dirt. Unsure whether to walk or creep in. I decide against listening covertly. Whatever must be said, can be said to me. I am no shrinking girl. If there is anything I desire more fiercely than truth, I cannot think of it.

'She stays with us! What else would we do with her? She has no one else now. It isn't safe for her to return. You've made enquiries with the district officials for that area?' says my mother, followed by a familiar voice.

'Gissur is making enquiries. As his wife, I am privy to many of these matters. I have dictated several letters, which he sent to those he considers discreet in his service.'

As I walk in, my mother turns. Next to her is Halladóra Einarsdóttir.

'Come, Þuriður, sit by the fire. Spring may be here, but it's cold still,' my mother's husband, Leif, says. 'You have met the Dean of Holt's wife, Halladóra.'

'Þuriður.' She turns her long neck to face me. 'We were talking about you, and your . . . predicament . . .'

I cannot dislike her. She holds herself proud, tall. She speaks to me as if I am able to reply.

I nod and sit.

The heat from the hearth is welcome.

'Please continue. Let Þuriður hear this. It concerns her after all. Halladóra and Gissur are great friends of ours. They have known of our . . . situation . . . and ensured our secrets were not carried over the mountains.' My mother throws me a small smile.

'The priest Síra Jón Magnússon preaches against your daughter in the pulpit,' the dean's wife continues, looking directly at me, 'my husband is reliably informed. The priest appears to be no less determined to see Þuriður returned to Eyri for interrogation.'

I shrug. This much I could guess at.

'But he can't reach her here?' Two pink spots appear on my mother's cheeks. I realize she is worried.

'He can't – for now at least,' Leif says. 'He doesn't have the support of all the district officials. There's little taste for the witch hunts that have burned through Europe, though the Danish authorities may force their hand.'

Here, my ears prick up. The lands beyond Iceland are unknown to me, though there have been rumours brought in from traders, of course.

My mother starts. 'The witch hunts?'

Leif nods. He looks between us.

'There they burn women as witches, thousands of them. Any woman thought to be practising magic is captured, and . . . forgive me . . . put to torture and burned at the stake or hanged in the marketplace. Many without trial. Many without evidence.'

From the sleeping area comes a cry then a snore. It sounds like Hrafn and one of his dreamings.

'But Iceland is different. Here only men are educated enough to be sorcerers. The small spells and charms of women are considered nothing in comparison, mere tinkering with magic . . .' my mother adds, hopeful.

'And so it used to be.' The dean's wife leans forward. 'But things have changed. Certain texts have been circulated by those priests educated in Copenhagen. There is the *Malleus Maleficarum*, which describes in great detail how it is women who weave magical snares, tempting the devil and cultivating heresy and sorcery. King James of Scotland and England commanded witches be burned in a Christian society. There is much darkness abroad, much hatred. Now, it seems, these ideas have travelled here along with timber and grain. We hear the witchfinder Þorleifur Kortsson has brought that deranged text, written by Heinrich Kramer, to the Westfjords. If this is true, then we must all look to our neighbours and friends. No woman is safe. We can only fight this together.'

Silence falls.

All except the fire. It spits and crackles. I think of my brother running from the flames.

I know I am in danger. Already branded a witch. Already outcast. Does this mean my mother should worry too? My half-sisters? My friends Anna, Freyja, Ólina, her daughter Kaðlin dreaming of becoming a newly-wed? Should they fear this too? I have missed them all, unable to reach them by letter or foot for months. Scared of putting them at risk if I tried. It was safer for them to know nothing about me or exactly where I had gone.

'Excuse me. I must continue with my work.' Leif gets up, dusts down his deep blue *treyja*, short jacket, and woollen breeches. 'We have many cases to hear at the local court in Mosvellir, which I must prepare for. Be careful, both of you. I can protect you for now, but I don't know for how long.'

We three women share a glance.

Complicit in fear.

'We must assume the worst, and you must continue to lie low here, Þuriður Jónsdóttir. Let's hope this wave of burnings from other lands will fizzle out before reaching our inlet.' Halladóra appears unconvinced.

'Thank you for coming. Please bring us any news you feel able to share. I know this compromises your position—'

'My position?' the dean's wife repeats. 'My position is as secure as any woman's in Iceland is possible to be, through ancient lineage and marriage. But it may not be enough to keep those around me safe. You might think to scratch away the markings, to remove any herbs or charms. There is danger coming. We must all beware.'

Later, after the fire has died down, we have much to think on, my mother and I.

'I've been waiting until we're alone.' She puts down her stitching: neat crosses forming a pattern on one of the girls' dresses.

'I want you to talk to me. To tell me everything you need to say. The children are sleeping. Speak to me, daughter. Speak and say your words so I can hear them.'

She settles back in her carved chair, her eyes never leaving my face.

Panic surges in like a storm-swell tide, swift and unsettling.

I shake my head.

My mother leans in.

'Speak, Þuriður. There is much you would say to me.'

Yes, there is everything to say! But I have been so long without words – for grief, for fury, for forgetting – and now I don't know how to find them again, how to begin.

'You're angry at me for leaving you and your brother. You suffered greatly thinking I was dead. You mourned me, and all the while I was alive. Here. With another. You hate me with a fury that is burning you inside. I can see it in your eyes. The flames of your anger are blacker than hell. They incinerate and destroy like the war gods of old. You love me too. I can also see this, though you try to hide it. Every day, you become more like the girl I knew, and so it's time. Time to speak. Time to reclaim your voice. Do it.'

The urge to run, to bolt away, strikes. Standing up, I throw a wild-eyed glance at the doorway, every sense in my body alert.

'You forget I know you, daughter. You always ran away when you were feeling frightened or when you didn't get your own way. You want to do it now, but let me ask you, what would it achieve? Only regret. Speak to me now and we can start over. You can let me love you again . . .' Her voice is tender, so gentle it shatters the barriers I have put up around my heart. Tears slide down my cheeks as if they too would escape.

Confused by her intuition, wanting this intimacy and hating her for knowing me too well, I stall like a horse before a ravine. If I step forward, I will leave, and then all that awaits is the same sorrow. I am sick of sorrow. I want to rise and rise again. Words begin to form in my mind.

Yes, you're right. But it wasn't just me. We all carried the absence of you, the loss. It was a gaping hole at the heart of our lives, whether my brother knew the truth or not. And what about him? Jón was only young. You left him too. He wept when he thought no one was watching. He suffered too, though he pretended not to. It is to both of us you must apologize, and yet only one of us is here to hear you.

Then a noise comes from my throat. Unexpected, rough. My

thoughts have begun to spill out in a cascade of small sounds, a whispering, croaking noise that says nothing of the hatred and hurt inside. My throat opens a little. I do not know what it is I am trying to vocalize. My thoughts have woven together with a warp and weft of their own. They are clogged with rage and fury and the wounds only a mother can inflict upon a daughter.

'That's it, Þuriður. Speak to me. Shout at me if that's what you want!'

But nothing else comes. I sound like I am choking.

Frustrated, I stand up, stamp my foot. A child at heart still.

I march down the corridor to the kitchen where one of my mother's servants is washing down the floor. Gesturing to her to hand over the broom covered in a length of fabric at the end, I swab down the floor that is already clean, trying to wash away my love for her, the love, stubborn and unbending, that refuses to leave.

42

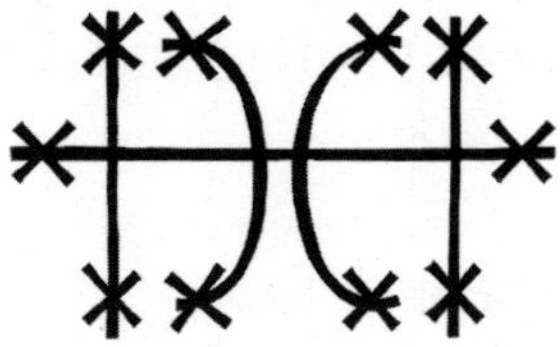

To the esteemed clergyman, Síra Jón Magnússon,

Grace and peace be with you from God, through the merits of Jesus Christ.

I, Dean of Holt, Gissur Sveinson, called and appointed to the spiritual care of this western part of Ísafjarðarsýsla, convey to the honourable servant of Christ, Síra Jón Magnússon, my wishes that he may have grace and peace from God through Jesus Christ. The sore anguish that lies upon you must be treated with earnestness, and I hope that the truth may be brought to light and that the consciences of those involved may be unburdened, and the suspicion of sorcery against the woman you do not name – which I treat with the utmost seriousness – allayed.

May God strengthen you and give victory to the truth, and I heartily commend you to His own glory in the name of Jesus, with my best wishes for your soul and body. In token whereof I herewith subscribe my name at Holt in Önundarfjörður, May 1657.

The Dean of Holt has replied. The letter lies on Síra Jón Magnússon's desk. There are stains from handling. A slight smudge where the author handed it to the messenger, the ink not fully dried.

The priest picks the letter up again. He scans the short message, the words looping across the parchment. Nothing has been said. No action has been taken. Disappointment, but not unexpected. He must go further. The quill is steady in his hand as he dips the nib into the well of ink and begins to write.

To the Dean of Holt, Gissur Sveinson,

May Almighty God have mercy upon you, bless you, and preserve you now and forever.

I, Jón Magnússon, a poor servant of God's word, feel compelled to inform you, my honourable and learned dean, of the witch that lives among you in your district. I hold her entirely responsible for the latest – and most malicious – acts of sorcery against me and beseech you to undertake such interrogations and punishments that your office demands. I will gather evidence, statements from those who witnessed with their own eyes and ears, the terrible crimes against God she committed here in Eyri. Her name will be known to you, as it is across the Westfjords, as one tainted by association with sorcerers. The purification of our district cannot be complete without eliminating her, the witch who follows in their wake. You will already know her name. It is Þuriður Jónsdóttir.

I intend to go to the highest in the land to seek righteous justice.

I commit you to the Lord and to the word of His grace, and likewise all those who are obedient to God in this life and in eternity. Amen.

(signed) Síra Jón Magnússon, preacher at the parish church of Eyri at Skutulsfjörður, May 1657

43

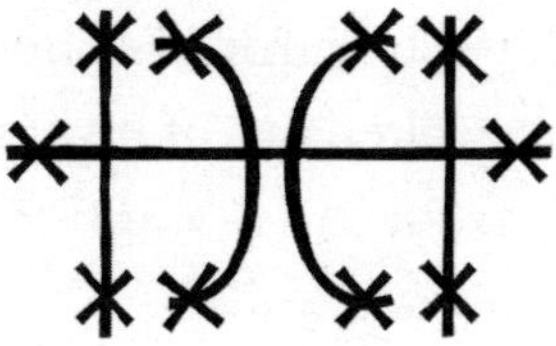

June 1657

I AM BUSY carding wool as my siblings bicker.

I draw the paddles together with swift motions, dragging at the soft *þel*, the downy inner wool that lies underneath the sheep's coarse hair, to make ready for spinning. The completed skeins lie in the *kembulár* at my feet, separated by colour.

Each winter evening was much like the next, none of us moving far from the croft. The first signs of spring came: green shoots poking through thawing snow, the sunrise earlier each day, the bitter chill softening. Still, we huddle indoors as we wait for summer, the children bored, restless.

'There was once a demon called Boneless,' Leif's mother, Birta, says. She looks up from the gloves she is darning. Her eager eyes dart around the *baðstofa*. A single lump of turf falls into the ashes, releasing a small shower of sparks.

'Nothing more than an old woman's invented stories,' Leif yawns. He is reading a letter, the parchment unrolled in his hands. Young

Hrafn is halfway to sleep. His head lolls against his wooden seat. The two girls, Guðrún and Þorgerður, stop bickering over a single knitted doll and wait.

'They call him Boneless, but none knows why as he has a rigid spine and legs like yours. He is a man, though small and slight and very wicked,' Birta continues.

My mother casts her eyes towards her children, who have frozen still. Even Hrafn has been jolted out of his slumber. They stare back at Birta now. The light from the fire and the fish-oil lamps dance flickering shadows on the stone walls.

My stepfather reads, frowning, seemingly oblivious to the story. The air suffocates with the cloying odour of fish bones, sheep's wool and soot.

'You can hear him when the wind is howling. He comes with the storms that rise up over the fjord. He comes in a whirl of snow and ice to steal children away from their God-fearing mothers. *Scratch, scratch* against the outer door, and you know he's there.'

She looks around, glancing first at her son, who ignores her, then at my mother, who arches an eyebrow, then at the children, who are spellbound. She looks at me as if she would frighten me too with her hoary old folktales. I shrug, hiding my smile. Birta is ever drawn to the dramatic, and now she has frightened her own grandchildren half to death.

'*Scratch, scratch*. Can you hear him? That's why we never open the door when night has fallen.'

A gush of wind. Hrafn whimpers. Guðrún is pale while her sister Þorgerður looks to me, eyes wide with entranced terror. I smile back to reassure her. The nights are long here, our imaginations endlessly fertile. She grins back, eventually. There is a new sort of contentment, a feeling I had not thought ever to experience again.

The wind rushes. The house appears to tremble, though this cannot be. It squats down in the earth, thick walls of stone above which sits a timber frame scavenged from the shoreline. Rain beats against the pane. Outside is darkness, lit only by starlight.

Little Hrafn runs over to me, his arms outstretched. I hug him, feeling his body trembling.

'Enough.' Leif does not put the letter down. He looks over at me. I have a knowing, an understanding.

Birta settles back, a self-satisfied grin on her face. Her mischief complete.

'Bed. Everyone. It's time for sleep.' My mother rises from her chair. Her face looks drawn in the low light. 'We'll have much work to do in the morning. The ewes will start lambing, if not tonight then soon. Sleep. No demons will be coming tonight. They have business elsewhere, with children far naughtier.'

She takes Hrafn from my arms and carries him into his bed, returning with a scowl.

'You shouldn't frighten them like that. They're good children. They're scared of the dark enough without your stories!'

Birta looks unrepentant. She gets up, awkward, complaining of her joints, bemoaning her sight, which is starting to fail her. Her rheumy eyes glance over at me before she tuts and grumbles as she climbs the ladder.

'I need to piss,' we hear her say. I stifle a laugh.

Leif does not look impressed. He looks over at me again, clears his throat.

My mother sits beside him as the two girls say their prayers before heading to bed.

There is a silence that falls between us. A burning log collapses in the hearth.

My stepfather, for I am reconciled to calling him that, glances back down at the parchment. I see small, neat, measured handwriting, which slants just a little to the right. An educated hand.

'Þuriður . . .'

I wait.

I can feel tension rise in the room. It is sudden, sharp, like the pricks of a fishbone needle.

'This concerns you.'

44

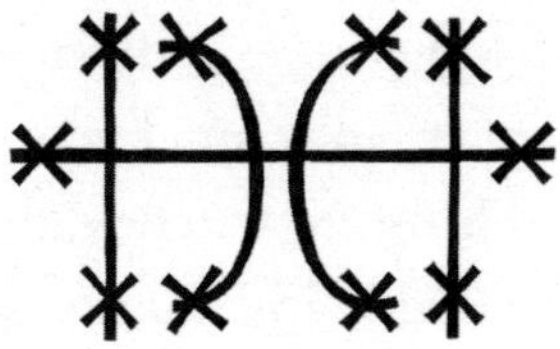

LEIF HANDS ME a letter. He holds another in his hand, inked words scratched into thick parchment.

He guesses I can read. I thank him silently for the acknowledgement. Most men would not do me the courtesy. For a moment, it appears the letter smoulders. I waft it around, before realizing it is a trick of the low candlelight. I glance down at the signature. My stomach knots when I see it was sent by Síra Jón Magnússon to the Dean of Holt.

He names me.

He wants justice.

I read the letter again. Leif flicks his gaze to mine once I have finished. My heart jolts.

'This is serious, Þuriður. You've been protected living here, with us, away from Kirkjuból, but I don't know for how much longer. Síra Jón has no jurisdiction here, but he has written to the witchfinder and says he will go to the highest in the land.'

I glance down at the text, so neat, so careful, so considered. Underneath it, I feel his urgency, his absolute focus. I feel his anger and his righteousness.

Should I run?

'With the thaw comes great danger. They will be able to travel here, if they convince those more powerful. I hardly need to tell you the kind of danger you're in. We were sorry for the loss of your father and brother.' Here he stops. It is the first time he has mentioned them. His voice is thick when he continues: 'I will do what I can to keep the law and Church away from you, as will the dean and his wife, but we cannot overrule Þorleifur Kortsson. He is master of the Vestfirðir. Let us hope he will tire of hunting witches and is in retirement in the north, counting his sheep and living out his days in Christ.'

My mother bursts out the second Leif stops speaking.

'We must stop them. I can't lose her again! I can't see my daughter burned as a witch. I lost my son. I will not go through that torment again.'

Tears flow down her face, outlining her delicate features. She wipes them away with a white hand. I stand up, drop the letter to the floor. It curls into a length of butter yellow. When my arms fold round her, it is like our roles have reversed, everted like the mountains and the fjord.

I have been caught in my own fury, blind to her grief. I start to understand how heavy the weight and heft of our family was upon her. She stayed for the first eight years of my life. Perhaps she did that for me. Staying with my father, leaving the way she did, I, of all creatures here, should understand the sacrifice. Did I not leave my home too? Did I not say a tearful farewell to Anna and Freyja and Ólina and all the sons and daughters of those I love? Did I not leave, without looking back, heading over the mountains afraid and alone?

What happens now? What do we do? Where should I go? Should I pack my things and head south, away from here?

I might survive. The snow has gone, leaving gushing streams and mud banks. I might survive the nights and find somewhere that could take me in. I might receive food and a bed in return for working on a farm where not too many questions are asked. Mostly likely I would not, and we all know this. Most likely, I would die of exposure by next autumn, or find myself at the mercy of a cruel master.

As if reading my mind, my mother grips my arms.

'Do not think to leave. Leif will do what he can and, until then, we wait. The witch-burning fever might not ignite again. Even Þorleifur Kortsson may say enough has been done and enough sorcerers have been killed already. Whatever happens, I will not let you go, and you see I cannot leave here . . .'

But you left me! Was I so easy to leave behind when you cannot walk away from your children by this man? Was I so easy to forget so you could start again?

My words will remain unsaid. This is the price of my silence. It is better that way.

Later, as the household sleeps, I open my mouth and consider the act of speaking. I feel my throat constrict and then expand. I feel my tongue resting on my teeth, my jaw slack, my mind whirring. How to begin?

First, I take a long breath in, filling my lungs. Then, I let it whistle out of my mouth, feeling the air escape, soft and silky. I breathe again. This time when it leaves, I drag the breath past my throat, making a low sound. The noise feels foreign, separate from me, as if a great beast is awakening within. I try again. This time, it is a hoarse sound. It catches at the back of my throat, making me cough.

Hrafn turns on his side, his eyes fluttering. The beast inside me, the one with the rattling breath, settles back to sleep: one eye open, watchful, waiting. Þorgerður is warm next to me. She rubs her nose, then falls back into slumber. I feel along my throat with my hand. Will words ever come back to me? Will I speak again, or is it a skill forever lost to me?

I think of the priest, of them all. I think of of my brother, his body alight, his face melting, running from the pyre as if outrunning the pain. I think of my mother. I imagine the movement of her skirt as she walked each step across the pasture away from me. The back of her head, her hair swaying. The long shadow thrown by sunlight that moved over tufted grass and moss alongside her. I think of my father and the lies he told me. The body that was never found. The drowning that never happened. The woman who lay forever on the bottom of the sea, swept into foreign oceans, far away from me. A jolt of anger.

The sound comes again. I had not meant to make it. A long hiss, like a serpent, escapes my mouth. I make it again, without thinking this time.

It is a start.

It is a beginning.

45

June 1657

THERE ARE HISSINGS in the priest's ear.

He looks up. The world has turned on its head. Where before he was upright, turning the pages of his Bible, waiting for the right passage to present itself for the sermon he is writing, he is now grounded. He is prostrate. Lying in the dust of the chapel floor of Eyrakirkja, staring up at the straight Danish timber roof.

His surplice is crumpled beneath him. He tries to stagger up, but his limbs feel weak. He discovers he is shaking. There are other things he notices: a cold sweat slick across his body that changes almost instantly to prickling heat. He is a furnace. He has been struck down – and there can only be one cause of this torment. Even from Holt, she has the power to inflict torments upon him.

He hears himself whimper, just like the servant girl who thrashed and convulsed in this chapel. Þuriður Jónsdóttir has cursed him too.

She must sense the case against her grows. He has begun collecting witness statements, the first that of servant girl Ingibjörg Ívarsdóttir.

He expected this. As the fight for justice strengthens, so too strengthens the wickedness of Þuriður Jónsdóttir.

After the witch fled, he could do nothing but wait until the thaws began and her hiding place was revealed. Months of hard winds and snow reaching beyond the window of the croft. A winter of freezing sermons, of dark days and nights, of storms that raged across the spit. But summer is almost here. Letters delayed by treacherous mountain passes and waist-high snow, have been delivered. His faith has shone through the long days and bitter nights. That too must grow stronger if he is to fight this cursed womanhood.

Yet still he lies, splayed, on the chapel floor.

He catches sight of the crudely carved statue of the Blessed Mary and the Christ child. They gaze upon him with their blank, wooden faces. He has the sudden urge to weep.

Lord. Bring me the means to rid Iceland of this woman and her powers. She is the devil incarnate and should be burned until there is nothing left, until her soul is cleansed and purified, until the blue of her eyes becomes blank and the whiteness of her hair crackles, black with flame and soot.

'Husband?'

A cool hand now on his forehead. The blurred form of his wife leaning over him. Her rounded belly makes her awkward.

'I . . . I . . .' Instead of words come indecipherable sounds.

'It is almost time for Mass. What has happened? What ails you?'

Þorkatla's face has lost its sallow hue. Her cheeks are flushed, her skin clear, her face fleshed out. He blinks. She looks different, changed.

She moves him to one of the pews at the front of the chapel. He sits for a moment, his bones aching.

At the edge of his vision, he sees a dog standing on two legs, prowling. From its jaw oozes drool, from its teeth comes the stench of carrion meat. It slinks away now, bloodstained teeth bared. He knows it is not real, at least he hopes it is not. It is not the first time he has been struck by delirium. Is this affliction *æðigaldur*, madness magic?

He looks back down at the ground as the shivering and hissings abate.

'Can you speak? What happened, husband?'

'Yes, yes, I can speak. I am well. My afflictions have been sent to test me . . .'

'Let me help you. Do you need water, tea, sustenance of any kind?'

'Nothing. I need nothing except God's grace.' He draws a still-trembling hand across his forehead. Feels the sweat that prickles.

'You have a sermon to give.'

Þorkatla looks around to see if anyone passes who might be prevailed upon to help, but there is no one within sight.

'People need spiritual guidance now more than ever. I must find the strength to give that guidance. I must be the one to summon all of God's light to drown out the darkness.' He clutches the back of the wooden pew, lifting himself back up.

'Each night I read the *Malleus Maleficarum* to you,' he says.

Þorkatla remains seated.

'Remember the warnings it gives, for it is a treasury of evil. Devils can be summoned and apparitions both imagined and real can infiltrate your soul. Satan can do this with natural power, but it is through witches he works in this world, in this place. Don't forget, wife. We must rise above these agonies and do what God commands of us . . .'

She nods.

He can see she is listening, but with only half an ear. He watches her hand stroke her belly, the shape of the child inside her.

'I am undefeated. Just a moment's weakness,' he murmurs, the black hound padding out of the chapel entrance, dissolving into the grey light.

Þorkatla eases herself up. Today, she looks tired. The baby is draining her strength. She begins to place peeling Bibles with roughened edges upon the pews that form two haphazard lines for the most important members of the small community to sit upon during the services. Behind them is standing room for everyone else. Those less fortunate will have to peer over their neighbour's shoulder to see the good Lord's works, those who can read.

The priest dusts the earth from his robe and picks up his catechism book, which he had been reading before this latest assault of witchcraft. He turns to face the altar. He prays. In time, he feels the love of heaven flow through him until, finally, he is, if not restored, then revived.

'Tomorrow, I ride to Þingvellir,' he says. 'There I will ask the assembly for permission to override the Holt district authorities and arrest the witch. I will force the hand of the dean. I will petition parliament at the summer meet, and, together, Church and state will unite in hunting her down.'

Before the sun has risen, Síra Jón Magnússon mounts one of the horses he gained from the Kirkjuból farmstead. The others have all gone lame, seemingly without cause. His wife, Þorkatla, watches him leave, shivering in the early-morning chill. She cradles her rounded waist. The final preparations are made, his leather bag secured, his horse pawing the ground, eager to walk. He clicks his tongue. The horse moves forward, tail swishing, neck and mane bobbing. They are witnessed by the soaring mountain range that seems to draw in around them. He does not look back.

She stays there until her husband is a small, moving dot in the distance. None of the nearby farmsteads are awake, though she hears cattle in their huts. With a last glance, she walks back into the croft she will manage with only a fool for a servant and the men who come and go. She looks back at the sky, laced with sunlight, and wonders when her husband will return. Until then, the hearth will smoke, the grain will rot and the milk sour, and she has no explanation for any of it. She does not feel the way she expected.

This life, this croft, this place, is all wrong. It hums with a vibration she does not like. She can feel it, as if it is itself a monster, a living creature that lies in wait. Of course, she cannot tell her husband or the servants this. They would think her mad, especially now all signs of witchcraft have been removed with crude force. No, she must keep these thoughts to herself. The watchful part of her. The sense that this place, these riches, are not blessed at all, but instead a curse.

46

THE RAVEN TAKES flight.

Each wing draws the air, pushes it behind the span of skeleton and feather. Far beneath, a woman with hair the colour of earth stands in front of a large turf croft. She stares into the distance where a man rides away, heading round the curve of the bay to Súðavik and far beyond. The raven, its sight blinkered for its prey, is intent only on searching the ravines and hillocks, the coastline and the rocky mountainsides that reach high above her. It looks for the moving, squealing, pounding hearts of the rodents and animals that lie in the bird's wind-tipped path. They run. They hide where they can, but the raven sees all.

If the woman notices the black bird gliding overhead, she does not look up, does not look back at it. Once or twice the raven's shadow falls upon her, slides over her tight belly, but she stares on and on, until there is nothing to see except land and sky.

The yearning, the aching disappointment, this woman feels will not touch the small beating heart of the raven, as obsidian as the rest of this creature. It flies. It claims the sky and all below it as its own. It carries death across the hillside and along the shore. All of the Westfjords are laid below this bird, spread out for pillage, for plucking morsels to fill its stomach in a glory of blood and bone.

The troubles of a woman, wife to a neglectful, duty-bound priest, is as nothing to this bird. Serene. At ease with its place in the world.

It chooses now to follow the horse and its rider until the small cluster of crofts lies far behind. It flaps again, rising higher, the smooth flow of the air rushing against its body. Far below, the horse gallops, the cloaked man clutching the reins, his face like stone, pushing his mount on and on as the day dawns.

47

I, INGIBJÖRG ÍVARSDÓTTIR, testify that I was present at Hnífsdalur on the day the fisherman's wife died in childbirth. I saw the following: at that time, Þuriður Jónsdóttir was attending the birth of the baby in the farmhouse. She washed her hands in a bucket of stream water and then came to the hut, where my cow had been labouring overlong. When she walked in, I saw immediately the black shapes around her. They flitted like moths or gnats, followed by demons on their hind legs walking around the skáli. They were fearsome, black and hairy. They had snarling mouths and long, pointed teeth. I was frightened and would not approach her while she laid hands on the cow. The calf was stillborn. The cow died not long after. I later discovered the woman died too, though not the child, who may now be a changeling.

The woman, Þuriður, was the daughter of the sorcerer Jón Jónsson, who cursed my father, making him sick almost unto death. This I wish to be known and made public.

(signed) Ingibjörg Ívarsdóttir, daughter of Ívar, a farmer, Hnífsdalur

48

September 1657

FOR WEEKS, MY mother has watched me, knowing I have thoughts of leaving. Without a plan, driven by a desire to confront the man who accuses me, I can wait no longer. I creep out before the household awakens one mist-dampened morning.

Why did I not go sooner? It is not an easy question to answer. In the past, I would have gone. I always acted alone, my father and brother occupied elsewhere. Now, I have roots that have tangled. A new family. I am a burden upon them if I stay or go, risking exposure and certain death on the mountain passes as autumn throws hailstones and showers, trembling winds and cold, cold nights. It was all of these things – and none of them.

I take food, enough for the journey, and my thickest shawl. Before I depart, I draw protective runes in the ashes as my mother once taught me. She will guess where I am going. The runes are my message to her. I cannot sit in her house weaving cloth to make clothing, forever waiting for news. I must go back to Kirkjuból. I must face Síra Jón

Magnússon. How I will do this without my voice, I do not know, but I will find a way. Every night as the others sleep, I have practised making small noises. Each time there is the possibility of a word, it seems to falter. I stutter and choke, but now and then sounds begin vibrating in my throat.

I will walk back over the mountains, across the ravines and craggy rockfaces, through pastures and valleys, until I am back in the place I was born. I will confront this priest. I cannot let him continue his war against me and mine. If he kills me, then who's to say he will stop there? In my heart, I know he will not. He will find a reason in his madness to hunt down my mother, my half-siblings, my friends, and so I must do something. The only question remaining is, what?

Each footstep is fuelled by fury. Each bringing me closer to Kirkjuból. Above me the harsh croak of the black bird that soars. Scrambling over rock, I feel the old beat of my heart, the pulsating rhythm of me. I have been buried too long in the hamlet with my mother, hiding away. I must stand and fight this man who seeks to destroy me. I must be visible, whatever the cost – and so it is time to rise against my foe.

It takes days to reach the valley. There is already snow on the headland. The nights are bitter cold. I shiver beneath my shawls. Every lungful of air is sweeter as I return along familiar paths. By the time I scramble down the side of the range closest to my old home, I have been travelling for four days or more. Night is falling as I walk across the valley, hoping I am hidden by sea mist and darkness.

Ahead lies the farmstead of Ari Björnsson, the home of my friend Anna. My heart feels sore as I run the last few lengths, knowing I will see her, hold her. Out of the gloom towards me comes a line of men. I stop, panting. All my senses reach out into the ether. Has word got to the priest somehow of my departure? Has he sent men to arrest me before I step foot inside the croft?

'We'll eat well tonight,' one of the black shapes that moves towards me says.

I wait. My breath stilling.

'Anna will smile on you, brother,' laughs another black shape. I exhale as I recognize Ari and Ólafur Björnsson. I hear their grunts as they lift barrels through the entrance, a sudden slant of candlelight glowing orange on the frosted grass.

Whatever Ari says in reply is lost as he walks into the low building. It is late for the men to fish at sea, the weather unpredictable, or more so with the likelihood of storms blowing up suddenly increasing as winter approaches. I imagine Anna's delight at their return. Being a wife to a fisherman is being a woman held hostage to the sea, hostage to its whims and rages, which can snatch a man under the waves in the blink of an eye.

Ari and Ólafur are busy bantering and laughing, stripping their sealskin protection from their limbs with the help of Anna when I step inside. Ólina is there too with Egil, as children and young people hover, all grown taller. All stop. Stare at me now as if I am a ghost come to haunt them.

'Þuriður! Is it really you?' Anna steps towards me, her face lit by a nearby fish-oil lamp. Ólafur looks as if I have slapped him, then he smiles, and I feel a sudden rush of joy.

I nod. I do not know what else to do. Awkward, suddenly.

In a second, she throws her arms round me. She clutches me and together, we sway, laughing like the men, crying like the old friends we are.

'But what are you doing here? Did you come alone?' Ólina is beside me.

'Ari, go and look outside. Check no one is watching the croft. Þuriður, my beloved friend, what are you doing here? It's too dangerous for you . . .' Anna and I touch foreheads like we used to as children.

'If the priest realizes you're here, he'll arrest you—'

'And us as well.' Ari glances at his wife. She shakes her head at him, but he is right.

'The priest spoke against you many times in the pulpit before he left . . .'

I cock my head, right ear near right shoulder. It is my way of asking 'why?' or 'where?' or anything that requires a question.

'We none of us know for sure where he's gone, but there's gossip. Margrét has said . . . Well, we'll talk about that later. Let's get you food and a bed, and make sure you're out of sight . . .' Anna smiles, but I see she has grown paler. A frown line appears between her brows. She does not quite catch my eye.

I tap her shoulder.

I stare pointedly at her.

What did Margrét say? Where has the priest gone? My hands reach for hers. I squeeze them just a little. *Tell me.*

Disappointment settles in my stomach. I had come to confront him. I have spent days walking, freezing, to get here – for nothing.

Around me, everything is the same. There is an overflowing basket of clothes still to wash, bunches of drying flowers hanging from the rafters.

'Sit. Eat.' Anna turns from me. She walks to the kitchen, returns a moment later with a dish of skyr and pitcher filled to the brim with cream-yellowed milk.

'It's good, fresh this morning,' she says, pouring the thick liquid into my cup. Ari the Younger is crawling at our feet.

She watches me as I gulp down the milk and spoon skyr into my mouth.

Meanwhile, the men talk about their bounty as they eat porridge made with moss and wait for some of their fresh catch to cook.

'The sea was bountiful, thanks to Ægir.'

'And we avoided being drowned in Rán's net . . .'

When I have eaten, she pulls up a chair.

'You can't stay. Not because we don't want you here – we do. But because they're after you. If they know you're here, they'll arrest you. Then there's nothing we can do to help you.'

Again, the clasped hand, the sweetness of my friend's touch.

'Freyja has gone to be wed. Her family thought it best she left here . . .'

I frown. What does this mean?

Before Anna can explain, Ari pulls up another seat opposite me, runs his freckled, roughened hand through his salt-encrusted hair. His expression is stern.

'I wish you could tell us why you're here, Þuriður.'

I withdraw my hands from Anna's. In my sacking bag is the letter my stepfather, Leif Árnason, showed me. I stole it from his desk as I crept out. My hands shake only a little when I hold it out to them.

Again, he and Anna share a glance. My friend takes the parchment, opens it, hands it to her husband as she does not read. He clears his throat and says the words. I can almost hear Síra Jón's voice emanating from the neat, slanting letters. When he has finished, Ari looks back at me.

'And so you're here to do what? To confront Síra Jón? This investigation is already underway. It's too late to march into church and demand he gives you back your house – or whatever it is you came here to do! He won't drop his investigation. You play into his hands by coming—'

'No, Þuriður, confronting him would be madness.' Anna looks at me, studying my expression.

I pout back at her, making her look at me with unmasked horror. Suddenly, my non-existent plan seems foolish. How would I have said what I needed to say to him? How would I have argued my case, except with stamping feet or impassioned gestures? How stupid of me. How ignorant to think I could persuade a man hell-bent on persecuting me.

Tell me where he's gone? Did Margrét tell you?

'This letter only proves what we already know.' Ari hands the letter back to me.

'The priest has gone to Þingvellir to ask the lawmen from all of Iceland to help him.'

To help him?

'With their permission,' says Anna, 'he can come to Holt with the sheriff's men and—'

'And burn you,' Ari finishes.

'She doesn't need to know that!' Anna glares at her husband.

Yes, I fucking do.

A wave of panic crashes over me.

Fokk, fokk, fokk.

Will he do that to me? Will he do that to us? I raise my hand to rub my cheek, but catch myself.

'If they discover you here, they'll take us too.' Ari frowns, folding the letter.

'They can't burn us all,' Anna says.

A flaming hunk of dried dung collapses, showering sparks and pieces of burning fuel out of the hearth.

They can't burn us all.

There is a pause, a stilling.

Anna and I stare at each other. I think of Freyja and Ólina, her daughters, Kristín and Kaðlin, her son, Gísli. I think of my mother, my half-siblings, my new stepfather. I think of all those whom I love.

If I could, I would say: *But they can. And they will.*

But, of course, I say nothing.

Instead, I reach down and sweep the glowing coals back into the rest of the low-burning cinders. With my finger, I trace a rune in the hearth. A line, straight; three smaller lines echoing the marks left by a raven's talons; the imprinted claw of that bird known as Huginn, Óðinn's ice-flecked raven. A link between the gods and men. A protection rune, warding off evil and mayhem, linking birth and death, and all else besides. A rune of power.

I look up to see Anna watching me.

'Have a care, Þuriður. The priest says openly that you're a sorceress. If you carry on with the magical ways . . .'

The old ways . . . I think.

My friend sighs when she sees the look on my face. I cannot tell, but I imagine there is obstinacy writ there. Pride and defiance too. She turns back to the fire, warms her hands, pulls little Ari onto her lap and nuzzles his unkempt blond hair as he wiggles in her arms.

'He's preached against me and Freyja, Ólina and even some of the serving girls.' Anna's voice is barely discernible above the crackle of the flames. 'He's whipping up a frenzy here in Eyri. That's why Freyja has been sent away. Her parents thought she wasn't safe here. They're probably right. He's done nothing so far except preach, when he's well enough, which is why we carry on. Our husbands protect us – for now. We keep going to church and praying loudly and often so there can be nothing else said against us. If you appear, then he may do more than just preach.'

Silence follows.

We none of us know what to say.

I should never have come. I put my friends in danger just being here, in their croft. I have been foolish and blind. My anger deflates. I missed them so much it blinded my decision to leave the safety of Holt. Guilt forms where there was rage and fury.

Anna sees the change in me. She gets up and comes to my side. I lean my head against her. She holds me until the feeling abates.

'Early tomorrow, you must go back. Ólafur will take you. We can say he has gone to trade fish further along the fjord and won't be back for several days. Stay with us tonight. Stay inside and we will eat together and remember when things were easy and the days sunny and long.'

Her meaning is clear: I am in great danger here and, worse, I have put my friends in danger too.

BANG! BANG! BANG!

A loud squeal from Ari the Younger. I stagger awake, dragged from unexpected slumber. I cannot open the door because I am not meant to be here. Like a fool, I cower in the corner, while Egil marches to the door, rubbing his eyes, hollering: 'What's this? Who wakes us before dawn?'

It is dark even though it cannot be long until morning. The season has turned. The nights of the midnight sun are but a memory.

BANG! BANG!

'Open up! It's life or death! Please open this door!'

I recognize Margrét's voice, though she slurs as if drunk on mead.

Egil yanks the door open. The servant who lived with my family for years falls into the room.

I am the first person she sees.

'What is it, Margrét? Are you well?' It is Anna's voice who greets her, yet my old servant stares at me with wild eyes. I see her face droops on one side, her prettiness rearranged by the seizure. Rannveig is beside her, face pale, looking between us all.

'Come!' she points at me. 'Come! We have need of your skills. The baby . . . the baby is stuck! It's not coming out and there's so much blood! It isn't yet her time, but her labour has started . . .'

Anna and I exchange a confused glance. I have no idea who she is talking about. Then in my mind comes the face of the priest's wife.

'Þorkatla . . .?' my friend says.

Before she has a chance to stop me, I run to the kitchen and collect some rags, a cauldron to boil water, the herbs for childbirth that are always kept on the shelf: ground *hvannarfræ*, angelica seeds; dried *birkilauf*, birch leaves; and *fjallagrös*.

I mutter, silently, internally, the prayer of Óðinn. *All father of many names, guide me on my path and grant me your wisdom. Send your ravens to my left and right. Send your wolves to my front and back. Protect me. Guide me.*

'You can't go there.' Anna follows me into the kitchen. 'You can't show your face.'

I'm going. You can't stop me.

'Þuriður should come.'

It is Rannveig. She is standing in the doorway.

'She knows what to do when there's a difficult birth.' If she wonders why I am here at all, she does not question us.

Anna shakes her head. She steps towards me.

'No, Þuriður. Please . . .'

I would say: *We cannot leave her to birth alone, no matter what has happened. We are women. This is our battleground. This is our war. We cannot leave her to die.* Even if I spoke those words, I know my friend would still try to stop me, but I am decided. I will walk into the den of the lion just like Daniel.

I nod to Margrét that I will follow her. My friend's face is aghast. She grabs her shawl and comes with us, Rannveig a few steps behind. Ari and Ólafur, who both appeared behind their brother, Egil, at the first sign of commotion, watch us leave, but say nothing. This is our work, women's work. It must be done by us.

We stride over to the croft that was once mine. Instantly, it feels different, as if there is a bad smell that lingers, the reek of the sick-room or the pungent, oily shorn wool that sits waiting too long to be washed. Inside: a woman howls. At the door, the servant hesitates, so I push past her and walk into the *baðstofa.* The first thing I notice when I climb the ladder up to the sleeping platform is the large cross that hangs above the bed.

'Am I dreaming? Is this a nightmare? God save me but the sorcerer's daughter is here . . .' Þorkatla Bjarnadóttir lies soaked in her own blood, fear pulsing, lapping against the walls.

'No, no no! Not her! Anyone but her!' But a contraction begins, and she is rendered as mute as I. The red of her blood shows black against pale thighs. I move fast.

'It's too soon for the baby to be born,' Margrét whispers through her lopsided mouth. Rannveig stands with her back to the wall as if she would rather be anywhere but here, but adds: 'My mother has another month or so to go.'

'She could've been wrong with her calculations. We can never know for sure when a child was conceived . . .' Anna's voice wavers.

'Get her out. Get her out!' the priest's wife shrieks.

I ignore her.

Anna begins to chant the birthing words.

'Get away from me, witch!' This time, she means Anna. Her face is whiter than death, her skin waxy, shiny like tallow.

Anna looks over at me. In the darkness, her face is unreadable.

A dark stain is spreading from the birthing woman, soaking into the mattress.

We do not have time to think about what she said.

I place a thick wad of rags underneath this woman who hates me. She tries to scrabble up upon her pillows, but is too weak. Her nightgown sticks to her like a shroud, slick with sweat. Another contraction, and so I take her arm. I breathe in the way she should breathe.

Quick breaths. One. Two. Three.

Then a longer exhalation before beginning again.

She tries not to look at me, but, as the pain builds, she grips my arm in turn. Begins to inhale and exhale as I showed her.

Hugrekki, þrek.

Courage, endurance. It is an enchantment of healing, an ancestral song to lure out the baby and save the mother's labours.

Hugrekki, þrek.

'Witchcraft!' Þorkatla says between gritted teeth. Another surge has begun. Her stomach tautens. Her breath shortens.

'No, not witchcraft. It is tradition among women. Please, try to trust us. These words help the child come. Try to save your strength,' Anna says.

The priest's wife turns her head to my friend, her eyes wide.

'I can hear you whisper spells,' she spits. 'You'll take my baby away and replace it with one from the *huldufólk*! Get them away from me. Get the witches away from me!' Þorkatla stares down the length of her body at me. I see the fright that has taken hold of her. She should be scared. She sits at the precipice of life and death itself, her child too.

I feel inside her. The baby, almost crowning, is stuck at the point where the pain is greatest. I throw a glance at Anna.

Hugrekki. Þrek.

Hugrekki. Þrek.

Something is wrong.

Hugrekki. Þrek.

More blood. It drips onto the wooden floor.

The head eases out, guided by my trembling hands. Finally, with a great heave and a deep, guttural sound emanating from Þorkatla's thin mouth, the infant slides out and into my arms. My heart is beating. Streaks of daylight paint the early-morning sky: a new day, as well as a new life. Except, already I know.

I hold the child. It is small: too delicate, too frail. I take a rag. I wipe away the birthing smears and look down into the tiny face of this child who will never breathe.

'Give me my child. Give him to me!' The priest's wife seems to lurch forward, reaching out from the bed. Blood covers her linen shift. Her thin thighs are shaking.

I walk with slow footsteps round to her, carrying her son. I cannot meet her eyes, wild and searching as they are. I hand her the infant that now lies, veined grey, skin peeling and cold, in her embrace.

'A boy . . . by the grace of God, a boy . . .' she says.

She has not realized yet.

Time seems to slow to this point as if it will never resume moving forward again. Outside: the shadow of a black wing, a beating span of feathers that soars up and away. Inside: knowledge dawning, words unspoken, unearthly silence.

Þorkatla kisses the top of the baby's head where the snaggle of downy hair should be. She peers down at his closed eyes, the pale eyelids, the tiny, upturned nose, the mouth closed as if sleeping.

'Why does he not cry?'

Her question is more an enquiry. It does not reflect the tragedy that unfolds around us. Anna and I look at each other. I shake my head, tears already forming, running down my cheeks.

'I wanted a boy for so long,' she says. 'One who looked like his father . . .'

I cannot bear to look.

'Why doesn't he cry for milk? Soak a rag in fresh milk from the cows, quickly!'

Why doesn't she understand? There is a gnawing in my belly. *Why doesn't she feel his absence?*

'He'll be hungry. Why isn't he hungry?'

The priest's wife stares round at us as if there is an answer. But the answer is lying in her arms. A child who came early. An infant who will forever reside with the gods, too precious to live in the world of men.

I will be glad to walk away tonight. There is too much sadness and longing in here. I can feel it leech from the walls and grasses of the roof. I wonder if I am to blame.

'When is Síra Jón back?' Anna asks Margrét, who stands dumbfounded as if she cannot believe what has happened. As if the baby will suddenly spring to life, squalling and crying for his mother's milk.

'Where is he?' Anna says, as soft as to a child.

'Síra Jón has gone to . . . to the parliament, the Alþingi, because he wants to arrest . . .' the serving girl says, then realizes her mistake. 'Anyway, he is due back any day. He's been gone a full month or two.'

It is nothing we did not already know.

'I see.' Anna turns to me.

'Go and get my husband, Ari.'

There is a sudden, agonized yell.

'My baby. My baby boy! He's . . . he's dead . . . The witch killed my baby!'

'Stillborn like the calf,' comes Margrét's stunned voice. She is looking at me, fear washing across her drooping features.

The room swims across my vision.

Þorkatla emits a wail unlike any I have heard before. It is a deep, visceral noise that speaks of pain, anguish, death. It is the sound of grief and longing. My instinct is to stay, to help this woman who has given birth to a stillborn son, but my friend is in front of me, urging me out of the doorway. I turn and see the expression on Þorkatla's face. It is a look that will stay with me forever. It is a 'why?' changing to a 'how?'. It is the turn of her head to stare after me as if I throttled her boy child with my own hands.

'Go and get Ari. You can't be here! Go. Now!'

I stumble out, past where the white feather once hung, where the stake carved with *galdrastafir* once stood. Anna's husband is waiting. He sits at the table, dressed, ready.

I point back at the farm I have come from. My skirts are drenched in blood. If Þorkatla survives the night, it will be a miracle. Ari nods, touches my shoulder, calls to Egil to accompany him. Directs Ólafur, who stands beside me, to take me back over the mountain to Holt.

I feel myself crumple into his waiting arms, before all goes black.

49

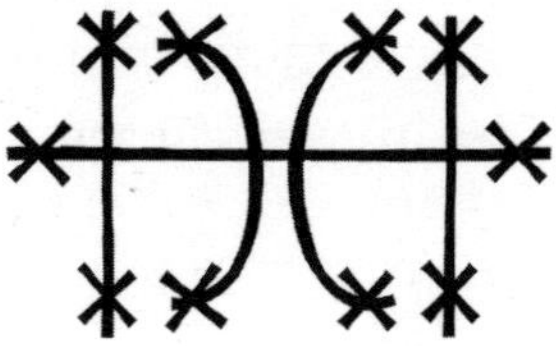

ANNO 1657

Regarding the charges of Síra Jón Magnússon against Þuríður Jónsdóttir

During the meeting of the Alþingi at Þingvellir, there came before the lögrétta that upstanding priest Síra Jón Magnússon, who believes he has been tormented for some time by assaults of the devil, for which he holds some persons responsible jointly with the devil.

He solicits the advice of the authorities as to how he should proceed, whether he should arraign and bring charges against those whom he considers suspect. A father and son have already been tried and burned for those acts of sorcery. But if there are still some persons as yet unpunished, who have an evil reputation for diabolical acts of this sort, or who are found to be sorcerers by some evidence or circumstance, then His Royal Majesty's directive obligates all persons in positions of authority, whether ecclesiastical or civil, each according to his rank and position, to report such matters as soon as they become aware of them, and to undertake legal proceedings and impose punishment. This they must do if they do not wish to be themselves liable to prosecution as accomplices.

And, according to the directive contained in His Royal Majesty's letter, it is commanded, charged and directed that authorities pursue this matter earnestly and justly, to the utmost of their ability.

50

FOR A LONG time, they lie together: mother and stillborn son.

Once the clawing shock of his birth abates, Þorkatla holds him, even though he is cold as stone. She kisses his tiny feet, his minuscule fingers, his eyelids, their soft lashes, the thin paleness of his skin, the wonder of him. She weeps for all that will now not be. She calls him Snorri because that is his name, forgetting the pain and the blood and the fear. Soon, they will take him from her: the child she prayed for. The child that took so long to conceive.

She tells her boy he is too good to walk this terrible earth, where witches and sinners dance by moonlight. She examines him to make sure he is human flesh and not a changeling, substituted by the sorcerer's daughter to be raised in the hidden world. She sniffs his head, checks his nose, his ears, his little legs. All is there, though small, fragile, faint. Her cheeks are dry, but, vaguely, she hears others crying. Her attention extends only to the slight weight of the infant lying in her arms. As the minutes pass, his colour changes from to grey to blueish. Þorkatla feels the wild pulse of hope. *Look*, she wants to say. *Look, there must be blood running in his veins! Look, he is coming back to life!* But he remains silent and still. She sees then it is a trick of the light, her yearning made manifest. Daylight streams in, dust motes dancing in the shafts of autumn yellow and gold, illuminating the brown-encrusted sheets, the wads of blood-soaked rags and moss gathered to staunch the rest.

As her body begins to return to itself, she whispers in his small ear, even though Anna opened the *skjár* to let his soul fly out and up to heaven. She tells him to remember he is loved. That God, not the devil, has called him home, though there had been no signs of this impending tragedy. The raven had not crowed on the gable of the croft. No candles had snuffed out without reason. There were no falling stars in the sky, or none she had seen. She tells Snorri that his death, therefore, is a matter between him and God, and he will have to take this question to Him who rules from beyond the cloud tops, as will she.

When the bed sheets have been changed, when Þorkatla's legs and belly have been swabbed with astringent herb-scented water, when the bowl containing the clotted red rags is whisked away, Anna stands beside her. The friend of the witch smells faintly of grass and flowers and the salt tang of fish. This woman touches her arm, strokes the side of her face with such gentle hands that the priest's wife can hardly believe she is a heathen and one who has muttered incantations during the birth. She speaks and, at first, her words do not find their way into Þorkatla's hearing. She is struck by the delicate beauty of this child who grew inside her for months, who died inside her too.

He looks like a cherubin, one of the angels who sit at God's feet, so perfect is he in all ways except he does not breathe.

'We must prepare him for burial.'

The priest's wife shakes her head. Tries to brush off this gentle woman's hand.

Anna strokes her hair then. She peeks down into the tiny bundle of linens.

'We must bury him, Þorkatla. The time has come to prepare him.'

'No.'

Doesn't this woman realize how wanted he was? How desperate Þorkatla was for him? Years of trying. Years of praying. Years of nothing except disappointment each time the moon glowed and her courses came. She cannot let go of him. He is her son. Her arms were made to hold him.

'You must do this. I'm so sorry, but you must prepare him. He must be taken to Eyrakirkja, and we must hope your husband returns to administer the last rites soon.'

'No, I cannot.' Her tears fall onto the small boy's face.

He looks just like he is sleeping. She dips her mouth to his wet forehead. So cold and strange, unmoving.

'Þorkatla, you must,' the friend of the witch repeats.

She kisses him for the last time.

When she relinquishes him to the care of this woman she barely knows, she feels like she has been ripped into shreds. She watches as Anna, so carefully, wraps him in a makeshift winding sheet, a length of cloth she had sent Margrét to her own croft to collect. This kindness confuses the priest's wife: witchery and magic replaced now with tenderness.

'Wait,' she says, trying to clamber out of the bed.

Anna looks at her with shock, holding the baby in her arms.

'You can't get up. You're too weak. Tell us what you need, and we'll fetch it for you.'

'The shearing scissors,' Þorkatla says. Her head spins. Her legs will not stop trembling.

'What for?' Anna says, frowning.

'To cut a lock of my hair to bury with him.'

The fisherman's wife looks back at her then nods, sends Margrét to the kitchen to find them. She hands Snorri back to his mother while she cuts a lock of Þorkatla's hair.

'I have some ribbon. Ari brought it for me from the Danish traders. Please, Margrét, please go back to my croft. It is kept inside a small wooden box next to my bed . . .'

Again, this kindness.

The world seems to have turned upon its head. Þorkatla feels a rush of emotion. Part grief, part sadness, part unity and accord. It is like having a friend. She tries to dismiss the feeling, but it stays: a well of love.

A flash of red. The servant girl dandles the ribbon in her hand. She slides it, reluctant, into Anna's. Anna winds the silk length round the lock of hair. The part of Þorkatla that will remain forever with her baby.

'I'll make sure he's buried with it,' the fisherman's wife says, tucking it inside the shroud.

This time, Þorkatla cannot bear to give him up. She promises him he will not be forgotten. His name will be forever on her lips. Her son. Her Snorri.

'One day, my son, I'll see you again and you'll be alive and free and running into my arms for the joy of seeing me, your mother, again.'

Anna takes him from her. Þorkatla falls back against the pillows, spent. A great cry rises inside her, one she cannot hope to keep silent.

On the fourth day, Snorri is moved to the church.

Þorkatla, who has not yet moved from her bed, declares she will walk with him to his resting place before the burial, even though she has not yet been churched. It is unheard of for a woman to enter a chapel without being given the blessings to redeem her 'unclean' state, but she will do it anyway. She will walk alongside the boy as her heart will do for as long as it beats inside her, even if it means defying the faith that sits at the heart of her life and her marriage. The two women, Anna and Ólina, who have kept vigil for the boy all night, who along with their husbands have taken turns to remain with him the past four nights, come to her now that the day is here.

They can leave the body without fear of evil spirits entering his corpse. They help her out of the bed, and though the bleeding is light now she notices there are fresh stains on the only spare set of linens.

Feeling weak as a newborn lamb, Þorkatla walks side by side with these women through the valley. The mountains look down on them. They seem to weep as the sky bleeds drizzle and fog. Slowly, they move. Ari the fisherman carries her child though he is a slight burden, hardly any weight at all, while the women hold her arms. At first, she tries to shrug them off. They may be neighbours, but they have never been friends. Yet here they are, beside her. Each clod of earth beneath her feet, each raindrop that slides down her hair, is shared with them.

When they reach the boat, she feels close to fainting. Snorri is passed to Anna, while Ari lifts Þorkatla as if she is but a small sack of grain brought over on a tall-masted ship by the Danes. He carries her onto the boat with such care she could weep for it. The rest clamber in. Without a word exchanged between them, they are rowed across the rippling bay.

Rannveig stands on the shore, watching them go. She says she has too many tasks and someone needs to stay at the farm. Þorkatla does not question her. Ever since the stillbirth, Rannveig stays away. She finds reasons to be out in the pastures or the *skáli* tending to the livestock, though there are farmhands aplenty for that. When Anna brought her in to say goodbye to the brother she never had, she paled. When offered the small bundle to hold, she shook her head. Instead, she came to Þorkatla's bedside, held her hand, as if soothing the living was more important than honouring the dead.

Þorkatla stares back at her daughter now. When the girl turns to walk home, she feels like a knife has pierced her chest.

51

THE JOURNEY IS arduous.

Long days in the saddle: winter fast approaching. Bitter nights spent listening to wolves howl across the endless landscape where once stood forests of aspen trees and birch. Síra Jón Magnússon gallops onward, leaving the plains that surround Þingvellir, heading north to Eyri. The time should pass slowly, but his heart rejoices with the pounding of the horse's hooves. He returns bearing the news that Sýslumaður Magnús Sigurdsson and witchfinder Þorleifur Kortsson are ordered to join him once again in a greater fight, one that will expose the very roots of witchcraft in the Westfjords. He will be celebrated. His name will forever be associated with the fight against sorcery.

He recalls how he walked into the large circle of lawmen that makes up the national parliament assembly, the Alþingi, his heart beating hard in his chest. Normally unruffled, he cleared his throat, looked around at the men who had travelled from every district in Iceland. He recalls each word he spoke to the throng, filled with earnest supplication, with the rightness of his thinking. He asked them for their support – and they gave it. A written decree was issued and signed by twelve good men, expressions grave, heads nodding. He can proceed without the authority of the Dean of Holt. He can proceed and bring the witch to justice.

The preacher praises God as he travels.

The way lies ahead, each bend in the path straightened, each rock and boulder unearthed. God shines His love down upon him like summer rain, and he will be victorious.

By the time he reaches the outskirts of Eyri, two weeks have passed. He is tired but exhilarated still. His horse slowed to a trot as they traversed the wilderness. Now they are home, and the final purge can begin. Together, they wind around the fjord, past that place of wickedness, heading along the length of the curving harbour to reach the spit. It is then he notices the people. Or the lack of them. There are none in the pastures or fields gathering in livestock. There are no horses nor men. Children usually run underfoot, but there are none to trouble his entrance back into the parish, the place where he will burn Þuriður Jónsdóttir: her name proof enough of her crimes against him.

It is then Síra Jón sees the church. A small crowd of people milling about. Some with caps held in their hands. What has happened?

As he comes closer, someone turns and points. Someone else mutters something. He can see faces turn to him.

'Síra Jón Magnússon is back!'

He looks around. Many from the congregation stand here, now, looking straight at the priest.

Someone is pushing their way through the mass of bodies. The stolid form of Sýslumaður Sigurdsson appears. He wears his broad-brimmed hat, though he is the only one. His pale eyes seek him out.

'What has happened here?' says Síra Jón. 'Has there been a death?'

The man looks back at him, and, for the briefest moment, Síra Jón sees pity. Not at all what he expected, especially from the sheriff.

A strange knot grows in his stomach. The priest drops down onto grit, brushing dust from the journey off his damp, heavy cloak.

'Speak, Sýslumaður Sigurdsson,' he says.

'Come with me,' he replies. His voice: gruff, low.

The people shuffle out of their way. As they approach, their eyes cast down. He searches the faces for that of his wife, and is relieved to find it, though she looks ill and wan, her eyes rimmed red, her skin white as fresh skyr. Then Síra Jón sees she stands with two women, who seem to be holding her up. Two women from Kirkjuból. Frowning, he walks over. Still, no one speaks. No one meets his eye. Someone puts their hand on his shoulder. It is unfathomable. Inside, candles are burning.

'Has there been a service?' the priest says, stepping into the chapel. Would the sheriff so overreach himself and hold Mass without his presence?

Then he sees the bundle.

Two candles sit on a plank at either end of the small shape. The plank sits between two pews: a laying out, a body waiting for burial. But it is so small. It looks like an animal has been shrouded in linen, which cannot be.

'What's this?'

He falters.

Þorkatla appears at his side. She looks gaunt. Her hair is falling from under her cap. She gestures towards the small shape, the form wrapped so neatly, tears rolling down her cheeks.

Stepping forward, Síra Jón places his hand on the cloth. He eases a corner of it back and he sees what it is they are here for.

A child.

Grey-faced, still, cold. Not at all what a child should be.

The priest steps back, dropping the end of the cloth covering, out of which peeps a flash of gaudy red satin, at odds with the stained linen shroud.

'Our child,' Þorkatla says.

'Our child,' he repeats, though it makes no sense to him at all.

The wife of the fisherman Ari steps towards them now. 'He came early. He couldn't be saved . . .'

'Get away from me,' he hisses. 'What is this to you?'

If the woman is afeared, she does not show it. She meets his eyes.

'I helped your wife deliver the child. She would've died without us there,' she says. Her voice is calm, strangely so. She shows no remorse, no shame.

'Us?'

His wife glances at the woman who should know better than to stand here, talking to him as if they are equals.

'Tell me, what does she mean by "us"? Who else was there? I command you to tell me. Why have you stepped inside this chapel without my blessing? You are unclean until the proper steps are taken!'

The fisherman's wife steps back, but she takes Þorkatla's arm again, as if this familiarity would be welcome.

'And let go of my wife!' He can hear his voice rising. Otherwise, there is silence in the church, an absolute emptiness of sound as everyone who has crowded inside stands still and watches.

'She means we had help, from other women. My daughter, Rannveig, was there, Margrét was there . . .'

He has an odd thought. He looks at his wife's face. He wonders if she is, at this point, deciding whether to lie to him or not. It is a strong feeling, and one he knows instinctively is correct. She tries to look away. The priest takes hold of her chin, pulls her features back to face his. Her eyelids flutter. She has deep charcoal shadows ringing her eyes. She looks as if she has not slept for days.

'Who else?'

Something is on the verge of exploding in his chest. There is anger building along with the deep pull of grief not yet formed. He wants to strike her.

'Who else?' he demands. His body shuddering with rage.

The priest's wife takes a step back, a whimper in her voice.

'The midwife . . . Þuriður Jónsdóttir was there. She helped the baby come, but he was dead, or he died in her arms, or—'

Before his wife finishes, he erupts.

'The witch Þuriður killed our child? Is this what you're telling me?'

Like the creep of fast-moving lava, his anger runs hot like blood.

'You allowed a woman known to be a sorceress practise witchcraft against my son! You're as damned as she! You're as culpable as she!'

His wife drops to her knees. She takes hold of the hem of his cloak, dirt-strewn and sodden.

'Forgive me,' she says.

Síra Jón Magnússon walks into the rectory. He almost stops to marvel how low the ceilings are, how damp the air, how dark it is. How he never before noticed the meagre state in which they lived. Instead, he drops to his knees, his hands already held, palms together, fingers reaching to heaven in supplication.

It is only then he allows himself to weep for the child they have lost, for the future that is no longer.

52

I, the undersigned, appointed to be a servant of God's word, publicly declare that I consider Þuriður Jónsdóttir to be fully responsible for renewed and violent acts of witchcraft, which have fallen upon my parish, my household and, above all, my own person.

She has sinned against my family in the most grievous way. The child born to my wife, Þorkatla Bjarnadóttir, our son, was found to be dead in the arms of this woman who has sent demons to inflict fresh sufferings upon me. Our child was killed at her hand, and we are bereft. Her hard-hearted malice has spread like a disease to my household. Where will it end? Þuriður Jónsdóttir defies the authority of the Church. She continues to practise those ways that are banned by the crown. Her wickedness must be purged. On the night of my son's killing, she ran away, declaring her guilt to all. I rode across the district, but could not find her. I wrote to every clergyman within Skutulsfjörður, but none had seen her. It appears she has landed back in the nest of wickedness she has created in Holt, because the learned and pious dean Gissur Sveinson has so far left my urgent letters unanswered. With the utmost promptness, Þuriður Jónsdóttir must be examined with regard to the suspicion of sorcery that is attached to her. The truth must be brought to light.

I make this declaration in the light of all those arguments and relevant antecedent events that may and will be adduced as pertinent to this affair, and that may be granted to me to recount consistently with truthfulness and the law. In token of this, I hereby sign my name by my own hand below.

(signed) Síra Jón Magnússon, preacher at the parish church of Eyri at Skutulsfjörður, November 1657

53

THE WITCHFINDER ARRIVES with the first flurry of hail.

Sea mist, thick and grey, rolls in off the shifting tides. Þorleifur Kortsson drops down from his horse. Síra Jón Magnússon's wife, Þorkatla, stands, shivering, at the doorway to the farmhouse. He touches the rim of his hat in greeting.

Inside, Sýslumaður Magnús Sigurdsson is already drinking coffee brewed by the bewitched maidservant, her face a grotesque reminder of the sorceress's power. Síra Jón Magnússon looks over and nods. They all know what comes next. Winter has come. Each day, the threat of snow grows greater, the skies darker. If they delay any longer, the mountain passes, already treacherous, will be impassable.

'Before we ride, let us pray,' the priest says.

The witchfinder bows his head as does the sheriff.

Three men at their prayers. Three men who will strike at the heart of this wretched business.

They are unaware that Þorkatla watches them. Oblivious to the fact that to her they seem blurred, their features opaque. The sounds that come out of her husband's mouth strike her as botched, irrelevant. She is a woman who does not know herself any more, except as a mother bereft. When she looks again at Rannveig, who still rejects her clumsy attempts to repair their rift, she recognizes grief rather than sullenness, because she feels it too. Did Rannveig feel ripped apart as she does now when the sorcerer's son was burned?

With shame, she watches her daughter as she carries laundry. She sees for the first time a young woman with feelings of her own. Rannveig's sadness has never been talked about, never soothed. Þorkatla cannot remember the last time she held her in her arms, comforted her. It is as if Snorri's death was a parting in the clouds of Þorkatla's life. For a brief moment, the sun shone through and illuminated everything. When did she last kiss her daughter's pale cheek? When last did they share a joke or read the Bible to each other?

Rannveig is kneeling now at the large hearth in the *baðstofa* as the men clatter away, scraping out the ashes and patting down piles of dried dung and pieces of foraged wood left in the stores. She does not appear to hear her mother approach.

'Daughter?' The priest's wife coughs a little. She can hear the men moving about outside, talking still, their boots on stirrups.

'Yes, Mother?' Rannveig does not look up. Her apron is stained black from kneeling by the remains of last night's fire.

Þorkatla has no idea what she is going to say. She has no notion of where to start, how to bridge the crevasse that yawns open between them. Her throat feels dry. Her tongue thick and slow.

Rannveig gets up off the floor, wiping her hair back off her face and leaving a long grey smudge.

'You've wiped dirt from the ashes on your forehead.' She reaches for her, but Rannveig turns away with a shrug.

'I'll clean it later when I've finished.'

This is not at all what the priest's wife wants to tell her. What she really wants to say is she loves her daughter. She understands her pain, at last. There it is. She already has a child. A grown woman almost, but a living, breathing girl, so precious she struggles to form the words that will communicate this. A sense of marvel grows within her chest underneath the spots of milk that leak so cruelly onto her blouse. Still, she says nothing.

Rannveig picks up the bucket.

The air is thick with things unsaid.

'Rannveig, please?'

'What is it, Mother? Go back to bed. You need rest after—'

'After Snorri died?' Þorkatla says.

'Yes, since he died.'

It is the first true thing they have said to each other for a long time.

'Are you well? Should I fetch Síra Jón?' Rannveig's face is puzzled.

'No, it's you I wanted to . . . to . . . It doesn't matter. You're busy. I'm sorry. I'm stopping you from your work.'

Rannveig throws her a strange look. Does her daughter know she paces the croft at night, unable to settle? She knows she looks odd, her hair unkempt, her care for the details of their lives vanishing almost completely. Þorkatla looks down at her crumpled skirt and blouse, and wonders again who that woman was. Will she ever fit those clothes again, be that person, think those thoughts? In answer to her own questions, she finds she does not care.

Rannveig puts down the bucket, takes her mother by the arm and steers her to the sleeping platform. When she lies down, Þorkatla traces the places where she gouged out the markings, hollows where there should be solid wood. She knows how the rafters feel. She too is hollowed out.

'Rannveig?'

'I promised I'd go with Margrét to Eyri today. She says the last ship before the winter storms has docked in the harbour and there may be grain to barter.'

The priest's wife watches as her daughter hurries back down the ladder, knowing, in the pit of her stomach, she is lost to her.

From outside comes the sound of horses, hooves padding on hard earth, followed by the priest and sheriff. There is an urgency to their actions. The end is coming.

54

November 1657

I CREEP TO my stepfather's desk and pick up his quill, a white goose feather, its nib newly sharpened.

The ink well is full. A pile of parchment, barely used, lies to one side. I find a piece, flatten out the calfskin membrane as best I can. Dipping the point into the ink, I hesitate before drawing the nib across the page. My letters are misshapen and crooked. They do not loop and flow like the priest's letters. They are awkward and stilted, but I can make out their meaning. I continue.

I, the undersigned, a pitiful and wretched being in the eyes of God and man, write to you, Gissur Sveinson, Dean of Holt, to demand an investigation . . .

The words flow from the quill. Jarring, halting words that contain both fury and reason. I will deliver this missive to the dean's croft under cover of darkness, and I will wait, like the hawk that watches the ground below for the mice that scuttle in tall grass. Then, I will swoop down, devouring all.

55

'PERHAPS SÍRA JÓN Magnússon has forgotten you?' my mother says the next day.

Together we sit spinning wool into thread. The afternoon light is fading though it is not long after noon. The river stones clack together as my mother draws a stick wound with weft-thread through the stationary warp yarns, each weaving through the other, crossing and recrossing like the fates.

No, that fucking priest won't ever stop. He's been waiting for the right moment. I can feel him crouching like a hungry fox in a pasture filled with sheep.

I bite off the length of thread.

I shake my head.

There is a knock at the door. Halladóra Einarsdóttir, the Dean of Holt's strident wife, appears. She wears a cloak of black velvet, already dusted with ice. Outside, her horse, a large black steed brought from Denmark, with reins of leather and a good riding seat, stamps the ground.

'I cannot stay, Gissur expects me, but I wanted to give you both some news. My husband received a letter today from the cleric in Súðavik,' she says, looking between us.

'Come in. Warm yourself. It's bitter out there,' my mother greets the visitor.

'No, thank you. I've come to warn you. The cleric writes with news of the witchfinder. He has come back to Eyri.'

My mother's face pales. 'What should we do? Should we leave Holt? Does Þorleifur Kortsson have jurisdiction here?'

'His power extends across the Westfjords and may overrule my husband here. I must go. I thought you should both know.'

Halladóra pulls her hood up over her hair. She nods at us both, before turning and leaving. We listen to her horse gallop away.

A cloud moves across the weak sunlight, throwing a veil of deepest grey on the small window. The chill air seeps under the door, and through the *skjár* in the roof and in the wall. A storm is on its way.

Suddenly, I can bear being inside no longer. Claustrophobic, restless, I stand up, my spinning forgotten. My mother puts down the yarn. It is white and brown, soft like autumn clouds on the paddle before snaking into threads.

My thickest shawl is draped over my chair, warming my back. I take it, pull it around me.

'Where are you going? It's getting dark . . .' my mother says.

Away.

Somewhere else.

I cannot bear to stay here, waiting.

Onward, I walk, across the pastureland. The wind flays, but still I walk. When I reach the sloping foot of the mountains, I am panting, but I do not stop. It is bitter cold. My face feels stung, sore. The air I breathe is ice-scented, colder than night.

Drawing in great inhalations of air, I reach the place where I stand

and let myself be buffeted, the raging force of the gods a match for the roaring of my heart.

I look up at the darkening sky, snow clouds lie heavy overhead. I shut my eyes and step forward, and again. The edge of the cliff is close, getting closer.

With another step, I could surrender to the gales. I could step into nothing.

It is then I open my eyes and see the raven.

It is then I hear the sound of horses' hooves, of men approaching.

It is then I remember how to scream.

PART FOUR

Dómur
Judgement

How fare the gods?
How fare the elves?
The dwarves, mountain-masters,
Feel tremors in the stone.

Hel's hound Garm howls.
His bonds will break.
Death comes for the gods
At Ragnarök.

Here comes Hyrm's corpse-ship
Over serpent-churned waves.
The pale eagle hymns;
Its beak will rend the dead.

Völuspá: Prophecy of the Völva

Now the wickedness of women is spoken of in Ecclesiasticus xxv: There is no head above the head of a serpent: and there is no wrath above the wrath of a woman. I had rather dwell with a lion and a dragon than to keep house with a wicked woman . . . All wickedness is but little to the wickedness of a woman . . . What else is a woman but a foe to friendship: an inescapable punishment, a necessary evil, a natural temptation, a desirable calamity, a domestic danger, a delectable detriment, an evil of nature, painted with fair colours!

Malleus Maleficarum, Part One, Question VI

A Thurs-rune I carve for you,
and three staves –
wantonness and frenzy
and torment;
I shall scrape it off,
as I scratched it on
if it becomes necessary.

Skírnismál, Poetic Edda

56

November 1657

I KNOW THEY will kill me.

They will drag me from this place, once a place of sanctuary, of wild solitude, and they will burn me. They will cast my soul into the depths of hell and rejoice as they do so. They will torture me as they say I have tortured them. They will steal my breath, as they say I stole his.

So why do I not step out into the empty air and end this?

Why, instead, do I turn to the men approaching, their hats pulled low over their foreheads, their thick woollen cloaks pulled tight against the gusting wind? I face them now. They scowl, their sly smiles vanishing at the sight of the raven's gift, a single black streak now dancing towards the rocks that reach to the darkening sky.

I wait with my head high.

Before me stand three men: the hunched form of Sýslumaður Magnús Sigurdsson, the black-clad witchfinder Þorleifur Kortsson and Síra Jón Magnússon, the priest, whose eyes glitter with a madman's zeal.

For a brief moment, we four stand stock-still as if enchanted, but the hex soon breaks. The air screams and with it come the winter storms. They are speaking now, but I cannot hear them. One struggles towards me. I realize they are afraid. Scared of me. Like children playing with a poppet, they are drawn to that which they fear.

Snow settles on my cloak. I feel the sharp ice taste of it on my lips. Will I ever see another winter? Will I ever see those I love again? I think not.

The witchfinder takes my arm. His touch is surprisingly gentle.

'Come now,' he says amid the whistling ferment that blows me towards my destiny.

57

I DO NOT struggle.

I allow my wrists to be bound by thick rope, then tied to the sheriff's horse. My obedience frightens the men more than if I fought back.

'What devilry is this?' Sýslumaður Magnús Sigurdsson mutters, mounting his mare with difficulty. He digs his leather heels into the side of the creature, and together we move off.

Dragged behind them, the rope cuts into my wrists. Wind tears at my face.

'Wait, she's fallen,' the priest says, bringing his horse to a standstill. His voice is sliced away by the storm that has engulfed the dying light of the winter sun.

'Whoa. Does it matter whether she walks or is dragged? She'll get there the same way,' shouts the sheriff as he looks over his shoulder.

'It matters,' says the witchfinder. 'We do not wish to make a martyr of her.'

Snow whirls, glinting white then grey as it lands in gathering darkness.

'Pick her up,' the priest commands.

I am on all fours as if I am a birthing woman. Wet snow soaks through my woollen mittens. My hair lies straggled and wild. My face stings. I pull myself back to my feet with difficulty, my skirts now sodden and cold. We move past the places I know: this tuft, that rock, this stream and pastures hidden under the flurry where the valley rises to meet the brooding mountains. I can only slip and stumble as a prisoner of these three men as they take me on the long journey towards the spit of land where my gaol lies.

A flash of iridescent plumage against the swirling maelstrom, wings in flight; beating together. They vanish as if they were never there, except for the space they leave behind that is filled with tumbling ice.

I am too slow. They wish to reach the other side of the mountains before the mountain pathways are impassable. The sheriff dismounts, grunts as he takes hold of me. His fat fingers grip my waist. I turn my face to him and spit full at him.

'She-devil!'

I allow myself to be hauled like a sack of grain onto his horse. He complains about the weight of me though I am small and skinny compared to his bulk. I bare my teeth as he twists me into position, making his small eyes register alarm.

'We should've brought more men. She's a witch and we know not the true extent of her powers,' he says.

'We must make do,' the priest replies, hunched against the gales. 'Tie her up. Quickly, or we'll all perish.'

His fingers fumble as he binds my ankles. I watch him, silent, still. Unnerved, he takes longer than he should. Inside, I rejoice at his fear.

I'll kill you for this.

'Why doesn't she fight back? What witchery is she conjuring? This storm must be hers. She was calling it up on that cliff,' the sheriff says.

Fucking idiots. I promise you all, if I survive, I'll come for you. I'll have my revenge, no matter how long it takes.

In the meantime, my silence is my only power.

We move. I am jolted, stomach on the horse's back, head and legs down the side of each flank. I am bruised and nauseous by the time we begin our descent. We travel many hours, a day or more. The sun that sets early and rises late has become a blur, a smudge on the horizon I cannot see. My sight is confined to the hooves of the horse that slip on the rocky passes.

Now and then, the men stop to give me stale water, or a morsel of *harðfiskur*, but nausea overcomes me, and I struggle to swallow the hard salted cod. The freezing air permeates every bone in my body, despite the thickness of my shawl and the warmth of the creature beneath me. I feel its pulse and hope the movement of the bony length of my body, jutting elbows and knees, have not hurt it. Drifting in and out of consciousness, I know we are close to my old home, to Kirkjuból, because I can taste the air: fresher, sweeter, bringing with it memories of weaving flower crowns in the summertime, of lying in thick, sun-scented grass with Anna and Freyja. Memories that wound now rather than heal.

Eventually, I am lifted off the horse like cargo from the Danish ships. The witchfinder Þorleifur Kortsson holds me upright as my legs tremble, barely able to stand. The light is weak, a pale yellow halo behind the cloud cover. The men talk, but I have heard enough of their bullish chatter, their ignorance and their stupidity. They gesture towards the harbour, and the boatman appears, rowing across the fjord that will soon be solid ice.

'Take her. We'll ride on with your horse and meet you on the other side.' The witchfinder and priest turn their horses and gallop away. I am pulled roughly into the boat by the pink-faced sheriff, shivering.

The oar breaks the spell of the water's surface as it dips and ploughs through the bleak waters of the fjord. Sýslumaður Sigurdsson sits opposite in this small wooden vessel. There is no sound except the grunts of the boatman, the muffled touch of the oar, the blustering wind-blown powder.

Of course, I know where we are going.

It is an irony not lost on me. I will sleep tonight where my father and brother lay, in filthy straw on a hard floor, in the Danish-store gaol.

Flinching against the cutting wind, the sheriff ignores me. His thick red coat with shining buttons keeps him warm enough, and he pulls his collar up. The boat nudges the shingle at the edge of the shoreline. In my confusion, I see a broken shadow eddying on the water, a wing that whips out of sight. I stumble as I step out, awkward, bound, chilled, though the ropes have been cut from my ankles.

The sheriff exchanges a few words, and coin, with the boatman. He takes hold of the rope and walks forward, pulling me behind him like cattle for slaughter. Ice crunches underfoot. My skirts are soaked up to my waist. The wind howls and throws a shower of hail. Candles bob in the small glow of the settlement's windows. In the distance, I see the shape of the large wooden cross that looms over the church entrance, black in the darkness. My face is numb, my fingers too. I stumble onward, led to the place I know they will keep me.

A place of sorrow. A place of bitter regret.

58

December 1657

THE DARKNESS IS absolute.

Even the small window up high shows not a sliver of moonlight. I can feel my fingers, the skin of my hands, the damp chill of the floor that seeps through my clothing. I can see but a glimmer of white from my hair that takes on a spectral hue in the black, black night. There is no candle stub to light these long waking hours. There is no fish-oil lamp either, no air except the musty, fetid inhalations while outside the wind screams its fury. There is not even a Bible to read by scant daylight.

My clothing is stained brown from dirt and sweat. The wild-flowers stitched into my skirt lie scuffed, their colours dimmed. There is nothing here except the filth of the straw and the overflowing chamber pot. I know there is a guard outside my cell because I watch him as he sleeps, his head nodding on his chest, the keys to my gaol lying against his thigh. A halberd rests against his knee. I know because I stare through the small window in the door: barred with iron.

When he awakes, he starts at the sight of me. Shouts at me to stay back. I recede, reluctant, an animal caged like those from other lands of which the Danish traders told stories. At night, I lie propped up against the wooden posts of the wall, just as my father and brother did. I have many hours to recall my visits to them both.

Will someone journey, as I once did, to find the twelve men who might swear the oath for me? Do my friends even know I am captured?

Like a ball of wool, our lives have unravelled. Generations of *seid-menn* now extinguished as easily as blowing out a candle.

And now it is my turn.

The nights barely ease into day as winter draws down. My fitful dreaming is full of the people I have loved: Anna, Freyja, my mother and siblings, Ólina, Þora, even Ólafur, and I find my thoughts straying to him often. At first, I counted each muted sunrise as they ground together: darkness into half-light, then back to darkness again. I scored a small line in one of the beams, marking with my nail until my finger bled. But the delirium of captivity soon rendered this counting obsolete. Soon, I could not decide between one low light and the next.

They are trying to break me, leaving me here for weeks stretching into months. Here alone, my courage is failing, my heart aching for all I have lost. Each day, I grow more desperate. My new-found family do not come, neither do old friends, and I begin to question if I am abandoned or simply forgotten. When the guard unlocks the door, metal lock scraping open, his footsteps echoing on the ground, I look up, hoping to see someone from Holt or Kirkjuból, but it is only ever my captor, and my heart drops to my stomach like a rock breaking off the mountainside. I long to see a familiar face, hear a friendly voice, but no one comes. Not even the witchfinder.

From minute to minute, I rage then weep. I even pray. The soft blueish light of snow is all that shines through the window. I wonder if I will ever feel warmth again, or sunlight on my face, or the shock of clear fjord water on my skin.

How much more of this?

59

January 1658

WHEN THE BLOW comes, it is a slug, a thick force, a fist ploughed into my cheek.

I topple. My face then my body hits the cold, damp floor. I feel around my mouth with my tongue to see if I have lost teeth and am relieved in a small way that nothing is missing. Then I scrabble to my feet, fetters allowing. I try to swing my chain at the gaoler who walked in with the men. This is a different gaoler, a stranger: broad, with red hair, pale brown eyes, a straggled beard and foul breath sour with mead. He is altogether a more spiteful beast.

He laughs.

'Wildcat! See how she dances!'

The chains rattle against the floor.

A month or more has passed since I was thrown into this small room and left to moulder. I have known this moment would come. I did not fear it. Instead, I gathered myself inwards, waiting for them to strike. I try again. This time, I catch his arm. He springs back from me, his face a picture of surprise. Then his expression changes. The shock leeches away, leaving fury, ugly and naked, on his face.

'The witch strikes back!' he shouts to the man standing in the shadowy corner of the room. Who else but the witchfinder lurks there, watching me, waiting, all in black, except for his buttons that are silver-coloured and shining. He says nothing. He holds up a gloved hand and the gaoler steps back. I see his reluctance and I smile.

'Enough,' says Síra Jón Magnússon. He steps out of the shadows too. I am surrounded, hackles rising, teeth bared, ready. A brazier has been lit. The heat is welcome, but I guess its purpose.

'You know why we're here. We want to know everything. Your maleficent ways, your rituals, your heathen practices. Spare us nothing for we come with the light of the Lord, and none shall harm us.' He holds up a cross made of metal. It reflects the flickering light of the flames that leap from the blackened grill.

'Tell us what you did, Þuriður Jónsdóttir,' the witchfinder says. His voice is lowered, pleasant, as if we are speaking as friends.

I glare at him.

'She doesn't speak. She's silent as the grave and no less deadly. All her spells are witched up inside her head!' The gaoler spits, landing grey spittle at my feet.

'Yes, this we know,' muses Þorleifur Kortsson, 'but we have many ways of changing her mind, of making her speak . . . She'll soon learn to loosen her tongue.'

He steps closer to me. He reaches out and with his gloved hand he takes a lock of my tangled hair, holds it as if it could leap to life and strangle him with its dirty white strands. How I wish it could.

'You are one of the *huldufólk*, or so the people here believe. But what say you to this? Will you break your silence to defend yourself? You face serious accusations! Síra Jón Magnússon, the preacher at

Eyrakirkja, says it was you all along. You were the witch who sent demons to molest him. You.'

He waits as if I will answer.

So you burned my father and brother for nothing? Do our lives mean so little to you? I already know the answer.

The witchfinder continues. He sits on a low stool, crosses his legs, leans towards me, head on hand, eyes narrowing.

'He says you are the one they spoke of at their burning. I saw you that day. You watched them burn without a sound, with no defence. Is that not proof enough of your wickedness?'

If I could swing the heavy links of this chain, I would smash them into his face, except the gaoler stands close, watchful.

'Or, upon their burning, their magic transferred to you? We do not yet understand the full workings of witchcraft, except that the devil himself is your master, and you his servant – and thus it has always been. What say you to my accusations? You must feel something, even a witch must feel *something*?'

I am no one's servant.

My feelings are my own and will never be revealed to you except in blood-lust and revenge. Do not the sagas tell us the gods went to war? Many have been slain in their honour – and many more will follow. Do not think your words frighten me, witchfinder. I may be young, but I have had a hard apprenticeship, a life you will never understand.

I return his gaze: fierce, bold, untamed. He peers at me as if truly he would know me. He is unlike any man I have met. I have known two sorts: the foolish, cruel kind like my kin and most of the men in this community, or the dutiful, steadfast kind, the fathers and husbands who speak well of their wives and children, even this priest who believes he is doing God's will. Yet this man is different. He is quiet, calculating, where the others bluster and boast. He is soft when others are hard, yet this may frighten me yet. He is a threat to me and mine.

I feel a trickle of blood run down the side of my mouth and know myself to be cut by the gaoler's blow.

'Her blood is dark red!' the gaoler says. 'It's not pale like the *álfar* . . .' He looks puzzled, as if, like a child, he really expects my veins to run with enchanted blood. 'Do you know what day it is, witch? It's January the sixth, the night when elves run wild across the land on galloping horses, when seals take human form and walk in from the sea. It's a night of elvish magic and sorcery.' His eyes search my face as if I will vanish, a disembodied spirit that will float away, curling like steam through the bars.

'Enough. This is fanciful talk,' the priest says, but he seems to grip the cross tighter.

'We are here to conduct this investigation in the name of Our Lord God in heaven. You have sinned most grievously. Unburden yourself. Return to the Lord, Þuriður Jónsdóttir. Even you may be welcomed back into his loving arms.'

Even me.

I smile a slow smile. I imagine I resemble more ghoul than woman.

'Red blood or not, she's a fucking witch. We're going to burn away your smile,' the gaoler says, turning to me: glaring.

Fuck you.

I move my arm to wipe my face, knowing I tremble. I cannot lift it. The chains hang heavy, the fetters cold, weighted. Fear has taken hold.

'Patience, my friend,' Þorleifur Kortsson says. His voice, soothing. 'Leave us now.'

The gaoler, reluctant, walks out, muttering as he goes. He throws me a look of pure hatred. If I could snarl, I would. The witchfinder continues.

'Tell us which charms and spells you've cast against the preacher. Tell us or we will force your confession.'

He points to the prongs sitting by the brazier's hungry flames. Picks them up, displaying them in his grip. It must be the angle he holds them, but the effect is to cast shadows of flame and smoke as if the witchfinder emits the sulphurous plumes of hell.

I feel my knees give way beneath me.

It is only a few minutes later when my sight returns. I find I can see each man's boots. I drag myself up enough to sit, but I am still unsteady. I picture the cuts on my father's face, my brother's bruises, the parts of their roughened fingers with missing nails that ran with blood. I remember how they dragged themselves from this floor when the questioning had begun. They were strong men, yet they were reduced to quivering shadows. Now they plan to do the same to me.

Þorleifur Kortsson faces me.

'Þuriður Jónsdóttir. Sorcerer's daughter. There are those who have spoken out against you. We have statements. We have proof of your deeds as witnessed by those who live and work around you. Ingibjörg Ívarsdóttir says you killed her cow and its calf by stroking the birthing animal. What say you to this? There are others, of course, but you shall learn of them in time. Did you kill the cow and its young? Did you kill the woman who gave birth moments earlier. Were they offerings to the dark one they call Satan? There is much you can help us with, if only you would speak.'

The witchfinder's voice is silken, as smooth as whey when it slides from the barrel.

'We may have a mind to be lenient, to help you, witch, if you could tell us how the devil contacts you. I might instruct the gaoler here to break your neck before the burning, to make your passage to hell easier. What say you? Will you find your voice and help us?'

A moan escapes my lips.

I feel my bladder release. I piss myself like the sheep when I walk too near.

'Speak now!' It is the priest. He looks agitated. He steps towards me, holding the cross just like a shield. 'Tell us how you made a pact with him! Did you fly at night to meet him? Did he come to you? Tell us everything and you may be forgiven.'

I watch Síra Jón Magnússon's mouth move, but I hear none of it. I have retreated somewhere beyond fear. I have crawled inside the recesses of my mind to find where there is peace, stillness. Closing my eyes, I see my mother's face, hear her voice as if she speaks from far away. She shakes her head from side to side, just like she did when I was a child and running wild across the pastureland, away from my chores, feeling the rush of air on my skin. I recall the solid warmth of her embrace, whispering love and stories into my ear. This comforts me, strengthens me. I would wish myself far away from this place, these questions, and the pain they promise me. Would wish myself dead rather than face the burning too. Yet the lure of a broken neck is not enough to open my mouth. If they are going to kill me, they will have my silence as reward, as my rebellion, as my revenge – and more besides.

60

Þorleifur Kortsson warms his hands, extending them towards the fire that crackles in his private chamber. Watched by Síra Jón Magnússon and Sýslumaður Magnús Sigurdsson, he takes his time to speak.

'Can we break her?' he says at last.

The priest and the sheriff glance at each other. The latter shrugs as if it is too much trouble either way.

'We will drive the devil from her!' Síra Jón leans forward, spittle-flecked mouth moving, eyes bright. 'There is none so righteous as he who wrestles with the forces of darkness. We shall be blessed by the battle, be not afraid.'

The priest's eager face belies his exhaustion. It is late. The night is black as pitch.

'There shall not be found among you anyone that maketh his son or his daughter to pass through the fire, *or* that useth divination, *or* an observer of times, *or* an enchanter, *or* a witch.'

'Deuteronomy, yes. She must confess before two witnesses to put her to death.' The witchfinder looks back at the fire.

'My master King Frederick desires a favourable outcome and fast. We have been slow here in Iceland to act against sorcery. The king is keen to . . . *rectify* . . . our unwillingness to act. The Danes, the Swedish, the Scots have not failed to take the harshest measures for decades now – and so must we. I will not return to Copenhagen without proof that we are carrying out the king's father's wishes. For his aunt, Anne of Denmark, was almost killed by a storm whistled up by witches in East Berwick, a land far from here but no less afflicted by maleficium.

'This outbreak of sorcery has gone on too long. He relies on me – *on us* – to bring the witch to heel. If she will not willingly confess, then we must seek a higher authority to enact the law. We must take her to trial at Þingvellir where she will face the Alþingi.'

'But torture a young woman?' Síra Jón clutches his cross, a frown creasing his brow.

'Think of her not as a maiden, but as a demon dressed in women's skirts,' Sýslumaður Sigurdsson unexpectedly interjects. 'The sooner it is done the better. We need a confession. It is a long journey to Þingvellir.'

The witchfinder watches the priest. Will he object when it is a woman, a young woman, facing those same techniques as her male kin: the prongs, the coals, the pliers?

Síra Jón Magnússon shifts on his seat. The sheriff yawns.

The witchfinder draws in a deep breath, looks away from the flames.

'My master demands an end to witchcraft in Iceland. I am tasked with razing it to the ground – and I cannot fail,' he says, staring down the priest.

Silence follows. Síra Jón Magnússon nods. A mutual understanding.

'Þuriður Jónsdóttir is the adoptive heir of the sorcerers' practices. I willingly go along with any good man who will destroy those who give everlasting suffering to me, whether she be a daughter of Eve, or a man. The attacks of witchcraft against me are not just a residue of the men who were burned. They have their source elsewhere – in the shape of this young woman . . .' The priest pauses. 'I will not object to whatever means are necessary . . .'

'Good. Tell only those whom you trust, only the godly among us. I don't want the witch wriggling out of the bars like a serpent when she learns of her fate.'

61

April 1658

'I HAVE GRAVE news.' The Dean of Holt, a measured, patient man, holds up the parchment he received that morning. His kindly face looks drawn, the lines on his forehead more pronounced.

Three sets of eyes, including his wife Halladóra's, stare back at him. The others are the girl's mother, Guðrún Símonsdóttir, and her husband, Leif Árnason. The dean, Gissur Sveinson, clears his throat. He would rather any news to impart than this to his dearest friends.

For months the question of where Þuriður Jónsdóttir vanished to has kept the gossips busy in Holt. Searches of the area were made after she disappeared from her mother's house at the start of winter – and did not come back. They found nothing. No body at the base of the cliffs she was known to walk. No trace of her at all. Snowfall covered any tracks she might have left. Some said she was spirited away by her kind, reviving the old rumours about her mother being one of the *álfar.* Gissur does not believe the old stories of elf folk who live lavish lives inside certain rocks or mountain stones, or at least he tries not to. He has never seen one, nor any of their famed riches, despite what the rumours suggest. The girl's mother is striking-looking sharing bone-white hair and translucent skin with her daughter, but he is man of the world enough to know that calves are born with no markings, with bleached skin and pink eyes, and other creatures too. God's imagination is limitless – and is not confined to fairy stories about elves and witches, and all manner of strange creatures.

'There is news of Þuriður?' Leif says. His wife, the girl's mother, grips his hand. She turns even paler if that is possible. The loss of her daughter a second time has aged her. She looks like a woman grieving, as well she should when she hears what comes next.

The dean nods.

'A letter has come from my contact in Súðavik. As you know, I sent word of your daughter's disappearance throughout the districts of the Westfjords. Finally, we have news, but you must prepare yourselves.'

His wife sits up even taller. She has a way of looking down her nose that intimidates even the most bullish farmhands and dignitaries.

Again, he clears his throat. He begins.

'As regards the information you requested about a certain woman known as Þuriður Jónsdóttir, if any should arise or her whereabouts be known, I write to you in haste.

'It has come to my attention that the girl in question is held at the Danish storehouse gaol in Eyri, where she is facing charges of sorcery brought about by the priest at Eyrakirkja, Síra Jón Magnússon, and led by Þorleifur Kortsson. I have made discreet enquiries, and I am sorry to say that the case will be taken to the next assembly of the Alþingi at Þingvellir. If I am able to assist your search in any other way, I remain your most humble servant . . .'

The dean stops reading. Guðrún collapses in upon herself like a poorly constructed turf house, the heavy burden of its roof breaking the structure. The dean and his wife exchange glances.

'What can we do? I must go there and beg the priest to free her,' the girl's mother says, tears already falling down her pale cheeks.

'You must do nothing of the sort! They're going to kill her,' says Halladóra. 'If you go to Kirkjuból, they'll fucking kill you too.'

His wife, nearing her fifties with silver hair pulled back into an embroidered cap, her fine woollen skirts arranged around her chair, sweeps her gaze around the *baðstofa*, alighting on each person in front of her. They have gathered in the dean's sprawling residence on the edges of the small settlement. Inside, the fire burns hot as snow falls heavy and thick outside the large wooden doors. Servants move from room to room, down the long corridor, bringing coffee and skyr. The space is the same size as Leif's, but it is richer still, with a large central table imported from Copenhagen surrounded by six chairs, each carved with intricate patterns, their seats plush with velvet cushions. The croft has a small glass window, the only one in this district to boast such a thing.

'But I must do something!' Guðrún says. 'I can't sit here and be told my daughter will be burned as a witch and do nothing! She deserves more than that. My son Jón deserved more – but I did nothing to save him. This time, I won't let my daughter down.'

'Unless you really are an elf woman and can spirit her out of that stinking gaol, then there's little you can do,' the dean's wife says. The two women regard each other: the mother of the witch, the wife of the dean. They share a long look that seems to encompass every slight, every injustice, every compromise a woman must make in a man's world such as this. They understand each other, even if they cannot help one another.

'This is the worst possible news,' Guðrún says, turning her head away. 'I wish she had perished on the mountainside. Death by exposure or from being smashed on the rocks below would've been preferable.'

'Don't speak of her death this way,' the dean says, his voice gruff.

'When no body was found, I hoped she'd run away to try to keep us safe, though I would never have wanted her to do that. I hoped she'd found sanctuary in another place, another farmstead, somewhere far from the reaches of the priest of Eyri. I was wrong. We have to get her out of there,' Guðrún says, her voice wretched. She looks back at the others. The only one who will meet her gaze is the dean's wife.

'You'll do nothing. If you go, they'll lock you up and tip you into the fire just as easily as your daughter. These are men who hate women. There are plenty enough of them. The burnings across Europe have shown us that, if little else. But there may be something *I* can do. The sheriff, Magnús Sigurdsson, is my nephew, and a lazy, arrogant man, but I will speak with him. I will tell him he must release her and stop this immediately. One day men will have to listen to the voices of women. Let's hope they do so today.'

Her husband nods his agreement.

'Prepare my horse,' she commands, waving away one of the men skulking around the edges of the room.

Within the hour, Halladóra Einarsdóttir mounts her horse, the leather reins in her hands, a thick cloak embellished with gilded thread around her shoulders. Alongside her, two burly manservants frown at the sky as white-grey clouds loom overhead. Halladóra looks down at the girl's mother, Leif Árnason and the dean himself. Her husband smiles up at her, kisses her hand.

'Godspeed, wife. Send word if you need assistance. I have duties here in Holt, but will join you if you need me,' he says, stepping back as a new flurry is hurled from the darkening skies. 'Take the Breiðadalsheiði, the mountain pass that leads direct to Eyri, and do not stop for anyone.'

Halladóra digs her heels into her horse's flanks. Three shapes canter across the pastureland, heading up into the mountains that will still be treacherous with slipping snow. All any of them left behind can do now is pray.

62

SÝSLUMAÐUR MAGNÚS SIGURDSSON is digging a stubborn piece of *harðfiskur* from his back tooth with a toothpick when his maidservant enters his chamber, bobs a curtsy.

'There's a visitor to see you,' the freckled girl says. The sheriff continues his quest for the tiny slice of fish that has become embedded in his gum, then looks up at her from his chair. She is ripe enough, though he has never been one for freckles. Most of the young servant girls he fumbles have the long blonde locks he prefers, but she will do, he thinks.

He smiles.

'Thank you. Who visits me at this hour?' It is late. The snow has, at least, stopped, but the air holds its chill, though the fire spits and smoulders in this, his private room.

'Oh, I didn't ask,' the servant, whose name he does not know, says, flustered.

Normally, he would snap at her, but the firelight and the good brandy imported from Copenhagen have left him feeling mellow. He feels a stirring in his breeches. He pats his leg.

'Come here, girl. Let me take a look at you. You say you're my maidservant, but you forget even the most basic tasks such as discovering the identity of my guests. What shall I do with you?' he leers. The girl moves closer, casting her eyes to the floor.

'You'll leave her alone, nephew, that's what you'll do.'

Halladóra Einarsdóttir stands in the entrance, the door pushed open, her hands folded in front of her bodice.

'Aunt!'

'You may go,' she says, pointedly, to the serving girl, who scurries out of the room, bobbing another curtsy as she goes.

'Haven't I told you before that the servants are not your playthings?' the dean's wife says, shutting the door behind her.

'I'll do what I like in my own chambers.' The sheriff pouts, annoyed at this uncalled-for interruption. 'And I won't have you ordering my staff around.'

'You will leave them alone or I will write to my sister, your mother. I am sure she would enjoy a trip to see you here. She may wish to stay for a few weeks, or even months . . .'

The sheriff scowls.

The thought of his mother being here, sniffing around his staff, changing his routines, ordering his servants around just as the Dean of Holt's wife has done, is too much to bear.

'Now that you're here, what do you want?'

'Is that any way to greet your aunt? Come, Magnús, embrace me, then we can talk.'

When Magnús Sigurdsson gives his aunt the customary kiss on the lips, she smells the taint of brandy, strong and earthy; feels the wet bristles of his beard.

He's drunk, she thinks. *This could work in our favour. He might be in the mood to be lenient.*

When the greetings are complete, the pair sit by the fire. Strong coffee is poured into two cups beside them. Halladóra eyes her nephew, takes a sip. The coffee is good. It burns her throat. She wonders if the girl Þuriður has eaten or drunk anything hot since she was arrested. She thinks, not for the first time, how strange it is that some men, her nephew included, can be so casually cruel to the women and girls they encounter. What makes them this way? It never fails to astonish her that they care about their wellbeing so little. She is grateful for the comforts afforded her by her high birth and her stubborn nature. These combined, along with a good husband by her side, mean her life has been very different to those who live theirs at the mercy of this ordinary tyranny – the tyranny of fathers, husbands, brothers, lawmen and priests.

'You have a young woman called Þuriður Jónsdóttir held prisoner here.'

Magnús Sigurdsson sniffs. 'I do, though, respectfully, what business is it of yours?'

She smiles imperiously at him. 'It is this young woman I have come to see you abou—'

'We've arrested a witch who'll be condemned to die for her sorcery,' he says, interrupting her, as if this settles the matter. He licks his lips. She knows he is thinking of the half-finished bottle of brandy sitting on the cupboard rather than her friend's daughter's plight.

Halladóra draws herself up in the chair. She leans forward. 'I want your word that she will have a fair trial, one where the correct procedures are carried out. You seem very sure she is guilty of the charge against her.'

An exaggerated sigh. 'Aunt, all due processes are underway. She will have the right to ask for twelve good men to swear the *tylftareiður*—'

'Yet you are confident they won't.' She stares back at him.

His turn to smile. He gets up, pours another measure of brandy.

'Your concern is heard and noted,' he replies, knocking back the drink in one gulp. 'But I cannot help a girl who won't speak . . .'

'You know as well as I that the *girl* has not spoken since her mother left. Whether by choice or whether she was struck dumb, no one can say. How can she ask twelve men to swear the oath of innocence if she cannot—'

'Will not—' the sheriff interrupts again.

'Speak?'

'Is there no one who will help her?'

'Why would anyone risk their neck to help a witch? Go back to your husband and your estate. Live out your days in peace and leave the law to men.'

Despite having the good fortune to be born in the highest social strata of Iceland, and receive learning alongside her brothers, Halladóra is used to being underestimated. With an irritated nod of the head, she rises.

It is clear the sheriff will be no help to her – or Þuriður.

'No man will swear the oath to save her wicked soul,' he says again. 'It's better for you if you forget about her. Go back home and pray to God this canker of witchcraft has spread no further in Holt.'

'Do you dare to threaten me, nephew?'

'Not at all, aunt. Merely to warn you. The law is clear. The woman held in my gaol is a sorceress and she will be tried and found guilty. Then she will die. The only thing you can do for her is beg the Lord it is a quick death. Since when does a woman married to a dean concern herself with a witch?'

'When she is innocent,' Halladóra snaps.

The silence that follows is impregnated with menace. What she does not say is that Þuriður reminds her of her younger self. Fierce. Wilful. Stubborn. The frailty of these virtues in a woman, so readily taken from them, so quickly suppressed and harmed. She was lucky.

She married a man who cherishes these traits. The younger woman is not so fortunate. She must fight for herself and her instincts alone. This is why she must help her. The sheriff stands, abrupt and angry.

'Aunt, I think you've said enough. I thank you to leave. This is not the business of women—'

'I think it very much the business of women when you arrest and torture them for nothing more than rumours of witchery!' Halladóra retorts. She wonders, briefly, if he will strike her. He would not dare, would he?

Her nephew's face has flushed red in anger. His eyes are fierce. If she was a lesser woman, she might be cowed by her relative, but she is neither of those things.

Instead, she glares back, looking down her straight nose at him, reminding him without needing words that he is shorter in stature.

'I wish you goodnight,' he says, his voice trembling with rage.

'You're holding an innocent woman in your gaol. I demand she is released immediately.'

This is not going the way she had hoped, but there is nothing for it but to try and make her idiot nephew see sense.

'I'll wager she is cold and hungry, and that is the best outcome. Have you beaten her? Or worse? Have any of your men defiled her or tortured her? I'm warning you, Magnús, if you harm a hair on the girl's head—'

'You'll what?' he sneers. 'What will you do, aunt? There's nothing you can do! Her trial is a mere formality. She'll be burned as she deserves to be. Your husband holds no sway here – and neither do you.'

The dean's wife breathes heavily. Her hand itches to slap this man who speaks to her with such impudence.

'We shall see,' she says. She turns and stalks out, leaving her nephew staring after her, his face pink and blotched under his greying beard.

She grabs her cloak from the serving girl, who hovers in the corridor.

'Stay away from him. He will use you for his pleasure then discard you, like the other serving girls who had the misfortune to work here,' Halladóra says, walking out.

At the end of the corridor is the wooden door of the gaol, with a large metal lock across it, and a small, barred window. Outside, sits a man, the gaoler. He yawns and stares back at her, blinking. He sits up, unsure whether to rise, clearly unsure who this finely dressed woman is except that she is a guest with status. Halladóra pauses. The girl Þuriður is there gazing back at her, silent. If she had not stopped, she would have missed her. The young woman looks like a shaft of moonlight in physical form. Her hair acts like an orb of light. An elf maiden in truth, peering from the shadows, her face dirty, her skin pale as death, her eyes glowing ice-blue from inside the dark, fetid cell.

Then, Þuriður is gone. Retreating back into the darkness of the prison.

63

HALLADÓRA EINARSDÓTTIR DOES not return home to her lands outside Holt.

She tells the men who accompanied her to rest, to take shelter in one of the winter fishing huts that straddle the harbour. She lies to them, telling them she will stay with her nephew, yet she has no intention of spending another second under his dissolute roof. After the men have left, she clicks her tongue, stroking her horse's mane. When she mounts, it paces but a little, unsettled for a moment because of the lateness of the hour. They do not usually ride so late, especially in winter.

'We have work to do,' she whispers to the beast with its long, shaggy mane and ears that twitch as she speaks. They move off on the gravel tracks leading along the spit towards the mainland, heading southwest. Her friend Guðrún has described it, and every dwelling and croft therein. Halladóra knows the croft belonging to Ari and Anna is the closest to Kirkjuból, the largest farmstead. She has visited this side of the mountain with her husband before, though on unofficial duties, and remembers asking about these farms and the land, never expecting she would now be asking for their help. Snow has started to fall again but she can see both crofts, candles alight inside, piercing the darkness. Her breath plumes, visible in the freezing air as they gallop onward by the light of the shy moon as it slips in front of the clouds.

Bang. Bang. Bang.

All is silent except for the screech of a fox somewhere on the mountainside making the restless sheep in their *skáli* skittish.

Bang! Bang! Bang!

Halladóra knocks harder, knowing this will frighten those within. Only ghosts and ghouls haunt the land at night, but she cannot wait till morning.

A tall, burly man opens the door a crack.

'Who's there? Who dares destroy our peace?'

'I must speak with a woman called Anna. She is the fisherman Ari Björnsson's wife. I come to warn her.'

The man looks her up and down, taking in, no doubt, her rich cloak, her fur gloves, her leather boots. If this is the wrong place, she may need to escape. She glances back at her horse, tied to the gate post.

'And who are you to ask for my wife, and at this time?' The man's manner, though gruff, is not unfriendly. The door opens a little more. Inside, it is dark except for the orange glow of the hearth fire.

'Please let me in. I am freezing and I must find Anna. This is important. I would not have come otherwise.'

A sudden gust of wind makes her horse whinny and stamp its foot.

'Yes, yes, come,' the man says, his eyes ringed grey in the dark.

A woman is standing by the steps leading to the raised platform. She has a woollen shawl wrapped around herself. She is slight, blonde plaits falling down each side of her face, just as Þuriður's mother described, though she would have known her only when she was a young girl.

'Shhh, you'll wake the children,' the woman whispers, putting her finger to her lips. 'Come this way, and we can talk. Go back to bed, husband. I'm safe enough.'

Ari looks between them. He nods but does not move.

'I'll stay. I'm here if you need me.' He pulls a chair from the table and sits down. The dean's wife sees a knife in its holder attached to his breeches.

'Thank you,' she says to the woman she hopes is Anna, Þuriður's great friend.

'I am sorry to alarm you – that was not my intention – but what I have to say concerns us all, assuming you are Anna?'

'I am. Do you have news of Þuriður? Come to the kitchen. It is warmer there.'

Anna leads the richly dressed older woman down the corridor to the kitchen.

Here, a serving girl sleeps on a pallet bed close to the hearth. She emits a snore, then turns over, smacking her lips, her muttering unintelligible.

'Don't mind her. She's a deep sleeper and won't hear anything we say between us. Sit down. Take off your cloak and dry it by the fire.'

Grateful to find the room is warm enough to divest herself of her sodden outer layers, Halladóra places her long cloak on a chair by the fire. She sits next to this woman who seems unfazed by her midnight guest.

Anna opens a door and retrieves a pot filled with milk, kept cold in an outbuilding close to the dairy. She pours it into a pan and places it upon the stove, where it hisses as she stirs it with a wooden spoon.

'Who are you and why have you come?' Anna says eventually, doling out the warmed milk into two cups, handing one to her.

The older woman takes the drink, grateful for the warmth of it. She sips, feeling the liquid run hot down her throat.

'Þuriður is in great danger,' she says.

'Where is she? We've spent months searching for her. She disappeared without trace. Who took her? What have they done to her?'

'She's held in the same gaol as her father and brother – and awaits the same fate.'

Anna cries out, spilling the milk. It soaks white into the wooden floor. Halladóra reaches for her hands, holding her steady.

'You must be quiet. We do not know who we can trust. My husband tells me privately there are witnesses for her sorcery who have written down their complaints as evidence against her. He learned this from those he can trust who live nearby. Shush now. Anyone could be listening with malice in their heart.'

Anna nods. Her eyes are wide, already filled with tears.

'They'll kill her, won't they?'

The dean's wife nods, then places her cup on the side of the hearth.

'Unless we fight.'

64

I AWAKEN.

For a brief moment, I do not know where I am. It is the stink of my own body that reminds me. I have not washed for months. Everywhere: filth.

The dean's wife came, but I do not have time to ponder this. The sound of the lock scraping open disrupts my thoughts. The tap of bootsteps on wooden boards. The clearing of their official throats tells me what is to come.

I look up. The witchfinder is there, standing above me. The brutish gaoler grins beside him. He carries a brazier, metal implements, a lit torch.

My time of waiting has ended. This time, the brazier will serve as more than a threat.

Pain is a thing of exquisite clarity, I have discovered. It sharpens every sensation, every thought, into searing, white-hot truth. It shapes every moment I live from now on. Every thought will form from the notion that they may do it again – and worse. If I survive this, I might one day forget, but I already know I will force myself to remember. I will lay claim to the savage truth of it, and I will have my revenge.

I say not a word though cursing words bubble inside me, desperate to be screamed into their faces, unleashed. No man will ever touch me this way again. I will make sure of it. I will call on the old gods, those of war and death and slaying. I will summon the blood-lust of my ancestors and I will rip apart my torturers' souls. Afterwards, they drag me into the corner of my hell hole onto lice-strewn straw, broken.

65

'DO YOU KNOW where Margrét is?' Síra Jón Magnússon says.

'She'll be at the stream. I gave her a basket of washing to finish,' Þorkatla replies. 'Do you need her?'

The priest's wife is folding linen at one end of the table, while the priest sits at the other, surrounded by the detritus of his work.

'Yes, it is most important. Find her, please, and bring her to me,' Síra Jón says, looking back down at the skins he has laid out, a candle stub on one corner, an ink well on another.

Not long afterwards, Margrét shuffles into the *baðstofa* with his wife. She attempts a curtsy, made clumsy by her listing gait.

'Leave us,' he says to Þorkatla, looking up at the maidservant. For a second, he wonders if his wife will disobey him. Her expression is mutinous.

'Thank you,' he offers. With a glance back at them both, she turns and walks down the corridor. When he can no longer hear her boot soles on the floor, Síra Jón points to the chair beside him.

Confused, Margrét sits. On the table is a sheaf of parchment, a newly sharpened quill in the priest's hand, a dish of ink.

'Sit. Please,' he says, gesturing with his other hand to the chair opposite him. 'You are going to tell me everything you saw. Everything. And I will write it down.'

I, Margrét Þorvaldsdóttir, testify that I was present at Kirkjuból, Skutulsfjörður, on the day Síra Jón Magnússon, accompanied by his wife, Þorkatla Bjarnadóttir, and stepdaughter Rannveig, moved into the Kirkjuból farm. I saw the following apparition above the farmstead: a red light was visible to me in the sky, round, and resembling the northern lights except it was redder, and it struck me that out of this light came darkness. I was afraid and covered my eyes with my hand. After a short while, I looked again and saw a ball of fire floating above the farmhouse. At that time, Þuriður Jónsdóttir was in a nearby farmhouse.

When Síra Jón arrived on horseback, I saw a black dog going after him. I watched as long as it was in sight, anxious to know what would come of this apparition, and expecting it would have its effect on the priest.

I also witnessed Þuriður Jónsdóttir perform acts of magic. She helped her father, Jón Jónsson the Elder, and brother, Jón Jónsson the Younger, with charms and spells when they were alive, blood being taken from her ankle for the business of strengthening curses and making them effective. One such act of magic was killing the wife of the priest's baby. It was newborn yet dead as she held it. I saw her lips move over the body. It was an enchantment. She took the boy child for the huldufólk, the hidden people. She breathed spells over it and sent its soul to the devil. This I saw with my own eyes.

I want this testimony of mine to be made public, whatever may be the outcome.

(signed) Margrét Þorvaldsdóttir, servant at the farm of Kirkjuból at Skutulsfjörðu, in the presence of Síra Jón Magnússon

When he has finished, the priest sits back. Allows himself a smile, though he cannot rejoice at the devil's work. He knows the witch-finder will be pleased with the day's efforts.

'What will you do?' Margrét says, licking her lips. 'Surely, the danger has passed now that Þuriður is captured. She can't send her witchery here no more.'

'If only it was so easy,' Síra Jón murmurs. 'You have done well. You are a godly, though afflicted, woman. God tests those he most loves.'

'Amen,' the maidservant says, uncertain. Her face is pale, a lopsided frown settling over her features.

66

June 1658

THE SMELL OF people and animals is ever the same: sweat, shit, mead, piss. The sounds come next: men's voices, horses whinnying, stall-holders calling out their wares. They have arrived in Þingvellir, a journey of two weeks from the Westfjords. It is here the parliament, the assembly known as the Alþingi, will put the witch to trial. There can only be one outcome.

Þorleifur Kortsson waves to a grubby-faced boy nearby. He runs over, dipping his head in deference.

'Tell me, where do we put the prisoner?' He flicks a coin in the boy's general direction.

'Follow the black stones down to the valley. There, you'll find the huts built specially. Throw me another coin and I'll take you there.'

The witchfinder raises an eyebrow. Another glint of metal and a coin lands in the grass at the boy's feet. He must be only fourteen winters or less, but already has the sharp eyes of a child used to hunger.

'Follow me,' he says and starts to whistle.

Behind the witchfinder rides Síra Jón Magnússon, and beside him the sheriff, Sýslumaður Magnús Sigurdsson, who appears to be leading a horse, attached to his own by a length of rope, carrying sacks of food and bedding. On closer inspection, a girl lies heavy over the horse's flank, unmoving.

Three men, four horses and one woman, condemned as a sorceress, move slowly among the throng towards the main arena where justice will be delivered in the coming days. Every official in Iceland, except those too infirm or aged, gather here to discuss the most pressing matters of state, to hear the most notorious and serious cases. It is a sea of men, horses and serving boys. There are no women except those kept as prisoners. When, finally, they reach the makeshift gaol constructed from found timber and stone, the witchfinder dismounts. This is where he will bring the witch to heel and wipe sorcery from this land. He glances over at the young woman sagging over the back of the fourth mare.

'Give her water and something to eat,' he says, throwing the reins to the boy.

67

I AM UNSURE if he means the boy to fetch food and water for the horse or for me.

The boy eyes me warily. I know I look like a hag: grime-streaked legs, wild, untameable hair, eyes too big for my sunken face, tattered rags once decorated with wildflowers and hanging off my small body, for I have seen my reflection in the limpid waters of a lake we camped by as we made our slow way here. I would believe me a demon – just as he does. I gesture for water, pat my lips, try to smile. He steps back, eyes wide with fear.

Water!

I try again but he shows no sign of understanding.

I see everything on a slant, still bent over the horse, sure I have rubbed the poor creature's flesh raw. All the world is angled. There are men walking around, stopping to speak with each other, faces stern. There are arguments and discussions, laughs and squabbles. The sun is in my eyes as I squint up at them. I imagine the horse is keen to offload the burden of me, though I am mere skin stretched over bone from months of eating little. I know we have arrived at the place where I will be confined until they present me to the men who will judge me. When I am lifted off and placed on the ground, I find my legs shake and I cannot stand up. Thirst devours me. I am light-headed with hunger too. My belly grumbles at the smell of the food, though I feel sick, nauseous, afraid.

The boy takes my arm with reluctance, leaning back because of the stench of me. I walk with difficulty, but with each step my body moves a little easier. The gentle summer breeze makes my skin pimple. A door is opened. I am shoved inside a windowless cell, one surrounded by the sounds of industry and men.

Someone shouts out as we enter: voice shrill, a woman begging to be freed. When the door is shut and bolted with a wooden plank, I am thrown into darkness again. My neighbour continues to curse and holler.

Sometime later, the door opens a crack, throwing a thin shaft of daylight onto the bare floor. I am hungry for light, for warmth. It is that I stagger to the door for. Instead, I am given a plate with meat, fish and a cup of water upon it. The smell makes my stomach turn. I turn away from the food. There are other forms of nourishment.

Óðinn, Loki og allir þær og þeir sem Valhöll byggja og byggt hafa frá heimsins upphafi, þá gefi mér það að mér veitist þessi hlutur . . .

Óðinn, Loki and all those who inhabit Valhöll, and have built the realm from its beginning, grant that which I ask . . .

A prayer, an invocation. Silent. Unheard. Seeping through the cracks in the doorframe, through the hastily formed roof. Do spells work if they are not spoken aloud? I do not know the answer to this. There is so much to which I do not know the answer.

How long must I wait?

68

ÞINGVELLIR SITS IN a wide, open valley, ringed in the far distance by mountains.

Síra Jón Magnússon is familiar with the assembly: the crowds of district officials discussing points of law, convicts brought here to face trial and punishment. It is an adjustment. From the small hamlet on a wind-battered spit to this, the epicentre of Iceland's justice system.

He sets down his things: his Bible, his bag containing clothing and food, in one of the shelters made from large lengths of cloth suspended between the tops of huge, jutting stones. Inside is a flattened area where he will sleep tonight. The annual meeting of the law council means there are many encamped here, and on the plains surrounding the ancient site.

Everywhere, men gather and discuss the trials that begin shortly. He looks around, recognizing some of the dignitaries. Nods to them. It has taken two weeks of travel across valleys, mountain passes, through streams and glacier melt, along fjords and inlets to reach this place where, finally, his troubles will end. He sees the hut where the young woman now moulders. His heart hammers in his chest. At last, it will all be over. He mutters a prayer of thanks to God, interrupted by a sudden swell of noise behind him, a surge of movement, as officials, churchmen, onlookers, gather by a small shallow pool. Suddenly, there is a shriek as a woman is half dragged out from the gaol.

'No! No! Help me!' Her voice is a strangled, pitiful thing. One of the guards strikes her.

She has dark hair, not unlike the colour of the priest's wife's. It lies in rats' tails down her back. She wears a thin linen shift stained brown with dirt. Her feet are bare. She shivers, eyes darting, wild like a bird.

'Stand back!' the guard commands the crowd that has come forward like moths to candlelight. 'Keep away from the adulteress!'

The priest walks over, puts his hands together. Prays again. This time, he beseeches God to save the soul of this creature who appears inhuman, a beast of the earth rather than a woman, a mother, a daughter.

When he has finished, he opens his eyes to find he is standing in a crowd of a hundred men or so: all waiting.

She cries out, her eyes screwed up, unused to daylight.

'Don't kill me!' she pleads as she is pushed roughly to the pebbled ground. The watching men stand just above, where the rocks are smoothed by footfall of centuries. They overlook Drekkinggarhylur, the deep pool that sits down off the track, fed by a stream from the Öxará river that rushes into the green-blue froth of water. She is crawling on her hands and knees. Then she rises, scratching at herself, drawing blood in a frenzy of panic. Síra Jón believes he can smell her fear, the guttural, feral stench of a woman's sweat and private parts. He tries to step back, but there are too many behind him. She grabs at one of the guards, but he kicks her away.

'Be still,' he says. 'Be quiet, whore.'

Then a man, one the priest recognizes as head of the gathered *lögmenn*, lawmen, steps forward.

'This woman has been found guilty of adultery and is condemned to die by the terms of the Great Edict of 1564. May God have mercy on her soul.' In his hand is a large sack. He gestures to the guards. Together, they take hold of the woman. She struggles, her cries muffled by the fabric as it is forced over her head, pulled down over her body.

'She stitched it herself. It is what all the women found to have fornicated out of wedlock must do. They make their own shroud,' the official standing beside the priest says. His pale eyes gleam.

A rope is wound round her until her arms are pinned to her side. From inside the sacking comes sobbing, a high wailing that seems to echo across the valley. Síra Jón watches, both repelled and fascinated. It is the first time he has seen a woman drowned thus. He mouths the Lord's Prayer. Feels the holy words like dust on his dry tongue.

Then a splash as she is pushed. Water slaps against the edges of the pool. The shock of her entry makes him jump. She writhes, kicking her bound legs and feet, thrashing and moaning, the water churning into white bubbles that travel upwards, breaking the surface. One of the guards stands with a long stick, his boots submerged in the dying woman's watery grave. He presses it down, pushing her back under the water. Her screams stop at last. There is a choking noise, a gushing, rippling sound. Then, silence.

The water moves still, the sides slick with the small tide-wash of her struggle. The reflection of the sky reappears gradually, reforming itself. In the middle, weighted down just beyond the shallows, the body wrapped in sacking lies motionless.

The priest has seen enough. He turns and almost stumbles into the man standing behind him. The witchfinder Þorleifur Kortsson does not trouble himself to move. He stares at Síra Jón. He appears to be smiling.

'Your first drowning,' he says, as if he relishes his shock.

The priest says nothing. His heart beats in his chest, his throat constricted. Did he not watch the Jón Jónssons burn, without flinching? Did he not root through their ashes, their immolated remains, to search for their organs, their brains, their hearts? So why this sudden terror? What could this adulteress's death possibly have to teach him?

The crowd begins to disperse. After all, there are statements to collate, witnesses to call, deals to be done, bribes to be paid. The business of the Alþingi must continue. The smooth mechanism of Icelandic law, of the long hand of the Danish crown reaching into this gnarly island of puckered lava sitting in the restless Grænland sea, must progress. Justice must be done.

That night, he sleeps, a fitful slumber.

He dreams of the witch Þuriður, slung over horseback, bruised and pitted with scars. He dreams of helping her off the horse, but, instead, her face turns to him, her odd gaze fierce: unrelenting. In front of his eyes, she begins to change. She elongates, her neck lengthening and lengthening, her tongue now forked, her eyes like slits. He shouts out as the serpent rises in front of him, preparing to strike, waving from side to side. He scrabbles back. He shouts again, then realizes a hand shakes his shoulder.

'Wake up! You're dreaming. You've woken half the camp!' It is the sheriff, who sleeps on a goatskin laid on the ground. His voice is coloured with sleep, but no less angry for it.

'It was a vision,' he says, tripping over his own words. The night sky is pale blue and pink, the sun never setting completely. He knows he will not rest again, too troubled is he by his nightmare. He gets up, brushes down his breeches, reaches for his surplice. He must find somewhere to kneel and pray. He must ready himself for today.

All the necessary legal preparations have been made. The evidence: the statements and eye-witness accounts have been compiled because the witch would not confess her crimes against him. It was extraordinary to watch her defy the great pain wrought upon her, the butchery enacted against her. Yet, silent she remained. He must prepare himself to meet his greatest foe: the devil in womanly form, a serpent who slithers under the guise of femininity.

He walks away from the men who grunt and snore, servants already running to collect water from the tributaries trickling through the plains, horses chewing grass from the mossy ground where they are tied up. He walks onward until the peace of the valley surrounds him. A screech overhead. He looks up to see a white-tailed eagle, its brown-grey plumage, its arching wingspan, its protruding beak and small, darting eyes, serene and focused as it plunges towards its prey.

69

ANNO 1658

The comments and observations of the lögmenn regarding the questions they consider most important to investigate in the case of Síra Jón Magnússon against Þuriður Jónsdóttir:

1. *Those persons who lived at Kirkjuból during the upbringing and maturing of Þuriður should be ascertained and questioned as to whether they are aware she ever studied or practised magic.*
2. *Is it known whether these dark arts were topics of conversation on the farm, or whether Þuriður was one of those who boasted of the exercise of them?*
3. *The timings of her trip to Hnífasdalur should be compared with the death of a woman, a cow and its calf, and the sufferings of the priest.*
4. *Is it true that any honest men saw the red light in the sky above the Kirkjuból farmstead, or saw the escort of devils that followed the priest when he rode home from Kirkjuból, being tormented*

thereafter by a swarm of gnats as a result of witchery made by Þuriður Jónsdóttir?

5. *What caused Þuriður to depart so suddenly from Skutulsfjörður where the priest was suffering?*

It is incumbent on everyone present to settle this as best they can, and clarify the points made, and commits all present to the protection of the good Lord.

For the proceedings at Þingvellir, 30 *June* 1658.

70

30 June 1658

CROUCHING IN THE darkness, I do not know if I have slept or not.

Today, I will be tried.

Today, I will die.

I know it is coming. I sniff the air and wonder if they will burn me here, or if there is a place nearby where a torch is kept lit, where wood and brush are bundled together and tied with rope, where ashes mingle with the fat of a melting body.

When the gaoler opens my door, this day's plate of meat and a cup of water in his hand, I sense the words before they leave his mouth.

'Eat. Your trial is today. I'll come back for you.'

He puts down the meal, as well as a small bundle of filthy cloth.

'Put that on,' he says.

Is it my burning robe?

No, I say without words, using my hand in a slicing action, a definitive answer. A clear answer, or so I believe, but he shrugs and bangs the door shut.

Once the door is closed, I scramble for the pot that sits full to the brim with the effect of the fear on my belly. I shit until the wave of terror has passed. Trembling, I wipe myself with a handful of damp straw. Peeling off my blouse and skirt, I stop for a moment, run my fingers along the faded, dirty embroidery of which I was once so proud. Soft colours of *maríusstakkur* and other wildflowers; petals, leaves, stems, dyed with squashed berries and lichen. Invisible stitches that were my blessing, taking the flowers with me wherever I went, even here. Their protection is worn, their magic faded. I remove the ragged clothing and know I will weep for the loss of their beauty, rather than my life.

I remember my mother, her eyes soft as she watched me stitch when I found her again, reborn to me from the dead. I recall her nod as she inspected my work, stroked the wildness of my hair, the wildness in us both.

When the guard comes back, I am ready.

I have not walked anywhere for months. My legs feel weak. They shake beneath me as I get up, wrists bound together with greasy rope, dirt and blood where my skin is rubbed raw. He cuts away the binding. A second of release before he shackles me in irons, though it is but a short walk to the assembly.

I follow behind him, slow, ungainly. I feel summer's gentle breath on my skin.

My gaoler does me the courtesy of stopping and waiting as I catch up. We walk on. The sheriff appears, falls in with us, the witchfinder too. The priest must be there already because I cannot see him. I walk head high, back straight as I can muster, the picture of defiance, though a wounded, feral one.

When I stagger, the gaoler stops again, waits. His kindness, such as it is, breaks me, but I keep moving, refusing to meet the stares of the men – and only men – who watch me as I walk. The laughter and arguments die away.

We reach a point where the crowd parts. Ahead, is the place where I will stand and hear what it is they will say against me. I feel small, as small as an insect in the *fjallagrös*, but I hold my gaze steady though my heart races, my body sweats, my throat seizes up.

Plains stretch away in all directions. There is an area of flat grassland. Around this, in a large circle, men are milling, talking, sharpening their knives, standing and drinking in small groups. All go quiet as I approach.

My feet are bare on the ground. I feel every dewdrop that glistens on the mush left by horses' and men's feet. I feel every undulation of the tufts of grass, moss and earth beneath me, as if experiencing it as a child for the first time. I relish the sensations as they will surely be my last.

There are *lögmenn*, all dressed in dark jackets and breeches. The brass shine of buckles, belts, buttons. The leather shine of boots. I think again of my appearance: my plain shift, straggling hair, bruised face and cracked lips, and know I resemble a sorceress in truth.

Squinting into the morning sunshine, I see Síra Jón Magnússon. He stands slightly at odds with the scene: his face eager. When he sees me, our eyes meet but it is he who looks away first.

The witchfinder stands by the man who must be the leader of the *lögmenn*. He is deep in conversation, but when I stop and turn to them he looks straight at me. Behind him, a grey cloud rolls over the sun. For a moment, we are cast into gloom, before the sun reappears in the sky.

My body shakes in earnest now. I feel queasy as faces turn, noses wrinkle. There are nudges and side glances. I am led out to the middle like cattle on market day. I see no one who is familiar, except for my persecutors. I thought I was used to the fact I have been abandoned, forgotten, by those I love. I realize now I had been hoping they would come. Hoping even just to lock eyes with someone who can say they love me, despite the accusations I now face. But no one is here for me. No one. No matter, I will face these bed-wetters alone. Anger flickers inside me.

I will soon know my destiny as if a *skáld* had writ my life in a saga. The saga of Þuriður Jónsdóttir, who dies today: a witch, a woman condemned. But there are no songs nor words. There is just me, surrounded by the great men of each district of Iceland, and the men who came for me, who hunted me, who will now burn me.

Þorleifur Kortsson steps forward, addresses the officials. 'We bring you the case of the witch Þuriður Jónsdóttir, who is accused of acts of malicious sorcery against this man, Síra Jón Magnússon, and others. She is a danger to all right-thinking men and women and must face the severest penalty.'

Will no one speak for me? Will no one help me? Where is my mother? Where are my friends?

There is a sudden breeze that sets me shivering again. I catch sight of an iridescent wing, a talon: arched. A trick of the light, a fevered imagining. A flash of movement crosses my vision. Horses, hard-ridden, snorting, the sheen of sweat on their flanks. It vanishes as quickly as it comes, leaving no trace. Then the witchfinder speaks again.

'What I present to the Alþingi today is proof that this woman who trembles before us is not only *likely* to have committed sorcery but is *incontrovertibly* a sorceress!'

Everywhere there comes the sound of loud whispers. The witchfinder pauses. He opens up his arms, clad in fine black wool. Looks around. He turns. His pale gaze sears into me. I try not to flinch. I stare back, refusing to lower my gaze.

'Þuriður Jónsdóttir, you are accused of witchcraft. How do you plead? Guilty or not guilty?'

There is a moment when the words rush to me. I feel as if I will faint.

I open my mouth. Nothing comes except a rush of air. A croak like the raven. A tremor at the base of my throat. Apart from that, nothing.

'Look. All assembled have witnessed her guilt! She cannot – or will not – speak!'

I try again.

A rasping sound escapes. A high note, then another.

I hear muffled laughter.

The priest stares up at the sky as if calling down his god. I feel rage boil up again, this time directed at myself.

I should have practised more. I have forgotten how to talk. It may well end my life. I shake my head but it only serves to amuse them more.

'All right-thinking men must agree that Þuriður Jónsdóttir's silence is proof of her guilt, though I will ask for the final time. Are you guilty or not guilty of the charge of witchcraft, a charge that will see you burn for your malice? You must say the words aloud for all here present to witness.' The witchfinder points at me, walks towards me until he is standing in front of me.

My head swims. I am shaking to my bones.

I open my mouth again and emit a soundless scream.

Þorleifur Kortsson glances over at Síra Jón Magnússon. Together, they share a look of triumph.

I want to shout my innocence, but the words will not come.

Then a sudden movement.

A series of gasps and exclamations.

A woman on horseback rears up, rides into the centre, stops alongside me.

'She pleads not guilty!' says Halladóra Einarsdóttir, taking off her hood, gazing down at me far below.

71

I WONDER IF I am hallucinating.

I have spent too long in the dark, yet Halladóra looks real enough. Her back is straight, her expression furious. She wears the *spaðafaldur* cap that arches high over her head, making her appear even taller. Her *faldbúningur*, national costume, is decorated with rich embroidery. Threads of gold wink in the sunlight on deep black velvet skirts with a tight bodice and ruff. Her voice rings out like the church choir on Sundays. I feel my heart lighten, my throat soften. I am seized with the desire to laugh and laugh. The Dean of Holt's wife, a woman known for her forthrightness, her absolute disregard for the pomposity of important men, is here, fighting for me. The thought is a splendid, shining thing.

'You have no proof. I have seen the observations of those who will judge her. I demand that evidence, *real evidence*, is presented to this court.'

No one seems to know what to do. Þorleifur Kortsson recovers first. Amid the silence that has now fallen, he steps towards her.

'You have no place here. This is a court. You are obstructing justice being done.'

'If that is so, then who here defends this woman? Who here speaks for her? If there is such a person, I will leave. If not, then I will stay.' Halladóra Einarsdóttir appears to be well aware of the effect she has on a certain type of man, the weaker, cowardly, cruel kind.

I watch them, laughing inside, as they shrink back. But neither the witchfinder nor the priest is cowed. Together, they step forward to challenge her.

'Women cannot be *seid-menn*, men of magic. The word itself is proof enough that women have no place in a witch trial!'

A titter of amusement.

My heart jolts. It sends blood around my veins as if awoken from an enchantment. The priest frowns. The witchfinder smiles a cold, heartless smile that chills me to my core. These men – and their kind – must be defeated or every woman on this isle will face a lifetime of fear and accusation, like our sisters across the seas.

'And yet here we are, with enough evidence to condemn this woman many times over,' Þorleifur Kortsson says, gesturing to the rolls of parchment in the priest's hands.

'Not here! Not in Iceland,' the dean's wife says, dismounting.

'We have witness statements,' the priest Síra Jón Magnússon says. 'I myself have written a statement. There can be no further evidence necessary. Madam, you have ridden a long way. You should return to your husband. Forget this witch. She has forfeited her life for her wickedness and spells.'

'I have seen the statements,' Halladóra says, ignoring him. 'They show no real proof, only gossip and conjecture. Show me the honest man who can say he has seen this woman perform magic! The honest man who saw the swarm of gnats that beset you and the red lights that were alleged to appear over Kirkjuból farmstead! Show me the honest man who saw Þuriður Jónsdóttir kill a cow and a woman with magic!'

She turns towards the priest.

'Síra Jón Magnússon, you have made many grave allegations, but there is no proof except the words of those who wish to harm her!'

The sky seems to darken. The glinting sunshine disappears. When the priest speaks, it is as if the clouds tremble.

'The evidence is clear!' His voice rings out across the circle of men. 'Þuriður Jónsdóttir is the daughter of notorious and proven *seid-menn* Jón Jónsson the Elder, and sister of Jón Jónsson the Younger, his apprentice. Both were burned to death for their crimes. From the ashes of the past, she has risen to continue their work. Her blood was used for the purposes of magic, for making spells and adding potency to rune-carving. She is – without doubt – a witch. She knew of the grimoires and magic-learning. I say it was she who cast the curses against me all along.'

The crowd stirs. All look at me. Do they imagine flames crackling up my legs, burning my hair to cinders, making my face and body droop as I melt down into the furnace? I feel sick. The faces blur. I must not faint. I must hold my ground. I glance at Halladóra, but she is staring back at him, her expression stone-hard.

'The guilt of this woman is plain for all to see,' the priest continues. He walks towards me. I stare back at him though the field seems to lurch and sway.

'Here she stands, without a tear shed. She does not drop to her knees in shame and humility! She stands as if she were the accuser not the accused! Who else could suffer a proceeding such as this without begging for mercy?'

I know I should defer. I know I should, but I cannot. Burn me, they will. Defile me, judge me. They can try, but I will never acquiesce. I am not my brother.

'You cannot pronounce guilt based upon the accused's nature! Because she does not fall to her knees for mercy means she is proud, yes. It does not mean she confesses.'

The dean's wife opens her mouth to carry on, but the witchfinder interrupts her.

'We will continue with the trial. Madam, you have no right to speak here.' He turns to the crowd. The first gossamer raindrops fall in a haze.

'I have here in my hands the parchments where the accused's guilt is recorded by witnesses. Not by gossips. No, these are writ by those who saw with their own eyes her evil deeds. I will read each to you and you must consider in all seriousness the nature of the claims and the likelihood of the truth of these accounts. Make no mistake, this is evidence, and it shall be used against her. But first I call upon one of those witnesses to speak to all assembled . . .'

I look at the priest, expecting him to speak. He says nothing. Stares down at his hands folded in front of his surplice.

Then the crowd parts again.

She stands, awkward, blushing, her strange slanting smile frozen on her face.

Margrét.

72

HER FAMILIAR SHUFFLING gait.

Each limp forward, an insult. My old maidservant, a girl I grew up with, comes to a halt in front of me. She does not raise her eyes to my face.

When she swears on the Bible held out to her by Síra Jón Magnússon, her slow speech is slurred. I see some of the men exchange glances.

Margrét, you shouldn't have come. It's an arduous journey. Your symptoms are worse. If only you'd let me treat you. And now, have they told you to do this? Did they force you?

The witchfinder begins.

'Please state your full name and where you reside,' he says.

'My . . . my name is . . .Margrét Þorvaldsdóttir.'

I glare at those who would mock her, the men with their eyebrows raised as she speaks. She may be here to condemn me, but she is unwell and – because of her low birth and status – reviled.

'I live at the Kirkjuból farmstead . . . I was there when . . . when Þuriður lived there, as well as her father . . . her brother too.'

She struggles, overawed by the proximity of every district official in the country. Her speech is worse than I remember. Her face droops alarmingly. She wipes a length of dribble from her chin with her hand as she speaks, and I wish I could do that for her with tenderness. She betrays me, and yet I would still care for her, cure her, if she would let me.

'And how long have you lived at Kirkjuból?'

Margrét blushes.

'Since I was small. I don't know how long exactly. I'm not rightly sure how many winters I've been alive . . .'

'And in what role were you there? What was the nature of your relationship with the accused?'

'As a maidservant.' She pauses. 'Though none has ever worked me as hard as my current mistress.'

A small ripple of laughter.

The witchfinder coughs, looks down at his sheaves of parchment. Is he unsettled? The witness seems unable to convince even herself of the charges.

'We were friends, in a way.'

'Friends?'

'Yes, sir, but when they killed her father and her brother, I was scared of her . . .'

All eyes turn to the priest.

Þorleifur Kortsson moves on quickly.

'Would you tell the court what you saw when you lived there with the accused and her kin.'

She throws a quick, sly glance at me.

Here it comes. She saw everything, heard everything.

I should hate her, but I cannot bring myself to do so. She is more a pitiable figure. A woman used by these lawmen, and discarded no doubt when she has said what they want her to say.

'They made spells, the men, I mean. They made lots of spells. All the time!' She wipes her mouth again, this time on the sleeve of her blouse.

'I saw them take blood from her ankle. They used it to make lots of charms, to make their curses stronger.'

'And were these men, the father and son known as the Jón Jónssons, assisted by the accused in any way other than the giving of her blood? Did you see her perform magic? Think very carefully about your answer.'

Margrét looks in the direction of the priest, panicked.

'Would you please answer the question?'

'I . . . I mean . . . no. I didn't see that. I don't think I did.'

'But you did see some things, didn't you? You saw other . . . visitations, as you have declared in your statement.'

Again, she looks over to where the priest is standing. He watches, his hands grasped together, but gives no response except a brief nod.

'Yes, I did, sir. I did . . . There was a red light in the sky when the priest and his family came to Kirkjuból and Þuríður had to leave. Then I saw a black dog running along by . . . by the fjord, or was it the spit?'

The witchfinder clears his throat.

'Let us assume you saw a black dog, and these red lights. How can you be sure they were manifestations of witchery performed by the accused?'

There is silence.

'I . . . I . . . It was her. I know it. She's always been different. If anyone made those spells, then it was her.'

'Who was it? Point to the person in this assembly you believe to have performed acts of sorcery against Síra Jón Magnússon.'

Margrét raises her arm.

It shakes as she points directly at me.

The assembly erupts.

Men shake their heads. Some nod and point in my direction too. I stand: defiant as I am able, without remorse.

Halladóra Einarsdóttir is the first to speak.

'Good men of the *lögrétta*, of Iceland. We have heard this young woman speak. She has many struggles of her own since her illness struck, but she has given her version of events. Indeed, it has been written down by Síra Jón Magnússon, the man most likely to benefit from her statement. Can any of us really believe that the lights and dogs were conjured up as if by a spirit? Can any of us really believe these writings as anything more than a young woman's fevered imagination? Margrét Þorvaldsdóttir has suffered greatly—'

'I call upon Síra Jón Magnússon,' the witchfinder says, interrupting the dean's wife again.

My stomach twists.

Faint with hunger, I sense it is over.

I watch him swear his oath on the Bible. The metal cross round his neck glints in a brief slant of sunlight that comes between the rain.

'I am the incumbent of Eyrakirkja in Ísafjarðarsýsla. My torments at the hands of the Jón Jónssons are well known to all, but it is my belief a greater mischief has been at work.'

Þorleifur Kortsson nods. 'Are you able to tell the court?'

'After the sorcerers were executed, I had a period of relief. I knew the Lord granted me freedom from the terrors and pains inflicted upon me by those who work with the devil.'

'So, when did it change?'

'When I went to inform the accused that I was to inherit her father's farmstead of Kirkjuból as recompense for my trials at his hand.'

'What happened after you saw her?'

'When I rode away, a swarm of biting gnats descended upon me. They came from no natural source, so vicious were they. They appeared from nowhere, conjured by a powerful witch. Then, when I stepped foot inside the chapel, the magic struck with violent force. By entering that holy space, I was thrown into a fight with the devil himself. I collapsed. My wife, Þorkatla Bjarnadóttir, was there and witnessed all.'

'Yet, there is no statement from your wife, is there, Síra Jón Magnússon? There is no witness account except your own, and you have much to gain by this young woman's death! Without Þuriður, your claim to Kirkjuból and its riches is undisputed!' The dean's wife raises her voice.

'This is not about money!' the priest retorts. 'These matters go far beyond a farm and its livestock. You are just a woman and do not understand the spiritual peril we are all placed in if Þuriður Jónsdóttir lives!'

'I understand completely,' Halladóra says, but again, the witch-finder's voice carries across the valley.

'Can you describe the accused's temperament? Her nature?'

'Wilful. Cold-hearted. Her wiles are those of a deceitful woman – but that is not all. A raven sits outside the gaol, never moving far. I have watched it, and every day it returns. It must be her familiar, just as the writings of learned priests in Germany say. She has a familial spirit, which is her conduit to the devil.'

My heart hammers.

Many gasp. Shake their heads.

From the corner of my eye I see the bird's wing again. A moment of flight. Shimmering coal-black and cawing. Raucous. A gore-streaked beak. A skull-picker, a bringer of death, an ebony foretelling.

'Let me repeat my question to you, Þuriður Jónsdóttir,' the witch-finder says.

Have I missed something? The world seemed to freeze for a moment, and all becomes a blur. Everyone stares at me.

'You are accused of witchcraft. What say you to this heinous allegation? What say you, sorceress? For it would be taken as a sign of guilt, would it not, if you chose not to speak?'

It would.

I see that.

I see also that as a woman I am expected to dim my light, to walk in this world of men at their command and do their bidding. *This* is why I am standing here. Because I refused.

I know the witchfinder's methods. He will use anything against me, and now he uses my silence. The men all murmur.

I shake my head again, bite my lip in frustration. I would pray, but not to their god. I could lower my eyes and cry for mercy, but they are not interested in my gestures. It is my words they want. My voice – the one I have denied for so long. I find I have opened my mouth. I pull out the aspen leaf given to me by my friend Anna when first I fled Kirkjuból. The plant for promoting eloquent speech. The plant for truth-telling. There are only dried pieces of it left. I have carried them in my skirt, in a small pouch, as fragments and desiccated powder. This morning, before they ordered me to change my gown, I placed what was left into my mouth. I spit it out now, thinking its magic dry, old, spent. Then, it happens.

The first sound that comes out is a long croak, then a low note and a crackle. I cough. I swallow. There is murmuring in the crowd. Bits of dried leaf make me cough again. My head burns with everything I wish to say. I shut my eyes, then I hear it.

'I . . . I . . . I. Am. Not . . .' The words scratch my throat.

'A . . . witch.'

The dean's wife turns to look at me as if for the first time. She smiles, a long, knowing smile. I would return it, but I find I have more to say.

The crowd falls silent.

'I. Am. Not . . . guilty.'

73

THE WORDS FEEL rough and raw as they bubble up from my stomach, my spleen, my heart. They start to spill out. My voice is rasping. The sound is odd, but I cannot stop. My voice rises.

'I. Am. Not. A. Witch.'

I hear myself and I could shout for joy, though this surely is my darkest moment. Síra Jón Magnússon drops to his knees and begins to pray as if my voice is a demon brought to life. The witchfinder stares at me as if I am already ablaze.

I hear whispers that become louder. They are not what I expect to hear.

'A miracle! The girl speaks!'

'They say she hasn't spoken for years!'

'She was beyond words! Surely, this is God's, not the devil's, work? The spirit of the Lord has moved her to speech! A miracle, surely?'

'Þuriður Jónsdóttir, unlike her father and brother, has always maintained her innocence,' Halladóra Einarsdóttir speaks into the shocked assembly. Even the priest and witchfinder appear dumbfounded.

'She has never been seen performing acts of witchcraft, as the first witness stated so clearly. A witness who *lived* with the accused!

'Good men of Iceland, I say to you that an innocent woman's life depends on your steady hand and benevolent judgement. Would you send a woman to her death upon such feeble claims? Even the priest himself offers only a judgement of her demeanour, something no man can ever know truly.'

Here a few of these good men laugh again.

Halladóra sweeps her hand around the arc of the onlookers.

'Have mercy, gentlemen. Have the courage to say no to these baseless accusations. We are not a nation of burnings, unlike so many others. Let us keep it that way, for the sake of our country and our future.'

'Pretty words,' Síra Jón Magnússon says. 'But they do nothing to defend this woman.' A sudden gust of wind and another shaft of light appears, tracing the priest's cross. He looks at me, glowering, and I realize this goes beyond justice or law. This is personal. He wants me dead. *Me*.

'In order to free her, now she has pleaded, she would need twelve men to swear the *tylftareiður* to prove her innocence. Where are these men? You'll find none here who'll take an oath and risk their immortal souls for a witch!'

'No, you are right,' the dean's wife says.

I look to her.

She capitulates. Is that the sign they will drag me to the pyre?

Halladóra Einarsdóttir walks over to the men of the law council, the *lögrétta*, who will decide my fate. She directs her speech to the leader, the man who stands at the front, his grey beard clipped short, his expression stern, lines around his eyes marking his age. He throws a look at the witchfinder. A man beholden to follow the law, even if he does not like it.

'If the oath is sworn, Þuriður Jónsdóttir is free to go?'

There is silence.

The wind whistles its bleak tune.

'Yes, this is true,' he says.

Þorleifur Kortsson steps over. 'But you do not have these men – you have said so yourself. We will retire and announce our verdict.'

'Indeed, you're right,' Halladóra says, turning to face him. 'Men won't swear the oath, but women will.'

74

FROM BEHIND THE men, they step.

My heart swells. Blood thrums in my veins. Here they come. Every woman I have loved.

My mother leads them to me. She walks across the grass, her head high, wearing her best skirt and blouse. Her hair is contained in her decorated cap. It shines in the damp haze of sunlight that streams through the clouds like fingers reaching from heaven. Beside her, Birta, whose eyes are fierce. Alongside her a woman I recognize from the spit, a fisherman's wife, her grey hair, lined face, neck held high. There is Ólina and her daughters, Kristín and Kaðlin, who are of age; my friends Anna and Freyja. There is Þóra Einarsdóttir, who scowls back at the crowd, walking with a stoop, her gnarled hand gripping a walking stick. There is Rannveig, who holds something in her hand. I squint until she is close enough to make out what it is: the loop of her hair, tied and left under my brother's pillow that I gave to her the day she stopped me to warn me. She told me to leave Kirkjuból. She grasped my hand and when she did so, I reached into my skirts with the other. I drew out the binding of her earthen-brown hair, the fragments of *sýkigras*, asphodel, with its tiny white petals that bound my brother and Rannveig together. We passed a look of sadness, of grief, of the understanding that is shared between women. Then we parted – and I soon discovered the wisdom of her warning.

She stands in front of me with the others. There are eleven women in total. I count them even as tears blur my vision. Not enough.

Together, we fought, but we have lost.

The priest and the witchfinder step over, their faces alight with triumph.

We need another, but there is no one else. There are no other woman here – except me – and I do not count.

This is the end of hope, that fleeting promise of freedom, of life.

It is Síra Jón Magnússon who announces the last arrival.

'Þorkatla?'

My eyes, cast down to my cold feet, rush upwards.

'What are you doing here?'

Another witness to speak for them, I assume. This time, my heart settles deep inside me. Terror comes now in waves. It is not death I fear. It is pain.

Þorkatla Bjarnadóttir walks towards us.

'Husband. I'm here to speak for Þuriður. I can't let you do this. This has to stop. It has to stop now.'

Síra Jón Magnússon's sallow face blanches white. He draws back his hair from his face. Disbelief and anger flit across his features.

'This is . . . This is . . . unconscionable! How dare you do this?' he says as if there is no one else here, as if he has forgotten that the assembly hears every word.

'Because it is right,' Þorkatla replies, her voice firm.

'We are twelve women together, and we are here to swear the *tylftareiður*,' the Dean of Holt's wife says to all present. There is a general look about the lawmen as if they have, collectively, been struck by thunder.

'But you're not men!' the priest shouts.

'We are aware of it,' Halladóra Einarsdóttir says. Around us there are snorts of amusement.

'Nowhere is it writ that women cannot swear the oath of innocence,' she continues, 'so we are here, to swear to all assembled, that Þuriður Jónsdóttir is not guilty of the crimes she is accused of.'

Sýslumaður Magnús Sigurdsson, who until now has been lurking behind the lawmen, steps forward.

'On whose authority?' he says.

'On our own,' Halladóra replies.

Up until this moment, the witchfinder has been as sure of his mission as if he is an apostle. He has considered himself a vessel of the Lord, an avenging missionary of the Old Testament with its brimstone, fire and dire warnings – though discharged in the name of Þorleifur Kortsson. He is an upholder of the one true God. Akin to a prophet, in his eyes. He has made it his personal mission to hunt witches and sorcerers, to eradicate those who are blemishes upon this land. He will not stop. He will use every wile or tool at his disposal for this one true purpose. Yet here is discord. Rebellion. An unfamiliar sensation assails him.

'Women?' Þorleifur hisses. 'Women swear the oath? It has never been done!'

The dean's wife appears to ignore him, addresses herself to the head lawman instead. An insult to the witchfinder. He finds he scrabbles for a reply, a situation to which he is also unused.

'It may never have been done before, but, as far as I am aware, and it is my husband I have to thank for this information, learned and wise in these matters as he is, there exists nothing in *Jónsbók* to say it cannot be sworn by a woman.'

The official is gaping, his mouth half open.

The witchfinder stands aghast. Surely his mission cannot unravel because of the women upon whom he has waged holy war. This is his legacy. This is how his name will be remembered for centuries to come. This is how he will win favour with the Danish king, favour that will translate into land and property and power.

How can this be? His mind races. His throat tightens. For the briefest moment, he understands how difficult it is to use vocal chords silenced by another. Before he can respond, the lawman speaks in a bluster:

'We will convene. We have much to discuss as men of . . . of law . . .We must check *Jónsbók* before we can agree whether these women can be oath-swearers. Keep the prisoner away from them. Take her back to the gaol.'

The witchfinder watches as Þuriður Jónsdóttir is led away, throwing him a look of triumph. She is shoved, more roughly than before, along the track back into the darkness, but this affords him only the smallest pleasure.

'We will find a way to convict her,' the witchfinder commands as the men retreat to talk in shocked, hushed whispers. The books of law are brought out, the *Hauksbók*, containing the sagas, the *Landslagabók*, containing the laws of the land. The law speaker is consulted. Heads and beards scratched. Sheaves of parchment rustle as they are carried by stern-looking men who shake their heads. The women stand, resolute.

'We *will* find a way,' the witchfinder says, his confidence returning now the witch is locked away.

'This rebellion must be part of her witchery,' he muses, imagining imps nipping at his heels as he strides over to gather, to talk, to scheme. The priest joins him, but not before further remonstrations with his wife, who appears un-humbled despite her shameful protest. Sýslumaður Magnús Sigurdsson is there too, his fur-lined jacket making his stomach protrude with even more prominence.

They are men of law, of reason, of power wielded for the good of their nation. Their cause is just, Þorleifur reflects as he watches officials and their assistants pore over the books, justice that is scribed by men, created by men, delivered by men. That, at least, is a comfort.

75

THE RAVEN SETTLES onto its perch on top of the makeshift gaol.

It ruffles its feathers, quivering in the soft summer air. All around are people, and beyond them mountains, plains, lakes and streams, teeming with life.

A sense beyond knowing keeps it here. It is bound, waiting, surveying the scene: the shape of darkness made flesh.

It calls to the river, to the fjord and ocean. It tells of the flight made by its kind, gathering stories and visions for Óðinn, the one-eyed, all-seeing father of the Norse gods. This bird is a shaman. A wandering spirit. A ghoul of the air.

It settles down. It waits. It knows there is not long to go.

76

IT MAY HAVE been minutes. It may have been hours or days.

When, finally, I am called, I wonder if these are the last steps I will take on this earth.

I do not fear death. I have seen so much of it: babies twisted in the womb, new mothers dying, their pale faces contorted, sheets soaked in their blood. I have seen death and the road to it, and it is the latter I fear most. The suffering.

They are waiting for me, but I only see my family and friends. They stand in the middle of the circle, together, unified. An army of women. They look undefeatable to my wretched, gaol-sore eyes. I am about to find out if that is an illusion, where hope turns sour as the burning fires roar. It is then I spot him. Red-gold hair. Soft eyes. The *solidity* of him that calms me inexplicably. Ólafur. He meets my gaze and smiles. There is a rushing sensation to my heart, a strange quality to the air. I blink and feel tears gather. My heart pumps and pumps.

My friends came and showed me what it is to be loved. In the moments I have left in life, I try to cherish this with every breath, life at its end.

The head lawman steps forward. By now, the tension in the assembly has risen.

'Are you innocent of these crimes?' he says to me.

I feel my stomach tighten.

'Yes, I . . . I am.'

My mother gasps.

My friends Anna and Freyja look at me with wide eyes. I have spoken. I have reclaimed my voice, though it is too late. They are all too late.

'Give her the Bible,' the lawman orders.

'She cannot swear on it! She is a witch and befouls all that is holy!' The priest steps forward but his wife, Þorkatla, takes his arm. Catches him.

A large leather tome is held in front of me.

I place my hand upon it. What care I for their god or mine? They are all tricksters, watching our feeble games, our envy and greed from above, laughing as they do so.

'By Almighty . . . God. I . . . swear . . . I . . . am . . . innocent.'

The words grate against my tongue, forming just enough. My throat is already dry, scraped by words expressed.

The leader turns to those assembled. 'She has sworn her *eiðstafur*, her oath, in front of all present.'

The witchfinder stares at me as if he would rip at my flesh with his teeth. Whatever is about to be said is done without his agreement.

The leader pauses. Clears his throat.

'The women shall be permitted to swear the *tylftareiður*. The law of Iceland is unclear on this matter. Until we find declarations that state they cannot do it, we must assume they can.'

There is a great noise from the crowd. It seems some would still see me burn.

My mother steps forward first.

She places her hand upon the Bible held by the priest, who turns his head away, his mouth twisted into a bitter line, as if he would rather perish than offer the holy book to women such as us.

My mother's voice rings out.

'I swear that Þuriður Jónsdóttir has not by word or deed, by magic or sorcery, inflicted, or had others inflict, the pains and torments upon the aforementioned Síra Jón Magnússon.' She breaks off, stares directly at my persecutor who stands so close. 'This I know to be true, so help me God.'

She turns. Looks at me, ice-blue eyes framed by pale lashes as if a reflection in a pool of still water.

Anna steps forward next.

Once she has sworn the oath she comes over and, with my mother, they stand beside me.

Each, in turn, steps forward. Each woman repeats the oath, swearing my innocence in all charges, leaving none out.

I watch, spellbound, as they finish and come to me.

Our sisterhood swells.

There are exclamations from the men assembled, but none tries to stop them.

When they have finished, there is a charge to the skies, as if thunder and rain will follow. I feel the vibration of it on my skin as if brushed by a feathered wing. I feel the beat of my pulse, and I begin to shake again. My breathing is short and quick. I feel a hand slide into mine, and I do not mind the pain of the sores. Anna takes one hand. Freyja the other. Each stands the other side of me. Ólina and the others behind. We are formed together, a single entity: lungs breathing, hearts beating, souls joining, coalescing, forging a new way, a new time.

The men look to each other. None seems to know what to say.

Síra Jón Magnússon explodes.

'This is unlawful! It is a sin against me and against God! She is a proven sorceress and I demand this trial be stopped, the verdict spoken. She has cast a spell against you all!'

I do not need to look at the witchfinder's face to know he agrees.

'She is a witch. I demand justice! I demand she is burned, and her ashes destroyed to end her sorcery!'

The leader of the *lögrétta* raises a hand to silence him.

Anna and Freyja grip my hands tighter.

'The law must stand. There will be no burning today.'

The witchfinder strides out of the circle.

I watch him go.

There are cries and screams, but women's voices this time. They soar to the heavens, filled with relief and joy and the long-felt residue of fear.

'The oath has been sworn and witnessed by the assembly. Þuriður Jónsdóttir, you are found not guilty of the charges of witchcraft and sorcery,' the leader of the lawmen ends.

'You are wrong! You are all wrong! May the Lord Himself judge you all for what you have done! The witch is laughing at you all!' The priest stands, hands aloft as if in the pulpit. Many nod, but they already drift away. There are other matters to which to attend. Other business to oversee. This will form part of the stories they tell over their campfires tonight, but that is all: the witch who fought back. The sorceress who was freed.

Exhaustion, as deep as the sea, fills me to the brim. I am full. I am complete. I am delivered by these women, and I am free.

My head spins. I could crumple like unwashed linen into a basket, but I am held. The fetters are unlocked. I make a cry and I feel warm arms around me. My tears wet my mother's cap as she holds me, then Anna's, then Freyja's.

'You spoke,' my mother says.

'Yes, I spoke.'

'And you won, Þuriður! I can hardly believe it!' Freyja says, her tawny eyes upon mine.

'Yes,' I reply. 'I won.'

The words are strange in my mouth, but they are good words, words of hope and future and life.

The priest shouts after us as we walk, slowly, each step feeling lighter and lighter as we go, back to the horses on which the women and Ólafur arrived. Margrét has shuffled away. Only Þorkatla remains in the centre. I glance back to see she has gone to her husband's side, is now walking him out of the assembly. She holds him as if she is holding a man with nothing left, and perhaps that is true.

77

Þorkatla Bjarnadóttir's husband rages until long into the night.

Even when the women have long since departed on horses borrowed from the Dean of Holt's stables, Síra Jón Magnússon froths and gesticulates, tears at the worn ruff round his neck, brandishes his Bible. Þorkatla waits, as any obedient wife must do, until the zenith of his anger is spent. She wonders if he will desert her, discard her, but says little, waiting for the storm of his feelings to pass as she clutches her small wooden cross. Rannveig left with the others, but before she departed, she touched her mother's arm, kissed her cheek. The first embrace for many months. It gave Þorkatla the strength to stay and face whatever came next.

'You betrayed me. You betrayed God,' he says at last, the heat of his temper gone, replaced by sullen accusation. 'Do you say nothing to this?'

'I am sorry,' she says, thumb rubbing the edge of the neckpiece, eyes to the floor.

'You are sorry. My wife is sorry!' The priest looks around as if they are surrounded by onlookers, but most are huddled elsewhere around campfires as the evening chill bites, cooking meat that sizzles and chars.

'You realize without your oath I would have vanquished Þuriður Jónsdóttir, a servant of the devil, a woman who killed your child—'

'*Our* child,' Þorkatla interjects. 'Our boy, Snorri, died, Jón. Can you not say his name?'

She waits for her husband to respond, but he continues to seethe, nose flaring.

'I believe our son has gone to God as he was too good to walk on this heathen earth. I do not know if the girl was to blame. She did not look like a powerful sorceress by the time the law and the witchfinder had finished with her.'

The priest stares at his wife as if seeing her for the first time. In the weeks following the stillbirth, he had avoided her as if she was an untended flame or a boiling pan that could scald him. He asked about her health. He instructed the witched servant Margrét to bring possets and blankets, but he retreated even further into himself. She knew it was grief, but even so. The betrayal – according to Þorkatla Bjarnadóttir – was wholly his. He stepped away from her when she needed his love the most, and, in doing so, he released her from that dutiful obligation by which every woman must abide. She saw him for the first time as a man flawed, who could not stand by her except as a self-directed conduit of a faith that had been tested sorely.

When she spied Rannveig running to speak to Þuriður that day the girl fled, she guessed it was to warn her. She saw something change hands, a token given to her daughter. She did not ask. It was enough to understand that her daughter would lie to her or refuse to answer, thus deepening their feud. She felt that knowledge like a hot poker in her breast. It pierced her.

Later, she searched for it, knowing she was betraying yet another part of their fragile trust, but unable to stop herself. Finally, she found it under Rannveig's pillow in the bed that had once belonged to the sorcerer's apprentice. Just a year ago, she would have had her daughter whipped for attempting to thwart her stepfather's campaign, for her love of this forbidden boy. The curl of brown hair, the same colour as her own, trembled in her grasp. She placed it back, her heart full, her feelings twisted and jarring. They were all liars: her daughter, her husband, herself. How, then, could she condemn her? Rannveig's secret lies with her still. She has taken it to God, trusting it will be used better by Him that way.

It was Anna who came to her, told her of the plan to travel to Þingvellir for the trial. A bold move. An unexpected request to join them. Without her, they could not swear the oath of innocence. At first, she was seized with a desire to refuse. It would serve them all right if she turned them down just when they needed her, but something had changed. Þorkatla could not find the spite she had once felt, buried as it was, underneath the purity of her love for the baby taken from her. Anna held her hand, and she let her do it. She begged her to go. Even though she shook her head, she knew she would join them. It surprised the friends of the witch, but no more so than her. Her husband had gone, left her alone yet again. She discovered she had a part to play, however small, in the unfolding of this business. It turned out it wasn't so small. She saved a life, and surely that should please God if not her husband.

Even as they rode the many days and nights, sore in the saddle, the priest's wife refused to believe she would betray her husband and do it publicly. But the sight of Þuriður Jónsdóttir and the new closeness to her daughter that she felt, riding alongside Rannveig, swayed her. She was a woman too. What was to stop them taking any of them, her and her daughter included, and using them this way?

*

Her husband is glaring at her, waiting for her to speak, when she pulls up her gaze. Þorkatla wonders what will happen now. The long ride back to Kirkjuból. The recommencement of their life together. The Masses, the sermons, the sleepless nights. It is enough to know she played her part in saving a woman's life. She has no intention of mixing with the others, of fraternizing with those she once considered enemies. She is resigned to her life. All is waiting. Waiting to join her son in heaven.

78

THE UNSEEN HAND pulls at the tangles of my hair.

Thick fingers jerk me back into the churning, restless water. Air seems to vanish from my lungs. I struggle against this tug again and again, as I have every time before this. This time, my scream does not stop. It does not disappear in a choking inhalation of air and water, mud and froth. It fills my chest, my lungs, my mouth and then it pours out: unstoppable, free.

I take a breath, and I shout again.

I can feel the hot air from deep inside me escaping with the noise. Too soon, the hand pushes down on me again. The panic rears, but this time it does not overwhelm me. I struggle against the strength of this attack, this drowning, and find I grip the rough, work-thick hand and dig my nails deep into it.

My limbs, deadened with cold, kick back. They wrestle and fight, claw and rip at whatever it is that pushes me back under.

My hair, in sodden stained clumps, comes free. I turn and I shove back, and I realize I can breathe.

My head lifts above the water, and somehow, somehow, I know I have survived. My eyes open. This is my familiar bed in my mother's croft. Sunlight washes the chamber, throwing shadows against grain-addled beams. A pitcher of water sits on a small round table. My things unpacked hastily after the journey, strewn over the floor, are being picked up and folded by the elder of my sisters. The last of the drowning dreams fades, and so I smile. I am alive.

79

THE REPLY TO my letter comes on a squally late-summer day.

My stepfather, Leif, hands the parchment to me. This time, he does not read it first.

'Thank you,' I say, reaching for the rolled-up missive.

I read it.

I put it down.

My stepfather waits.

'I wrote to Gissur Sveinson, the . . . the Dean of Holt, before they took me.' I am still learning how to speak again. 'I complained of the . . . the . . . attacks by Síra Jón Magnússon upon me. I said I . . . I . . . could not stand silent and let him continue his pursuit of me, and so I wrote . . . saying that, if his accusations were to be judged true, death would be my . . . my lot.

'I said I want . . . redress . . . for the false suspicions laid upon me, that resulted in me being . . . thrown from my home, from . . . from the place I was born, and cast out from my . . . my life in Kirkjuból . . .'

Leif leans forward in his chair.

'I said it should . . . should not be possible for someone to . . . accuse an innocent person, and . . . and escape without penalty! I . . . I said I want him to face justice.'

My mother walks into the *baðstofa*. She is carrying a basket of plants plucked before the autumn storms come. Behind her comes Hrafn, who wipes his nose using his sleeve and scampers over to me. I scoop him up onto my lap with one arm, the other holds this letter, the response from the dean.

'What's this?' my mother says. She stands next to her husband, the late-summer light rendering her hair silvery white. She unties her cap, letting her hair tumble freely down her back. She wears a blouse I have embellished with leaves and delicate petals, with the herb thyme. On my skirt is a blueish faded thistle, embroidered the winter before I was taken.

'Þuriður has received a reply from Gissur Sveinson,' my stepfather says, taking my mother's hand after she places the basket on the table. 'She wrote before she was arrested, demanding that Síra Jón be held accountable for his campaign against her.'

My mother's eyebrows, such that they are, so pale and white, shoot upwards.

'You did what?'

I nod.

'The dean has . . . replied,' I say. I scan the words. A feeling rises within me. It is a yearning I have not allowed myself to feel, a calling for my home, a reaching for something that has been denied me. It overcomes me now. I feel a choking sensation in my throat.

'What does he say?' Leif says, leaning forward, yet still.

I hold the parchment. My hand shakes only a little.

'He says I may bring a charge against the priest.' My voice is clear this time. I hear its power, its dominion over this. I feel the scales tip the other way, the weighted side dropping towards me, like counting coin for trading.

'I am taking Síra Jón Magnússon to court.'

80

November 1658

SÍRA JÓN MAGNÚSSON stares back at me as if he cannot believe what is taking place.

We stand either side of the assembly, which convenes this time in Mosvellir, the local court. Men wearing black stand around, each no doubt curious to see this strange event: a woman once declared a witch suing her accuser. If my gaze was made of fire, this priest would be scorched to blackness. All the rage, the fury, the injustice of the past two years surges through me as I prepare to speak.

'This priest persecuted me for two years. He burned my father and my brother. He drove me from my home and took all the livestock due to me from my father's estate. He rendered me outcast from my community and tainted all those who knew me with the same accusations,' I say, my words ringing out into the bleak chill of this November day.

'This cannot go on! I have been found innocent. Twelve women travelled to Þingvellir, a long and difficult journey, to swear my innocence on the Holy Bible. The law had no choice but to acquit me.

'Síra Jón Magnússon's allegations were shown to be false, yet it is still true that the priest has all but destroyed my life. He nearly had me burned. He has made unfounded allegations against the women of Kirkjuból, who have done nothing wrong except support me, and we will stand it no longer! I will not be silent. The time has come for women to speak out, to rise against terror such as the priest has inflicted upon me and mine. Who will he point the finger at next? Who else will suffer the same fate at his hand? My voice is my own, and I use it to condemn him!'

I rejoice in the sound of me. The words that fly from my mouth with ease. The clarity of them, the direction and flow of them. They have power. They are changing the course of my fate. I can feel their presence as if they too are bystanders, watching this most unusual case unfold.

I stand. My head high, my voice clear. I stand, my friends and family beside me.

They can't burn us all.

They will not burn us all.

'I demand the court gives me back what is rightfully mine: my croft and my animals. I am fighting for what was taken from me by a man determined to blame me for the afflictions he suffers. Would anyone here deny me what is mine? Would anyone here declare the verdict of the Alþingi, our supreme national parliament, wrong or mistaken? No!

'I am proved innocent of witchcraft. I counter his charges. I say he should be punished for falsely declaring me a sorceress. His accusations were baseless. I say he should be removed from *my* home, from *my* farm, and return to *his* church to ask God for forgiveness!'

The dean, a thoughtful man, wearing a neat cap, a long cloak with a wool collar, a short white beard and eyes that veer somewhere between green and grey, holds up his arms to quell the noise as, all about, people talk and whisper.

'I was urged to take your case by my esteemed and noble wife, and I have heard your arguments, Þuriður Jónsdóttir. You have felt wronged on many counts over the past two years. You wrote to me a year ago to state your case and demand the priest be punished. You have since endured months in the most wretched state, in gaol, alone, cold, tortured and then tried as a witch. You were exonerated at the hearing in Þingvellir. The *tylftareiður* was sworn and you were declared innocent of the charges laid before you.'

He walks around. Comes to face Síra Jón Magnússon. His wife stands beside him. She refuses to meet my gaze. I have wanted to thank her, but the old divide is back. Her actions that day in Þingvellir are now just a memory; a temporary truce has ended.

The priest is hunched, thin. His hand shakes when he raises it. He looks at once puzzled and afraid. His eyes, when they meet mine, have lost much of their intensity, their fierce stare.

'I deny Þuriður Jónsdóttir's claims. I deny her,' he says, his voice flat.

Where is the fire of retribution? Where is the rage and the fury he vented at the assembly only five months ago? He is a man lost, a man changed, a man defeated.

'Is that all you will say? Do you still claim this woman is not innocent?' Gissur Sveinson says.

Síra Jón nods and it is as if all that is left are the ashes of his convictions.

'The court has been convened to hear the case of Þuriður Jónsdóttir against her accuser, Síra Jón Magnússon. I can see no satisfaction from the defendant as to the correctness of the result of the case. By the swearing of the oath, the parliament saw fit to pronounce this woman innocent, and not the source of the torments Síra Jón has suffered. Yet still, against their judgement, he thinks otherwise.'

My heart skips. My pulse quickens.

Was I right to fight back when no others have done so before me?

Will they punish me for my temerity, for being a woman who will be silent no longer?

The wind blows cold, and so I pull my cloak around me. I have finer things now. My stepfather is a generous man, and my mother likes to see me shod in good leather boots and a thick cloak. I am wearing a silk cap, already embroidered. *Þistill*. Thistle, their blue spikes and curling leaves in tiny stitches as if growing along the seam.

The Dean of Holt turns to me.

'This woman has been wronged. Her complaint holds. I pronounce that I see no reason why she should not return to her farmhouse in Kirkjuból. The crimes of her father and brother should never have been held against her. Her croft should never have been forfeited. The matter is now ended. The complainant's right to her family home is reinstated by the laws of this district. However, these laws do not extend to Kirkjuból, except as a moral duty. This court demands Síra Jón Magnússon leave the farm within seven days as an act of righteousness. May it sit on the conscience of those here present and may they be seen to do the right thing as a result of this session. In the absence of Þorleifur Kortsson, who is attending to other matters in the north of Iceland, and Sýslumaður Magnús Sigurdsson, who in any case has no jurisdiction here, either, I pronounce this case closed. Judgment is delivered.'

There is gasping.

There is clapping behind me where my friends and my family stand.

The priest looks confused. He steps away, led by his wife. For the briefest moment, our eyes meet: two women from two communities, forced together by circumstance. She nods and in that small gesture I understand they will leave, return to the spit, give me back my home.

There are some shakings of heads from some of the men, but I see none of it. I am soaring. I feel I have taken flight, looking down upon the gathering from a great height, wings outstretched.

It is over.

81

THE RAVEN LEAVES its branch.

It picks up a current of air, strong and swift, and rises, wings aloft, spanning the void into which it soars. Below, small shapes, people – women and men – leaving the flat valley plain where so many had gathered. The dispersing mass, the bone-white hair that flows down the young woman's back, the women who huddle together laughing and crying, are as nothing to the bird. The scene below is no different to the sound of gushing stream water or the dance of wind through long grass. It cares not for the trials and troubles of people. Instead, it spies a small brown mouse hiding by a rock. It sees the tail of a rat that moves away quickly into a small hole in the tuft of moss, too fast for the bird. It flaps, moving each great weighted wing up and down in awkward symphony, and rises higher, to look further. Here, it can see the ravines and valleys, the mountains peppered with early snow. It spies the serpentine movement of a creature, scaly and silver-bright, as it slips out of the ocean waves and back into the sea depths.

Its shadow runs the contours of the hillocks and plains as it flies onward. Below, the woman with her distinctive translucent skin, her veins showing blue, her hair as white as the glacier-freeze, looks up. In one hand, she holds something. It is solid, indistinct, the shape of a book. If she spots the raven, it pays little attention. It has seen a nesting seabird. It changes direction, swoops towards the straggle of bush and branches, talons outstretched, hungry for its kill.

Epilogue

Summer 1660

MY FATHER AND brother stumbled over their spells from the day I was old enough to understand what it was they were doing. I watched them don the pelts of foxes and draw the sigils and runes, consulting their grimoires by candlelight. I saw them try – and fail – to cast those curses. Oh, how they failed! They butchered ravens and sea mice, winding the entrails of small animals round posts hammered into the earth. The feathered heads of birds, the gaping gills of fish, the bleached skulls of sheep, all attached to stakes, for one thing or another. How I laughed inside even as they tried and tried.

It has always been so easy for me.

I consult the wind or the sea. I watch the white-tipped waves, the circular crested motion of the ocean, the whipped briny air. I hear the terns shriek, the air change, the signs that are all around, yet my father and brother were oblivious to them all. Was it magic I cast when I conjured up the storm as a child or was it fate that so small a boat foundered, even as my father carved signs, thinking he had the power to deal death at sea to his enemy?

Many times have I wished something into being. A baby breeched comes out alive, though my wishing could not save its mother. Others born healthy and strong, though not always. A stillborn child in a house I cursed. Is this magic? Even now, I cannot be sure.

What is sure is that I took my father's grimoire, the one I kept back when the priest seized my father's possessions. I read it by candlelight, learning each spell, each charm, each malignant verse by heart.

It was there I found how to use *þistill*, thistle, dried to seal its potency. I took it. I carved the sign to bring malfortune into its stalks. I whispered silent words over it the night before I was commanded to leave my home, knowing to burn it would only increase its power. I walked widdershins round the croft – once, twice, three times – to unleash this spell upon the priest and his wife. To bring unhappiness, pain, suffering to all inside the walls that were once mine. To bring them not a single day's peace while they lay in my beds, ate at my table, burned my wood in my dwelling. I left each dried stalk with its soft blue-purple head in places where their powers would be strongest: above the entrance, so the spell would enter with them every time they walked through my door; under the bed in which I knew the priest and his wife would sleep; inside the rafters, tucked into spaces in the stone walls so the very air they breathed contained my enchantments. *Þistill*: spiked, prickled, for hexing and other malefica besides.

I used my knife, the ceremonial one with a brass handle I bribed the gaoler to give back to me after it was taken from my brother when they arrested him. I carved runes and sigils into the beams, into staves: *þjófastafir*, thief staves, to injure those who had stolen from me; *óttastafur*, terror staves, to strike fear into the priest and all who lived there. I hexed my own home, making sure the skyr curdled, the hearth smoked, the livestock remained restless, the fish ruined.

Did my spells work? Who can tell? I felt the hum of their sly magic in my dreams as I visited the priest's wife, as I hovered in the croft, a spirit woman with revenge and anger in her heart. I rejoiced with the power of it. They took everything from me, and so I did the same.

Did I also unleash demons upon the priest? It is hard to say. I wished for them. I was reckless with my dreams. In them, I saw the spirits of my father and brother, and so I guided them to the croft of the priest. I knew how much Síra Jón hated and feared us. I sent black dogs to sit outside the church. I sent demons to make mischief, but surely it was just idle dreaming, reckless ill-wishing, invisible to all except the seer Randiður Ólafsdóttir, though it appears I fooled even her. Though what did she see? Was it an old woman's imaginings or did she really spy the spirits I cast in hatred and vengeance?

I called to the Dean of Holt's wife from my cell, knowing she was the only one who could help. When our eyes locked in the Danish store prison that night while in the sheriff's custody, I knew she had answered that call. I had wished her into being – and she came. My father and brother boasted of their powers, but perhaps all along it was me.

Did the women who swore the *tylftareiður* know me as a witch? A woman with knowledge all of my own? Who knows. What is more important, and has always been more important, is that we stand together against those who would crush us for who we are, for being women who dare to think for ourselves. Already, we are an indomitable sisterhood. Already, we weave magic into our fabrics, brew it into our mead. Anywhere where our menfolk do not tread, there is women's magic hidden in plain sight.

So why could I not save my kin? This question remains unanswered. I tried to dream of flight, of them turning into cawing ravens and leaping up and out of the gaol window. Maybe it was too late. I did not desire their release enough, forgotten as I was by them, ignored and abandoned after my mother left. My father could hardly bear to look upon me, so close is my resemblance to her. I believed it was grief. I know now it was injured pride. I was both a consolation and an offence. I dampened myself down: invisible, still, silent.

The day I walked away from Mosvellir, a woman of means, a woman free in her own right, I held that grimoire. It was like a talisman. I had carried it with me since leaving Kirkjuból. All that was contained within it settling under my skin, through each layer of parchment, until it lodged in my heart and became mine. I did not read the spells, I *absorbed* them. Did I damn myself along the way? I dare not give an answer as I hold my sleeping son in my arms, rocking him gently, the danger long passed.

It is enough to know my husband, Ólafur, looks at me with love-longing in his eyes. It is enough to bring a healthy child into this world, a son I call Snorri in memory of he who left a woman un-mothered, by my spells, by the fates, the gods or the cruelty of nature.

It is enough to look at the rune bowl on my shelf, its rune stones within. Now, they pulse with energy. They lie, if not expectant, then waiting.

Waiting for my son to take on the mantel of his inheritance, to step out into the world a true *seid-mann*: my legacy, my revenge and my delight.

A Short Note about Witch Trials in Iceland

BY 1683, A total of twenty-two people had been executed as witches in Iceland. Of these, there is only one confirmed case of a woman being burned, Þuríður Ólafsdóttir. She was burned with her son, Jón Helgason, in the Westfjords in 1678.

In 1654 in Trékyllisvík, three men were burned for sorcery: Þórður Guðbrandsson, Egill Bjarnason and Grímur Jónsson. The case was brought by Þorleifur Kortsson, who brought several other witch trials to the national parliament in the years following, resulting in the death by burning of men at Þingvellir.

The vast majority of those accused, and convicted, were men, in stark contrast to the witch trials that swept across Western Europe alongside the Reformation. Some estimates suggest up to 60,000 women were executed as witches during this period in Europe.

Author's Note

THIS BOOK IS based on the Kirkjuból Affair, an infamous witch trial that took place in the Westfjords of Iceland in 1656. While some of the characters are based on actual historical figures, their portrayals are fictitious, as are many of the events that surround them. There is no offence intended to any living descendant of any of the characters.

I have drawn on letters, documents and extracts from trial procedures, taking those parts that serve the narrative. The place names are all true to life. Eyri, the spit of land arching into the Djup, is now encompassed by the modern town of Ísafjörður, while the farmstead known as Kirkjuból, situated south of the harbour, is no longer in existence. Icelandic folk tales and legends are rich and numerous. I have borrowed some and created my own, taking the appearance of elves, *álfar*, from Snorri Sturluson's chapter 'Gylfaginning' in *Edda* (1995), where he states, 'The light elves are fairer than the sun to see, and the dark elves blacker than pitch.' I have bestowed upon the young woman at the heart of this story, Þuriður Jónsdóttir, this description. Her muteness is an invention of mine, a way of revealing the impact of her backstory and her fight for freedom, literally finding her voice in a time when women were denied one.

I have changed characters' names to mitigate the confusion of similar and repeating names for different people in the text. I discovered during this part of the process that Þorkatla Bjarnadóttir's daughter's full name was Rannveig Snorradóttir, her father, the former priest, was named Snorri Hákonarson, hence the name chosen for the son born to the priest and his wife. Though, in reality, Snorri lived and was thrown out of the priesthood due to fathering an illegitimate child, I have chosen to give a living legacy of this story to my protagonist. Indeed, there is evidence to show that Þuriður Jónsdóttir was recorded as alive in the 1703 census. Síra Jón Magnússon died in 1696 after resigning his parish in 1689.

What is extraordinary about this period in Icelandic history is that the instigator of the Kirkjuból trials, a Lutheran pastor, Síra Jón Magnússon, wrote a diatribe against the sorcerers he persecuted. *Píslarsaga* (Passion Story/And Though This World with Devils Filled: A Story of Sufferings) charts the pastor's torments as he suffered what he believed to be demonic attacks by *seid-menn* Jón Jónsson the Elder and Younger. He later accused the daughter/sister Þuriður of the same crimes.

I am greatly indebted to so many authors, researchers and academics who have examined texts from this tumultuous period, and none more so than Michael Fell, who translated *Píslarsaga* by Jón Magnússon. I owe thanks to academic, politician and writer Ólína Þorvarðardóttir for her work *Brennuöldin* (the Burning Times), and to Stephen Flowers' work *The Galdrabók: An Icelandic Book of Magic*.

When a character like Þuriður forms herself on the page, I have learned not to question but to let her speak for herself in her actions and desires. Throughout this book, I asked myself what might happen if a witch fought back. I hope her story is an answer to that central question, and to the enduring necessity of giving forgotten women a voice.

Set against sweeping religious and social change, this is a story of a woman who stands up to the patriarchal forces that range against her: Church, community, state. I cannot help but acknowledge that I write this in strange times. Women's rights are eroded and suppressed throughout the world. Þuriður's fight is becoming our own. This is a story of female empowerment in an age of oppression and brutality, of a woman holding her own, told against the achingly beautiful and harsh wilderness of seventeenth-century Iceland. How much of her story will become ours in the years to come?

Glossary

Gods, Goddesses, Legends and Myths

Ægir the personification of the sea in Norse mythology

Flóki Hrafna-Flóki Vilgerðarsson was a Norwegian written about in the Landnámabók manuscript, who sailed north to Iceland in 868

Huginn Raven messenger for the Norse god Óðinn

Muninn Raven messenger for the Norse god Óðinn

Norns the three goddesses, Urðr, Verðandi and Skuld, who spin the threads of fate at the base of Yggdrasil

Nykur the horse-like water spirit who rides the unwary to their death

Óðinn or Odin, also known as the All-Father, the Lord of the Dead and king of the Norse gods

Rán a giantess goddess associated with the darkest, deepest parts of the sea, known for pulling sailors into the ocean and drowning them

Valhöll or Valhalla, also known as the Hall of the Slain, the place where warriors live when killed in battle

Várblót the Spring sacrifice of the Old Norse calendar, now the Spring Equinox

Yggdrasil the central sacred ash tree, which connects the nine worlds in Norse mythology

Þórr or Thor, also known as the Lord of Thunder

Places

Bær near Hrútafjörður, a hamlet by 'Ram's Fjord' where witchfinder Þorleifur Kortsson resided

Bolungarvík small fishing town on the northernmost tip of the Westfjords peninsular

Breiðadalsheiði the mountain pass that leads over the mountains from Holt to Eyri

Danmörku Denmark

Drekkinggarhylur pool at Þingvellir where women were drowned for adultery, incest or infanticide at the parliament sessions

Eyrakirkja Eyri Church

Eyri meaning 'spit of land'. Modern-day Ísafjörður

Grænland Greenland

Hnífsdalur is a small village and is part of the municipality of Ísafjörður

Holt in Önundarfjörður, a fishing village in Flateyri district

Ísafjarðarsýsla Ísafjarður County

Kirkjuból largest farmstead that lay south-east of the harbour and Eyri

Mosvellir settlement near to Holt where the local court was held

Mount Hekla an active volcano believed by Icelanders to be the gateway to hell. In Icelandic *hekla* means 'cloak', possibly referring to the clouds covering the summit

Seljabrekkum killing stones. The execution site on the south side of the Djup near the (now gone) Kirkjuból farmstead

Skutulsfjörður westernmost fjord branching off the main fjord, Ísafjarðardjúp, where Eyri (now Ísafjörður) was situated

Súðavik coastal fishing town

Trékyllisvík Westfjords coastal community where three men burned as witches in 1654

Vestfirðir Westfjords

Þingvellir ancient seat of Icelandic parliament

Icelandic Vocabulary

æðigaldur madness magic

Ægishjálm Helm of Awe – a magical symbol drawn to induce terror and defeat enemies

Ægishjálm er ég ber, milli brúna mér I bear the Helm of Awe between my brows

akrlengd 'acre-long' – the length of a field of arable land

álfar elves

Alþingi Supreme National Parliament of Iceland

andskotans damn it

baðstofa originally a 'bath house' or sauna, it came to mean the main, communal room which was heated where families passed entire winters

birkilauf birch leaves

burnirót rose root

eiðstafur oath

faldbúningur Icelandic national costume

farðu til helvítis go to hell

fjallagrös mountain grass (a variety of moss)

fjölnir rune, derived from one of the names of Óðinn to create malevolent spells

fokk fuck

frétrunir, golnisþey, hagallinn blá and ***augnaþuss*** runes

galdrabækur books of magic, grimoires

galdrabók book of magic, grimoire

galdraletur magical lettering

galdrastafir magical runes or symbols

glímagaldur magic to ensure victory in wrestling

harðfiskur dried fish, usually cod or haddock

Hauksbók fourteenth-century Icelandic manuscript collated by Haukr Erlendsson, including Icelandic sagas

hrafn raven

hugrekki courage

huldufólk the hidden people, elves

hvannarfræ angelica

Jólblot Yule festivities

Jónsbók the lawbook, the law of Iceland

kembulár a wooden box without a lid used for storing carded wool

Landslagabók the book of the law of the land

ljónslappi Alpine lady's mantle, a medicinal herb

lögmenn lawmen

lögrétta the law council

maríusstakkur lady's mantle

mjöll fresh-fallen snow

mömmu mummy

Naustahvilft the troll seat

níðstöng a cursing pole

óttastafur staves to strike fear in enemies

pallur platform or raised part of the floor

sæll vertu/sæl vertu masculine and feminine forms of greeting from a visitor to their host: 'be happy', with the reply given by the host, ***komdu sæll/sæl***, meaning 'come happy'

seid-menn men of magic

siginn fiskur half-dried fish, hung for two weeks then boiled (lowered fish)

sigurskufur willow bark

síra sir or master, often used as a title for priests (reverend)

skafrenningur thick snowfall, already settled

skáld poet

skáli the huts or sheds used to house cattle or as outhouses

skjár a window screen made of an animal membrane, the amniotic sack of a sheep or cow

slátur blood sausage, made using the casing of a sheep's stomach and filled with sheep's blood, grains, fat and onions

spaðafaldur traditional Icelandic cap that arches high over the head

stafur stave

sýkigras asphodel

sýslumaður district sheriff

treyja short jacket

tylftareiður oath of innocence, sworn by twelve people

umfeðmingur vetch plants

útburður ghosts of children born out of wedlock and left in a forest or on a mountainside to die

vallhumall yarrow

vegvísir a sigil of warning

vindgapi magical rune to direct the wind

Þakka þér kærlega fyrir mig I thank you very much

þel the soft inner wool of an Icelandic sheep

þistill thistle

þjófastafir runes against thieves

þrek endurance

þumlungar inches, used to indicate smallness (thumb-sized) stature or as an insult referring to a man's penis

Traditional Icelandic Folk Song

Móðir mín í kví, kví,
Kvíddu ekki því, því;
ég skal ljá þér duluna mína,
duluna mina að dansa í,
ég skal ljá þér duluna mína,
duluna mina að dansa í . . .

Mother of mine in the pen,
You don't need to worry about it because
I will lend you my cloak,
My cloak in which to dance.
I will lend you my cloak,
My cloak in which to dance . . .

The song is a lullaby sung by the ghost of an abandoned baby. It was the practice to leave illegitimate children out in the forest to die of exposure. The ghost child sings to its mother, telling her she can borrow the child's rags to dance in.

Bibliography

Björn, A. *Icelandic Plant Magic: Folk Herbalism of the North*. Great Britain. Erebus Society, 2022

Ellison, R. C. 1993. 'The Kirkjuból Affair: A Seventeenth-Century Icelandic Witchcraft Case Analysed'. *Seventeenth Century*, 8 (2): 217–43. doi:10.1080/0268117X.1993.10555361

Ellison, R. C. 'A Prophet Without Honour: The Brief Career of Erlendur Ormsson'. *Saga Book*, XXIV, Part 5, 1994–1997, pp. 293–310

Flowers, S. E. *The Galdrabók: An Icelandic Book of Magic*. Second Revised Edition. Texas: Rûna-Raven Press, 2005. Citation from this edition reproduced on p. 289.

Gibson, M. *Witchcraft: A History in 13 Trials*. London: Simon & Schuster UK, 2023

Gunnlaugsson, H. (director). *Myrkrahöfðinginn*. [Film]. Iceland: Icelandic Film Corporation, 1999

His Majestie King James I of England, *Daemonologie*, 1597. London: Aziloth Books, 2012

Hreinsson, V. (ed.). *Egil's Saga*: 'The Complete Sagas of Icelanders'. Vols I–V. Edited by Vidar Hreinsson, Robert Cook, Terry Gunnell, Keneva Kunz and Bernard Scudder. Translation, Leifur Eiríksson Publishing, 1997

Jónasson, B. *A Little Book About the Runes*. London: Gudrun Publishing Ltd, 2001

Jónsson, M. *Galdrar og siðferði í Strandasýslu á síðari hluta 17. Aldar*. Hólmavík: Strandagaldur, 2008

Jónsson, M. *Galdrar og guðlast á* 17. Öld: Sögufélagið, 2021

Jónsson, M. *A Witchfinder's Archive in 17th-century Iceland*. Hufnagel, S., Ólaffsson, D., Sigurðardóttir, Þ. (eds.). *Paper Stories – Paper and Book History in Early Modern Europe*. Berlin/Boston: De Gruyter, 2023

Kent, H. *Burial Rites*. London: Pan Macmillan, 2013

Krämer, H. *Malleus Maleficarum* (Hammer of Witches). Translated by P. G. Maxwell-Stuart. Manchester: Manchester University Press, 2007

Krämer, H. *Malleus Maleficarum – The Hammer of Witches*. London: DigiCat Publishing, 2022

Krämer, H. *The Hammer of Witches: A Complete Translation of the Malleus Malleficarum*. Translated by C. S. Mackay. Cambridge: Cambridge University Press, 2009/2012

Krämer, H. *The Hammer of Witches: Malleus Maleficarum*. Translated by Montague Summers. e-artnow, 2017. Citations from this edition reproduced on pp.198 and 288.

Levack, B. P. *Witchcraft in Continental Europe*. New York: Taylor & Francis, 2001

Magnússon, J. *Píslarsaga* (*Passion Story/And Though This World with Devils Filled: A Story of Sufferings*). Translated by Michael Fell. New York: Peter Lang Publishing, 2007

Rafnsson, M. *Angurgapi: The Witch Hunts in Iceland*. Hólmavík: Strandagaldur, 2002

Rafnsson, M. *Rún*. Museum of Icelandic Sorcery & Witchcraft, 2014. A facsimile of a grimoire.

Rafnsson, M. *The Exhibition of Sorcery and Witchcraft*. Hólmavík: Strandagaldur, ongoing

Rafnsson, M. *Tvær galdraskræður: Two Icelandic Books of Magic*. Hólmavík: Strandagaldur, 2021

Richardson, N. 2014. 'Völuspá: The Seeress's Prophecy'. The Junket, 6 January. Available at: https://thejunket.org/2014/01/archive/voluspa-the-seeresss-prophecy/ Citations from this edition reproduced on pp. 3, 121, 197, 287.

Róbertsdóttir, A. R. *Icelandic Herbs and Their Medicinal Uses*. Translated from the Icelandic by S. Smith. Berkley, California: North Atlantic Books, 2013/2016

Sigmundsdóttir, A. *Icelandic Folk Legends: Tales of Apparitions, Outlaws and Things Unseen*. Reykjavík: Little Books Publishing, 2019

Sigmundsdóttir, A. *The Little Book of the Icelanders in the Old Days*. Reykjavík: Little Books Publishing, 2014

Sigurðsson, A. *Museum of Hidden Beings: Mythological Beings of Icelandic Folk Tales*. Reykjavík: Salka, 2016

Sturluson, S. *Edda*. Translated and edited by A. Faulkes. London: J. M. Dent, 1995

Thorsson, O., Scudder, B. (eds.). *The Sagas of Icelanders*. London: Penguin Books Ltd, 2005

Zarrillo, D. *The Icelandic Witch Craze of the Seventeenth Century*. The College of New Jersey, 2018

Þorvarðardóttir, Ó. *Brennuöldin, Galdur og galdratrú í málskjölum og munnmælum*. Reykjavík: Háskólaútgáfan, 2000

Þorvarðardóttir, Ó. *Merkingarheimur og skynjun, Sekt og sakleysi í Píslarsögu Síra Jóns Magnússonar, Tímarit Máls og menningar*, 4.92, pp. 37–72. timarit.is

Þorvarðardóttir, Ó. *Visindavefurinn: Er vitao hvada sjúkdómur hrjdi Jón pumlung?* visindavefur.is/The Science Web. 2014

The Museum of Icelandic Sorcery and Witchcraft located in Hólmavík is an extensive source of magical and witchcraft history. The museum has an online log of primary sources of those executed during the witch craze and those involved in the trials: www. http://holmavik.is/galdrasyning/executed.php

Bible quotes are taken from the King James Bible.

Acknowledgements

As an eleven-year-old, I sneaked Jean Plaidy books from the library, reading way past my bedtime, absorbed in the shimmering worlds of the past: poisoner queens, thwarted loves and powerful women. I wish that girl who longed to write those books could have known that one day I'd be thanking all the incredible, talented people who have supported the genesis of this, my second novel.

I am indebted to so many, but none more so than my agent, Jane Graham Maw. This book would not have been written without your absolute conviction in me as a writer. Thank you for nurturing my craft as a novelist, for encouraging me to find my voice writing fiction. It was you who inspired me to apply for the Faber Academy Writing a Novel course, and, in doing so, pushed me into doing what I have always dreamed of: writing historical fiction.

Thank you to my dream editorial team at Transworld, Olamide Olatunji-Bello and Imogen Nelson. You made this a better novel and pushed me further than I ever expected or imagined. I am truly honoured to have worked with you to create the magic that underlies this novel. You both shaped this into something I am deeply proud to have written. I extend this gratitude to everyone at Transworld, Penguin Random House, to Oliver Martin, Melissa Kelly, to all in the rights, sales and design teams who have championed this book. I have been privileged to work with such a dedicated, passionate team.

In researching *They Can't Burn Us All*, I have spent time in Iceland, and owe a debt of thanks to many people who kindly and enthusiastically translated and signposted documents, books, experts, archivists and researchers. They include Jóna Símonía Bjarnadóttir, Director of the Westfjords Heritage Museum in Isafjörður, and Herbert Snorrason and Anna Björg, also at the Westfjords Heritage Museum. I am grateful to Jón Jónsson – author, folklorist and founder of the Museum of Icelandic Sorcery and Witchcraft in Hólmavik – for giving me your time translating and discussing Icelandic sorcery. I am hugely grateful to the CEO of the museum, Anna Björg Þórarinsdóttir, for your generosity in making introductions and welcoming me so openly into this field of research. Thanks also to author, academic and politician Ólína Þorvarðardóttirfor so generously offering your published works as an expert on the Kirkjuból Affair, and to Kristinn Valdimarsson at the National State Archives of Iceland, and Hrund Gunnsteinsdóttir, author of *InnSæi*. I want to send particular thanks to Ester Bíbí Ásgeirsdóttir of Kvikmyndasafn Islands, the National Film Archive of Iceland, for kindly allowing me access to the film *Myrkrahöfðinginn* by Hrafn Gunnlaugsson, and to Hrafn's son Aron for so graciously gifting several of Hrafn's iconic films when I knocked on the door of the director's surreal art house in Reykjavík! Thank you to Norse mythology expert and author Andreas Kornvall, who shared extensive knowledge of the fertile imagery and mythology of sagas, staves and sorcery in seventeenth-century Iceland, and to knitter and artist Halla Lilja, and Elín S. Sigurðardóttir of Heimilisiðnaðarsafnið, the Textile Museum in Blönduós.

Eternal thanks go as ever to my parents for helping in all the ways you do, to my partner and son for tolerating me spending so much time wrapped inside the world I created, and to my coven: your wisdom, witchery and warmth runs through this novel like the threads in Þuriður's weaving.

About the Author

Cathryn Kemp is a *Sunday Times* bestselling author and ghost writer, with a prolific career writing celebrity, inspirational, true-crime and nostalgia titles. Her memoir, *Coming Clean*, won the Big Red Read Prize for Non-Fiction, and Cathryn's first novel, *A Poisoner's Tale*, won the HWA Debut Crown Award 2025. *They Can't Burn Us All* is her second work of historical fiction.

She is currently restoring a glorious wreck of a Victorian villa on the south coast along with her husband, son, puppy and familiar, a ginger cat.

cathryn_kemp
cathrynkemp
author.cathryn.kemp